The Bristling Wood

Katharine Kerr
The Bristling Wood

A Foundation Book

Doubleday
New York London Toronto Sydney Auckland

A FOUNDATION BOOK
Published by Doubleday, a division of
Bantam Doubleday Dell Publishing Group, Inc.
666 Fifth Avenue, New York, New York 10103

FOUNDATION, DOUBLEDAY and the portrayal of the
letter F are trademarks of Doubleday, a division of
Bantam Doubleday Dell Publishing Group, Inc.

Library of Congress Cataloging-in-Publication Data
Kerr, Katharine.
　　The bristling wood/Katharine Kerr.—1st ed.
　　　p.　cm.
　　"A Foundation book."
　　I. Title.
PS3561.E642B7　1989　　　88-30132
813'.54—dc19　　　　　　　CIP

ISBN 0-385-24275-1
Copyright © 1989 by Katharine Kerr
ALL RIGHTS RESERVED
PRINTED IN THE UNITED STATES OF AMERICA
MARCH 1989
FIRST EDITION

BG

In memoriam: Raymond Earle Kerr, Jr.,
1917–87,
an officer and a gentleman

Acknowledgments

As usual, I owe many people many thanks:

Pat LoBrutto, my editor and one of the best in the business, who keeps going to bat for me even as this project grows longer and longer.

Elizabeth Pomada and Michael Larsen, my agents, who are friends far more than business acquaintances.

Marta Grabien, who gave me invaluable help in acquiring my computer system.

Nic and Deborah Grabien, who went beyond the call of friendship to install the new computer once acquired.

Jon Jacobsen, my best critic and supporter, who no doubt would be a silver dagger himself did he live in Deverry.

Alice Brahtin, my mother, who much to her surprise found she actually likes the peculiar things I write.

And as always, Howard Kerr, my husband.

A Note on the Pronunciation of Deverry Words

The language spoken in Deverry is a member of the P-Celtic family. Although closely related to Welsh, Cornish, and Breton, it is by no means identical to any of these actual languages and should never be taken as such.

Vowels are divided by Deverry scribes into two classes: noble and common. Nobles have two pronunciations; commons, one.

A as in *father* when long; a shorter version of the same sound, as in *far*, when short.

O as in *bone* when long; as in *pot* when short.

W as the *oo* in *spook* when long; as in *roof* when short.

Y as the *i* in *machine* when long; as the *e* in *butter* when short.

E as in *pen*.

I as in *pin*.

U as in *pun*.

Vowels are generally long in stressed syllables; short in unstressed. Y is the primary exception to this rule. When it appears as the last letter of a word, it is always long whether that syllable is stressed or not.

Diphthongs generally have one consistent pronunciation.

AE as the *a* in *mane*.

AI as in *aisle*.

AU as the *ow* in *how*.

EO as a combination of *eh* and *oh*.

EW as in Welsh, a combination of *eh* and *oo*.

IE as in *pier*.

OE as the *oy* in *boy*.

UI as the North Welsh *wy*, a combination of *oo* and *ee*. Note that OI is never a diphthong, but is two distinct sounds, as in *carnoic* (KAR-noh-ik).

Consonants are mostly the same as in English, with these exceptions:

C is always hard as in *cat*.

G is always hard as in *get.*

DD is the voiced *th* as in *thin* or *breathe,* but the voicing is more pronounced than in English. It is opposed to TH, the unvoiced sound as in *th* or *breath.* (This is the sound that the Greeks called the Celtic tau.)

R is heavily rolled.

RH is a voiceless R, approximately pronounced as if it were spelled *hr* in Deverry proper. In Eldidd, the sound is fast becoming indistinguishable from R.

DW, GW, and TW are single sounds, as in *Gwendolen* or *twit.*

Y is never a consonant.

I before a vowel at the beginning of a word is consonantal, as it is in the plural ending *-ion,* pronounced *yawn.*

Doubled consonants are both sounded clearly, unlike in English. Note, however, that DD is a *single letter,* not a doubled consonant.

Accent is generally on the penultimate syllable, but compound words and place names are often an exception to this rule.

I have used this system of transcription for the Bardekian and Elvish alphabets as well as the Deverrian, which is, of course, based on the Greek rather than the Roman model. On the whole, it works quite well for the Bardekian, at least. As for Elvish, in a work of this sort it would be ridiculous to resort to the elaborate apparatus by which scholars attempt to transcribe that most subtle and nuanced of tongues. Since the human ear cannot even distinguish between such sound pairings as $B>$ and $B<$, I see no reason to confuse the human eye with them. I do owe many thanks to the various Elven native speakers who have suggested which consonant to choose in confusing cases and who have labored, alas often in vain, to refine my ear to the Elven vowel system.

A Note on Dating

Year 1 of the Deverry calendar is the founding of the Holy City, or, to be more accurate, the year that King Bran saw the omen of the white sow that instructed him where to build his capital. It corresponds roughly to 76 C.E.

For the profit of kings, well did he attack the hosts
of the country, the bristling wood of spears,
the grievous flood of the enemy.

—*The Gododdin of Aneirin,* Stanza A84

Prologue

Spring, 1065

Often those who study the dweomer complain that it speaks in
riddles. There is a reason for this
riddling. What is it? Well, that
happens to be a riddle of its own.
—*The Secret Book of
Cadwallon the Druid*

Out in the grasslands to the west of the kingdom of Deverry, the concepts of "day" and "month" had no meaning. The years flowed by, slowly, on the ebb and swell of the seasons: the harsh rains of winter, when the grass turned a bluish green and the gray sky hung close to the earth; the spring floods, when the streams overflowed their banks and pooled around the willows and hazels, pale green with first leaves; the parching summer, when the grass lay pale gold and all fires were treacherous; the first soft rains of fall, when wildflowers bloomed briefly in purple and gold. Driving their herds of horses and flocks of sheep, the People drifted north in the summer's heat and south in the winter's cold, and as they rode, they marked only the little things: the first stag to lose his antlers, the last strawberries. Since the gods were always present, traveling with their folk in the long wandering, they needed no high holidays or special feasts in their honor. When two or three alarli, the loosely organized traveling groups, happened to meet, then there was a festival to celebrate the company of friends.

Yet there was one day of the year marked out from all the others: the spring equinox, which usually signaled the start of the floods. In the high mountains of the far north, the snows were melting, sending a tide down through the grasslands, just as another tide, this one of blood, had once swept over them from the north in the far past. Even though individuals of their race lived some five hundred years on the average, by now there were none left who'd been present in those dark years, but the People remembered. They made sure that their children would always remember on the day of the equinox, when the alarli gathered in groups of ten or twelve for the Day of Commemoration.

Even though he was eager to ride east to Deverry, Ebañy Salomonderiel would never have left the elven lands until he'd celebrated this most holy and terrifying of days. In the company of his father, Devaberiel Silverhand the bard, he rode up from the seacoast to the joining of the rivers Corapan and Delonderiel, near the stretch of primeval forest that marked the border of the grasslands. There, as they'd expected, they found an alardan, or clan meet. Scattered in the tall grass were two hundred painted tents,

red and purple and blue, while the flocks and herds grazed peacefully a little distance away. A little apart from the rest stood ten
unpainted tents, crudely stitched together from poorly tanned
hides.

"By the Dark Sun herself," Devaberiel remarked. "It looks like
some of the Forest Folk have come to join us."

"Good. It's time they got over their fear of their own kind."

Devaberiel nodded in agreement. He was an exceptionally handsome man, with hair pale as moonlight, deep-set dark blue eyes,
slit vertically like a cat's, and gracefully long pointed ears. Although Ebañy had inherited the pale hair, in other ways he took
after his mother's human folk; his smoky gray eyes had round
irises, and his ears, while slightly sharp, passed unnoticed in the
lands of men. They rode on, leading their eight horses, two of
which dragged travois, loaded with everything they owned. Since
Devaberiel was a bard and Ebañy, a gerthddyn—that is, a storyteller and minstrel—they didn't need large herds to support themselves. As they rode up to the tents, the People ran out to greet
them, hailing the bard and vying for the honor of feeding him and
his son.

They chose to pitch the ruby-red tent near that of Tanidario, a
woman who was an old friend of the bard's. Although she'd often
given his father advice and help as he raised his half-breed son
alone, Ebañy found it hard to think of her as a mother. Unlike his
own mother back in Eldidd, whom he vaguely remembered as
soft, pale, and cuddly, Tanidario was a hunter, a hard-muscled
woman who stood six feet tall and arrow-straight, with jet-black
hair that hung in one tight braid to her waist. Yet when she greeted
him, she kissed his cheek, caught his shoulders, and held him a bit
away while she smiled as if to say how much he'd grown.

"I'll wager you're looking forward to the spring hunt," he said.

"I certainly am, little one. I've been making friends with the
Forest Folk, and they've offered to show me how to hunt with a
spear in the deep woods. I'm looking forward to the challenge."

Ebañy merely smiled.

"I know you," Tanidario said with a laugh. "Your idea of hunting
is finding a soft bed with a pretty lass in it. Well, maybe when
you're fully grown, you'll see things more clearly."

"I happen to be seventy-four this spring."

"A mere child." She tousled his hair with a callused hand. "Well, come along. The gathering's already beginning. Where's your father gotten himself to?"

"He went with the other bards. He'll be singing right after the Retelling."

Down by the river, some of the People had lashed together a rough platform out of travois poles, where Devaberiel stood conferring with four other bards. All around it the crowd spread out, the adults sitting cross-legged in the grass while restless children wandered around. Ebañy and Tanidario sat on the edge near a little group of Forest Folk. Although they looked like the other elves, they were dressed in rough leather clothes, and each man carried a small notched stick, bound with feathers and colored thread, which were considered magical among their kind. Although they normally lived in the dense forests to the north, at times they drifted south to trade with the rest of the People. Since they had never been truly civilized, the events that they were gathered to remember had spared them.

Gradually the crowd quieted, and the children sat down by their parents. On the platform four bards, Devaberiel among them, took their places at the back, arms crossed over their chests, legs braced a little apart, a solemn honor guard for the storyteller. Manaver Contariel's son, the eldest of them all, came forward and raised his arms high in the air. With a shock, Ebañy realized that this would be the last year that this bard would retell the story. He was starting to show his age, his hair white and thin, his face pouched and wrinkled. When one of the People aged, it meant death was near.

"His father was there at the Burning," Tanidario whispered.

Ebañy merely nodded his acknowledgment, because Manaver was lowering his arms.

"We are here to remember." His highly trained voice seemed to boom out in the warm stillness.

"To remember," the crowd sighed back. "To remember the west."

"We are here to remember the cities, Rinbaladelan of the Fair Towers, Tanbalapalim of the Wide River, Bravelmelim of the Rainbow Bridges, yea, to remember the cities, and the towns, and all the marvels of the far, far west. They have been taken from us, they lie in ruins, where the owls and the foxes prowl, and weeds and thistles crack the courtyards of the palaces of the Seven Kings."

The crowd sighed wordlessly, then settled in to listen to the tale that some had heard five hundred times or more. Even though he was half a Deverry man, Ebañy felt tears rise in his throat for the lost splendor and the years of peace, when in the hills and well-watered plains of the far west, the People lived in cities full of marvels and practiced every art and craft until their works were so perfect that some claimed them dweomer.

Over a thousand years ago, so long that some doubted when the Burning had begun, whether it was a thousand and two hundred years or only a thousand and one, several millions of the People lived under the rule of the Seven Kings in a long age of peace. Then the omens began. For five winters the snows fell high; for five springs, floods swept down the river. In the sixth winter, farmers in the northern province reported that the wolves seemed to have gone mad, hunting in big packs and attacking travelers along the road. The sages agreed that the wolves must have been desperate and starving, and this coupled with the weather meant famine in the mountains, perhaps even some sort of blight or plague that might move south. In council the Seven Kings made plans: a fair method of stockpiling food and distributing it to those in need, a small military levy to deal with the wolf packs. They also gathered dweomerfolk and sages around them to combat the threats and to lend their lore to farmers in need. In the sixth spring, squadrons of royal archers went forth to guard the north, but they thought they were only hunting wolves.

When the attack came, it broke like an avalanche and buried the archers in corpses. No one truly knew who the enemies were; they were neither human nor elvish, but a squat breed like enormous dwarves, dressed in skins, and armed only with crude spears and axes. For all their poor weapons, their warriors fought with such enraged ferocity that they seemed not to care whether they lived or died. There were also thousands of them, and they traveled mounted. When the sages rushed north with the first reinforcements, they reported that the language of the Hordes was utterly unknown to them. Half-starved, desperately fleeing some catastrophe in their homeland, they burned and ravaged and looted as they came. Since the People had never seen horses before, the attackers had a real advantage, first of surprise, then of mobility once the elves grew used to the horrifying beasts. By the time that they realized that horses were even more vulnerable to arrows than men, the north was lost, and Tanbalapalim a heap of smoking timbers and cracked stone.

The kings rallied the People and led them to war. After every man and woman who could loose a bow marched north, for a time the battles held even. Although the corpse fires burned day and night along the roads, still the invaders marched in under the smoke. Since he pitied their desperation, King Elamanderiel Sun-Sworn tried to parley with the leaders and offered them the eastern grasslands for their own. In answer, they slew his honor guard and ran his head onto a long spear, which they paraded in front of their men for days. After that, no mercy was offered. Children marched north with bows to take the places of their fallen parents, yet still the Hordes came.

By autumn the middle provinces were swept away in a tide of blood. Although many of the People fell back in a last desperate attempt to hold Rinbaladelan on the coast, most fled, taking their livestock, rounding up the horses that had given the invaders such an edge, loading wagons and trekking east to the grasslands that the Hordes despised. Rinbaladelan fought out the winter, then fell in the spring. More refugees came east, carrying tales the more horrible because so common. Every clan had had its women raped, its children killed and eaten, its houses burned down around those too weak to flee. Everyone had seen a temple defiled, an aqueduct mindlessly toppled, a farm looted then burned instead of appropriated for some good use. All summer, refugees trickled in—and starved. They were settled folk, unused to hunting except for sport. When they tried to plant their hoarded seed grains, the harsh grasslands gave them only stunted crops. Yet in a way few cared whether they lived another winter or not, because they were expecting that the enemy would soon follow them east. Some fled into the forests to seek refuge among the primitive tribes; a few reached what later became Eldidd; most stayed, waiting for the end.

But the Hordes never came. Slowly the People learned to survive by living off their flocks and herds while they explored what the grasslands had to offer them. They ate things—and still did—that would have made the princes of the Vale of Roses vomit; lizards and snakes, the entrails of deer and antelope as well as the fine meat, roots and tubers grubbed out wherever they grew. They learned to dry horse dung to supplement the meager firewood; they abandoned the wagons that left deep ruts in the grassland that now fed them in its own way. They boiled fish heads for glues and used tendons for bowstrings as they moved constantly from one foraging ground to another. Not only did they survive, but children were born, replacing those killed in flash floods and hunting accidents.

Finally, thirty-two years after the Burning, the last of the Seven Kings, Ranadar of the High Mountain, found his people again. With the last six archers of the Royal Guard he rode into an alardan one spring and told how he and his men had lived among the hills like bandits, taking what vengeance they could for their fallen country and begging the gods to send more. Now the gods had listened to their grief. While the Hordes could conquer cities, they had no idea how to rebuild them. They lived in rough huts among the ruins and tried to plant land they'd poisoned. Although every ugly member of them wore looted jewels, they let the sewers fill with muck while they fought over the dwindling spoils. Plague had broken out among them, diseases of several different kinds, all deadly and swift. When he spoke of the dying of the Hordes, Ranadar howled aloud with laughter like a madman, and the People laughed with him.

For a long time there was talk of a return, of letting the plagues do their work, then slaughtering the last of the Hordes and taking back the shattered kingdom. For two hundred years, until Ranadar's death, men gathered nightly around the campfires to scheme. Every now and then, a few foolhardy young men would ride back to spy. Even fewer returned, but those who did spoke of general ruin and disease still raging. If life in the grasslands hadn't been so harsh at first, perhaps an army might have marched west, but every year, there were almost as many deaths as births. Finally, some four hundred and fifty years after the Burning, some of the younger men organized a major scouting party to ride to Rinbaladelan.

"And I was among them, a young man," Manaver said, his voice near breaking at the memory. "With twenty friends I rode west, for many a time had I heard my father speak of Rinbaladelan of the Fair Towers, and I longed to see it, even though the sight might bring my death. We took many quivers of arrows, for we expected many a bloody skirmish with the last of the Hordes." He paused for a twisted, self-mocking smile. "But they were gone, long dead, and so was Rinbaladelan. My father had told me of the high temples, covered with silver and jet; I saw grassy mounds. He told of towers five hundred feet high made of many-colored stones; I found a broken piece here and there. He told of vast processions down wide streets; I traced out the grassy tracks. Here and there, I found a stone hut, cobbled out of the ruins. In some, I found skeletons lying unburied on the floor, the last of the Hordes."

The crowd sighed, a grief-torn wind over the grassland. Near the front a little girl squirmed free of her mother's lap and stood up.

"Then why didn't we go back, if they were all dead?" she called out in a clear, high voice.

Although her mother grabbed her, the rest of the gathering laughed, a melancholy chuckle at a child's boldness, a relief after so much tragedy. Manaver smiled at the little girl.

"Back to what, sweet one?" he said. "The kingdom was dead, a tangle of overgrowth and ruins. We'd brought our gods to the grasslands, and the grasslands became our mother. Besides, the men who knew how to lay out fine cities and smelt iron and work in stone were all dead. Those of us who survived were mostly farmers, herdsmen, or foresters. What did we know about building roads and working rare metals?"

Her mouth working in thought, the girl twisted one ankle around the other. Finally she looked up at the dying bard.

"And will we never go back, then?"

"Well, 'never' is a harsh word, and one that you should keep closed in your mouth, but I doubt it, sweet one. Yet we remember the fair cities, our birthright, our home."

Even though the People sighed out the word "remember" with proper respect, no one wept, because none of them had ever seen the Vale of Roses or walked the Sun Road to the temples. With a nod, Manaver stepped back to allow Devaberiel forward to sing a dirge for the fallen land. The songs would go on for hours, each bard taking a turn and singing of happier and happier things, until at last the alardan would feast and celebrate, dancing far into the night. Ebañy got up and slipped away. Since he'd heard his father practice the dirge for some months, he was heartily sick of it. Besides, his Deverry blood pricked him with guilt, as it did every year on the Day of Commemoration.

By talking with Deverry scholars, Ebañy had pieced together something about the Burning that no one else knew. Since it would only lead to hatred between his two races of kinfolk, he kept the secret even from his father. The Hordes had been driven south by the great influx of the people of Bel, as the Deverry men called themselves, when they'd come from their mysterious homeland over a thousand years ago. Although to the People's way of thinking the Deverry men were a bloodthirsty lot, in the old days they'd been ruthless conquerors, hunting their enemies' heads to decorate the temples of their gods. In their wanderings before they founded their holy city, they'd swept through the far north, slaughtering, looting, enslaving some of the strange race, even, before they passed down the valley of the Aver Troe Matrw to their new lands. And the Hordes had fled before them, fled south.

"You never lifted a sword against us, O men of Deverry," Ebañy whispered aloud. "But you slaughtered my father's people sure enough."

With a little shudder, he ducked into the tent, where the sun came through the dyed leather and turned the air to ruby. Since they'd arrived late for the alardan, piles of tent bags and gear lay scattered on the leather ground cloth. Idly he picked up a few bags and hung them from the hooks on the tent poles, then sat down in the clutter to poke through a canvas bag of the Deverry sort. Down at the bottom he found a tiny leather pouch, opened it, and took out a simple silver ring. A flat band about a third of an inch wide, it was engraved with roses on the outside and words in Elvish characters but some unknown language on the inside. The roses caught the reddish light and seemed to bloom, double hybrids of the cultivated sort now found only in Deverry.

"And are you spoil from Rinbaladelan or Tanbalapalim?" he asked it. "The only roses my people know now are the wild ones with their five meager little petals."

The ring lay mute on his palm, a gleaming paradox. Although it possessed no dweomer of its own, it was tied to the dweomer. Many years ago, a mysterious, nameless wanderer had given it to Devaberiel as a present for one of his as yet unborn sons. Now the omen reading of a dweomerwoman showed that it belonged to Rhodry, the youngest of the three and, like Ebañy, a half-breed. But unlike Ebañy's, Rhodry's mother was no pretty village lass, but one of the most powerful noblewomen in the kingdom. Rhodry could never learn the truth about his real father, who had given Ebañy the task of taking the ring to him.

"And what am I supposed to tell him when I find him?" he grumbled aloud, because talking came much easier to him than thinking. "Oh, well, this peculiar personage said it was yours, but I can't tell you why. Of course, I don't know why it's yours—no one does —so, dear brother, I won't be lying to you when I make my most feeble excuses. One dweomer says it encircles your Wyrd, and another working says that your Wyrd is Eldidd's Wyrd, and so here we are, in the land of vagaries, nuances, and secrets. Ah, by the gods, doesn't my elvish curiosity ache to know the truth!"

With a laugh, he slipped the ring back into its wrapping, then put that pouch into the one he carried around his neck. Soon he would be riding into the lands of men, where thieves prowl, and he would need a better hiding place for the ring than an open canvas sack. Thinking of the journey ahead of him, he went outside and wandered down to the riverbank, where the Delonderiel rolled by, flecked with gold in the lowering sun. Distantly he heard his father's voice, firm and clear in its sorrow as the stanzas marched on. He stared at the river and used it to focus his mind, until at last his dweomer scryed Rhodry out, a pale image of him at first, then a clear picture.

Rhodry was standing on the ramparts of a rough stone dun and looking out over countryside where patches of snow still lay under dark pine trees. He was wrapped in a cloak, and his breath came in a frosty puff. Now that Ebañy knew they shared a father, he could see what had eluded him the summer before, when he'd met Rhodry by chance and wondered why this young warrior looked so familiar. Although Rhodry had raven-dark hair and cornflower-blue eyes, they looked enough alike to be what they were, brothers. As he studied the resemblance, Ebañy found himself grumbling again.

"So I'm not supposed to tell you the truth, brother, am I? What am I supposed to do, smash every mirror within your reach? Rhodry has to think himself human and a Maelwaedd, says my master in dweomer. Oh, splendid! Then I'd best hand over this ring and disappear before you look too closely at my face!"

In the vision, Rhodry's image suddenly turned and seemed to be staring right at him, as if he were listening to his faraway kin. Ebañy smiled at him, then widened the vision, switching his point of view this way and that around the countryside to the limits of the scrying, about two miles away from its focus. He saw sharp rocky hills, covered with pine, and here and there among them small farms. Most likely Rhodry was in the province of Cerrgonney, then, a good five hundred miles away at the very least.

"It's going to be a long summer's riding, then, Ebañy, lad," he told himself. "On the other hand, it would be a wretched shame to leave before the feasting's over."

Although it was cold up on the ramparts of Lord Gwogyr's dun, Rhodry lingered there a few moments longer and looked out over the Cerrgonney hills without truly seeing them. For a moment he wondered if he were going daft, because it seemed he'd heard someone talking to him though he was the only man on the walls. The words had been indistinct, but someone had called him brother and talked of giving him a gift. In irritation he tossed his head and decided that it had only been some trick of the wind. Since the only brother he knew of hated him with his very soul, it was unlikely that he'd be giving him any gift but a dagger in the back, and those words—if words they were—had sounded warm and friendly.

Leaning back against the damp stone, he pulled his silver dagger from his belt and looked at it while he idly thought of his elder brother, Rhys, Gwerbret Aberwyn, who had sent him into exile some years before. Although the dagger was a beautiful thing, as sharp as steel but gleaming like silver, it was a mark of shame, branding him a dishonored mercenary soldier who fought only for coin, never for honor. It was time for him to wander down the long road, as the silver daggers called their lives. Although he'd fought well for Lord Gwogyr last fall, even taking a wound in his service, a silver dagger's welcome was a short one, and already the chamberlain was grumbling about having to feed him and his woman. Sheathing the dagger, he glanced up at the sky, cold but clear. It was likely that the snows were long past.

"Tomorrow we'll ride," he said aloud. "And if you were thinking of me, brother, may the thought turn your guts to fire."

Far to the south, in a little town in Eldidd, an event was happening that would indeed bring Gwerbret Rhys the sort of pain his younger brother had wished upon him, even though Rhodry had no way of knowing it. Dun Bruddlyn, a fort only recently disposed upon its lord, Garedd, was filled with a tense sort of bustle. While the lord himself paced restlessly in his great hall with a goblet of mead in his hand, his second wife, Donilla, was giving birth up in the women's hall. Since this was her first child, the labor was a long one, and Tieryn Lovyan, as well as the other women in attendance, were beginning to worry. Her face dead white, her long chestnut hair soaked with sweat, Donilla crouched on the birthing stool and clung to the thick rope tied from one of the beams far above. Her serving woman, Galla, knelt beside her and wiped her face every now and then with a cloth soaked in cold water.

"Let her suck a bit of moisture from a clean rag," said the herbman who was attending the birth. "But just a bit."

Another serving lass hurried to get clean cloth and fresh water without a moment's hesitation. Not only was old Nevyn known as the best herbman in the kingdom, but it was widely rumored that he had the dweomer. Lovyan smiled at the lass's awe, but only slightly, because she knew full well that the rumors were true. When she glanced at Nevyn in a questioning sort of way, he gave her a reassuring smile, then spoke to Donilla. His ice-blue eyes seemed to bore into her soft brown ones and capture her very soul. With a sigh she relaxed as if some of the pain had left her.

"It'll be soon now, my lady." His voice was very soft and kind. "Breathe deeply now, but don't bear down on the babe. It'll be coming soon."

Donilla nodded, gasped at a contraction, and let out her breath in a long, smooth sigh. Although Lovyan had given birth to four sons herself, she couldn't remember her own labors being this difficult. Perhaps I've just forgotten, she thought. One does forget the pain, and so oddly soon. Restlessly she paced to an open window and looked out on the bright spring day while she considered the irony. Poor Donilla had been so eager to have a child; now she was probably wishing that she truly had been barren. When the younger woman moaned again, Lovyan winced in sympathy.

"It's crowning, my lady!" Nevyn crowed in victory. "Soon, very soon. Now—bear down."

Lovyan stayed at the window until she heard the high-pitched wail, a good, healthy cry at that. She turned around to see Nevyn and the serving woman laying Donilla down on the pallet prepared by the stool and laying the babe, still attached by the cord, at her breast. With trembling fingers the lady stroked the soft fuzz on her child's head and smiled in wide-eyed triumph.

"A son, Your Grace!" she croaked. "I've given my lord another son."

"And a fine healthy one, at that," Lovyan said. "Shall I go tell his lordship the good news?"

Donilla nodded, her eyes on the tiny face already nuzzling at her breast.

As she went downstairs, Lovyan's heart was heavy, and she felt badly about it. Of course Donilla deserved this moment of tri-

umph, of vindication. After ten years of a childless marriage, her
first husband had cast her off as barren, a bitter humiliation for
any woman to bear, worse than the heartbreaking thought that
she would never have children. Now she had her son, and everyone in Eldidd knew that she wasn't the barren one. Unfortunately,
her small triumph had important political consequences, of which
her second husband seemed to be painfully aware. Garedd was a
man of middle years, with two sons and a daughter by his first
marriage; a solid sort with gray in his blond hair and mustaches,
he was genuinely pleased at Lovyan's news, breaking out into a
laugh and yelling that he had a son to his warband across the hall.
Then, almost instantly, he wiped the look of triumph off his face.

"My apologies for gloating, Your Grace," he said. "But it takes a
man that way."

"You don't need to apologize to me, cousin," Lovyan said wearily. "Nor to Rhys, either, though I'd advise you to stay away from
Aberwyn for a while."

"I was planning to, truly."

There lay the crux of the matter; Gwerbret Rhys had been Donilla's first husband, the one who had shamed her as barren because
he had no heirs for his vast rhan, one of the most important in the
entire kingdom. If he died childless, as now seemed most likely,
Eldidd could well break out into open war as the various candi-
dates tried to claim the gwerbretrhyn for their own clan. Although
Lovyan was fond of her cousin and his wife, she was here to witness the birth because of its political implications. Since she was
the tieryn of Dun Gwerbyn, with many vassals and large holdings,
her time was too valuable for her to ride around the countryside
playing at midwife for her vassals' wives. But it had been necessary that she see with her own eyes that, truly, Donilla had given
birth to a child.

"Do you think Rhys will adopt a son?" Garedd said.

"I have no idea what Rhys will or won't do anymore, for all that
he's my firstborn son. An adopted heir won't have much of a
chance in the Council of Electors anyway. The sensible thing for
him to do would be recall Rhodry from exile."

Garedd raised one questioning eyebrow.

"I haven't given up hope yet," Lovyan snapped. "But truly, my
lord, I understand your skepticism."

In another half hour, Nevyn came down to the great hall. A tall
man with a thick shock of white hair and a face as wrinkled as old

burlap, still he moved with strength, striding up to the table of honor and making Garedd a smooth bow. When he announced that the lord could visit the lady, Garedd was off like a flushed hare, because he loved his young wife in an almost unseemly way. Nevyn accepted a tankard of ale from a page and sat down beside Lovyan.

"Well," he remarked. "She had a remarkably good first birth for a woman her age. Knowing you, you're pleased in spite of yourself."

"Just that. I was always fond of her. If only some other beastly man had cast her off."

Nevyn gave her a thin smile and had a well-deserved swallow of ale.

"I'll be leaving tomorrow," he said. "Going to Dun Deverry. Now that I have a nephew at court, I can hear some of the gossip from the king's councils."

"Nephew, indeed! But I'm glad he's there, all the same. I'm beginning to think that our only hope is to get our liege to override Rhys's sentence of exile. It's happened before."

"Gwerbrets have also risen in rebellion against such meddling. Do you think Rhys will?"

"I don't know. Ah, by the Goddess herself, it aches my heart to think of war coming to Eldidd, and all over my two squabbling sons!"

"The war hasn't started yet, and I'm going to do my cursed best to make sure it doesn't."

Yet he looked so weary that she was suddenly frightened. Even though he was the most powerful dweomerman in the kingdom, he was still only one man. He was also caught up in political intrigue that—or so it seemed to her—his magical calling would ill equip him to handle.

"Ah well," she said at last. "At least the child himself was born with good omens. They always say it's a lucky lad who's born the first day of spring."

"So they do, and let's hope this spring is as well omened for us all."

The absent way he spoke made her realize that he very much doubted it would be. She was hesitating, half wanting to ask more, half afraid to hear the truth if he should tell her, when a page came over to her. The young lad looked utterly confused.

"Your Grace? There's a noble lord at the gates. Should I ask you what to do, or go find Lord Garedd?"

"You may ask me, because I'm of higher rank. If I were of the same rank as Garedd, you'd have to go find him. Now. Which noble lord is it?"

"Talidd of Belglaedd, Your Grace. He said the strangest thing. He asked if he was welcome in the dun that should have been his."

Beside her Nevyn swore under his breath.

"Oh ye gods," Lovyan said feebly. "He *would* turn up right now! Well, lad, run and tell him that indeed he's welcome in the dun called Bruddlyn. Tell him that exactly and not a word more."

As soon as the page was on his way, Nevyn turned to her with the lift of a quizzical eyebrow.

"It all goes back to Loddlaen's war," she said, her voice heavy with weariness. "Talidd's sister was Corbyn's wife. She went back to her brother before the war even started, because having Loddlaen in the dun was driving her daft, and I can't say I blame her for that, frankly. But then, after Corbyn was killed, I attainted this demesne because she'd left her husband. All my loyal men would have grumbled if I hadn't. I offered her a settlement of coin and horses, but Talidd refused to let her take a copper or a filly of it."

She broke off because the subject of this explanation was striding into the great hall, stripping off his cloak and riding gloves as he did so. Talidd of Belglaedd was a heavyset man of forty, with gray hair still streaked with blond, and shrewd green eyes. Tossing his cloak to the page, he came over and made the tieryn a deep bow. His bland smile revealed nothing at all.

"I'm surprised to see you here, my lord," Lovyan said.

"I came to congratulate Garedd on the birth of a child. The page tells me it's a lad."

"It is, and a healthy one."

"Then Dun Bruddlyn has yet another heir, does it?" Talidd paused to take a tankard of ale from a serving lass. "Well, the gods may witness the justice of that."

Lovyan debated challenging him then and there. If she'd been a man, and thus able to fight her own duels, she might well have done it, but as it was, she would have to call for a champion. Answering that call would be the captain of her warband, Cullyn of Cerrmor, who was without doubt the best swordsman in all Deverry. It seemed rather unfair to sentence Talidd to certain death for a few nasty remarks.

"I choose to ignore that, my lord," Lovyan said, and she put ice in her voice. "If you feel injured, you may put your case before the gwerbret, and I shall come to court at his order."

"The gwerbret, Your Grace, happens to be your son."

"So he is, and I scrupulously raised him to be a fair-minded man."

At that Talidd looked down abruptly at the table, and he had the decency to blush. In the duel of words, Lovyan had scored the first touch.

"I'm surprised you'd come here just to pour vinegar in an old wound," she said.

"The matter's of great moment for the gwerbretrhyn, isn't it? You forget, Your Grace, that I hold a seat on the Council of Electors."

Lovyan *had* forgotten, and she cursed herself mentally for the lapse. Talidd had a sip of ale and smiled his bland, secretive smile at her and Nevyn impartially.

"I was hoping I'd be in time to witness the birth," he said at last. "I take it there were witnesses not of this household."

"Myself and the herbman here."

"And none, my lady, would dare dispute your word, not in open court or in private meeting." The smile grew less bland. "We may take it as a given that, indeed, the Lady Donilla's not barren, no matter what seemed to be the case before."

Lovyan gave him a brilliant smile and hated his very heart.

"Just so, my lord. I take it as another given that you'll be summoning the council with this news as soon as ever you can."

Talidd left well before the evening meal with the remark that he had a better welcome nearby. He sounded so martyred, so genuinely injured, that Nevyn felt like kicking him all the way out of the great hall. For Lovyan's sake, he refrained. Instead he went up to look in on Donilla, who was by then resting in her own bed with the swaddled babe beside her. In some minutes Lovyan joined him there, her expression as placid as if she'd never heard Talidd's name, and made a few pleasantries to the younger woman. Nevyn left when she did, following her to the chamber in the suite that had been allotted to her on this visit. Although plain, it was obviously furnished with Dun Bruddlyn's best; her cousin and his lady both had reason to be grateful for her gift of this demesne, as she remarked.

"Although it's turning out to be a troubled gift, sure enough," Nevyn said. "I didn't realize Talidd felt so strongly."

"Him and half the lords in the tierynrhyn. I knew there'd be trouble when I gave it to Garedd, but there'd have been trouble no matter what I did. Well, I suppose if I'd apportioned it to you, no one would have grumbled, but you didn't want it, and so here we are."

"Come now, Lovva! You almost make me feel guilty."

"I like that 'almost.' But truly, whenever an overlord has land to give, there's bound to be injured feelings. I only wish that Talidd didn't have a seat on the council. Ah ye gods, what a nasty thing this is becoming! Even if Rhys's wife did have a babe now, no one would believe it was his."

"Just so. I—"

With the bang of a door and a gleeful howl of laughter, a child of about two came charging into the chamber with a nursemaid in pursuit. She was slender for her age, with a mop of curly, raven-dark hair and violet eyes, almost as dark a purple as an elf's—all in all, a breathtakingly beautiful child. With a gurgle, she threw herself into Lovyan's exalted lap.

"Granna, Granna, love you, Granna."

"And I love you, too, Rhodd-let, but you're being naughty and interrupting."

Rhodda twisted in her lap and looked solemnly at Nevyn. The family resemblance was profound.

"I'd almost forgotten about Rhodry's daughter. She certainly hasn't inherited her looks from her mother's side, has she?"

"None, but Maelwaedd blood tends to be strong, and Olwen, poor lass, was one of those blond and bland sorts. Rhodry's bastard might have a very important role to play in what lies ahead, so I keep her with me at all times—to supervise her upbringing, of course." For all her talk of political purposes, she kissed the top of the child's head with a genuine fondness, then motioned to the nursemaid. "Now let Mistress Tevylla take you away and give you some bread and milk. It's almost time for bed."

Although Rhodda whined, begged, and finally howled, Lovyan held firm and scooped her up bodily to give her to her nurse, who was hovering by the chamber door. Nevyn hadn't truly noticed her before, but he saw now that she was a striking woman of about thirty, with dark hair, dark eyes, and almost severely regular features. Once she and her small charge were gone, Nevyn asked about her.

"Tevva?" Lovyan said. "A charming woman, and with a will of steel, which she needs around Rhodda, I assure you. She's a widow, actually, with a son of her own, who's—oh ye gods, I don't remember his age, but old enough for Cullyn to be training him for the warband. Her man was a blacksmith down in my town, but he died suddenly of a fever two winters ago. Since she had no kin, the priests recommended her to my charity, and I needed a woman for Rhodda. That child is a worse handful than even her father was." She sighed, and since they were alone, she could be honest. "I suppose it's the Elven blood in their veins."

"I'd say so, for all that Rhodda doesn't have much of it."

"A full quarter, let us not forget. Don't fall for your own lies about a trace of Elven blood in the Maelwaedds."

"Well, it's not a lie, because there is one, but of course it doesn't apply here. I take it you plan to make the child a good marriage someday?"

"An influential marriage, certainly, and I plan to teach her how to make any marriage suit her own purposes. If she can learn to channel all that willfulness, she'll be a woman to reckon with in Eldidd, illegitimate or not."

Although Nevyn agreed with vague words rather than burden her further, he privately wondered if the child could ever be tamed and forced into the narrow mold of a noble-born woman. Sooner or later, her wild blood was going to show.

Before he left Dun Bruddlyn, Nevyn made a point of scrying out Rhodry and, when he found him well, telling Lovyan so. As he rode out, leading his pack mule behind him, he felt a dread that was as much logic as it was dweomer warning. The summer before, he and those others who studied the dweomer of light had won a series of victories over those who followed the dweomer of darkness. They had not only disrupted an elaborate plot of the dark masters but had also ruined one of their main sources of income, the importing of opium and various poisons into the kingdom. The dark ones would want revenge; they always did, and he reminded himself to stay on guard in his travels. Of course, it was likely that they'd scheme for years, trying to lay a plan so clever and convoluted that it would be undetectable. It was likely, but at the same time, the dweomer warnings came to him in a coldness down his back. Since the dark masters were so threatened, they would doubtless strike back as soon as they could. The only question was how.

And yet, other, more mundane matters demanded his attention as well. The gwerbretrhyn was too rich, too desirable, to stay peaceful if the line of succession should be broken. As much as he hated involving himself in the schemings and feudings of noble clans, Nevyn knew that his duty to Rhodry's dweomer-touched Wyrd also imposed on him a duty to Rhodry's rhan and to his innocent subjects, who preferred peace to war, unlike noble-born men like Talidd. He would fight with every weapon he had to keep Aberwyn safe. For all that Lovyan was skeptical about his political skills (and he knew full well that she was), he was better armed for this fight than any man in the kingdom, right down to the wisest of the high king's councillors. Oh, I learned a trick or two that time, he thought to himself, and our Rhodry was right in the middle of that little mess, for all that he was a humble rider then, and an outlawed man! Although it had been well over a hundred years ago now, he knew what it was to battle for the throne of not merely a gwerbret, but a king.

Part One

Deverry and Pyrdon, 833–845

When Dilly Blind went to the river,
To see what he could see,
He found the King of Cerrmor
A-washing his own laundry . . .

—Old Eldidd folk song

ONE

The Year 833. Slwmar II, king in Dun Deverry, received a bad wound in battle. The second son of Glyn II, king in Cerrmor, died stillborn. We took these as bad omens. Only later would we realize that Bel in His wisdom was preparing peace for his people . . .

The Holy Chronicles of Lughcarn

The flies were the worst thing. It was bad enough to be dying, but to have the flies so thick was an unjust indignity. They clustered buzzing round the wound and tried to drink the blood. It hurt too much to try to brush them away. The wound was on his right side, just below the armpit, and deep. If someone could have stitched it for him, Maddyn supposed, he might have lived, but since he was all alone in the wild hills, he was going to die. He saw no reason to lie to himself about it: he was bleeding to death. He clutched the saddle-peak with his left hand and kept his right arm raised, because the wound blazed like fire if he let his arm touch it. The blood kept oozing through his shattered mail, and the big shiny blue-black flies kept coming. Every now and then, a fly bit his horse, which was too exhausted to do more than stamp in protest.

Maddyn was the last rider in his warband left alive. Since when he died, the enemy victory would be complete, it seemed honorable to try to postpone their victory for a while; it seemed important then, as he rode slowly through the golden autumn haze, to cheat them of their victory for twenty minutes more. Ahead, about a mile away, was a lake, the surface rippled gold and shining in the sunset. Along the edge stood white birches, rippling in the rising wind. He wanted water. Next to the flies, being thirsty was the worst thing, his mouth so dry that he could barely breathe. His horse ambled steadily for the lake. It wouldn't matter, his dying, if only he could drink first.

The lake was coming closer. He could see the rushes, dark strokes against bright water, and a white heron, standing one-legged at the edge. Then something went wrong with the sun. It wasn't setting straight down, but swinging from side to side, like a lantern held in someone's hand as they walked. The sky was dark as night, but the sun kept swinging back and forth, a lantern in the night, back and forth, wider swings now, up up high up all the way to noon about him all the way above him and blazing. Then there was darkness, the smell of crushed grass, the flies buzzing and the thirst. Then only darkness.

A lantern was burning in the darkness. At first, Maddyn thought it was the sun, but this light was too small, too steady. An old man's face leaned over him. He had a thick mane of white hair and cold blue eyes.

"Ricyn." His voice was low but urgent. "Ricco, look at me."

Although Maddyn had never heard that particular name before, he knew somehow that it was his, and he tried to answer to it. His lips were too dry to move. The old man held a golden cup of water to his lips and helped him drink. The water was sweet and cold. I won't die thirsty after all, Maddyn thought. Then the darkness came again.

The next time that he woke, he realized that he wasn't going to die. For a long time, he lay perfectly still and wondered at it: he wasn't going to die. Slowly he looked around him, for the first time wondering where he was, and realized that he was lying naked between soft wool blankets on a pile of straw. Firelight danced over the walls of an enormous stone room. Although his wound still hurt, it was nicely bound with linen bandages. When he turned his head, he saw the old man sitting at a rough wooden table by the stone hearth and reading in a leather-bound book. The old man glanced up and smiled at him.

"Thirsty, lad?"

"I am, good sir."

The old man dipped water from a wooden barrel into the golden cup, then knelt down and helped him drink.

"My horse?" Maddyn said.

"He's safe and at his hay." The old man laid a hand on Maddyn's forehead. "Fever's broken. Good."

Maddyn just managed to smile before he fell asleep. This time, he dreamt of his last battle so vividly that it seemed he could smell the dust and the horse sweat. His warband drew up on the crest of the hill, and there were Tieryn Devyr and his men waiting across the road—over a hundred to their thirty-seven, but they were going to make the hopeless downhill charge anyway. Maddyn knew it by the way Lord Brynoic laughed like a madman, lounging back in his saddle. There was naught they could do but die; they were trapped, and they had naught left to live for. Even though he felt like a fool for doing it, Maddyn started thinking about his mother. In his mind, he could see her clearly, standing in the doorway of their house and holding out her arms to him. Then the horn blew for the charge, and he could only think of riding. Down the hill, on and on, with Devyr's men wheeling to face them—the clash came with a shriek from both sides. In his dream Maddyn relived every parry and cut, choked again on the rising dust, and woke with a cry when the sword bit deep into his side.

"Here, lad." The old man was right beside him. "All's well now."

"Can I have some water?"

"All you want."

After Maddyn gulped down six cupfuls, the old man brought him bread and milk in a wooden bowl. Since his hands were shaking too badly to hold a spoon, the old man fed him too, a spoonful at a time. The best feast in the gwerbret of Cantrae's hall had never tasted as good as that meal did.

"My thanks," Maddyn said. "Truly, I owe you the humblest thanks I can give for saving my life."

"Saving lives is somewhat of a habit of mine. I'm an herbman."

"And wasn't that the luck of my life, then!"

"Luck?" The old fellow smiled in a sly sort of way. "Well, truly, it may have been, at that. My name is Nevyn, by the by, and that's not a jest; it truly is my name. I'm somewhat of a hermit, and this is my home."

"My name is Maddyn, and I rode for Lord Brynoic. Here, do you realize that I'm an outlawed man? By every black-hearted demon in the hells, you should have let me bleed to death where I fell."

"Oh, I heard me of Brynoic's exile, sure enough, but the pronouncements of tieryns and suchlike mean little to me. Cursed if I'll let a man die when I can save him just because his lord overstepped himself at court."

With a sigh, Maddyn turned his head away. Nearby was his shield, leaning against the wall, and a tidy stack of his other gear, including his small ballad harp, wrapped safe in its leather sack. The sight of the fox device stamped on everything he owned made tears burn in Maddyn's eyes. His whole warband, all his friends, men he'd ridden with for eight years now—all dead, because Lord

Brynoic had coveted another man's land and failed in his gamble to get it.

"Did the tieryn bury our dead?" he whispered.

"He did. I found the battlefield some days after I brought you home. From the sight of the slaughter, I'm surprised that even one man escaped."

"I ran like a coward. I made the charge and got my wound. I knew I was dying, then, and I just wanted to die alone, somewhere quiet, like. Ah ye gods, I never dreamt that anyone would save me!"

"No doubt it was your Wyrd to live."

"It was a harsh Wyrd, then. I'm still an outlawed man. I threw away the last bit of honor I had when I didn't die with my lord and my band."

Nevyn made a soothing remark, but Maddyn barely heard him. For all that his shame bit at him, deep in his heart he knew he was glad to be alive, and that very gladness was another shame.

It was two days before Maddyn could sit up, and then only by propping himself against the wall and fighting with his swimming head. As soon as he was a bit stronger, he began wondering about the strange room he was in. From the smell of damp in the air and the lack of windows, he seemed to be underground, but the fire in the enormous hearth drew cleanly. The room was the right size for that massive hearth too, a full fifty feet across, and the ceiling was lost above him in shadows. All along the wall by his bed was a carved bas-relief, about ten feet above the floor, that must have at one time run around the entire room. Now the severely geometric pattern of triangles and circles broke off abruptly, as if it had been defaced. Finally, on the day when he was strong enough to feed himself for the first time, it occurred to him to ask Nevyn where they were.

"Inside Brin Toraedic. The entire hill is riddled with chambers and tunnels."

Maddyn almost dropped his spoon into his lap. Since Lord Brynoic's dun was only about five miles away, he'd seen the hill many a time and heard all the tales about it too, how it was haunted, plagued by demons and spirits, who sent blue lights dancing through the night and strange howls whistling through the day. It certainly looked peculiar enough to be haunted, rising straight out of an otherwise flat meadow, like some old giant long ago turned to stone and overgrown with grass.

"Now, now." Nevyn gave him a grin. "I'm real flesh and blood, not a prince of demons or suchlike."

Maddyn tried to return the smile and failed.

"I like to be left alone, lad," Nevyn went on. "So what better place could I find to live than a place where everyone else is afraid to go?"

"Well, true enough, I suppose. But, then, there aren't any spirits here after all?"

"Oh, there's lots, but they go their way and I go mine. Plenty of room for us all."

When Maddyn realized that the old man was serious, his hands shook so hard that he had to lay down his bowl and spoon.

"I couldn't lie to you," Nevyn said in a perfectly mild tone of voice. "You'll have to shelter with us this winter, because you won't be fit to ride before the snows come, but these spirits are a harmless sort. All that talk about demons is simple exaggeration. The folk around here are starved for a bit of color in their lives."

"Are they now? Uh, here, good sir, just how long have I been here, anyway?"

"Oh, a fortnight. You lay in a fever for a wretchedly long time. The wound went septic. When I found you, there were flies all over it."

Maddyn picked up his spoon and grimly went on eating. The sooner he got the strength to leave this spirit-plagued place, the better.

As the wound healed, Maddyn began getting out of bed for longer and longer periods. Although Nevyn had thrown away his blood-soaked clothes, Maddyn had a spare shirt in his saddlebags, and the old man found him a pair of brigga that fit well enough. One of the first things he did was unwrap his ballad harp and make sure that it was unharmed. With his right arm so weak, he couldn't tune it, but he ran his fingers over the sour, lax strings to make sure they still sounded.

"I'm surprised that Lord Brynoic would risk a bard in battle," Nevyn remarked.

"I'm not much of a bard, truly, more a gerthddyn who can fight. I know a good many songs and suchlike, but I never studied the triads and the rest of the true bard lore."

"And why not?"

"Well, my father was a rider in our lord's warband. When he

was killed, I was but thirteen, and Lord Brynoic offered me a place in the troop. I took it to avenge my father's death, and then, well, there never was a chance to study after that, since I'd given my lord my pledge and all."

"And do you regret it?"

"I've never let myself feel regret. Only grief lies that way, good sir."

Once he was strong enough, Maddyn began exploring the old man's strange home, a small complex of caves and tunnels. Beside the main living quarters, there was another stone room that the herbman had turned into a stable for his horse, Maddyn's, and a fine brown mule. The side of that room crumbled away, leading back to a natural cave, where a small spring welled up, then drained away down the side of the hill. Just outside the stable door was the gully that had given Brin Toraedic its name of "broken hill," a long, straight cleft slicing across the summit. The first time he went outside, he found the air cold in spite of the bright sun, and the chill worked in his wound and tormented him. He hurried inside and decided to take Nevyn's word for it that winter was well on its way.

Since the herbman had plenty of coin as well as these elaborate living quarters, Maddyn began to wonder if he were an eccentric nobleman who'd simply fled from the civil wars raging across the kingdom. He was far too grateful to ask such an embarrassing question, but scattered across the kingdom were plenty of the noble-born who weaseled any way they could to get out of their obligations to the various gwerbrets claiming to be king of all Deverry. Nevyn had a markedly courtly way about him, gracious at times, brusque at others, as if he were used to being obeyed without question. What's more, he could read and write, an accomplishment rare for the simple herbman he claimed to be. Maddyn began to find the old man fascinating.

Once every few days, Nevyn took his horse and mule and rode down to the nearby village, where he would buy fresh food and pack in a mule load of winter supplies: hay and grain for the stock, or cheeses, sausage, dried fruit, and suchlike for the pair of them. While he was gone, Maddyn would do some share of the work around the caves, then sleep off his exertion. On a gray morning with a sharp wind, Nevyn mentioned that he'd be gone longer than usual, because one of the village women needed his healing herbs.

After the old man left, Maddyn swept the stable refuse into the gully, then went back for a rest before he raked it out onto the hillside. He laid a bit more wood on the hearth, then sat down close by to drive the chill from his wound.

For the first time since the battle, he felt too strong to sleep, and his neglected harp called him reproachfully. When he took her out of her leather bag, the lax strings sighed at him. On a harp that size, there were only thirty-six strings, but in his weakened state, tuning her seemed to take him forever. He struck out the main note from his steel tuning bar, then worked over the strings, adjusting the tiny ivory pegs while he sang out the intervals, until sweat ran down his face. This sign of weakness only drove him on until at last the harp was in reasonable tune, but he had to rest for a few minutes before he could play it. He ran a few trills, struck a few chords, and the music seemed to give him a small bit of his strength back as it echoed through the huge stone-walled room. The very size of the place added an eerie overtone to every note he played.

Suddenly, at his shoulder, he felt the White Lady, his agwen, she who came to every bard who had true song in him. As she gathered, he felt the familiar chill down his back, the stirring of hair at the nape of his neck. For all that he called himself a gerthddyn, her presence and the inspiration she gave him were signs that the kingdom had lost a true bard when Maddyn had pledged for a rider. Although his voice was weak and stiff that morning, he sang for his agwen, a long ballad, bits of lyric, whatever came to his mind, and the music soothed his wound as well as a healing poultice.

All at once, he knew that he wasn't alone. When he looked up, expecting to see Nevyn in the doorway, no one was indeed there. When he glanced around, he saw nothing but fire-thrown shadows. Yet every time he struck a chord, he felt an audience listening to him. The hair on the back of his neck pricked like a cat's when he remembered Nevyn's talk of spirits. You're daft, he told himself sharply; there's naught here. But he had performed too many times to believe himself. He knew the intangible difference between singing to empty air and playing to an attentive hall. When he sang two verses of a ballad, he felt them, whoever they were, leaning forward to catch every word. When he stopped and set the harp down, he sensed their disappointment.

"Well, here now. You can't be such bad sorts if you like a good song."

He thought he heard someone giggle behind him, but when he turned, there was nothing there but the wall. He got up and walked slowly and cautiously around the room, looked into every corner and crack—and saw nothing. Just as he sat down again, someone else giggled—this time he heard it plainly—like a tiny child who's just played a successful prank. Maddyn grabbed his harp only in the somewhat fuddled thought of keeping it safe, but when he felt his invisible audience crowd round him in anticipation, he was too much of a bard to turn down any listeners, even incorporeal ones. When he struck the strings, he was sure he heard them give a little sigh of pleasure. Just because it was the first thing that came to mind, he sang through the fifty chained stanzas that told of King Bran's sea voyage to Deverry, and of the magical mist that swept him and his fleet away at the end. By the time that the enchanted ships were safe in the long-lost, mysterious harbor in the far north, Maddyn was exhausted.

"My apologies, but I've got to stop now."

A sigh sounded in regret. Someone touched his hair with a gentle stroke, like a pat on a dog; someone plucked at his sleeve with skinny-feeling fingers. The fire blazed up on the hearth; a draft swirled around him in preternaturally cold air. Maddyn shuddered and stood up, but little hands grabbed his brigga leg. The harp strings sounded in a random run down as someone tried them for itself. The very shadows came alive, eddying and swirling in every corner. Fingers were touching his face, stroking his arm, pinching his clothes, pulling his hair, while the harp strings rang and strummed in an ugly belling.

"Stop that, all of you!" Nevyn yelled from the door. "That's a wretched discourteous way to treat our guest!"

The little fingers disappeared. The fire fell low, as if in embarrassment. Maddyn felt like weeping in relief as the herbman strode in, carrying a pair of saddlebags.

"Truly, it was a nasty way to behave," Nevyn went on, addressing the seemingly empty air. "If you do that again, then Maddyn won't ever play his harp for you."

The room went empty of presences. Nevyn tossed the saddlebags down on the table and gave Maddyn a grin. With shaking hands, Maddyn set his harp down and wiped the sweat from his face on his sleeve.

"I should have warned you about that. They love music. My apologies, lad."

Maddyn tried to speak, failed, and sat down heavily on the bench. Behind him, a harp string twanged. Nevyn scowled at the air beside it.

"I said stop it!"

A little puff of wind swept away.

"Aren't you going to ask me a few questions, Maddyn lad?"

"To tell you the truth, I'm afraid to."

The old man laughed under his breath.

"Well, I'll answer anyway, question or no. Those were what men call the Wildfolk. They're like ill-trained children or puppies, all curiosity, no sense or manners. Unfortunately, they can hurt us mortal folk without even meaning to do so."

"I gathered that, sure enough." As he looked at his benefactor, Maddyn realized a truth he'd been avoiding for days now. "Sir, you must have dweomer."

"I do. How does that strike you?"

"Like a blow. I never thought there was any such thing outside of my own ballads and tales."

"Most men would consider me a bard's fancy, truly, but my craft is real enough."

Maddyn stared, wondering how Nevyn could look so cursed ordinary, until the old man turned away with good-humored laugh and began rummaging in his saddlebags.

"I brought you a bit of roast meat for your supper, lad. You need it to make back the blood you lost, and the villager I visited had some to spare to pay for my herbs."

"My thanks. Uh, when do you think I'll be well enough to ride out?"

"Oho! The spirits have you on the run, do they?"

"Well, not to be ungrateful or suchlike, good sir." Maddyn felt himself blush. "But I . . . uh . . . well . . ."

Nevyn laughed again.

"No need to be ashamed, lad. Now as to the wound, it'll be a good while yet before you're fit. You rode right up to the gates of the Otherlands, and it always takes a man a long time to ride back again."

From that day on, the Wildfolk grew bolder around Maddyn, the way that hounds will slink out from under the table when they realize that their master's guest is fond of dogs. Every time

Maddyn picked up his harp, he was aware of their presence—a liveliness in the room, a small scuffle of half-heard noise, a light touch on his arm or hair, a breath of wind as something flew by. Whenever they pinched or mobbed him, he would simply threaten to stop singing, a threat that always made them behave themselves. Once, when he was struggling to light a fire with damp tinder, he felt them gather beside him. As he struck a spark from his steel, the Wildfolk blew it into a proper flame. When he thanked them automatically, he realized that he was beginning to take spirits for granted. As for Nevyn himself, although Maddyn studied the old man for traces of strange powers and stranger lore, he never saw any, except, of course, that spirits obeyed him.

Maddyn also spent a lot of time thinking over his future. Since he was a member of an outlawed warband, he would hang if Tieryn Devyr ever got his hands on him. His one chance at an honorable life was slim indeed. If he rode down to Cantrae without the tieryn catching him, and then threw himself upon the gwerbret's mercy, he might be pardoned simply because he was something of a bard and thus under special protection in the laws. Unfortunately, the pardon was unlikely, because it would depend on his liege's whim, and Gwerbret Tibryn of the Boar was a harsh man. His clan, the Boars of the North, was related to the southern Boars of Muir, who had wheedled the gwerbretrhyn out of the king in Dun Deverry some fifty years before. Between them, the conjoint Boar clans ruled a vast stretch of the northern kingdom and were said to be the real power behind a puppet king in the Holy City. It was unlikely that Tibryn would bother to show mercy to a half-trained bard when that mercy would make one of his loyal tieryns grumble. Maddyn decided that since he and the spirits had worked out their accommodation, he would leave the gwerbret's mercy alone and stay in Brin Toraedic until spring.

The next time Nevyn rode to the village, Maddyn decided to ride a ways with him to exercise both himself and his horse. The day was clear and cold, with the smell of snow in the air and a rimy frost lying on the brown stubbled fields. When he realized that it was nearly Samaen, Maddyn was shocked at the swift flowing of time outside the hill, which seemed to have a different flow of its own. Finally they came to the village, a handful of round, thatched houses scattered among white birches along the banks of a stream.

"I'd best wait for you by the road," Maddyn said. "One of the tieryn's men might ride into the village for some reason."

"I don't want you sitting out in this cold. I'll take you over to a farm near here. These people are friends of mine, and they'll shelter you without awkward questions."

They followed a lane across brown pastureland until they came to the farmstead, a scatter of round buildings inside a circular, packed-earth wall. Out in back of the big house was a cow barn, storage sheds, and a pen for gray and white goats. In the muddy yard, chickens pecked round the front door of the house. Shooing the hens away, a stout man with graying hair came out to greet them.

"Morrow, my lord. What can I do for you this morning?"

"Oh, just keep a friend of mine warm, good Bannyc. He's been very ill, as I'm sure his white face is telling you, and he needs to rest while I'm in the village."

"We can spare him room at the hearth. Ye gods, lad, you're pale as the hoarfrost, truly."

Bannyc ushered Maddyn into the wedge-shaped main room, which served as kitchen and hall both. In front of a big hearth, where logs blazed in a most welcome way, stood two tables and three high-back benches, a prosperous amount of furniture for those parts. Clean straw covered the floor, and the walls were freshly whitewashed. From the ceiling hung strings of onions and garlic, nets of drying turnips and apples, and a couple of enormous hams. On the hearthstone a young woman was sitting cross-legged and mending a pair of brigga.

"Who's this, Da?" she said.

"A friend of Nevyn's."

Hastily she scrambled up and dropped Maddyn a curtsy. She was very pretty, with raven-black hair and dark, calm eyes. Maddyn bowed to her in return.

"You'll forgive me for imposing on you," Maddyn said. "I haven't been well, and I need a bit of a rest."

"Any friend of Nevyn's is always welcome here," she said. "Sit down, and I'll get you some ale."

Maddyn took off his cloak, then sat down on the hearthstone as close to the fire as he could get without singeing his shirt. Announcing that he had to get back to the cows, Bannyc strolled back outside. The woman handed Maddyn a tankard of dark ale, then sat down near him and picked up her mending again.

"My thanks." Maddyn saluted her with the ale. "My name's Maddyn of . . . uh, well, just Maddyn will do."

"Mine's Belyan. Have you known Nevyn long?"

"Oh, not truly."

Belyan gave him an oddly awestruck smile and began sewing. Maddyn sipped his ale and watched her slender fingers work deftly on the rough wool of a pair of brigga, Bannyc's, by the large size of them. He was surprised at how good it felt to be sitting warm and alive in the presence of a pretty woman. Every now and then, Belyan hesitantly looked his way, as if she were trying to think of something to say.

"Well, my lord," she said at last. "Will you be staying long with our Nevyn?"

"I don't truly know, but here, what makes you call me lord? I'm as common-born as you are."

"Well—but a friend of Nevyn's."

At that Maddyn realized that she knew perfectly well that the old man was dweomer.

"Now here, what do you think I am?" Maddyn had the uneasy feeling that it was very dangerous to pretend to dweomer you didn't have. "I'm only a rider without a warband. Nevyn was good enough to save my life when he found me wounded, that's all. But here, don't tell anyone about me, will you? I'm an outlawed man."

"I'll forget your name the minute you ride on."

"My humble thanks, and my apologies. I don't even deserve to be drinking your ale."

"Oh, hold your tongue! What do I care about these rotten wars?"

When he looked at her, he found her angry, her mouth set hard in a bitter twist.

"I don't care the fart of a two-copper piglet," she went on. "All it's ever brought to me and mine is trouble. They take our horses and raise our taxes and ride through our grain, and all in the name of glory and the one true king, or so they call him, when everyone with wits in his head knows there's two kings now, and why should I care, truly, as long as they don't both come here a-bothering us. If you're one man who won't die in this war, then I say good for you."

"Ye gods. Well, truly, I never thought of it that way before."

"No doubt, since you were a rider once."

"Here, I'm not exactly a deserter or suchlike."

She merely shrugged and went back to her sewing. Maddyn wondered why a woman her age, twenty-two or so, was living in her father's house. Had she lost a betrothed in the wars? The question was answered for him in a moment when two small lads, about six and four, came running into the room and calling her Mam. They were fighting over a copper they'd found in the road and come to her to settle it. Belyan gave them each a kiss and told them they'd have to give the copper to their gran, then sent them back outside.

"So you're married, are you?" Maddyn said.

"I was once. Their father drowned in the river two winters ago. He was setting a fish trap, but the ice turned out to be too thin."

"That aches my heart, truly. So you came back to your father?"

"I did. Da needed a woman around the house, and he's good to my lads. That's what matters to me."

"Then it gladdens my heart to hear that you're happy."

"Happy?" She thought for a moment. "Oh, I don't think much of things like happiness, just as long as the lads are well."

Maddyn could feel her loneliness, lying just under her faint, mocking smile. His body began to wonder about her, a flicker of sexual warmth, another sign that life was coming back to him. She looked at him steadily, her dark eyes patient, self-contained, almost unreadable.

"And what will you do now?" she said. "Ride on before the snows come?"

"Nevyn doesn't think I'll be fit by then, but sooner or later I have to go. It'll mean my life if I stay. They hang outlawed men."

"So they do."

Belyan considered him for a moment more, then got up briskly, as if she'd come to some decision, and strode out of the room through a blanket-hung door in one of the wickerwork walls. He was just finishing his tankard when she returned, carrying a shirt, which she tossed into his lap when she sat back down.

"That was my husband's," she said. "It's too small for Da, and it'll rot before the lads grow to fit it. Take it. You need a shirt that doesn't have foxes embroidered all over it."

"Ye gods! I forgot about that. No wonder you thought I was a deserter, then. Well, my humble thanks."

He smoothed it out, studying with admiration the sleeves, stiff with finely embroidered interlace and spirals, and at the yokes, floral bands. It had probably been her husband's wedding shirt, because it was unlikely that her man had owned two pieces of such fancy clothing, but still, it was a good bit safer for him to wear than one with his dead lord's blazon. He took off his old shirt and gave it to her.

"Do you want this for the cloth? You can mend the lads' tunics out of it."

"So I can. My thanks."

She was looking at the scar along his side, a thick clot of tissue in his armpit, a thinner gash along his ribs. Hurriedly he pulled the new shirt over his head and smoothed it down.

"It fits well enough. You're generous to a dishonored man."

"Better than letting it rot. I put a lot of fancy work into that."

"Do you miss your man still?"

"At times." She paused, considering for a few moments. "I do, at that. He was a good man. He didn't beat me, and we always had enough to eat. When he had the leisure, he'd whittle little horses and wagons for the lads, and he made sure I had a new dress every spring."

It came to that for her, he realized, not the glories of love and the tempests of passion that the bard songs celebrated for noble audiences. He'd met plenty of women like Belyan, farm women, all of them, whose real life ran apart from their men in a self-contained earthiness of their work and their children. Since their work counted as much as their men's toward feeding and sheltering themselves and their kin, it gave them a secure place of their own, unlike the wives of the noble lords, who existed at their husbands' whims. Yet Belyan was lonely; at times she missed her man. Maddyn was aware of his body, and the wondering was growing stronger. When she smiled at him, he smiled in return.

The door banged open, and shouting and laughing, the two lads ushered in Nevyn. Although he joked easily with the boys, the old man turned grim when he reached Maddyn.

"You were right to stay out here, lad. I like that new shirt you're wearing."

Belyan automatically began rolling the old one up, hiding the fox-blazoned yokes inside the roll.

"Tieryn Devyr is up at Brynoic's dun," Nevyn went on. "He's going to assign the lands to his son, Romyl, and give the lad part of his warband to hold them. That means men who know you will be riding the roads around here. I think we'll just go home the back way."

For several days after, Maddyn debated the risk of riding on his own, then finally went down to see Belyan by a roundabout way.

When he led the horse into the farmstead, it seemed deserted. The wooden wagon was gone, and not even a dog ran out to bark at him. As he stood there, puzzling, Belyan came walking out of the barn with a wooden bucket in one hand. Maddyn liked her firm but supple stride.

"Da's taken the lads down to market," she said. "We had extra cheeses to sell."

"Will they be gone long?"

"Till sunset, most like. I was hoping you'd ride our way today."

Maddyn took his horse to the barn and tied him up in a stall next to one of the cows, where he'd be out of the wind and, more importantly, out of sight of the road. When he went into the house, he found Belyan putting more wood in the hearth. She wiped her hands on her skirts, then glanced at him with a small, secretive smile.

"It's cold in my bedchamber, Maddo. Come sit down by the fire."

They sat down together in the soft clean straw by the hearth. When he touched her hair with a shy stroke, she laid impatient hands on his shoulders. When he kissed her, she slipped her hands behind his neck and pulled him down to her as smoothly as if she were gathering in a sheaf of wheat.

The winter was slow in coming that year. There was one flurry of snow, then only the cold under a clear sky, day after day of aching frost and wind. Although the pale sun managed to melt the first snowfall, rime lay cold and glittering on the brown fields and in the ditches along the roads. Maddyn spent the days out of sight in Brin Toraedic, because Lord Romyl's men were often out prowling the roads, riding back and forth to the village to exercise their horses and to get themselves out of the dun. Maddyn would sleep late, then practice his harp by the hour with the Wildfolk for an audience. Sometimes Nevyn would sit and listen, or even make a judicious comment about his singing or the song itself, but the old man spent much of his day deep within the broken hill. Maddyn never got up the nerve to ask him what he did there.

One afternoon when Nevyn was gone, Maddyn remembered a song about Dilly Blind, the trickiest Wildfolk of them all. Since it was a children's song, he hadn't heard it in years, but he ran through it several times and made up fresh verses when he couldn't remember the old. The Wildfolk clustered close and listened enraptured. When he finally finished with it, for the briefest of moments he thought he saw or perhaps did indeed see them, little faces, little eyes, peering up at him. Then, suddenly, they were gone. When Nevyn returned later, Maddyn mentioned his vision—if such it was—to the old man, who looked honestly startled.

"If you do start seeing them, lad, for the sake of every god, don't go telling people about it. You'll be mocked within a bare thread of your life."

"Oh, I know that, sure enough. I'm just puzzled. I never had so much as a touch of the second sight before."

"Truly? That's odd, because bards so often do have the sight. But anyway, lad, you're doubtless picking it up just from being here with us. Suppose you laid your sword down close to the fire in the hearth. In time, the blade would grow hot, even though it wasn't in the fire itself. Being in a center of dweomer power can do that to a man with a sensitive mind."

With a little shudder Maddyn looked around the towering stone chamber. A center of power? he thought; truly, you can feel it sometimes.

"Well," Maddyn said at last. "It was a strange chance that brought me here."

"Perhaps. But naught happens to a dweomerman by chance, especially not in these cursed and troubled times."

"I take it the wars ache your heart."

"Of course they do, dolt! If you had any sense, they'd ache yours."

"Well, good sir, I've never known anything but war. Sometimes I wonder if the days of the old kingdom are like the tales in some of my songs—splendid to hear, but never true."

"Oh, they were real enough. There was a time when a man could ride the roads in peace, and the farmers gather in their crops in safety, and a man have a son and feel sure that he'd live to see the lad live to be grown and married. Good days, they were, and I pray constantly that they'll come again."

Maddyn felt a sudden longing to know that kind of life. Before, he'd wanted battle glory and honor, taken it for granted that there would always be wars to provide them, but all at once he wondered if glory were the great prize he'd always believed it to be. Later, when he went out to walk on the top of the hill, he found that the snow had been falling all morning. For miles around, the world was soft and white under a pearly gray sky, the trees etched against the horizon, the distant village snug under a breath of smoke from its chimneys. He'd seen views like it a hundred times and thought nothing of them, but now it was beautiful, so beautiful that he wondered if he'd ever really looked at anything before he'd ridden up to the gates of the Otherlands.

At night, whenever the weather allowed, Maddyn rode down to see Belyan. At first he was afraid that Bannyc would resent this outlaw who'd ridden in and taken his daughter, but the old man regarded him with a certain pleasant indifference. Her sons were a different matter. The younger found him a nuisance, and the elder frankly hated him. Maddyn took to arriving late at the farm, when he could be sure they were asleep, because Belyan made it clear that the lads came first in her heart—fair enough, he thought, since they both knew he'd be riding on in the spring. Yet whenever he held her in his arms, the spring seemed very far away.

Once the snows came in force, it was hard to ride down to her bed as often as Maddyn wanted. One night, after a frustrating week of being snowbound in the hill, he left early and pushed his horse hard through the heavy drifts. He stabled his horse, then climbed in through Belyan's chamber window, pushing the oiled hides aside and cursing while she laughed at him. Although she had a freestanding clay stove in the chamber, it was still bitter cold. He threw off his cloak, pulled off his boots, then got into bed before undressing the rest of the way.

"Your chamber's as cold as the blasted roads!"

"Then come over to my side of the bed. It's nice and warm."

When he took her in his arms, she turned to him greedily with a simple, direct passion that still took him by surprise. She didn't know how to be coy and flirtatious like the other women he'd had. When would she have had the time to learn, he supposed, and it didn't bother him one whit. Later, as he lay drowsing between sleep and waking, he found himself considering staying in the spring. Bannyc would be glad to have an extra man to help work the farm; Bell would be glad to have him in her bed every night; the lads could gradually be won over. While Maddyn didn't love her, he liked her, and it would do well enough all round. Yet he didn't dare stay. For the first time, he saw clearly that he was indeed running for his life. Any lord in Cantrae who recognized him would turn him over to Devyr for hanging. He was going to have to ride west, ride fast and far enough to find a lord who'd

never heard of him or Lord Brynoic and one who was desperate
enough for men to take him on with no questions asked. Most
likely, he'd end up riding for one of the enemy sides in the long
wars, a Cerrmor ally or an Eldidd lord. He kissed Belyan awake
and made love to her again, simply to drown his thoughts of the
future ahead of him.

That night the snow was so bad that Maddyn risked staying till
morn. It was pleasant, sleeping with his arms around her, so pleasant that he was tempted to risk doing it often, but when he came
out of her chamber in the morning, he found some of Bannyc's
neighbors there, eating bread and drinking ale while they chatted
by the hearth. Although they were pleasant to him, Maddyn had
the grim experience of finding himself the undoubted focus of
four pairs of eyes and—no doubt—a good bit of future gossip. If
any of that gossip reached the wrong ears, he would be in danger.
After that, he rode only at night and left her house well before
dawn.

Yet for all his precautions, the night came when Maddyn ran
across some of Romyl's men. Just at midnight, he was picking his
way across the fields on his way back to Brin Toraedic. A cold
wind drove torn and scudding clouds across the sky, alternately
covering and sailing free of a full moon. He could see the hill
close, a jagged blackness rising out of the meadow and looming
against the sky, when he heard the jingle of bridles carrying in the
clear night air. Horses snorted; hoofbeats were trotting fast down
the road. Nearby was a leafless copse, an imperfect shelter, but the
best Maddyn could find. As he guided his horse into the trees, the
branches dropped snow, scattering over his hood and cloak.
Maddyn sat as still as he could and waited. He refused to make an
obvious dash for the hill. If he were going to be caught, he didn't
want Nevyn hanged with him.

Trotting in tight formation, six riders came down the road.
When they were directly abreast of the copse, they paused and
wheeled their horses into a ring to argue about which direction to
take at the crossroads ahead. Maddyn could clearly hear that they
were more than a bit drunk. In an almost tangible swirl of concern and bewilderment, the Wildfolk clustered around him to listen as the argument in the road went on and on. Then Maddyn's
horse stamped, shivering uncontrollably in the cold with a jingle
of tack. One of the riders turned in the saddle and saw him.

Maddyn urged his horse slowly forward; he would rather surrender, he realized, than put Nevyn and possibly Belyan at risk.

"Danger," he whispered to the Wildfolk. "Tell Nevyn."

He felt some of them rush away, but the others crowded round, a trembling of small lives like gusts of warmer air.

"You!" the rider called. "Come forward!"

With a sinking heart, Maddyn recognized Selyn, one of Devyr's men, who knew him well. With Selyn at their head, the riders trotted over, spreading out in a semicircle to surround and trap him. Since it was a hopeless situation, Maddyn rode out to meet them. In the moonlight, he could just see an exaggerated surprise on Selyn's face.

"Maddyn! Oh, by the gods!" His voice was a frightened hiss. "It's long past Samaen."

One of the others yelped sharply, like a kicked hound. The group pulled their horses to an abrupt halt, just as Maddyn felt the Wildfolk rushing about him in panic, lifting and trembling the edges of his cloak and hood.

"Now, here, Maddo lad, don't harm us. I used to be a friend of yours. It was only my lord's orders that ever made us lift a sword against you. May peace be yours in the Otherlands."

As Selyn began edging his nervous horse backward, the truth hit Maddyn: Selyn, who thought he was dead with all the rest of Brynoic's warband, could only assume that he was seeing Maddyn's spirit. The thought made him laugh aloud. It was the perfect thing to do; the entire squad began edging their horses backward, but they never took their terrified eyes off Maddyn's face. Such profound attention was more than any bard could resist. Maddyn tossed his head back and howled, a long eerie note, sending his trained voice as far and high as he could. A rider shrieked, and the sound broke the squad.

"Spirits!" Selyn screamed. "Save yourselves."

With a giggle of pure, delighted malice, the Wildfolk threw themselves forward among the horses. In the moonlight Maddyn could see them: a thickening in the air like frost crystals, little faces, little hands, fingers that began pinching every horse and rider they could reach. The horses kicked and plunged; the riders yelled, slapping at their mounts with their reins as they desperately tried to turn them. When Maddyn howled a second time, the horses lurched sideways and charged for the road at a gallop with their riders clinging to their necks. Maddyn sat in his saddle and

sobbed with laughter until the Wildfolk returned. In a companionable crowd, he rode back the hill, whose legend had just grown a
good bit larger. As he led his horse into the stable, Nevyn came
running to meet him.

"What's all this about danger?"

"All over now, good sir, but it's a pretty tale. I think I'll make a
song about it."

First, though, he simply told the tale to Nevyn over a tankard of
mulled ale, and the old man laughed his dry chuckle that always
sounded rusty from long disuse.

"The battlefield where your warband fell is only about five miles
from here, certainly close enough for a haunt. One thing, though,
if they ride back in the morning, they'll see the hoofprints of your
horse." Nevyn looked at a spot close to his right knee. "Do us a
favor, will you? Take some of the lads and go out to the field. Do
you remember the tracks Maddyn's horse made? . . . You do?
Splendid! Sweep those away like a good lad, but leave all the other
tracks where they are. We'll have a good jest on those nasty men."

Maddyn could feel that the crowd was gone, except for a tiny
blue sprite. All at once, he saw her clearly, perched on his knee
and sucking her finger while she stared up at him with alarmingly
vacant green eyes. When she smiled, she revealed a mouth full of
needle-sharp, bright blue teeth.

"Oho!" Nevyn said. "You see her, don't you?"

"I do, at that. Will I go on seeing the Wildfolk after I leave here?"

"I'd imagine so, but I don't truly know. I haven't come across a
puzzle like you before, lad."

Maddyn had the ungrateful thought that if he were a puzzle,
then Nevyn was the greatest riddle in the world.

The next afternoon, Nevyn rode down to the village to hear the
gossip and brought back the tale of Maddyn's meeting with the
squad in its new and doubtless permanent form. Lord Romyl's
men had foolishly ridden by Brin Toraedic in moonlight, when
every lackwit knows you should avoid the hill like poison during
the full moon. There, sure enough, they'd seen the ghosts of Lord
Brynoic's entire warband, charging across the meadow just as
they had during the last battle. Yet in the morning, when the riders
came back to look, they found the hoofprints of only their own
horses.

" 'And what did they think they'd find?' the tavernman says to me," Nevyn said with a dry laugh. "Everyone knows that spirits don't leave tracks."

"So they *did* come back, did they? I'm cursed glad you thought of that."

"Oh, it's one thing to be spirit-plagued by moonlight, quite another to think things over in the cold light of dawn. But they found naught for all their looking, and now none of Lord Romyl's men will ride near the hill, even in daylight."

"Isn't that a handy thing?"

"It is, but ye gods, you warriors are a superstitious lot!"

"Oh, are we now?" Maddyn had to laugh at the old man's indignation. "You show me a world full of spirits, send those spirits out to run me an errand, and then have the gall to call me superstitious!"

Nevyn laughed for a good long time over that.

"You're right, and I apologize, Maddyn my lad, but surely you can't deny that your average swordsman believes that the strangest things will bring him luck, either good or ill."

"True, but you just can't know what it's like to ride in a war. Every time you saddle up, you know blasted well that maybe you'll never ride back. Who knows what makes one man fall and another live in a battle? Once I saw a man who was a splendid fighter —oh, he swung a sword like a god, not a man—and he rode into this particular scrap with all the numbers on his side, and you know what happened? His cinch broke, dumped him into the mob, and he was kicked to death. And then you see utter idiots, with no more swordcraft than a farmer's lad, ride straight for the enemy and come out without a scratch. So after a while, you start believing in luck and omens and anything else you can cursed well turn up, just to ease the pain of not knowing when you'll die."

"I can see that, truly."

Nevyn's good humor was gone; he looked saddened to tears as he thought things over. Seeing him that way made Maddyn melancholy himself, and thoughtful.

"I suppose that's what makes us all long for dweomer leaders," Maddyn went on, but slowly. "You can have the best battle plan in the world, but once the javelins are thrown and the swordplay starts, ah by the hells, not even the gods could think clearly. So call it superstition all you want, but you want a leader who's got a touch of the dweomer about him, someone who can see more than you can, and who's got the right luck."

"If being lucky and clear-sighted made a man dweomer, lad, then the world would be full of men like me."

"Well, that's not quite what I meant, good sir. A dweomer leader would be different, somehow. Doubtless none exist, but we all want to believe it. You'd love to ride for a man like that, you tell yourself, someone the gods favor, someone you can believe in. Even if you died for him, it'd be worth it."

Nevyn gave him such a sharp look that Maddyn hesitated, but the old man gestured for him to go on.

"This is incredibly interesting."

"Then my thanks, truly. Now, Slwmar of Dun Deverry's a great and generous man, but he's not a dweomer leader. I always had trouble believing he was the true king, frankly, even though I always pledged him that way because my lord did. He used to walk among us men every now and again, talking to us and calling us by name, and it was splendid of him, but he was just an ordinary sort of lord, not a true king."

"Indeed? And what should the true king look like, then?"

"Well, there should just be somewhat of the dweomer about him. You should just be able to tell he's the true king. I mean, he doesn't have to be as tall as one of the gods, or as handsome, either, but you could look at him and know in your very soul he was meant to rule. He'd have splendid good luck, and the gods would send omens of the things he was going to do. By the hells, I'd follow a man like that to the death, and most of the kingdom would, too, I'll wager."

With a wild, half-mad grin, Nevyn got up and began pacing furiously back and forth in front of the hearth.

"Have I said somewhat stupid?" Maddyn said.

"What? You've just said the best thing I've heard in many a long year, actually. Lad, you can't know how glad I am that I dragged you back from the gates of the Otherlands. My thanks for making me see what's been under my nose all along. I'll tell you one great fault of the dweomer. You get so used to using it and looking in strange places for stranger lore that you forget to use the wits the gods gave you in the first place!"

Utterly confused, Maddyn could only stare at him as he cackled and paced back and forth like a madman. Finally Maddyn went to bed, but when he woke restlessly in the middle of the night, he saw Nevyn standing by the hearth and smiling into the fire.

Over the next couple of snowbound weeks, Nevyn spent much time brooding over the idea that Maddyn had so inadvertently handed him, a splendid repayment for his healing. Although complex in its details, the plan was peculiarly simple at its core and thus possible. At the moment, things looked as if the wars might rage until the end of time, ravaging the kingdom until there wasn't a man left fit to fight. After so many years of civil war, after so many leaders slain and buried, so many loyal followers wiped out, it seemed to men's minds that each of the claimants had as good a right as the next one to the throne. When it came to figuring bloodlines and genealogies, even the priests had a hard time telling who was most fit to be king of all Deverry. The lords, therefore, pledged to the man who seemed to offer an immediate advantage, and their sons changed the alliance if the advantage changed.

But what if a man appeared who impressed his followers as the true king, a dweomer leader, as Maddyn said, whom half the kingdom would follow to the throne or the grave? Then at last, after one final gruesome bloodbath, the kingdom would come to peace. Dweomer leader, is it? Nevyn would think; give me a decent man, and I'll make him look dweomer soon enough. It would be easy—disgustingly easy as he thought about it—to surround a good-looking man with glamour, to manipulate the omens around him, to pull a few cheap tricks just like the one that the Wildfolk had pulled on Selyn and his friends. They would have the troops on their knees and their lords along with them, all cheering the one true king. He realized, too, in those nights of brooding, that he shouldn't have been surprised that Maddyn would bring him the idea. In his last life, as young Ricyn down in Cerrmor, he'd been the captain of a warband pledged to just such a dweomer leader, Gweniver of the Wolf, whose madness and undoubted piety to the Dark Goddess had combined to blaze her round with false glamour like a fire.

Thinking about her and her grim fate made Nevyn wary. Did he have the right to subject another man to the forces that had torn her fragile mind apart? He would have to be very careful, to wait and scheme until he found a candidate strong enough for the burden. He wondered, too, if he would even be allowed to use dweomer for such a purpose. He spent long hours in meditation, stripped his soul bare and begged for aid from the Lords of Light. In time, his answer grew slowly in his mind: the kingdom needs peace above all else, and if somewhat goes wrong, then you will be the sacrifice. That he could accept, thinking of himself as the servant of and the sacrifice for the king he would create.

The permission given, it was time to plan. While Maddyn was away at Belyan's, or sleeping his boredom away, Nevyn would talk through the fire to the other dweomerfolk of the kingdom, particularly Aderyn in the west and a woman who bore the honorary name of Rommerdda in the north. Everyone was so weary of war that they were eager to throw their dice on Nevyn's long gamble.

"But we can't do this alone," Rommerdda remarked one night. "We'll have to win over the priests. Can we?"

"I intend to start turning the earth for this particular garden in the spring. At the same time, we can start scouting around for the proper prince."

As her image danced in the firelight, Rommerdda looked skeptical. She wore her long white hair done in two braids like a lass of the Dawntime, and her face was even more wrinkled than his, so old, so exhausted that Nevyn knew she would never see the end of this work they were planning. Of all the dweomer folk in the kingdom, only he and Aderyn had unnaturally long lives, each for their separate reasons. There would, however, soon be another Rommerdda to take up the task in hand.

And it was going to be a hard one: find the right man, then lay the proper omens for his coming with the aid of the priests. Once the kingdom lived for the day when the true king appeared, then Nevyn could orchestrate his moves. As he brooded over the details, Nevyn began to long for spring. The sooner he got started, the better.

TWO

The year 834. This was the year of the first omens of the coming king. A two-headed kid was born in a village near our temple. It died soon after, because a kingdom with two kings cannot live. In the sky we saw a vision of a great horse, running before a storm, and coming from the west. Although the omen was duly recorded, only later did we realize its import . . .

The Holy Chronicles of Lughcarn

Spring came too fast that year for Maddyn's liking. Every morning, he would walk up on the hill and search the sky for weather omens. Although he would have to stay until the snows were well past, at the same time he had to be well away before the real spring, when the riders would be swarming on the Cantrae roads for the summer muster. First came the rains that melted the last of the snow and turned the world to brown muck; then the nights grew warmer until it seemed a hardy man could sleep beside the road without freezing. Yet he found excuses to stay until the pale grass began to come out in sheltered valleys. That very night, he rode down early to see Belyan.

When he climbed through her window, he found her still up, fussing over the fire in the clay stove. She gave him a distracted sort of kiss.

"Take off those boots before sitting on the bed, will you, love? I don't want muck all over the blankets."

Maddyn leaned into the curve of the wall and began to pull them off.

"Spring's here," he said. "Will it ache your heart when I ride?"

"It will, but not half as badly as seeing you hanged would ache it."

"True enough. But, Bell, I wish I could stay, and all for your sake. I want you to know that."

"It would be splendid, having you with us on the farm, but I don't see how we could keep you hidden. A few of our friends already know I've got a man, and in a few months, the whole village will know."

When he looked up, he found her smiling, her dark eyes as calm as always.

"Oh, by the hells, what have I done? Gotten you with child?"

"What did you think would happen after all the rolling around we've done? I'm hardly barren, am I? Oh, here, don't look so troubled, love. I've wanted another babe for ever so long now. I'm just glad we had the time for you to give me one."

"But I have to desert you! I don't even have the wretched coin for the midwife."

"Oh, the midwife's a friend of mine, so don't trouble your heart over that. I can tend a babe on my own, but I couldn't have gotten one without a bit of help, could I?" She laid her hands delicately on her stomach. "Oh, I do hope it's a daughter, but if it's a son, shall I name him after you?"

"Only if you truly want to. I'd rather you gave him my father's name. It was Daumyr."

"Then Daumyr it is, if it's a lad. Well, either way, I hope it has your curly hair."

Maddyn hesitated with a troubling suspicion rising in his mind. He'd always known she didn't truly love him, but he was beginning to wonder if he'd just been put out to stud.

"Bell? Will you miss me when I'm gone?"

Somewhat startled, she considered the question.

"Well, I will," she said at last. "A bit."

When Maddyn left that night, the air was warm with the moist rich smell of spring earth. At the hilltop he dismounted and stood looking out over the dark countryside, the glitter of streams in the moonlight, the distant mound of the sleeping village, and far away, the gleam of the lake where the gates of the Otherlands had almost opened to receive him. I've been happy this winter, he thought; ah, curse both false kings and their balls, too!

In the morning Maddyn led his horse down the gully one last time. Overhead, white clouds sailed by, sweeping their shadows over the pale grass on the muddy moorland. When they reached the foot of the hill, Nevyn handed him a worn leather pouch, jingling with coin.

"Take it without arguing, lad. I didn't save your life only to have you starve on the road."

"My thanks. I wish I could repay you for everything you've done for me."

"I'll wager you will. Your Wyrd brought you to me once, and I suspect it'll do so again, but in some strange way that neither of us can understand."

Although Maddyn wanted to head straight west and put Cantrae behind him as soon as he could, he was forced to turn south, because the hills between Cantrae and Gwaentaer province were still snowy this time of year. He went cautiously, avoiding the main road that ran beside the Canaver down to Dun Cantrae, sticking to winding farm lanes and what wild country there was. The only people he allowed to see him were farmers, who, like Belyan, cared less for the honor of war than they did for the coppers he spent for food. After four days of this careful riding, he was at the Gwaentaer border at a place roughly parallel with Dun Cantrae. Here the hills were low and rolling, dotted with small farms and the winter steadings of the horse breeders who roamed with their herds all summer in the pasturelands. This time of year, every house bustled with activity. Mares were foaling; hooves needed shoeing; gear needed repairing; food had to be packed against the first long spring ride. No one had time to notice or to care about a solitary rider with a warrior's saddle but a farmer's shirt.

Just at dusk one warm day Maddyn came to the pillar stone that marked the boundary between the two gwerbretrhynau. As he rode past, he let go a long sigh of relief. Although he was still an outlaw, his neck was a good bit safer now. Once, back in that peaceful and now near-mythical past, every gwerbret in the kingdom would have honored Tibryn's decree of outlawry, but now in the midst of the long-bleeding wars, fighting men were too valuable for lords to go driving them away with awkward questions. For the first time in weeks he felt relaxed enough to sing. Two Wildfolk came for the song, the blue sprite perching on his saddle peak and showing him her pointed teeth, a gnarled brown gnome who was new to him dancing in the road beside his horse. Maddyn was so glad to see them that he almost wept. At least one small part of his magical winter would travel with him.

As it turned out, he soon had human company, and in a way that he never would have expected. The morning after he passed the boundary stone, he came to the last of the hills and paused his

horse for a moment to look down and over the vast green plain of
Gwaentaer, the wind's own country indeed, where the trees that
the farmers laboriously planted soon grew leaning, as if they
shrank in continuous fear away from the constant whistling of the
wind. Since the day was sparkling clear, he could see for miles
over the land, softly furred with the first green of grass and winter
wheat, dimpled here and there with tiny ponds or the round steadings of the widely separated farms. He could also see a well-
marked road running dead west, and on it, not more than a mile
ahead of him, a solitary rider.

Something was wrong with the man. Even from his distance
Maddyn could see it, because the fellow was riding doubled over
in the saddle, and his horse was picking his own way, ambling
slowly, pausing every now and then to snatch a tuft of grass from
the side of the road before its rider would come to himself and get
it back under control, only to slump again a few moments later.
Maddyn's first impulse was to ride on by a somewhat different
route and not burden himself with anyone else's troubles, but then
he thought of Nevyn, risking his own life to heal and shelter an
outlawed man. With a chirrup to his horse, he started off at a brisk
trot. The rider ahead never heard him coming, or else he cared not
a whit if he were followed, because he never turned nor even
looked back the entire time that Maddyn was closing with him.
Finally, when Maddyn was close enough to see that the entire
back of the man's shirt was thick with rusty-brown dried blood,
the fellow paused his horse and sat slumped and weary, as if inviting Maddyn to have a clear strike at him and be done with it.

"Here," Maddyn said. "What's wrong?"

At that the rider did turn to look at him, and Maddyn swore
aloud.

"Aethan, by all the gods! What are you doing on the Gwaentaer
road?"

"And I could ask the same of you, Maddo." His voice, normally
deep and full of humor, was rasped with old pain. "Or have you
come to fetch me to the Otherlands?"

Maddyn stared for a moment, then remembered that everyone
in Cantrae thought him dead.

"Oh, I'm as much alive as you are. How were you wounded?"

"I'm not. I've been flogged."

"Ah, horse dung and a pile of it! Can you ride any farther?"

Aethan considered this for a long moment. He was normally a

handsome man, with even features, dark hair just touched with gray at the temples, and wide blue eyes that always seemed to be laughing at some jest, but now his face was twisted in pain, and his eyes were narrow and grim, as if perhaps he'd never laugh again.

"I need a rest," he said at last. "Shall we sit awhile, or are you riding on and leaving me?"

"What? Are you daft? Would I run out on a man I've known since I was a cub of fifteen?"

"I don't know anymore what men will do, and women neither."

In a nearby meadow they found a pleasant copse of willows planted round a farmer's duck pond, with the farmer nowhere in sight. Maddyn dismounted, then helped Aethan down and watered the horses while his friend sat numbly in the shade. As he worked, he was wondering over it all. Aethan was the last man in the kingdom that Maddyn would have expected to get himself shamed, flogged, and turned out of his warband. A favorite of his captain, Aethan had been a second-in-command of Gwerbret Tibryn's own warband. He was one of those genuinely decent men so valuable to any good warband—the conciliator, everyone's friend, the man who settled all those petty disputes bound to arise when a lot of men are packed into a barracks together. The gwerbret himself had on occasion asked Aethan's advice on small matters dealing with the warband, but now here he was, with his shame written on his back in blood.

Once the horses were watered, Maddyn filled the waterskin with fresh drink and sat down next to Aethan, who took the skin from him with a twisted smile.

"Outlawed we may be, but we still follow the rules of the troop, don't we, Maddo? Horses first, then men."

"We need these mounts more than ever, with no lord to give us another."

Aethan nodded and drank deep, then handed the skin back.

"Well, it gladdens my heart that you weren't killed in Lord Devyr's last charge. I take it you found a farm or suchlike to hide in all winter."

"Somewhat like that. I was dying, actually, from a wound I took, when a local herbman found me."

"Gods! You've always had the luck, haven't you?"

Maddyn merely shrugged and stoppered up the skin tight. For a moment they merely sat there in an uncomfortable silence and watched the fat gray ducks grubbing at the edge of the pond.

"You hold your tongue cursed well for a bard," Aethan said abruptly. "Aren't you going to ask me about my shame?"

"Say what you want and not a word more."

Aethan considered, staring out at the far flat horizon.

"Ah, horseshit," he said at last. "It's a tale fit for a bard to know, in a way. Do you remember our gwerbret's sister, the Lady Merodda?"

"Oh, and how could any man with blood in his veins forget her?"

"He'd best try." Aethan's voice turned hard and cold. "Her husband was killed in battle last summer, and so she came back to her brother in Dun Cantrae. And the captain made me her escort, to ride behind her whenever she went out." He was quiet, his mouth working, for a good couple of minutes. "And she took a fancy to me. Ah, by the black ass of the Lord of Hell, I should have said her nay—I blasted well knew it, even then—but ye gods, Maddo, I'm only made of flesh and blood, not steel, and she knows how to get what she wants from a man. I swear to you, I never would have said a word to her if she hadn't spoken to me first."

"I believe you. You've never been a fool."

"Not before this winter at least. I felt like I was ensorceled. I've never loved a woman that way before, and cursed if I ever will again. I wanted her to ride off with me. Like a misbegotten horseshit fool, I thought she loved me enough to do it. But oh, it didn't suit her ladyship, not by half." Again the long, pain-filled pause. "So she let it slip to her brother what had been happening between us, but oh, she was the innocent one, she was. And when His Grace took all the skin off my back three days ago, she was out in the ward to watch."

Aethan dropped his face into his hands and wept like a child. For a moment Maddyn sat there frozen; then he reached out a timid hand and laid it on Aethan's shoulder until at last he fell silent and wiped his face roughly on his sleeve.

"Maybe I shouldn't be too hard on her." Aethan's voice was a flat, dead whisper. "She did keep her brother from killing me." He stood up, and it was painful to watch him wince as he hauled himself to his feet. "I've rested enough. Let's ride, Maddo. The farther I get from Cantrae, the happier I'll be."

For four days Maddyn and Aethan rode west, asking cautious questions of the various farmers and peddlers that they met about the local lords and their warbands. Even though they sometimes heard of a man who might be desperate enough to take them in without asking questions, each time they decided that they were still too close to Cantrae to take the risk of petitioning him. They realized, however, that they would have to find some place soon, because all around them the noble-born were beginning to muster their men for the summer's fighting. With troops moving along the roads they were in a dangerous position. Maddyn had no desire to escape being hanged for an outlaw only to end up on a rope as a supposed spy.

Since Aethan's back was far from healed, they rode slowly, stopping often to rest, either beside the road or in village taverns. They had, at least, no need to worry about coin; not only did Maddyn have Nevyn's generous pouch, but Aethan's old captain had managed to slip him money along with his gear when he'd been kicked out of Dun Cantrae. Apparently Maddyn wasn't alone in thinking the gwerbret's sentence harsh. During this slow progress west, Maddyn had plenty of time to watch and worry over his old friend. Since always before Aethan had watched over him—he was, after all, some ten years Maddyn's elder—Maddyn was deeply troubled to realize that Aethan needed him the way a child needs his father. The gwerbret might have spared his life, but he'd broken him all the same, this man who'd served him faithfully for over twenty years, by half beating him to death like a rat caught in a stable.

Always before Aethan had had an easy way with command, making decisions, giving orders, and all in a way that made his fellows glad to follow them. Now he did whatever Maddyn said without even a mild suggestion that they might do otherwise. Before, too, he'd been a talkative man, always ready with a tale or a jest if he didn't have serious news to pass along. Now he rode wrapped in a black hiraedd; at times he didn't even answer when Maddyn asked him a direct question. For all that it ached Maddyn's heart, he could think of nothing to do to better things. Often he wished that he could talk with Nevyn and get his advice, but Nevyn was far away, and he doubted if he'd ever see the old man again, no matter how much he wanted to.

Eventually they reached the great river, the Camyn Yraen, an "iron road" even then, because all the rich ore from Cerrgonney came down it in barges, and the town of Gaddmyr, at that time only a large village with a wooden palisade around it for want of walls. Just inside the gate they found a tavern of sorts, basically the tavernman's house, with half the round ground floor set off by a wickerwork partition to hold a couple of tables and some ale barrels in the curve of the wall. For a couple of coppers the man brought them a chunk of cheese and a loaf of bread to go with their ale, then left them strictly alone. Maddyn noticed that none of the villagers were bothering to come to the tavern with them in it, and he remarked as much to Aethan.

"For all they know we're a couple of bandits. Ah, by the hells, Maddo, we can't go wandering the roads like this, or we might well end up robbing travelers, at that. What are we going to do?"

"Cursed if I know. But I've been thinking a bit. There's those free troops you hear about. Maybe we'd be better off joining one of them than worrying about an honorable place in a warband."

"What?" For a moment some of the old life came back to Aethan's eyes. "Are you daft? Fight for coin, not honor? Ye gods, I've heard of some of those troops switching sides practically in the middle of a battle if someone offered them better pay. Mercenaries! They're naught but a lot of dishonored scum!"

Maddyn merely looked at him. With a long sigh Aethan rubbed his face with both hands.

"And so are we. That's what you mean, isn't it, Maddo? Well, you're right enough. All the gods know that the captain of a free troop won't be in any position to sneer at the scars on my back."

"True spoken. And we'll have to try to find one that's fighting for Cerrmor or Eldidd, too. Neither of us can risk having some Cantrae man seeing us in camp."

"Ah, horseshit and a pile of it! Do you know what that means? What are we going to end up doing? Riding a charge against the gwerbret and all my old band someday?"

Maddyn had never allowed himself to frame that thought before, that someday his life might depend on his killing a man who'd once been his ally and friend. Aethan picked up his dagger and stabbed it viciously into the table.

"Here!" The tavernman came running. "No need to be breaking up the furniture, lads!"

Aethan looked up so grimly that Maddyn caught his arm before he could take out his rage on this innocent villager. The tavernman stepped back, swallowing hard.

"I'll give you an extra copper to pay for the damage," Maddyn said. "My friend's in a black mood today."

"He can go about having it in some other place than mine."

"Well and good, then. We've finished your piss-poor excuse for ale, anyway."

They'd just reached the door when the tavernman hailed them again. Although Aethan ignored him and walked out, Maddyn paused as the taverner came scurrying over.

"I know about one of them troops you and your friend was talking about."

Maddyn got out a couple of coppers and jingled them in his hand. The taverner gave him a gap-toothed, garlic-scented grin.

"They wintered not far from here, they did. They rode in every now and then to buy food, and we was fair terrified at first, thinking they were going to steal whatever they wanted, but they paid good coin. I'll say that for them, for all that they was an arrogant lot, strutting around like lords."

"Now that's luck!"

"Well, now, they might have moved on by now. Haven't seen them in days, and here's the blacksmith's daughter with her belly swelling up, and even if they did come back, she wouldn't even know which of the lads it was. The little slut, spreading her legs for any of them that asked her!"

"Indeed? And where were they quartered?"

"They wouldn't be telling the likes of us that, but I'll wager I can guess well enough. Just to the north of here, oh, about ten miles, I'd say, is a stretch of forest. It used to be the tieryn's hunting preserve, but then, twenty-odd years ago it was now, the old tieryn and all his male kin got themselves killed off in a blood feud, and with the wars so bad and all, there was no one else to take the demesne. So the forest's gotten all overgrown and thick, like, but I wager that the old tieryn's hunting lodge still stands in there someplace."

Maddyn handed over the coppers and took out two more.

"I don't suppose some of the lads in the village know where this lodge is." He held up the coins. "It seems likely that some of the young ones might have poked around in there, just out of curiosity, like."

"Not on your life, and I'm not saying that to get more coin out of you, neither. It's a dangerous place, that stretch of trees. Haunted, they say, and full of evil spirits as well, most like, and then there's the wild men."

"The what?"

"Well, I suppose that by rights I shouldn't call them wild, poor bastards, because all the gods can bear witness that I'd have done the same as them if I had to." He leaned closer, all conspiratorial. "You don't look like the sort of fellow who'll be running to our lord with the news, but the folk who live in the forest are bondsmen. Or I should say, they was, a while back. Their lord got killed, and so they took themselves off to live free, and I can't say as I'll be blaming them for it, neither."

"Nor more can I. Your wild men are safe enough from me, but I take it they're not above robbing a traveler if they can."

"I think they feels it's owing to them, like, after all the hard work they put in."

Maddyn gave him the extra coppers anyway, then went out to join Aethan, who was standing by the road with the horses' reins in hand.

"Done gossiping, are you?"

"Here, Aethan, the taverner had some news to give us, and it just might be worth following down. There might be a free troop up in the woods to the north of us."

Aethan stared down at the reins in his hand and rubbed them with weary fingers.

"Ah, horseshit!" he said at last. "We might as well look them over, then."

When they left the village, they rode north, following the river. Although Aethan was well on the mend by then, his back still ached him, and they rested often. At their pace it was close to sunset when they reached the forest, looming dark and tangled on the far side of a wild meadowland. At its edge a massive marker stone still stood, doubtless proclaiming the trees the property of the long-dead clan that once had owned them.

"I don't want to be mucking around in there when it's dark," Aethan said.

"You're right enough. We'll camp here. There's plenty of water in the river."

While Aethan tended the horses, Maddyn went to gather firewood at the forest edge. A crowd of Wildfolk went with him, darting around or skipping beside him, a gaggle of green, warty gnomes, three enormous yellow creatures with swollen stomachs and red fangs, and his faithful blue sprite, perching on his shoulder and running tiny hands through his hair.

"I'll have to play us a song tonight. It's been a while since I felt like music, but maybe our luck is turning."

Yet when it came time to play, Maddyn's heart was still so troubled that he found it hard to settle down to one ballad or declamation. He got the harp in tune, then played scraps and bits of various songs or practiced runs and chordings. Aethan soon fell asleep, lying on his stomach with his head pillowed on folded arms, but the Wildfolk stayed to the last note, a vast crowd of them, stretching out beyond the pool of firelight across the meadow. Maddyn felt awed, as if he were playing in a king's court, the great hall crowded with retainers. When he stopped, he felt more than heard a ripple of eerie applause; then suddenly, they were gone. Maddyn shuddered profoundly, then put the harp away.

After he banked the campfire, Maddyn paced a little ways into the meadow out of restlessness and nothing more. He could see the forest edge, looming dark not far from them, and even more, he could feel its presence, like an exhalation of wildness. He was sure that more than human fugitives lived there. It occurred to him that while the long wars were a tragedy for human beings, to the Wildfolk they were a blessing, giving them back land that men had once taken and tamed. As he stood there in the silent meadow, it seemed that he heard faint music, an echo of his own. Again he shuddered convulsively, then hurried back to his safe camp.

On the morrow the blue sprite woke him just at dawn by the expedient method of pulling his hair so hard that it hurt like fire. When he swatted at her, she laughed soundlessly, exposing her needle-sharp teeth. Nearby Aethan was still sleeping, but restlessly, turning and stretching like a man who'll wake any moment.

"Listen carefully, little sweet one," Maddyn said to the sprite. "Somewhere in that forest are a whole lot of men like me and Aethan, warriors with swords. They'll have lots of horses, too, and they live in a stone house. Can you lead me there?"

She thought for a long moment, then nodded her agreement and promptly disappeared. Maddyn decided that either she'd misunderstood or had simply forgotten, but as soon as they were ready to ride, she reappeared, dancing and leaping on the riverbank and pointing to the north.

"I don't suppose that misbegotten tavernman gave you any directions to this place," Aethan said.

"Well, he had a confused idea or two. I'll try to lead us there, but don't be surprised if it's a bit roundabout."

It was a good thing that Maddyn had put in his warning, because the Wildfolk's idea of leading someone left much to be desired. As soon as the men started riding north, two gray gnomes appeared to join the sprite, but they kept pinching either her or each other and distracting her both ways from her task. Once they were all well into the forest, the Wildfolk disappeared, leaving the men to follow a rough deer track for several miles. Just when Maddyn had given up on them, they flashed back into being, perching on his horse's neck and saddle peak and pointing off to the west down a narrow and rough track indeed. Although Aethan grumbled (and a welcome sign of returning life it was), Maddyn insisted on following it, and every time the path branched, he faithfully went the way she pointed. By noon, Maddyn was hopelessly lost, with no choice but to follow where the Wildfolk led. Hopping from tree to tree, they grinned, giggled, and pointed in various directions, but Maddyn always followed the blue sprite, who threatened to bite the gray fellows whenever they contradicted her.

"Maddo, I hope to every god and his horse that you know what you're doing."

"So do I. I've got the ugly feeling I may have gotten us lost in here."

Aethan groaned with a drama worthy of a bard. Just as Maddyn was thinking that he'd spoken the bitter truth, the sprite led them to a big clearing, ringed round with stumps of trees. Out in the middle was a hut built of logs, piled up whole to form a square structure—a house different from any that Maddyn had ever seen. The roof was neatly thatched with branches, and a wisp of smoke trailed lazily out of the smoke hole in the roof.

"What in the three hells have you found?" Aethan sputtered. "That's not big enough for a band of mercenaries."

"So it's not. More likely it's some of those runaway bondsmen the taverner mentioned."

At the sound of their voices, a man came out. He was one of the shortest men Maddyn had ever seen, not more than five feet tall, but he had broad shoulders and heavy arms like a miniature blacksmith, and his legs were in perfect proportion to the rest of him. His long black beard trailed past the round collar of the wool tunic he wore over brigga. He carried a long woodsman's ax like a weapon. When he spoke, his voice was rough with a heavy guttural accent. "And just who are you, lads?"

"Naught but a pair of lost travelers," Maddyn said.

"Thieves, more like." The fellow hefted the ax. "And what brought you into these wretched woods in the first place?"

"We were looking for a mercenary troop," Aethan broke in. "A tavernman in Gaddmyr said there might be one quartered in this forest."

"All we want to do is see if they'll take us on," Maddyn said. "I swear it, we're not thieves, and I don't know what a hermit like you would have that's worth stealing, anyway."

The man considered with his ax at the ready. When Maddyn noticed the blade, he nearly swore aloud in surprise. Although the metal gleamed exactly like silver, it had an edge as sharp as steel by the look of it, and it carried not one nick or bite.

"Now, here," Aethan said. "We'll be more than glad to leave you alone if you'll only show us the way out of these blasted woods."

"Go back the way you came, of course."

"Good sir, we're lost," Maddyn said, and quickly, because he didn't like the black look on Aethan's face.

"Indeed? You found me easily enough."

"Well, I was following one of the . . ." Maddyn broke off just in time.

As if she knew he was thinking of her, the blue sprite popped into existence, settling on his shoulder and kissing his hair. The fellow frankly stared and lowered his ax to lean on it like a walking stick. Quickly he darted a conspiratorial glance at Aethan, who of course had seen nothing, and then gave Maddyn a grudging smile.

"Well, perhaps I could take you to the old lodge after all, but your horses look worn out from all these wretched trees. There's a spring over there, by that bit of stump. Give them a drink first. My name's Otho, by the by."

"And I'm Maddyn, and this is Aethan. My thanks for your help. Do you know this troop?"

"Somewhat. I did a bit of work for them this winter, fixing buckles and suchlike. I'm a smith, you see."

It was Maddyn's turn to stare. What was a smith doing out in the middle of a wilderness? Then it occurred to him that Otho might have some dishonor of his own behind him.

"Now, Caradoc—that's their leader—isn't a bad man, considering what he is," Otho went on. "He wants me to ride south with him when they go. I've been thinking it over."

While Aethan watered the horses, Otho went into his cabin, then reappeared wearing a leather vest over his tunic and carrying a different ax, one with a long handle banded with metal and obviously made as a weapon, which he used to good advantage for clearing brush and overhanging branches. The trail was so narrow and twisty that the men had to lead their horses. It was about the middle of the afternoon when they came into a vast clearing of some five acres and saw the high stone walls of what once had been a noble's hunting lodge. The wooden gates were long since rotted away, letting them see the broch, still in reasonable repair, and a collection of tumbledown sheds inside.

As they walked up, Caradoc himself came out to meet them. Otho introduced him, a tall, slender man with the long, ropy arms of a born swordsman and the high cheekbones and pale hair of a southern man. He seemed about Aethan's age, in his mid-thirties, and for all that he was a dishonored man, there was something impressive about Caradoc, the proud way he stood, the shrewd way he looked men over with eyes that seemed to have seen a lot of life.

"Since you're looking for bodies to sell," Otho said, "I brought you a couple."

"Interesting." Caradoc gave them each a pleasant smile. "Here's Aethan with a Cantrae boar on his shirt, and Maddyn dressed like a farmer but carrying a sword. I looked like the pair of you once. Left a warband down in Cerrmor a bit . . . well, sudden, like. Never did bid a proper farewell to my lord. I'll wager, Aethan, that there's scars on your back, judging from the stains on your shirt."

"More than a few. Cursed if I'll tell you why."

"I'd never ask. Now, here's the terms, lads. I'll take anyone on for a summer. If you can't fight, then you'll die in a scrap, and we'll be rid of you. If you can fight, then you get an equal share of the coin. And remember: I'm the leader of this pack of dogs. You give me one bit of trouble, and I'll beat the shit out of you. Scribe that deep into your ugly hearts: you ride at orders, or you don't ride."

It was obvious that Caradoc meant what he said as soon as they went into the dun. Instead of the banditlike pile of filth that Maddyn had been dreading, the camp was as clean as a great lord's barracks. There were thirty-six men in the troop, and their gear was well tended, their horses good, healthy stock, and their discipline tighter, in fact, than that of Maddyn's old warband. As Caradoc introduced the new recruits around, the other members of the band paid him such strict and respectful attention that Maddyn began to wonder if he were noble-born. Otho came along with them, listening to Caradoc and stroking his beard in thought, but he said naught a word until they all went outside again so that Maddyn and Aethan could unsaddle their horses and unload their gear.

"Well, Otho," Caradoc said. "We'll be pulling out soon. Coming with us to Eldidd?"

"I might, at that. I've gotten used to a bit of company, especially company that can pay a smith better than the stinking bondsmen in this forest."

"So we can, and you'll like Eldidd well enough once we get there."

"Hah! I've got my doubts about that. They always say that there's elven blood in Eldidd veins."

"Not *that* again!" Caradoc mugged a doleful expression. "As much as I admire your craft, good smith, I have to say that your wits are a bit thin in places. Elves, indeed!"

"Mock all you want, but elven blood makes a man unreliable."

"It'd make any man unreliable to have a myth in his clan's quarterings." Caradoc ran one finger down the silvery blade of Otho's ax. "But talk about elves all you want, just so long as you keep working your witchcraft on metals. When we're all as rich as lords and the most famous free troop in all of Deverry, you're going to make us swords out of that warlock's metal of yours."

"Hah! You'd have to be a king to afford that, my friend. You'll be blasted lucky if you ever get rich enough to have so much as a dagger out of it."

After Maddyn and Aethan had their horses settled and fed in the stables, one of the men, Stevyc by name, came to help them carry their gear into the broch. When he picked up the big leather bag that held Maddyn's harp, he broke into a grin.

"Which one of you is the bard?"

"I am," Maddyn said. "But not much of one, a gerthddyn, truly, if that. I can sing, but I don't have a true bard's lore."

"And who gives a pig's fart who some lord's great-great-great-grandam was? This is a bit of splendid luck." Stevyc turned, calling out to Caradoc. "Here, Captain, we've got a bard of our own."

"And next we'll be eating off of silver plates, like the great lords we are." Caradoc came strolling over. "But a bard would have come in handy this winter, with the pack of you causing trouble because you had naught better to do. Well and good, then, Maddyn. If you sing well enough, you'll be free of kitchen work and stable duty, but I'll expect you to make up songs about our battles just like you would for a lord."

"I'll do my best, Captain, to sing as well as we deserve."

"*Better* than we deserve, Maddyn lad, or you'll sound like a cat in heat."

After a rough dinner of venison and turnips, Maddyn was given his chance to sing, sitting on a rickety, half-rotted table in what had once been the lodge's great hall. He'd only done one ballad when he realized that his place in the troop was assured. The men listened with the deep fascination of the utterly bored, hardly noticing or caring when he got a bit off-key or stumbled over a line. After a winter with naught but dice games and the blacksmith's daughter for entertainment, they cheered him as if he were the best bard at the king's court. They made him sing until he was hoarse, that night, and let him stop only reluctantly then. Only Maddyn and Otho knew, of course, that the hall was filled with Wildfolk, listening as intently as the men.

That night, Maddyn lay awake for a long while and listened to the familiar sound of other men snoring close by in the darkness of a barracks. He was back in a warband, back in his old life so firmly that he wondered if he'd dreamt those enchanted months in Brin Toraedic. The winter behind him seemed like a lost paradise, when he'd had good company and a woman of his own, when he'd had a glimpse of a wider, freer world of peace and dweomer—a little glimpse only; then the door had been slammed in his face. He was back in the war, a dishonored rider whose one goal in life was to earn the respect of other dishonored men. At least Belyan was going to have his baby back in Cantrae, a small life who would outlive him and who would be better off as a farmer than his father would be as a warrior. Thinking about the babe, he could fall asleep at last, smiling to himself.

On the day that Maddyn left Brin Toraedic, Nevyn spent a good many hours shutting up the caves for the summer and loading herbs and medicines into the canvas mule packs. He had a journey of over nine hundred miles ahead of him, with stops along the way that were crucial to the success of his long-range plans. If he were to succeed in making a dweomer king to bring peace to the country, he would need help from powerful friends, particularly among the priesthoods. He would also need to find a man of royal blood worthy of his plans. And that, or so he told himself, might well be the most difficult part of the work.

The first week of his journey was easy. Although the Cantrae roads were full of warbands, mustering to begin the ride to Dun Deverry for the summer's fighting, no one bothered him, seemingly only a shabby old herbman with his ambling mule, his patched brown cloak, and the white hair that the local riders respected as a sign of his great age. He followed the Canaver down to its joining with the river Nerr near the town of Muir, a place that held memories some two hundred years old. As he always did when he passed through Muir, he went into the last patch of wild forest—now the hunting preserve of the Southern Boar clan. In the midst of a stand of old oaks was an ancient, mossy cairn that marked the grave of Brangwen of the Falcon, the woman he had loved, wronged, and lost so many years ago. He always felt somewhat of a fool for making this pilgrimage—her body was long decayed, and her soul had been reborn several times since that miserable day when he'd dug this grave and helped pile up these rocks. Yet the site meant something to him still, because, if for no other reason, it was the place where he'd sworn the rash vow that was the cause of his unnaturally long life.

Out of respect for a grave, even though they could have no idea of whose it was, the Boars' gamekeepers had left the cairn undisturbed. Nevyn was pleased to see that someone had even tended it by replacing a few fallen stones and pulling the weeds away from its base. It was a small act of decency in a world where decency was in danger of vanishing. For some time he sat on the ground and watched the dappled forest light playing on the cairn while he wondered when he would find Brangwen's soul again. His meditation brought him a small insight: she was reborn, but still a child. Eventually, he was sure, in some way Maddyn would lead him to her. In life after life, his Wyrd had been linked to hers, and, indeed, in his last life, he had followed her to the death, binding a chain of Wyrd tight around them both.

After he left Muir, Nevyn rode west to Dun Deverry for a firsthand look at the man who claimed to be king in the Holy City. On a hot spring day, when the sun lay as thick as the dust in the road, he came to the shores of the Gwerconydd, the vast lake formed by the confluence of three rivers, and let his horse and mule rest for a moment by the reedy shore. He was joined by a pair of young priests of Bel, shaven-headed and dressed in linen tunics, who were also traveling to the Holy City. After a pleasant chat, they all decided to ride in together.

"And who's the high priest these days?" Nevyn asked. "I've been living up in Cantrae, so I'm badly out of touch."

"His Holiness, Gwergovyn," said the elder of the pair.

"I see." Nevyn's heart sank. He remembered Gwergovyn all too well as a spiritual ferret of a man. "And tell me somewhat else. I've heard that the Boars of Cantrae are the men to watch in court circles."

Even though they were all alone on the open road, the young priest lowered his voice when he answered.

"They are, truly, and there are plenty who grumble about it, too. I know His Holiness thinks rather sourly of the men of the Boar."

At length they came to the city, which rose high on its four hills behind massive double rings of stone walls, ramparted and towered. The wooden gates, carved with a wyvern rampant, were bound with iron, and guards in thickly embroidered shirts stood to either side. Yet as soon as Nevyn went inside, the impression of splendor vanished. Once a prosperous city had filled these walls; now house after house stood abandoned, with weed-choked yards and empty windows, the thatch blowing rotten in dirty streets. Much of the city lay in outright ruin, heaps of stone among rotting, charred timbers. It had been taken by siege so many times in the last hundred years, then taken back by the sword, that apparently no one had the strength, the coin, or the hope to rebuild. In the center of the city, around and between two main hills, lived what was left of the population, scarcely more than in King Bran's time. Warriors walked the streets and shoved the townsfolk aside whenever they met. It seemed to Nevyn that every man he saw was a rider for one lord or another, and every woman either lived in fear of them or had surrendered to the inevitable and turned whore to please them.

The first inn he found was tiny, dirty, and ramshackle, little more than a big house divided into a tavern room and a few chambers, but he lodged there because he liked the innkeep, Draudd, a slender old man with hair as white as Nevyn's and a smile that showed an almost superhuman ability to keep a sense of humor in the midst of ruin. When he found out that Nevyn was an herbman, Draudd insisted on taking out his lodging in trade.

"Well, after all, I'm as old as you are, so I'll easily equal the cost in your herbs. Why give me coins only to have me give them right back?"

"True-spoken. Ah, old age! Here I've studied the human body all my life, but I swear old age has put pains in joints I never knew existed."

Nevyn spent that first afternoon in the tavern, dispensing herbs for Draudd's collection of ailments and hearing in return all the local gossip, which meant royal gossip. In Dun Deverry even the poorest person knew what there was to know about the goings-on at court. Gossip was their bard, and the royalty their only source of pride. Draudd was a particularly rich source, because his youngest daughter, now a woman in her forties, worked up in the palace kitchens, where she had plenty of opportunities to overhear the noble-born servitors like the chamberlain and steward at their gossip. From what Draudd repeated that day, the Boars were so firmly in control of the king that it was something of a scandal. Everyone said that Tibryn, the Boar of Cantrae, was close to being the real king himself.

"And now with the king so ill, our poor liege, and his wife so young, and Tibryn a widower and all . . ." Draudd paused for dramatic effect. "Well! Can't you imagine what we folk are wondering?"

"Indeed I can. But would the priests allow the king's widow to marry?"

Draudd rubbed his thumb and forefinger together like a merchant gloating over a coin.

"Ah, by the hells!" Nevyn snarled. "Has it gotten as bad as all that?"

"There's naught left but coin to bribe the priests with. They've already gotten every land grant and legal concession they want."

At that point Nevyn decided that meeting with Gwergovyn—if indeed he could even get in to see him—was a waste of time.

"But what ails the king? He's still a young man."

"He took a bad wound in the fighting last summer. I happened to be out on the royal road when they brought him home. I'd been buying eggs at the market when I heard the bustle and the horns coming. And I saw the king, lying in a litter, and he was as pale as snow, he was. But he lived, when here we all thought they'd be putting his little lad on the throne come winter. But he never did heal up right. My daughter tells me that he has to have special

food, like. All soft things, and none of them Bardek spices, neither.
So they boil the meat soft, and pulp apples and suchlike."

Nevyn was completely puzzled: the special diet made no sense at
all for a man who by all accounts had been wounded in the chest.
He began to wonder if someone were deliberately keeping the
king weak, perhaps to gain the good favor of Tibryn of the Boar.

The best way to find out, of course, was to talk to the king's
physicians. On the morrow he took his laden mule up to the palace, which lay on the northern hill. Ring after ring of defensive
walls, some stone, some earthworks, marched up the slope and cut
the hill into defensible slices. At every gate in every wall, guards
stopped Nevyn and asked him his business, but they always let a
man with healing herbs to sell pass on through. Finally, at the top,
behind one last ring, stood the palace and all its outbuildings and
servant quarters. Like a stork among chickens, a six-story broch,
ringed by four lower half-brochs, rose in the center. If the outer
defenses fell, the attackers would have to fight their way through a
warren of corridors and rooms to get at the king himself. In all the
years of war, the palace had never fallen to force, only to starva-
tion.

The last guard called a servant lad, who ran off to the royal
infirmary with the news that an herbman waited outside. After a
wait of some five minutes, he ran back and led Nevyn to a big
round stone building behind the broch complex. There they were
met by a burly man with dark eyes that glared under bushy brows
as if their owner were in a state of constant fury, but when he
introduced himself as Grodyn, the head chirurgeon, he was soft-
spoken enough.

"An herbman's always welcome. Come spread out your wares,
good sir. That table by the window would be best, I think, right in
the light and fresh air."

While Nevyn laid out packets of dried herbs, tree barks, and
sliced dried roots, Grodyn fetched his apprentice, Caudyr, a sandy-
haired young man with narrow blue eyes and a jaw so sharply
modeled it looked as if it could cut cheese. He also had a club foot,
which gave him the rolling walk of a sailor. Between them the two
chirurgeons sorted through his wares and for starters set aside his
entire stock of valerian, elecampane, and comfrey root.

"I don't suppose you ever get down to the seacoast," Grodyn said
in a carefully casual tone of voice.

"Well, this summer I'm thinking of trying to slip through the battle lines. Usually the armies don't much care about one old man. Is there somewhat you need from the sea?"

"Red kelp, if you can get it, and some sea moss."

"They work wonders to soothe an ulcerated stomach or bad bowels." Nevyn hesitated briefly. "Here, I've heard rumors about this peculiar so-called wound of our liege the king."

"So called?" Grodyn paid busy attention to the packet of beech bark in his hand.

"A wound in the chest that requires him to eat only soft food."

Grodyn looked up with a twisted little smile.

"It was poison, of course. The wound healed splendidly. While he was still weak, someone put poison into his mead. We saved him after a long fight of it, but his stomach is ulcerated and bleeding, just as you guessed, and there's blood in his stool, too. But we're trying to keep the news from the common people."

"Oh, I won't go bruiting it about, I assure you. Do you have any idea of what this poison was?"

"None. Now here, you know herbs. What do you think this might be? When he vomited, there was a sweetish smell hanging about the basin, rather like roses mixed with vinegar. It was grotesque to find a poison that smelled of perfume, but the strangest thing was this: the king's page had tasted the mead and suffered not the slightest ill effect. Yet I know it was in the mead, because the dregs in the goblet had an odd rosy color."

Nevyn thought for a long moment, running over the long chains of lore in his memory.

"Well," he said at last. "I can't name the herbs out, but I'll wager they came originally from Bardek. I've heard that poisoners there often use two different evil essences, each harmless in themselves. The page at table doubtless got a dose of the first one when he tasted the king's mead, and the page of the chamber got the other. The king, alas, got both, and they combined into venom in his stomach."

As he nodded his understanding, Grodyn looked half sick with such an honest rage that Nevyn mentally acquitted him of any part in the crime. Caudyr, too, looked deeply troubled.

"I've made special studies of the old herbals we have," the young chirurgeon said. "And never found this beastly poison. If it came from Bardek, that would explain it."

"So it would," Nevyn said. "Well, good sirs, I'll do my best to get you the red kelp and what other emollients I can, but it'll be autumn before I return. Will our liege live that long?"

"If no one poisons him again." Grodyn tossed the packet of beech bark onto the table. "Ah ye gods, can you imagine how helpless I feel? Here I am, fighting to undo the effects of one poison while someone is doubtless scheming out a way to slip him a second!"

"Wasn't there any inquiry into this poisoning?"

"Of course." Abruptly Grodyn turned guarded. "It found out naught, though. We suspect a Cerrmor spy."

Oh, I'll just wager you do! Nevyn thought to himself; that is, if there are Boars in Cerrmor, anyway.

Their business over, Nevyn put on a good show of expressing the gossipy interest that any visitor to the palace would have in seeing the place where the king lived. Caudyr, who seemed to be a good-hearted lad, took him on a tour of the semi-public gardens and outbuildings. It took only the slightest touch of Nevyn's dweomer to sense that the palace was filled with corruption. The omen came to him as the smell of rotting meat and the sight of maggots, crawling between the stones. He banished the vision as quickly as he could; the point was well made.

As they were walking to the front gate, they saw a noble hunting party returning: Gwerbret Tibryn of the Boar, with a retinue of servants and huntsmen behind him and his widowed sister at his side. As Nevyn led his mule off to the side out of the way of the noble-born, he noticed Caudyr watching the Lady Merodda wistfully. Just twenty, the lady had long blond hair, bound up in soft twists under the black headscarf of a widow, wide green eyes, and features that were perfect without being cold. She was truly beautiful, but as he watched her, Nevyn loathed her. Although he couldn't pinpoint his reasons, he'd never seen a woman he found so repellent. Caudyr was obviously of the opposite opinion. Much to Nevyn's surprise, when Merodda rode past, she favored Caudyr with a brilliant smile and a wave of her delicately gloved hand. Caudyr bowed deeply in return.

"Now here, lad," Nevyn said with a chuckle. "You're nocking an arrow for rather highborn game."

"And don't I just know it? I could be as noble as she is, but I'd still be deformed."

"Oh, my apologies! I meant naught of that sort."

"I know, good sir, I know. I fear me that years of being mocked have made me touchy."

Caudyr bowed and hurried away with his rolling, dragging limp. Nevyn was heartsick over his lapse; it was a hard thing to be handicapped in a world where women and men both worshipped warriors. Later that day, however, he found out that Caudyr bore him no ill will. Just after sunset Caudyr came to Nevyn's inn, insisted on buying him a tankard, and sat them both down at a table in a corner, far from the door.

"I was wondering about your stock of herbs, good Nevyn. You wouldn't happen to have any northern elm bark, would you?"

"Now here! I don't traffic in abortifacients, lad."

Caudyr winced and began studying the interior of his tankard.

"Ah well," the lad said at last. "The bark's a blasted sight safer than henbane."

"No doubt, but the question is why you're doing abortions at all. I should think that every babe these days would be precious."

"Not if it's not sired by your husband. Here, please don't despise me. There's a lot of noblewomen who spend all summer at court, and well, their husbands are off on campaign for months at a time, and well, you know how things happen, and well, they come to me in tears, and—"

"Shower you with silver, no doubt."

"It's not the coin!"

"Indeed? What is it, then? The only time in your life that women have come begging you for somewhat?"

When tears welled in Caudyr's eyes, Nevyn regretted his harsh accuracy. He looked away to give the young chirurgeon a chance to wipe his face. It was the infidelities more than the abortions that bothered Nevyn. The thought of noblewomen, whose restricted life gave them nothing but their honor to take pride in, turning first to illicit affairs, then to covering them over, made him feel that the kingdom was rotting from the center out. As for the abortions, the dweomer lore teaches that a soul comes to indwell a fetus only in the fourth or fifth month after conception; any abortion before that time is only removing a lump of flesh, not a living child. By the time a noblewoman was in her fifth month, Nevyn supposed, her indiscretion would be known already, and so doubtless Caudyr was solving their little problems long before the fetus was truly alive.

"Now one moment." Nevyn was struck by a sudden thought. "You're not using ergot, are you, you stupid little dolt?"

"Never!" Caudyr's voice rose in a sincere squeak. "I know the dangers of that."

"Good. All it would take is for one of your noble patients to die or go mad, and then you'd be up to your neck in a tub of horseshit good and proper."

"I know. But if I didn't find the right herbs for these ladies, they'd be cast off by their husbands, and probably end up smothering the babe anyway, or they'd go to some old witch of a farmwife, and then they *would* die."

"You split hairs so well you should have been a priest."

Caudyr tried to smile and failed utterly, looking like a child who's just been scolded when he honestly didn't know he'd done a wrong thing. Suddenly Nevyn felt the dweomer power, gathering round him, filling his mouth with words that burned straight out of the future.

"You can't keep this sort of thing quiet. When the king dies, his murderers will need a scapegoat. It's going to be you, because of this midnight physic you've been dispensing. Live ready to flee at the first sign that the king is sinking. Can Tibryn of the Boar find out about your unsavory herbs?"

"He could, the lady Merodda . . . I mean . . . ah ye gods! Who are you, old man?"

"Can't you tell dweomer when you hear it? The Boar will take his sister's evidence, turn it against you, and have you broken on the wheel to avert suspicion from himself. If I were you, I'd leave well before the end comes, or they'll hunt you down as a regicide."

Caudyr jerked to his feet so fast that he toppled both his tankard and Nevyn's, then fled, racing out of the tavern door. Although old Draudd gave Nevyn a questioning look, he also shrugged as if to say it was none of his affair. Nevyn retrieved the tankards from the floor, then turned on the bench so that he could look directly into the peat fire smoldering on the tavern hearth. As soon as he bent his mind to Aderyn, his old apprentice's image appeared with his enormous dark eyes and his gray hair swept up in two peaks at his forehead like the horns of a silver owl.

"And how's your scheme progressing?" Aderyn thought to him.

"Well enough, I suppose. I've learned one very important thing. I'd rather die than put any Cantrae king on the throne."

"Is it as bad as all that?"

"The palace stinks like the biggest dung heap on the hottest day of the longest summer. I can't see how any young soul could grow up there without being corrupted from birth. I'm not even going to bother talking to the priests here. They're corrupt, too, and doubtless in new and unusual ways."

"I haven't seen you this angry in about a hundred years."

"Naught's been so vexing in a hundred years. The most honorable man I've met here is an abortionist. Does that give you a hint?"

Floating about the fire, Aderyn's image rolled its eyes heavenward in disgust.

Caradoc and his band of mercenaries left the deserted hunting lodge soon after Maddyn and Aethan joined the troop. Although everyone was speculating about where they would go, the captain told no one until the morning of their departure. Once the men were mounted and formed up in neat ranks that would have done the king's guard credit, Caradoc inspected them carefully, then pulled his horse up to face them.

"It's Eldidd, lads. We've got too many men who can't let themselves be seen around Dun Deverry to take a hire on Slwmar's side, and I don't dare be seen in Cerrmor. I've hoarded some coin from the winter, seeing as our lodging was free and all, so I think we can ride straight there."

Although no one cheered this prospect of leaving home for a foreign land, no one muttered in discontent, either. Caradoc paused, as if waiting for grumblers, then shrugged and raised his hand.

"Otho the smith's meeting us on the road with a wagon. Forward . . . march!"

With a jingle of tack the troop executed a perfect turn in ranks and began to file out the dun gate, two by two. As a mark of honor to a bard, Maddyn rode next to Caradoc at the head of the line. Over the next few days, as they worked their way southwest as quickly as possible, he had plenty of chances to study his new leader. The biggest puzzle that ate at his bardic curiosity was whether or not Caradoc was noble-born. At times, when the captain was discussing some point of the royal law or giving orders with his firm authority, Maddyn was sure that he must have been born the younger son of a lord. Yet when it came to coin, he had all the grasping shrewdness of an old peasant woman, an attitude he never would have learned among the nobility. Occasionally Maddyn dropped hints or half-questions about the past into their conversation, but Caradoc never rose to the bait. When the troop camped for the night, Caradoc ate alone like a lord, and Maddyn shared a fire with Aethan and a small crowd of Wildfolk.

After a week of riding, the troop crossed the Aver Trebyc at a point about a hundred miles west of Dun Deverry. Caradoc gave orders that the men were to ride armed and ready for trouble. He sent out point men and scouts ahead of the main body of riders, because they were approaching the border between Cerrmor-held and Cantrae-held territory. The precautions paid off with a rather strange prize. On the second day of riding armed, when they were finally getting close to the Eldidd border, the troop stopped for the noon rest in a grassy meadow that had never known plow or herd. When the point men came back to change the guard, they brought with them a traveler, an unarmed man with rich clothing, a beautiful riding horse, and an elegant pack mule that had obviously been bred from the best stock. Maddyn was surprised that the poor dolt had survived unrobbed for as long as he had. The young, sandy-haired fellow looked so terrified that Maddyn supposed he was thinking similar thoughts.

"He says he comes from Dun Deverry," the point man said. "So we brought him along in case he had any interesting news."

"Good," Caradoc said. "Now look, young fellow, we're not going to slit your throat or even rob you. Come have a meal with me and Maddyn here."

With a most discourteous groan, the stranger looked around at the well-armed troop, then sighed in resignation.

"So I will, then. My name's . . . uh . . . Claedd."

Caradoc and Maddyn each suppressed a grin at the clumsiness of the lie. When the stranger dismounted, Maddyn saw that he had a clubfoot, which seemed to ache him after so many days in the saddle. As they shared a meal of flatbread and cheese, the supposed Claedd told them what little he knew about the troop movements around the Holy City. The current rumor was that the northern forces were planning to make a strong strike along the eastern borders of the Cerrmor kingdom.

"If that's true," Caradoc said thoughtfully, "we'll have no trouble getting a hire in Eldidd. Probably the Eldidd king will want to take the chance to raid into Pyrdon."

"Oho!" Claedd said. "Then you're a free troop! Well, that's a relief."

"Oh, is it now? Most men would think the opposite." Caradoc shook his head, as if he were utterly amazed at the innocence of this lad. "Well and good, then. Who's chasing you? It's safe to tell me. I've sunk pretty low, lad, but not so low that I'd turn a man in for the bounty on his head."

Claedd concentrated on shredding a piece of flatbread into inedible crumbs.

"You don't have to tell me if you don't want to," Caradoc said after a moment. "But think about traveling with us. You'll be a blasted sight safer. Ever had a fancy to see Eldidd?"

"That's where I was trying to go, and you're right enough about it being safer. I've never swung a sword in my life. I'm a . . . uh . . . a scholar."

"Splendid. Maybe I'll need a letter written some fine day."

Although Claedd managed a feeble smile at the jest, his face stayed deadly pale. Yet, when the troop rode out, he came with them, riding by himself just behind Otho's wagon. At the night camp, Maddyn took pity on him and offered to let him share their fire. Although he brought out food from his mule packs, Claedd ate little of it, merely sat quietly and watched Aethan polishing his sword. When, after the meal, Caradoc strolled over for a chat, Claedd again said little as the captain and the bard talked idly of their plans in Eldidd. Finally, though, at a pause he spoke up.

"I've been thinking about your offer, Captain. Could you use a troop chirurgeon? I finished my apprenticeship only a year ago, but I've had an awful lot of practice at tending wounds."

"By all the ice in all the hells!" Maddyn said. "You're worth your weight in gold!"

"Cursed right." Caradoc cocked his head to one side and considered the young chirurgeon. "Now, I'm not a curious man, usually, and I like to leave my lads their privacy, like, but in your case, I've got to ask. What's a man with your learning doing traveling the long lonely roads like this?"

"You might as well know the truth. First of all, my name's Caudyr, and I was at the court in Dun Deverry. I mixed up a few potions and suchlike for some highborn ladies to rid them of . . . ah, well . . . a spot of . . . er, well . . . trouble now and again. The word's gotten out about it in rather a nasty way."

Caradoc and Aethan exchanged a puzzled glance.

"He means abortions," Maddyn said with a grin. "Naught that should vex us, truly."

"Might even come in handy, with this pack of dogs I've got," Caradoc said. "Well and good, then, Caudyr. Once you've shown me that you can physic a man, you'll get a full share of our earnings, just like a rider. I've discovered that a lord's chirurgeon tends his lord's men first and the mercenaries when he has a mind to and not before. I've had men bleed to death who would have lived if they'd gotten the proper attention."

Idly Maddyn happened to glance Aethan's way to find him staring at Caudyr in grim suspicion.

"Up in Dun Deverry, were you?" Aethan's voice was a dry, hard whisper. "Was one of your highborn ladies Merodda of the Boar?"

In a confession stronger than words, Caudyr winced, then blushed. Aethan got to his feet, hesitated, then took off running into the darkness.

"What, by the hells?" Caradoc snapped.

Without bothering to explain, Maddyn got up and followed, chasing Aethan through the startled camp, pounding blindly after him through the moon-shot night down to the riverbank. Finally Aethan stopped and let him catch up. They stood together for a long time, panting for breath and watching the silver-touched river flow by.

"With a bitch like that," Maddyn said finally. "How would you even know that the babe was yours?"

"I kept my eye on her like a hawk all winter long. If she'd looked at another man, I'd have killed him, and she knew it."

With a sigh Maddyn sat down, and after a moment, Aethan joined him.

"Having a chirurgeon of our own will be a cursed good thing," Maddyn said. "Can you put up with Caudyr?"

"Who's blaming him for one single thing? I wish I could kill her. I dream about it sometimes, getting my hands on her pretty white throat and strangling her."

Abruptly Aethan turned and threw himself into Maddyn's arms. Maddyn held him tightly and let him cry, the choking ugly sob of a man who feels shamed by tears.

Two days later the troop crossed the border into Eldidd. At that time, the northern part of the province was nearly a wilderness, forests and wild grasslands broken only by the occasional dun of a minor lord or a village of free farmers. Plenty of the lords would have liked to hire the troop, because they were in constant danger of raids coming either from the kingdom of Pyrdon to the north or from Deverry to the east. None, however, could pay Caradoc what he considered the troop was worth. With thirty-seven men, their own smith, chirurgeon, and bard, the troop was bigger than the warbands of most of the lords in northern Eldidd. Just when Caradoc was beginning to curse his decision to ride that way, the troop reached the new town of Camynwaen, on the banks of an oddly named river, the El, just as the spot where the even more strangely named Aver Cantariel flows in from the northwest.

Although there had been a farming village on the site for centuries, only twenty years before had the gwerbret in Elrÿdd decided that the kingdom needed a proper town at the joining of the rivers. Since the war with Pyrdon could flare up at any time, he wanted a staging ground for troops and a properly defensible set of walls around it. Finding colonists was no problem, because there were plenty of younger sons of noble lords willing to risk a move to gain land of their own, and plenty of bondsmen willing to go with them since they became free men once they left their bound land. When Caradoc's troop rode into Camynwaen, they found a decent town of a thousand round houses behind high stone walls, turreted with watchtowers.

About a mile away was the stone dun of Tieryn Maenoic, and there Caradoc found the kind of hire he'd been looking for. Although Maenoic received maintenance from the gwerbret to the south, there was a shortage of fighting men in his vast demesne, and he had a private war on his hands. Since the authority of his clan was fairly new, he was always plagued with rebellions. For years now the chief troublemaker had been a certain Lord Pagwyl.

"And he's gathered together a lot of bastards like himself," Maenoic said. "And they claim they'll ask the gwerbret to give them a tieryn of their own and not submit to me. I can't stand for it."

He couldn't, truly, because standing for it would not only take half his land away but also make him the laughingstock of every man in Eldidd. A stout hard-muscled man, with a thick streak of gray in his raven-dark hair, Maenoic was steaming with fury as he strode back and forth, looking over the troop, who were sitting on their horses outside the gates to Maenoic's dun. Caradoc and Maddyn followed a respectful distance behind while the lord judged the troop's horses and gear with a shrewd eye.

"Very well, Captain. A silver piece per week per man, your maintenance, and of course I'll replace any horses that you lose."

"Most generous, my lord," Caradoc said. "For peacetime."

Maenoic turned to scowl at him.

"Another silver piece per man for every battle we fight," Caradoc went on. "And that's paid for every man who dies, too."

"Far too much."

"As it pleases your lordship. Me and my men can just ride on."

And over to your enemies, perhaps—the thought hung unspoken between them for a long moment. Finally Maenoic swore under his breath.

"Done, then. A second silver piece per man for every scrap."

With an open and innocent smile, Caradoc bowed to him.

Maenoic's new-built dun was large enough to have two sets of barracks and stables built into the walls—a blessing, because the mercenaries could be well separated from Maenoic's contemptuous warband. At meals, though, they shared the same set of tables, and the warband made barely tolerable comments about men who fought for money and quite intolerable comments about the parentage and character of such who did so. Between them Caradoc and Maenoic broke up seven different fistfights in two days before the army was at last ready to ride out.

After he called in all his loyal allies, Maenoic had over two hundred and fifty men to lead west against his rebels. In the line of march, Caradoc's troop came at the very end, behind even the supply wagons, and ate dust all day long. At night they made camp by themselves a little way off from the warbands of the nobleborn. Caradoc, however, was summoned when the lords held a council of war. He came back to the troop with solid news and gathered them around him to hear it.

"Tomorrow we'll see the first scrap. Here's how things stand, lads. We're coming to a river, and there's a bridge there. Maenoic claims the taxes on it, but Pagwyl's holding out. The scouts say Pagwyl's going to make a stand to prevent the tieryn from crossing, because once he crosses against Pagwyl's will, it's his bridge again in everybody's eyes. We'll be leading the charge—of course."

Everyone nodded, acknowledging that they were, after all, the disposable mercenaries. Maddyn found himself troubled by a strange feeling, a coldness, a heaviness. It took him a long time to admit it, but then he realized that he was quite simply afraid. That night he dreamt of his last charge up in Cantrae and woke soaked with cold sweat. You coward, he told himself; you ugly little coward! The reproach burned in his very soul, but the truth was that he had almost died in that last charge, and now he knew what it felt like to be dying. The fear choked him as palpably as if he'd swallowed a clot of sheep's wool. What was worst of all was knowing that here was one thing he could never share with Aethan.

All night, all the next morning, the fear festered so badly that by the time the army reached the bridge, Maddyn was hysterically happy that the battle was at hand and soon to be over. He was singing under his breath and whistling in turn when the army crested a low rise and saw, just as they'd expected, Lord Pagwyl and his allies drawn up by the riverbank to meet them. There was a surprise, however, in the men who waited for them: a bare hundred mounted swordsmen, eked out by two big squares of common-born spearmen, placed so that they blocked any possible approach to the bridge itself.

"Oh, here," said Maddyn, forcing a laugh. "Pagwyl was a fool to rebel if that's all the riders he could scrape together."

"Horseshit!" Caradoc snapped. "His lordship knows what he's doing. I've seen fighting like this before, spearmen guarding a fixed position. We're in for a little gallop through the third hell, lad."

As Maenoic's army milled around in confusion, Caradoc led his men calmly up to the front of the line. The enemy had picked a perfect place to stand, a long green meadow in front of the bridge, bordered by the river on one side of their formation and on the other, the broken, crumbling earthwork of some long-gone farmer's cattle corral. Three rows deep, the spearmen stood shield to shield, the spearheads glittering around the chalk-whitened oval shields. To one side of the shield wall, the mounted men sat on restless horses, ready to charge in from the side and pin Maenoic's men between them and the river.

"Horseshit and a pile of it," Caradoc muttered. "We can't wheel round the bastards without falling into the blasted river."

Maddyn merely nodded, too choked for breath to answer. He was remembering the feel of metal biting deep into his side. Under him, his horse tossed its head and stamped as if it, too, were remembering their last charge. When Caradoc trotted off to confer with Maenoic, Aethan pulled up beside Maddyn; he'd already settled his shield over his left arm and drawn a javelin. While he followed the example, Maddyn had to work so hard to keep his horse steady that he suddenly realized that the poor beast did re-member that last charge. He had a battle-shy horse under him and no time to change him.

The spearmen began calling out jeers and taunting the enemy for scum on horseback, screaming into the sunlight and the wind that blew the taunts into jagged, incomprehensible pieces of words. Some of Maenoic's men shouted back, but Caradoc's troop merely sat on their horses and waited until at last their captain left the lord's side and jogged back, easy in his saddle, a javelin in his hand.

"All right, lads. We're riding."

There was a gust of laughter in the troop as they jogged forward to join him. Maenoic's own men pulled in behind, but the rest of the army wheeled off, ready to charge the enemy riders positioned off to the side. With an odd jingling shuffle, like a load of metal wares jouncing in a cart, the army formed up. Caradoc turned in his saddle, saw Maddyn right next to him, and yelled at him over the noise.

"Get back! I want to hear our bard sing tonight. Get back in the last rank!"

Maddyn had never wanted to follow an order more in his life, but he fought with himself only a moment before he shouted back his answer.

"I can't. If I don't ride this charge, then I'll never have the guts to ride another."

Caradoc cocked his head to one side and considered him.

"Well and good, then, lad. We might *all* be doing our listening and singing in the Otherlands, anyway."

Caradoc turned his horse, raised his javelin, then broke into a gallop straight for the enemy lines. With a howl of war cries, the troop burst after him, a ragged race of shrieking men across the meadow. Maddyn saw the waiting infantry shudder in a wave-ripple of fear, but they held.

"Follow my lead!" Aethan screamed. "Throw that javelin and wheel!"

Closer—a cloud of dust, kicked-up bits and clods of grass—the infantry shoving together behind the line of lime-white shields—then there was a shower of metal as Caradoc and his men hurled javelins into the spearmen. Shields flashed up, caught some of the darts, but there was cursing and screaming as the riders kept com-ing, throwing, wheeling, peeling off in a long, loose circle. Maddyn heard battle yells break out behind as the reserve troops charged into Pagwyl's cavalry. Snorting, sweating, Maddyn's horse fought for the bit and nearly carried them both into the river. Maddyn drew his sword, slapped the horse with the flat, and jerked its head around to spur it back to the troop.

The first rank of Maenoic's men were milling blindly, waving swords and shouting, in front of the shield wall. Caradoc galloped among his troop, yelling out orders to re-form and try a charge from the flank. Maddyn could see that Maenoic's allies had pushed Pagwyl's cavalry back to expose the shield wall's weakest spot. In a cloud and flurry of rearing horses, the troop pulled around and threw itself forward again. Maddyn lost track of Aethan, who was shoved off to the flank when Maenoic's men, blindly pulling back to charge again, got themselves mixed up with the charging mercenaries. One or two horses went down, their riders thrown and trampled, before Caradoc sorted out the mess into some rough order. Maddyn found himself in Maenoic's warband. For one brief moment he could see Caradoc, plunging at the flank of the shield wall with a mob behind him. Then his own unit rode forward for the charge.

On and on—the shield wall was trembling, turning toward its beleaguered flank, but it held tight directly ahead of Maddyn. From the men behind him javelins flew. Maddyn's horse bucked and grabbed for the bit; he smacked it down and kicked it forward. A split-second battle—of nerve, not steel—Maddyn saw the slack-jawed face of a young lad, his hands shaking on his braced spear, his eyes suddenly meeting Maddyn's as he galloped straight for him. With a shriek the lad dropped his spear and flung himself sideways. As the man next to him fell, cursing and flailing, Maddyn was in. Dimly he saw another horseman to his right. The shield wall was breaking. Swinging, howling with an unearthly laughter, Maddyn shoved his horse among the panicked spearmen. Ducking and bobbing in the saddle like a water bird, he slashed out and down, hardly seeing or caring whom or what he was hitting. A spearhead flashed his way. He caught it barely in time and heard his shield crack, then shoved it away as he twisted in the saddle to meet another flash of metal from the right. Always he laughed, the cold bubble of a berserker's hysteria that he could never control in battle.

His horse suddenly reared, screaming in agony. As they came down, the horse staggered, its knees buckling, but it couldn't fall.

All around was a press—panicked infantry, trapped cavalry, horses neighing and men shouting as they shoved blindly at one another. Desperately Maddyn swung out, cutting a spearman across the face as his dying horse staggered a few steps forward. All at once the line broke, a mob-panicked scuffle of men, throwing spears down, screaming, pushing their fellows aside as they tried to get away from the slashing horsemen. Maddyn's mount went down. He had barely time to free his feet from the stirrups before they hit the ground hard, a tangle of man and horse. Maddyn's shield fell over his face; he could neither see nor breathe, only scramble desperately to get up before a retreating spearman stuck him like a pig. On his knees at last, he flung up his shield barely in time to parry a random thrust. The force of the blow cracked the shield through and sent him reeling backward to his heels. He saw the spearman laugh as he raised the spear again, both hands tight on the shaft to drive it home for the kill; then a javelin flew into the press and caught the man full in the back. With a scream, he pitched forward, and the men around him ran.

Staggering, choking on dust and his own eerie laughter, Maddyn got to his feet. Around him the field was clearing as the horsemen charged the fleeing infantry and rode them down, slashing in blind rage at men who could no longer defend themselves. Maddyn heard someone yell his name and turned to see Aethan, riding for him at a jog.

"Did you throw that dart?" Maddyn called out.

"Who else? I've heard you laugh before, and I knew that cat's squalling meant you were in trouble. Get up behind me. We've won this scrap."

All at once, Maddyn's battle fever deserted him. He felt pain, bad pain, cracked ribs burning like fire. Gasping for breath, he grabbed at Aethan's stirrup to steady himself, but the movement made the pain stab him into crying out. With a foul oath, Aethan dismounted and caught him round the shoulders, a well-meant gesture that made Maddyn yelp again.

"Hard fall," Maddyn gasped.

With Aethan shoving him from behind, Maddyn managed to scrabble his way onto the horse. He kept telling himself that riding was better than walking, but he hung on to the saddle peak with both hands to brace himself against the motion as Aethan led the horse out of the death-strewn welter of the battlefield. As they went by, he saw some of Caradoc's men looting the dead, friend and enemy alike.

Up the riverbank the chirurgeons and their apprentices were waiting for the wounded. Aethan took Maddyn over to Caudyr, then went back to the field to pull more wounded men out of the dead and dying. When he tried to walk to the chirurgeon's wagon, Maddyn fell, then lay on the ground for an hour while Caudyr frantically worked on the men who were far worse off. At times Maddyn drowsed, only to wake with an oath for his burning ribs; the sun was hot, and he sweated copiously inside the mail he couldn't remove by himself. All he could think about was water, but no one had time to bring him any until Aethan returned. He fetched him a drink, unlaced the mail and helped him slide it off, then sat down beside him.

"We've won good and proper for all the good it does us. Maenoic's got Pagwyl's body at his feet, and his allies are all suing for peace right now."

"Is Caradoc alive?"

"He is, but not a lot of the godforsaken rest of us are. Maddo, we're down to twelve men."

"Ah. Can I have some more water?"

Aethan held the waterskin so he could drink again. Only then did he truly understand his friend's words.

"Oh ye gods! Only twelve?"

"Just that."

After another hour Caudyr came, his shirt blood-soaked down the front and up to his elbows. All he could do for Maddyn's ribs was to bind them with a wet linen band. As it dried in the sun, it would tighten enough to let him sit up. Maddyn's left shoulder was also a mass of bleeding, ring-shaped bruises: the mark of his own mail, pressed right down through his clothes when he'd fallen. Caudyr washed them down with a slop of mead from a wooden cup. Maddyn shrieked once, then bit his lower lip to keep from doing it again. Caudyr handed him the cup.

"Drink the rest of this," Caudyr said. "I put some painkilling herbs in it, too. It'll take the edge off."

The stuff was bitter and stinking, but Maddyn got it down a few sips at a time. He was just finishing the cupful when Caradoc came over and half sat, half fell next to him. Caradoc's sweaty face was spattered with some other man's blood, and his eyes were dark and exhausted. With a long sigh he ran grimy hands through his hair.

"This is the worst scrap I've ever fought." The captain's voice was halfway between a growl and a whisper. "Well, what else did I expect? That's what we're for, this dishonored pack of dogs, thrown out ahead of everyone. It's going to happen again, lads. Again and again."

Since the herbed mead was making Maddyn's head swim, he had to bend all his will to understand what Caradoc was saying. Aethan put one arm around him and helped him sit up.

"It's a fine short life we're going to have," the captain went on. "Ah, horseshit and a pile of it! Now listen, Maddo. I know you rode into that scrap with no guts for it, and I honor you. That's enough. You've proved you're not a coward, so stay out of it from now on. A bard's too valuable a man to lose."

"Can't. What kind of honor would I have?"

"Honor?" Caradoc tossed his head back and howled with high-pitched laughter. "Honor! Listen to you! You don't have any honor, you god-cursed little bastard! None of us do. Haven't you listened to one piss-poor word I've been saying? No noble lord sends men with honor into a suicide charge, but they sent us, and I took it because I had to. We've got as much honor as a pack of whores: all that counts is how good we fuck. So stay out of it from now on." He laughed again, but the pitch was closer to his deep-voiced normal tone. "Listen, when my Wyrd takes me, I want to know that there's a man still alive who can take over whatever's left of the troop. You pack of whoreson bastards are the only thing I have in life, and blasted if I know why, but I want to know the rotten-assed troop will last longer than I do. From now on, bard, you're my heir."

Caradoc got up and strode away. Maddyn slumped back and felt the world spin around him.

"Do what he says," Aethan growled.

Maddyn tried to answer but fainted instead.

By the time the army returned to Maenoic's dun, another man in Caradoc's troop had died. That left eleven, plus Caradoc himself, Otho, and Caudyr, to huddle dispiritedly in a corner of a barracks that had once housed nearly forty of them. The war over, Lord Maenoic turned generous, telling Caradoc that he was welcome to his shelter until his remaining wounded (Maddyn and

Stevyc) were ready to ride. He also promptly paid over the negoti-
ated wages and even added a couple of silver pieces as a bonus.

"Bastard," Caradoc remarked. "If he hadn't hired me to do it for
him, he would have had to lead that charge himself, and his piss-
proud noble lordship knows it."

"He'd be dead, too," Maddyn said. "He's not half the man on the
field that you are."

"Don't flatter the captain, you whelp of a bard, but as a cold,
hard assessment, like, you're right enough."

After a day or two in bed, Maddyn was well enough to go down
to the great hall for dinner. Caradoc and his men sat together as
far away from the rest of the warband as they could, drank hard,
and said next to nothing, not even each other. Occasionally Caradoc would try to joke with his demoralized pack, but it was a hard
thing to smile in answer to him. When Maddyn grew too tired to
sit up, the captain helped him back to the barracks. Otho was
already there, twining the rings of a bit of shattered mail by lantern light.

"I've been thinking, smith," Caradoc said. "Remember our jest
about the silver daggers? We've got a good bit of extra coin. Is it
enough to make us some?"

"Mayhap, but how am I going to work metal on the road?"

"We'll be sheltering here for at least one week, and if Maddyn
and Stevyc groan and moan like dying men, we can eke out another. There's a forge here in the dun, and the blacksmith says it's
a good one."

Otho considered, running gnarled fingers through his beard.

"You need somewhat to pick the lads up a bit," the dwarf said at
last.

"I do, and my own spirits could use a little raising, for that
matter. A silver dagger—it's a nice bit of jewelry for a man to
wear." Caradoc paused to stare into the hearth fire for a long moment. "I'm beginning to get an idea. Do you know this troop is
going to survive? By being the rottenest pack of black-hearted bastards Eldidd has ever seen, by making it an honor to become a
silver dagger, an honor to a certain kind of man, I mean. Someone
like our Aethan. He's as death-besotted and hard a man as I've ever
seen. I wouldn't cross him myself. Never wanted to die with a slit
throat in a brawl."

Maddyn was shocked to the heart. Caradoc was right about
Aethan, he realized; his old friend would never again be the man

who used to laugh and jest and solve all the little problems of the Cantrae warband. It hurt worse than his cracked ribs, thinking about it.

"When you break a man down to naught, he turns into an animal," the captain went on, somewhat meditatively. "Then if you give him somewhat to live for, he turns into a man again, but it's a hard kind of man, like the blade of a sword. That's the kind of lads I want, and the silver dagger's what they're going to live for." All at once he grinned, his hiraedd lifting. "Oh, they'll beg us for it, one fine day, but by every sticky hair on the Lord of Hell's ass, they're going to have to earn it. What kind of metal do you need, Otho? I'll ride into town on the morrow and see if I can buy it for you."

"You won't! You'll give me the coin and let me see if I can find what I need. No man learns the formula for this alloy—I cursed well mean it."

"Have it your way, then, but I want a dagger for every man we've got left, and, say, five more for new recruits—if I can find men worthy of the things, that is."

"Then I'll get started on it right away." All at once, Otho grinned, the first smile Maddyn had ever seen on his face. "Ah, it's going to feel so good, doing a bit of smelting and mixing again."

Otho was as good as his word. On the morrow, he first bribed Lord Maenoic's blacksmith into letting him use the dun forge, then rode off into town with his wagon. He returned late in the day with sundry mysterious and heavy bundles, which he refused to let any man touch, not even to help him unload. That very night, he shut himself up in the forge and stayed there for a solid week, sleeping beside his work, if indeed he slept at all. Once, in the middle of the night, when Maddyn went down to the ward to use the privy, he heard hammering coming from the forge and saw red light glowing through the window.

On the morning when the daggers were finished, Caradoc decided that it was time to leave Maenoic's hospitality. Not only were Maddyn and Stevyc both healed, but he wanted Otho to display his handiwork someplace where he could avoid awkward questions about it. After a last farewell to the lord, the troop saddled up and rode out, but they went only a half mile down the road before they turned off it, jogging out into a wild meadow and forming a rough circle about the smith and his wagon.

"Get 'em out, Otho," Caradoc said. "Dismount, men, so you can see clearly."

The troop clustered round while a proud if somewhat weary Otho unpacked a large leather sack. Nestled in straw were daggers for each of them, beautiful weapons, with a blade that glowed like silver but was harder than the finest steel. Maddyn had never handled weapon or tool with such a sharp edge.

"You won't have to polish those much, neither," Otho said. "They won't tarnish, not even in blood. Now, if any of you wants a mark or device, like, graved onto it, I'll do it, but you're paying me a silver piece for the job."

"This'll do to cut a throat with, won't it?" Aethan said to Maddyn.

"Blasted right. I've never had a knife I liked more."

As solemnly, as carefully as priests performing a rite, the troopers drew their old daggers and replaced them with the new. Although Caradoc seemed to be hardly watching, his eyes lazy and heavy-lidded, Maddyn knew that he was judging the effect of the gesture. The men were smiling, slapping each other on the back, standing straight for a change, their morale better than it had been in days.

"Well and good, then," Caradoc said. "We're all silver daggers now, lads. Doesn't mean a lot, I guess, except that we fight like sons of bitches, and we earn our hire."

Spontaneously the troop cheered him, ragged remnant though it was. When they remounted, they all formed of their own accord into a tight military order and trotted down the road to Camynwaen, where Caradoc had promised them a day of liberty before they started searching for a new hire. Near the west gate they found an inn that seemed big enough to shelter the lot of them, but the skinny, trembling innkeep announced that it was full.

"The stable looks empty to me," Caradoc said. "We'll pay you the going price."

"And what if you wreck the place? The wretched coin won't do me one bit of good then."

"And what if we wreck it without paying you first?"

Although he moaned and wrung his hands, the innkeep gave in quickly. In truth, he did have some custom, enough so that Aethan and Maddyn ended up sharing a small chamber tucked under the roof. While they ate their noon meal in the tavern room, the entire troop talked about women. Caradoc dispensed what was left of their wages along with some orders.

"We're in a town we may visit again someday, so you keep your paws off any lasses who don't want you, and your fists out of the faces of decent citizens, and I don't want to hear about anyone puking their guts out in a townsman's garden, either. Do it in the gutters, and leave their daughters alone."

After one hurried goblet of mead, Maddyn and Aethan went out for a stroll. By then it was midafternoon, and the streets were full of townsfolk, hurrying about their business. They all took one quick look at the pair of mercenaries, then either crossed the street or turned down an alleyway to avoid them. After a leisurely circuit of the town, they found a little tavern next to the baker's and went in. They had the place pretty much to themselves, except for the serving lass, a tousled sort of blonde with a soft, round face and heavy breasts. When she brought them tankards of dark ale, she lingered with an impartial smile for them both. Not bad, Maddyn thought, and he could tell from Aethan's predatory eyes that he agreed.

"What's your name?" Aethan asked.

"Druffa, and what's yours?"

"Aethan, and this is Maddyn. You don't happen to have a friend as pretty as you, do you? We could all sit down and have a bit of a chat."

"Chat indeed. And I suppose you lads are interested in a nice game of carnoic or gwyddbwcl."

"Do you have a better sort of game in mind?"

"I might. It depends on how generous you are."

Aethan raised a questioning eyebrow in Maddyn's direction.

"What about that friend?" Maddyn said.

"Well now, most of them would be busy this time of day. It's a pity you didn't come by at night, like."

"Ah, by the hells, then why bother?" Aethan said with a shrug. "Why don't you just come back to our inn with us? We've got a proper bed, better than a hayloft, and we'll buy a skin of mead."

Caught between drunkenness and fastidiousness, Maddyn shot him a foul look, but Aethan was paying strict attention to the lass. Druffa giggled in a pleasurable surprise.

"It might be rather amusing," she announced. "I'll go get the mead and just tell Da where I'm going."

When she minced off, Aethan turned to Maddyn with a shrug. "Wet fur, dry fur—does it matter?" His voice cracked. "They're all bitches anyway."

Maddyn finished the ale in his tankard in two long gulps. He had the vague thought of slipping away on the street, letting Aethan have this lass and finding himself another, but he was too drink-muddled to find his way back on his own in this unfamiliar town. When they came round to the back door of the inn, Aethan paused long enough to lean Druffa against the wall and kiss her. Maddyn found the sight exciting in a troubling sort of way. He made no protest when the lass suggested they all go upstairs.

Yet once they were in the quiet chamber, Maddyn's shyness returned in force. He barred the door behind them and rummaged in a saddlebag for a wooden cup, while Aethan untied the mead skin. Druffa giggled and took it away from him.

"Let's leave the drinking for later. You promised me a bit of fun, Aethan."

"So I did. Take off that dress, then."

With a peal of giggles, Druffa began to untie her highly inappropriate virgin's kirtle. The cup clutched in his hand, Maddyn watched as she undressed—slowly, smiling at the pair of them the entire time. When she stepped out of the underdress to reveal soft, pale skin and dark nipples, he felt the sexual tension in the room like a stroke across his groin. She gave Aethan one kiss, then turned to Maddyn, took the cup out of his hand, and kissed him, too, drawing them both after her to sit down on the bed.

It was several hours after sundown before they let her make her escape, pleading exhaustion between giggles. In a drunken, satisfied gallantry, Maddyn put on enough of his clothes to escort her downstairs and press a clutch of coppers into her hand. Although he may have been overpaying her, he felt she'd earned it. When he staggered back into the chamber, he found the candle burning itself out in the lantern and Aethan sound asleep and snoring on his side of the bed. Maddyn took off his brigga, threw a blanket over Aethan, then blew out the candle and lay down. The room spun slowly and majestically around him in a gold-flecked darkness. *And what would old Nevyn think of me now?* he thought; *well, thanks be to the gods, he'll never know what became of me.* Then he fell asleep as suddenly as he'd blown out the candle.

When he left Dun Deverry, Nevyn headed straight south, following the open road that ran beside the Belaver. He'd gone no more than five miles when he met a mounted patrol of five of the king's riders, coming right for him. Automatically, thinking little of it, he pulled off to the side to let them pass, but their leader hailed him and trotted over, blocking his path.

"That's a fine mule you've got there, herbman. He's going to see the king's service, too."

"Oh, is he now?" Nevyn looked deep into the man's eyes and sent a soothing flow of magnetic force out of his aura. "You don't want this mule. He comes up lame too often to be of use to you."

"Do you think I'd fall for such a clumsy ruse?" He started to laugh, then merely shook his head, his eyelids drooping. "Clumsy ruse. I don't want that mule."

"Truly, you don't want this mule."

The warrior yawned, shook himself, then turned his horse around.

"Come on, lads, we don't want that mule. He comes up lame too often to be of any use to us."

Although they looked puzzled, the others obeyed him without question and trotted after as he headed back toward Dun Deverry. In a bad temper, Nevyn rode on, and this time he kept a good watch out for mounted men. The incident made him think over his proposed route. Although he'd been planning on riding to Eldidd, he disliked the idea of having to ensorcel endless patrols of confiscating warriors the whole way there. Thanks to the war, he could no longer simply take a ship from Cerrmor, but just possibly there were less legitimate ships than ran the border far out to sea where few could catch them. Even though it was a good bit out of his direct route, he decided to swing by Dun Mannanan and see what he could find.

At that time Dun Mannanan was a pleasant-looking little town of some two thousand souls, whose round houses marched up from the harbor in tidy semicircles. Despite the war every house looked oddly prosperous, with fresh thatch, nicely whitewashed walls, and a handsome cow and a flock of hens in every yard. The town's one inn was clean and tidy, too, with a proper stable out back. It was quite a surprise, then, when he went into the tavern room and found the innkeep cooking stew at a hearth where the spit across the fire, the kettle itself, and the long spoon were made of bronze, not iron. When he commented about it, the innkeep snarled under his breath.

"You won't find a bit of good iron all along the Cerrmor coast, good sir. Naught can come south through the Cantrae battle lines, you see, and our wonderful king and his wonderful warbands have to have shoes for their misbegotten horses and swords and suchlike. So they strip every bit of iron they can find, right down to the rotten buckle on your belt, and if you ask for repayment, you get it in bruises." He paused to spit into the fire. "Even the plowshares are tipped with bronze, and they don't plow as deep, I tell you. So there's less of a yield every year, and the misbegotten king still takes the same taxes out of it."

"I see. Ye gods! I never dreamt things had gone as far as all this."

"I only wonder how far they'll go. Soon enough we'll all have gold hinges on our privy doors—it'll be cheaper than iron." His laugh was not a pleasant one.

As the evening wore on, a fair amount of customers drifted into the inn. As soon as they realized that Nevyn was an herbman, he had custom of his own and set up something of a dispensary on a table in the curve of the wall, out of the tavernman's way. When he was done, a young sailor named Sacyr, who'd bought herbs to ease a bad hangover, settled down next to him and insisted on buying a round of ale so that he could start developing his symptoms all over again.

"Will you be staying in Dun Mannanan long, sir?"

"I won't, truly. I'm hoping to find a ship going to Morlyn—on the Eldidd border, you know—one that has the draft to take my horse and mule. There are some valuable herbs that only grow in that part of the kingdom."

Sacyr nodded, taking the lie with the faith of the ignorant, and considered the question.

"Well, I do know a man who's running a good-sized boat west. He might be stopping in Morlyn."

"Stopping there? How much further west can you go these days?"

Looking suddenly stricken, Sacyr devoted himself to his tankard.

"Now, here." Nevyn dropped his voice to a whisper. "I'd truly like to get to Eldidd, and I'll pay well for my passage. Is that at all possible?"

"It just might be. Wait around here a bit."

In about an hour, a stout, graying man in the checked brigga of a merchant appeared, pausing in the tavern door and looking around carefully before he came any further. When Sacyr hailed him, he strolled over to the table, but he had a cautious eye for Nevyn.

"Sit down, Cabydd," Sacyr said. "There's coin in it."

With a small smile, the merchant sat. Sacyr leaned across the table to whisper.

"This herbman has a great desire to get to Eldidd. He needs a ship that can carry stock. I don't suppose you'd know of such a thing."

"Well." Cabydd paused to size Nevyn up. "It's a dangerous trip, good sir. I can't guarantee your safety if the Eldidd war galleys catch us."

"Ah, I see." Nevyn was quite sure that he could do the guaranteeing, though he didn't dare tell Cabydd that, of course. "But slipping across the border by land won't be much safer, and it'd be a cursed sight longer."

"True enough. But what if you came across from the west, right by Cannobaen?"

"Perfect! That's exactly where I want to go."

"Well and good, then. How many head of stock do you have?"

"Only one horse and a mule."

"Oh, well now, that's no trouble at all. You see, I've got a cattle boat that'll hold a hundred head easy, but we'll be running empty on the westward trip."

"I think I begin to understand. You've found a less than patriotic Eldidd man who's selling you war horses for the Cerrmor army."

"Not an Eldidd man." Cabydd leaned close to whisper. "Some of the Westfolk. Ever heard of them? They're a strange lot. They crop their babies' ears like calves, and they speak this language that'd break your jaw, but they raise beautiful horses. But best of all, they hate the men of Eldidd with a passion, so they sell at good prices to supply Eldidd's enemies."

Nevyn caught his breath. Although he knew that the elves never forgot a grudge, he was surprised at how far they would go to satisfy one.

On the next night, Nevyn went down to the dark, silent harbor at about the middle of the third watch, when the tide was turning to run out. At the end of a long wooden pier, muffled lanterns winked with a narrow beam beside the squat shape of the cattle boat. Nevyn coaxed his animals across the gangplank and settled them in solitary splendor in the hold, then came back up on deck. Cabydd showed him the low cabin, built on deck like a hut, that they would share: two narrow bunks bolted to the wall, and a tiny table and bench, bolted to the floor.

"The lads sleep on deck, but we do put up an old tent if it rains," Cabydd remarked. "The ship has to look shabby, you see, and I have to look poor." He shuddered briefly. "Let's pray to Mannanan ap Lier to keep the Eldidd galleys away! Once we pass Cerrmor, we'll pick up an escort—you'll see—but I've no desire to find myself in the middle of a sea battle."

Even though the wind was brisk, it took them two full days to reach Cerrmor in the lumbering, awkward boat. They never put into the harbor, because a sleek Cerrmor war galley was already waiting for them. Cabydd ordered the sails down and let the boat drift while the galley manoeuvered alongside and grappled on. The rowers, all free men and marines, rested at their oars while their captain made the precarious jump up to the cattle boat's deck.

"We'll follow the usual plan," he said to Cabydd. "You stay about fifteen miles out to sea. We'll follow a parallel course, just in sight of you. We'll meet at the usual harbor near the Westfolk's camp."

"Done, then, but come in our way every now and then so I can see that we haven't lost you."

As long as they were in Deverry waters, the two ships sailed close together, but about noon of the next day, Cabydd and his crew turned the cattle boat's clumsy nose out to sea and wallowed along against the tide until the galley's captain hailed them and told them they'd gone far enough out. Although Cabydd turned again, the galley kept going, heading out to sea. From that point on, Cabydd spent most of his time in the bow, keeping watch himself rather than trusting one of his men.

Four long anxious days and nights on the open sea brought them finally far enough west to turn back inland. Soon the Cerrmor galley joined them, and they sailed together to a tiny harbor, little more than a bite out of the chalk cliffs, with a short, rickety pier. Although the cattle boat edged in beside it, the galley headed straight for the sandy beach. As the high carved prow scraped on land, the marines jumped over the side, grabbed the gunwales in well-trained unison, and ran her up onto the sand.

"Well, Nevyn," Cabydd said. "Will you shelter on board tonight?"

"My thanks, but it's just a bare hour past noon. I'll be on my way."

As soon as Nevyn got his horse and mule on deck, they smelled land and practically bolted for it. He led them across the soft sand to the scrubby grassland just beyond the beach, then returned to fetch his saddles and mule packs. A couple of the sailors helped him carry the gear over.

"Look." One of the lads pointed. "Westfolk."

On golden horses two men and a woman were riding up, sitting easy in their elaborately stamped and tasseled leather saddles, their pale hair like moonlight to their mounts' sun. The sailors dumped Nevyn's gear near his stock, then ran back toward their ship as if they thought the elves would eat them or suchlike. When Nevyn called out a friendly greeting in Elvish, the woman turned her horse and trotted over, though the two men continued on to meet the marines.

"Greeting, elder one," she said in the same tongue. "You speak too well to be a merchant."

"No, I'm not. I'm a friend of Aderyn of the Silver Wings. Do you know him?"

"I know of him, but never has the honor been mine to meet him. Do you study the moonland lore, too?"

"Yes. I'm going to be traveling east from here, going to Eldidd. Will I be safe on the road?"

"A man like you is always safe among the People, but watch out for the Eldidd swine. You never know what *they'll* do."

"Oh yes." Nevyn agreed for politeness' sake. "I'm surprised you'll trade with my people at all."

"The longer the war goes on, the more Eldidd men die. Besides, they won't be trying to take our lands as long as there's fighting to the east." She raised her hand in mock salute. "May there be a king in Cerrmor for a hundred years!"

Although he was planning on going to Eldidd eventually, Nevyn's real destination lay just to the west of the border, where out to sea rise the three drowned peaks that form the islands of Wmmglaedd. Nevyn rode along the sea cliffs through meadows of tall, windswept grass for the rest of that day and on into the next, when he reached the low hills where neither men nor elves lived. On the third day, he came through a narrow pass to a wide, rocky beach, where the slow waves washed over gravel with a sad mutter, as if the sea were endlessly talking to itself. A scant two miles offshore, he saw the dark rise of the main island against the silver glitter of the Southern Sea.

Since the tide was at its full, Nevyn had to wait before he could cross over. He led his animals down to the two stone pillars that marked the entrance to the stone causeway, still underwater at the moment, and watched the waves lapping at the carved notches. Sure enough, the tide was turning, as each wave fell a little lower than the one before. Crying and mewling, seabirds swooped down as if to take a look at him, the graceful gulls, the occasional osprey, and the ungainly pelicans who were sacred to the god Wmm. As he idly watched the birds, Nevyn thought over the job ahead of him, convincing the priests of the Water Temple to aid the dweomer in the work of healing the torn kingdom. He was oppressed by doubts; thinking about his elaborate scheme in cold blood made it seem daft.

As the waves fell back, the long causeway emerged, streaming water like a silver sea snake. Nevyn waited until the sun and wind had dried it off, then led his balky stock across. Snorting, they picked their hooves up high on the unfamiliar footing. Ahead the island rose up, about ten miles long and seven wide, with a low hill standing in the midst of meadows of coarse sea grass. Since the day was sunny (a rare thing at Wmmglaedd), he could just pick out the temple buildings themselves as he went across. At the end of the causeway stood a stone arch, carved with panels of interlace and roundels decorated with pelicans, and an inscription: "Water covers and reveals all things."

Just as Nevyn left the causeway for solid land, a young priest came hurrying across the meadow to meet him. A blond lad of about sixteen, he was dressed in dark brigga and a linen overshirt of an ordinary cut, but on the yokes of the shirt, where a lord's blazon would go, were orange pelicans.

"Welcome, good traveler. What brings you to the water temple of Wmm?"

"I need the help of the oracles of the god. My name is Nevyn."

"And mine's Cinrae. The god gives oracles to all who ask."

The temple complex was a good mile away across the windblown meadow. As they walked along, Cinrae said not a word more, and Nevyn wondered about him and his reasons for choosing this lonely life so young. He was a good-looking boy, though his slender face was chapped and red from the continual sea wind, but his blue eyes were oddly distant, a bit wistful, as if he felt that ordinary life had nothing to offer him. In the shelter of the hill rose a high stone broch and, scattered around it, some storage sheds, two small round houses, and a stables. A few wind-gnarled trees cast small patches of shade; a few flowers struggled to bloom in the shelter of walls. The wind sighed around the buildings and swirled the sandy dust in a perpetual scour. Out beyond the complex Nevyn could see kitchen gardens, a field of barley, and some white cows at pasture. Although the pious made donations to Wmm when they wanted his advice, the coin would never have been enough to provision the temple. Cinrae pointed to a small round hut with a freshly thatched roof right by the stable well.

"That's the guesthouse, good sir. I'll put your baggage in there after I've stabled your horse and mule. See the big house over there? That belongs to the high priest, and you can pay him your respects straightaway."

"My thanks, and I will. Is Adonyc still the head of the order here?"

"Oh, he died ever so long ago. Pedraddyn was called to replace him."

As so often happened, Nevyn was caught by surprise at just how fast the time seemed to go—for other men. He remembered Pedraddyn as an earnest acolyte not much older than Cinrae, but the man who greeted him at the door of the high priest's residence had a thick streak of gray in his dark hair and the slow, solid walk of a man secure in his years and his position.

"By the feet and feathers of the holy birds! Can it truly be Nevyn?"

"It is, at that. Do you remember me? Why, it must have been twenty years ago that I was here."

"It was, but you made quite an impression on me. It's a marvel to see you looking so hale. You must be the best testimonial for your herbs that ever a man could have, or is it the dweomer that keeps you so fit?"

"The dweomer, truly, in its own way. It gladdens my heart to see you, too."

Pedraddyn ushered him into a spare stone room that held one table, one bench, a narrow cot, and a vast set of shelves, stacked with codices and scrolls in leather cases. In the pink sandstone fireplace a peat fire smoldered to take off the sea chill. When the high priest clapped his hands, a servant came in the back door. He was a man in his thirties, dark-haired, and he had the worst scar on his face that Nevyn had ever seen, thick knots and welts of shiny scar tissue that ran through his left cheek and clotted at the corner of a mouth twisted in a perpetual parody of a smile.

"Davyn, get our guest and me some spiced milk. Then you can do what you'd like until dinner."

With a silent nod he left by the same door.

"He can't speak clearly," Pedraddyn said to Nevyn. "He was an Eldidd sailor once. We found him washed up on our beach and bleeding half to death from those wounds. That was about six years ago now. He begged to stay here with us, and I can't say I blamed him for wanting out of the wars. A silent man makes a good servant for a priest."

After Davyn brought the milk, priest and sorcerer sat down together by the fire. Nevyn had a sip of the sweet milk and wished that the priests of Wmm weren't forbidden to drink ale and mead.

"With your skill in dweomer, I'm surprised you'd come to us for an oracle."

"The oracle I need concerns the entire land of Deverry and Eldidd, not merely my own doings, Your Holiness. I also came to ask your aid in a certain peculiar matter. Tell me, does it ache your heart to see the wars raging and no end in sight?"

"Do you truly need to ask? It would ache the heart of any sane man."

"Just so. We who serve the dweomer of light have joined together, and we have a plan to end the wars, but we can't do it without the help of those who serve the gods. I've come to beg you to help put the one true king upon his throne."

Pedraddyn's eyes widened like a child's.

"Who is he?" he whispered.

"I don't know yet, but you have every important genealogy and noble bloodline stored away in your records. Once Great Wmm gives us an omen, surely we can interpret it with the help of the archives."

"I see. And once you know his name?"

"Then the dweomer will put him on his throne. Let me tell you my scheme."

Pedraddyn listened quietly at first, then flung himself out of his chair and began pacing back and forth in sheer excitement.

"It could work!" the priest burst out. "With the help of the gods, and the dweomer behind it, we could do it. The cost, though—by my most holy lord, a good many men will die in such a war."

"Will it be any more than are dying already? At least this war will put an end to it, or so we can hope. What hope do we have now?"

"None, sure enough. On the morrow we'll consult the god."

Dinner that night was served in the broch in a vast round room, smoky from the torches and the peat fire, that served as refectory and kitchen both. The five priests, their three servants, and whatever guests there were all ate together at two long tables with no show of rank. Even the high priest got up to fetch himself more milk and stew if he wanted them. The quiet talk was of books and gardening, the religious exercises of the priests and the slow life of the island. Nevyn envied them. His life would soon revolve around kings and warfare, politics and death—the very things he'd tried to leave behind when he chose the dweomer road, as he remarked to Pedraddyn.

"The man who runs from his Wyrd finds it waiting for him, or so the proverb goes," the priest said. "But yours seems to be an unusually fast runner."

After a pleasant night in the clean, comfortable guesthouse, Nevyn woke to a world turned gray by fog. It lay so thick on island and sea that land and water seemed the same element. In the windless damp, every word spoken hung in the air like a tuft of sheep's wool caught on a bramble. When Cinrae came to fetch him, the lad was wearing an orange cloak with the hood up against the damp.

"I hope the fog doesn't bother you, aged sir."

"It doesn't, lad, but my thanks for your concern. I've got a good heavy cloak of my own."

"Good. I like the fogs. They make a man feel safe, somehow."

Cinrae led the way through the gray-shrouded complex and out to the gardens, where Pedraddyn was waiting. Although it was only about a hundred yards away, the top of the broch was lost in fog. Without speaking they walked up the grassy hill to the small round temple at the top. Inside was a single plain room of worked stone, with eight freestanding pillars set around and eight small oil lamps on the altar. Pedraddyn and Nevyn knelt before the altar while Cinrae lighted the lamps, an eerie pale glow in the heavy air. It seemed that the fog had followed them inside and hung over the altar and the niche behind, where there was a statue of Wmm, or Ogmios, as he was known in the Dawntime. The god was sitting cross-legged on a stool, with his right hand raised in benediction and his left holding a reed pen. As the light flared up, his calm face seemed to smile at his worshippers. Cinrae knelt down beside Nevyn and stared at his god in sincere devotion.

Pedraddyn prayed aloud, asking the god to favor Nevyn's request and to grant them both wisdom, and he went on at a good length, his voice echoing through the room. Although the usual worshipper would have been listening to the priest and little more, Nevyn had the skills to make a direct link with the force—or the part of the Innerlands, if you prefer—that Wmm represented. In his mind he built up a thought form of the god behind his statue, carved it from the blue light, worked and perfected it until the image lived apart from his will. Then he used a trick of the mind to force his imaginings out through his eyes until he saw it standing behind the altar. Slowly, the god force that Pedraddyn was summoning came to ensoul it. Nevyn knew he was successful when Cinrae cried out, a sob of joy, and raised his hand to greet what he saw as a visitation of the god. Nevyn felt a bit dishonorable, as if he'd tricked the lad, but on the other hand, the image did represent a truth.

At the end of the prayer, the three of them sat for a long moment of silence. A bit at a time, Nevyn withdrew the force he'd put into the actual image and thanked the god for appearing to them. Cinrae's devotion kept it alive a little longer, but soon the unstable etheric substance went its own way, spinning off, swirling, and dissolving as the god force left its temporary home. Cinrae sobbed once under his breath, like a child who sees his mother go off to work in the fields but knows he can't call her back. Pedraddyn rose and closed the temple working with a short chant, then clapped his hands eight times in slow, stately succession.

"We are blessed," Pedraddyn said. "He has appeared to us."

Again, Nevyn felt rather shabby. He felt sorry for the priests, particularly young Cinrae, who would never know the truth about the object of his devotion, never realize that he could learn to call the god at will. Yet, as he thought about it, perhaps it was better that way. How, after all, can one love an objective natural force that can be summoned in cold blood to ensoul an artificial image? In a way, there's little room for love in the dweomer, which is why mankind needs priests like Cinrae.

Silently, in single file, they left the temple and walked down the far side of the hill. The fog still lay thick, but through the clinging damp came the distant boom and echo of wave striking rock. As they picked their way through a vast meadow of coarse sea grass, the waves grew louder and louder, until at last they reached the cliff at the far side of the island. Down below, across a graveled beach, great rocks rose jagged out of the swirling white surf. The ocean crashed over them with sheets of spray like birds' wings, then flowed all white and foaming through the narrow channels between.

"Behold the voices of the god!" Pedraddyn cried.

The ocean roar answered him with a hundred tongues. As they slowly made their way down the damp, treacherous stairs cut into the side of the rocky cliff, the roar and boom of the surf grew so deafening that it seemed to echo inside Nevyn's mind as well as in his ears. At the tide line the three of them knelt on the slimy gravel and raised their hands palm outward to the oracle. Each great wave swept in like an omen, spraying over the rocks and swirling with white foam up almost to their knees.

"O mighty Wmm," Nevyn called out. "We beg you: guide us in choosing the one true king of all Deverry. O mighty Wmm, put the true king on the throne and no other. O mighty Wmm, lend us your power to tell truth from falsehood."

One after the other, the waves swept in from the gray, misty ocean that might have broken on Eldidd's shore or on that of the Otherlands, for all they could tell. The voices roared and boomed incomprehensible answers to Nevyn's question. All at once, Cinrae sobbed and rose slowly to his feet, his eyes staring all-unseeing in deep trance. When he spoke, his thin lad's tenor had changed into a voice as deep and hollow as wave on rock.

"Look in the north and west. The lad who will be king has been born in the north and west. The king of all Deverry and all Eldidd has been born in a lake among the fishes and the water reeds. He who will give peace trains for war."

With a sharp cry Cinrae fainted, falling forward headlong as the god left him. Nevyn and Pedraddyn raised him up, then carried him away from the tide line to the tenuous shelter of the foot of the cliff. Pedraddyn stripped off his own cloak and wrapped it around the boy.

"Nevyn, he's the priest you get only once in a hundred years, if that. He'll succeed me and surpass me a thousand times. I thank the god every day for bringing him here."

"So you should, and for his sake, too. I don't know what would have happened to him if he hadn't found the way of the god."

"Oh, his family thought he was a bit simpleminded, sure enough. They brought him here to ask the god's advice when he was but a tiny lad, and he's never left. Sometimes I wonder if there's some Westfolk blood in our Cinrae, but of course I couldn't possibly go asking his kin a shameful thing like that." He laid a fatherly hand on the boy's cheek. "He's icy cold. I wish we could get him away from the damp."

"Naught easier. Just give him to me."

Nevyn called on the spirits of the elements, an almost automatic task there in that rage and vortex of elemental force, and asked them to support the lad's weight. With their help, he picked Cinrae up like a sack of grain and carried him up the steps without even having to pause for breath. He brought the lad well away from the edge, then laid him down gently in the cushioning grass while Pedraddyn stared in utter amazement. In a few minutes Cinrae tossed his head this way and that, then opened his eyes.

"I can walk soon, Your Holiness," he whispered.

"When you're ready, lad, and not before." Pedraddyn knelt down beside him. "And someday soon you'll learn how to control the force of the god."

Nevyn walked a few steps away and turned to look over the distant swirl of fog and ocean. The voices of the god echoed softly in the distance. North and west, he thought; I would have been wasting my time if I'd gone to Cerrmor. He had no doubt that the omen was a true one; reinforced by the ritual and the dramatic physical setup of the oracle, Cinrae's raw psychic talent had tapped in deep to the Deverry racial soul. Born in the midst of reeds and fishes—that particular phrase bothered him, but he was sure that in time everything would become clear. All in all, he was well pleased. Only later did he remember that ominous phrase, king of all Deverry *and* of all Eldidd, and wonder just what mighty forces he had set in motion.

That afternoon, while Cinrae slept, Nevyn and Pedraddyn went to the Chamber of Records, which occupied the entire second floor of the broch. Aided by another neophyte, they sat at a table by a window and pored over dusty codex after dusty codex of genealogies. As they compiled lists of heirs, both direct on the male line and indirect through the sons of royal women, one name reappeared three times: Maryn, marked prince of the small kingdom of Pyrdon, related vaguely to the Eldidd throne, tightly to the Cantrae claimant through his mother, and most directly indeed to the Cerrmor line through Prince Cobryn, Dannyn's son. Realizing that a man of Dannyn's line might someday hold the throne of all

Deverry made Nevyn shudder with the dweomer cold. It was just the sort of irony that the Lords of Wyrd seemed to love.

"This lad interests me." Nevyn tapped the name with a bone stylus. "Do you know anything about him?"

"I don't. Pyrdon's a long way away. At times I even have trouble getting correct information for my records."

"You don't think the lad might be dead or suchlike?"

"I doubt that. Usually someone will make an effort to tell me of a thing as important as the death of a marked prince. I only meant that I've never laid eyes on the lad or his mother. I saw his father once when Casyl was . . . oh, twelve, I'd say. He impressed me as a nice child, but still, who knows what's happened since then?"

Since, if their plan was to succeed, they would need the help of at least one powerful priest of Bel, Nevyn headed directly back to Deverry rather than going hundreds of miles out of his way to Pyrdon. He gave the job of looking over young Prince Maryn to Aderyn, who was roaming with his alar near the border of the kingdom. Nevyn had just crossed into Deverry proper when Aderyn contacted him through his campfire.

"I think we've found our claimant." Aderyn's image was smiling, but in a thoughtful sort of way. "Pyrdon's a harsh place, but it's the right sort of harshness, the kind that keeps a man mindful that he needs other people to survive. I was most impressed with King Casyl; he has an honor that's rare even in the best of times. The young prince seems bright beyond his years, but he's only five, so it's a bit early to tell how he's going to turn out. He seems healthy, though. It would be a pity if he died in childhood."

"True-spoken, but then Casyl might have another son or two yet. I hate storing all my mead in one skin."

"So do I, but we've got to. The whole problem is that we've got too beastly many would-be kings."

"Just so. What about the omens?"

"They couldn't be more right. Dun Drwloc is Casyl's primary residence, and that's where the young prince was born. It's a fortified island, right out in the middle of a lake."

"Excellent! My thanks for your help. I'm on my way to Lughcarn. I remember the high priest of Bel there as being a decent, honorable man—well, if he hasn't up and died on me, anyway."

Since it was far enough from the Cerrmor border to be spared the worst ravages of war, Lughcarn was still prosperous, and the biggest city left in Deverry. The center of the iron workings, it was continually dusted with fine dark ash from its smelters, forges, and of course the big beehive ovens where wood was turned into charcoal. In the still summer air, the haze hung over the city and turned the sky yellow. Nevyn made his way to the center of town, where the temple of Bel stood among soot-dusted ancient oaks. He was well known there, and neophytes came running to take his horse and mule as soon as he entered the sacred grove. Much to his relief, Olaedd the high priest was very much alive, though severely troubled by pains in his joints. A neophyte ushered Nevyn into Olaedd's chamber, which was bare except for a narrow, hard pallet on the floor and one chair.

"You'll forgive me if I don't rise, Nevyn. The pain in my back is bad today."

"You've got to get yourself a proper bed. It doesn't have to be soft or some such sinful thing; you've just got to get out of the draft."

"I'll consider it, then."

The neophyte brought Nevyn a low stool, then took himself away. Nevyn launched straight into his plans. The priesthood of Bel was in the perfect position to interpret oracles and omens in the "correct" way, simply because so many men came to them with puzzling dreams or events. When the time came, too, they would be the ones to proclaim the new king and marry him to the sovereignty of the kingdom.

"And I've no doubt he'll reward the temples once he's gained the throne," Nevyn finished up.

"No doubt, oh no doubt, but why are you coming to me instead of the high priest of the Holy City?"

"I was recently there. I heard Gwergovyn is the new high priest."

"Um. He is, of course, my superior, no matter what I may think of him."

For a moment they considered each other, each wondering just how much could be said aloud. Since he was running the lesser risk, Nevyn spoke first.

"I realize that traditionally the priesthood of Deverry has always claimed supremacy, but as I remember, anyway, it's only tradition —not law—that gives them their place."

"True enough." Olaedd's dark eyes blinked once. "So it is, truly."

"That tradition might be badly shaken if the priesthood there supports the wrong claimant to the throne."

"While Lughcarn supports the right one?" Olaedd put the tips of his fingers together and studied his arched hands for a moment. "In just an eightnight there'll be a convocation of the northern temples here in Lughcarn."

"Won't the Dun Deverry priesthood send an envoy?"

"Of course, but there are always ways for a few trustworthy men to talk privately. Ride back when the convocation's over. We'll speak of this matter again."

Nevyn went to a small village about ten miles north of the city and camped in a farmer's barn on the pretense of gathering herbs in the neighborhood. Since not only the farmer in question but the whole village was glad to have an herbman nearby, he was soon well known. During his second week there, the miller's little daughter came running to tell him that a marvel had happened: one of the goats had given birth to a two-headed kid. Mostly because she expected him to, Nevyn went to look and found most of the village crowded round the pen. Weighed down by its deformity, the kid couldn't even stand, while its mother bleated in a hopeless sort of way even as she licked it clean.

"It doubtless won't live the day," Nevyn remarked to the miller.

"Couldn't agree more. Do you think someone bewitched my goats?"

"I don't." Nevyn was about to launch into a long discussion of the interrelationships of the four humors in animals when he got a much better idea. "The gods sent it as an omen, I'll wager. Here, can an animal with two heads live? Of course not. So, then, can a kingdom with two kings do much better?"

The crowd nodded sagely at this display of erudition.

"I'll wager you're right," the miller said. "I'll send my eldest lad to the local priest about this."

"Do that. He'll find it interesting, I'm sure."

When he returned to Lughcarn, Nevyn found that indeed the news of the two-headed goat had preceded him. As soon as Olaedd and he were alone, the priest mentioned it.

"Now, even though you were the one to interpret the omen for the village, I'm sure Great Bel sent it. Your interpretation is the same as I'd give, too. If the civil wars go on much longer, there won't be any kingdom to fight over, just a pack of minor lords, each squabbling over his borders. We discussed this at length during the convocation. After all, if there's no king, who will protect the temples?"

"Just so."

Olaedd looked absently away for a long moment, and even when he spoke, he didn't look directly at Nevyn.

"There was some small discussion of Gwergovyn. It seems that there are some who are less than pleased with his presidency over the Holy City."

"Ah. I wondered if that might be the case."

"There are some good reasons for this dissatisfaction, at least if certain rumors are to be believed." Again the long pause. "I do not think that they need concern you. Let me only say that I found them most distressing."

"I have perfect faith in Your Holiness's judgment."

"My thanks. You may, however, count on the northern temples for any aid we can render you. Ah, at times I feel so weary! We're talking of a plan that will take many years, but who better to start a plan than old men who have the wisdom to pick the young men to finish it?"

"Just so. I take it none of the priesthood in the Holy City will be consulted?"

Olaedd smiled, answering the question the only way such things can be answered: by silence.

Late in the autumn, when the trees stood stark beside the road and the morning sky smelled of snow, Nevyn returned to Brin Toraedic. Since the caves were musty and damp from being shut up so long, he lit fires and sent the air elementals sweeping through the chambers to cleanse the fetid air, then took his mule and went down to the village to buy food. When he rode in, everyone ran over to greet him. They all knew what his real work was and were proud to have something that no other village did, or at least, none that they knew of: their own local sorcerer. While he packed up some cheese, a ham, and barley for porridge, Nevyn also heard the summer's worth of gossip, much of which concerned Belyan, big with a bastard child and not telling a soul who the father was. When Nevyn took his stock over to the blacksmith's to be reshod, the smith's wife, Ygraena, invited him in for a drop of ale.

"Have you seen our Belyan yet?" she remarked, ever so casually.

"I knew about the child before I left. I'll be going out to the farm to buy dried apples, so I'll see how she fares then."

"I've no doubt she'll have an easy time of it. I'll admit to being ever so envious of the way she has hers, just like a cat." She hesitated, her eyes as shrewd as ever Olaedd's were. "Here, good Nevyn, some people are saying that she got this child from one of your spirits."

When he laughed so hard that he choked on his ale, Ygraena looked bitterly disappointed: such a lovely theory, and all exploded.

"I assure you that the lad was real flesh and blood, and hot enough blood at that, judging from what's happened to Bell. If she's keeping her own counsel about it, well, she always was a close-mouthed lass."

Belyan had the baby just four days later. Nevyn was sweeping out his caves when the oldest lad came running to tell him that Mam was starting to have the new baby. By the time he packed a few herbs and rode down, Ygraena's prediction had come true: Bell's new son was already born, and an easy time he had coming, too. While the midwife washed the babe and got Belyan comfortable, Nevyn and Bannyc sat by the fire.

"And how do you feel about this new cub in the litter?" Nevyn said.

"Well, I wish she would have married some lad if she wanted a babe that bad, but Bell was always too headstrong for me to handle. He's healthy, the midwife says, and so he's welcome enough. You can always use another pair of hands around a farm."

With a deep heave of a sigh, Bannyc went out to tend his goats. Nevyn stretched his feet out to the warmth of the fire and thought of Maddyn. Quickly enough his image grew in the fire, a tiny figure at first, then swelling until Nevyn could comfortably see the entire scene around him. Maddyn was sitting in a dirty tavern room with about a dozen other men, all of them drinking hard and laughing. At their belts each had a dagger with an identical pommel decorated with three silver balls. When one of the men idly drew his to gouge a splinter out of the table, Nevyn could see that it was some peculiar metal, a kind of silver, he thought, but the vision was not sharp or detailed enough for him to be sure. What did seem obvious was that Maddyn had found himself a place in a mercenary troop. Nevyn's first thought was pity; then it occurred to him that such a troop, one with no fixed loyalties, might be very useful for the work he had ahead. He made a mental note to keep better track of Maddyn in the future.

Later, Nevyn went in to see Belyan, who was sitting up in bed with the babe at her breast. A big baby, easily eight pounds, Daumyr had a soft crown of fine blond hair, and he was sucking eagerly with an occasional bird chirp of satisfaction.

"I'll be getting the true milk soon," Belyan said. "The way this hungry little beast is nursing."

"No doubt. Do you miss his father?"

Belyan considered while she changed the babe to her other breast.

"A bit," she said at last. "What with all I had to do around the farm, I hardly thought of him all summer, but now that winter's almost here, I find myself remembering him. I hope he's safe and well, wherever he is. It's better to wonder where he is than to go visit his grave."

"It is, at that, truly."

With a smile, Belyan gently stroked the baby's hair.

"He's a bit different than my other lads were when they were born, and he'll doubtless look different, with Maddyn's curly hair and all, but in time, he'll grow to be like us. It's a bit like needlework, having a babe. You've got your cloth, and you've got your colors of thread, but it's up to you how the pattern grows."

Nevyn suddenly smiled. She'd just handed him the missing piece of his plan. What better way to have a true and noble king than to raise the prince? Maryn was still young and malleable; he needed tutors, and he would respond to the proper influence. One of us can find a way into the court, Nevyn thought; we'll make sure the lad grows up well while we lay the rest of the groundwork.

That night, Nevyn walked on the hill just as the full moon was at her zenith. Clouds came in from the north, casting moving shadows across the sleeping countryside. For too long now, darker shadows had killed all joy in Deverry. Nevyn smiled to himself. Deep in his heart, he saw the coming peace and the victory of the light.

THREE

The year 837. Olaedd the high priest died in the spring. Retyc of Hendyr was appointed high priest by the northern conclave. In the summer a little lad with falling sickness was brought to the temple. He had a seizure at Retyc's feet and cried out that the king was coming from the west. When he awakened he repeated that the king was in the west, but he could give no reason why he said it. Retyc declared the speaking a true one . . .

—The Holy Chronicles of Lughcarn

Up on the dais of the great hall, Ogretoryc, king of all Eldidd and what little of Deverry he could hold with his army, was sitting in his high-backed carved chair. Behind him hung a finely worked tapestry depicting Epona riding with her retinue of godlets in the Otherlands. To either side the tapestry were long banners in blue and silver cloth, with the Dragon of Eldidd appliqued in green. At the king's feet lay a blue and green carpet, covering a floor of inlaid slate. His bard sat nearby; his picked guard stood behind him; two pages waited with a golden goblet and a pitcher of mead. The king, however, was asleep, slumped to one side and snoring, a line of drool running from his toothless mouth down his wrinkled, flabby chin. Out in the circular expanse of the hall, the noble lords, their warbands, and the king's own men went on with their feasting and tried to ignore their liege lord.

Because they were mercenaries, the silver daggers were seated in the back and to one side of the hall, where they caught the drafts from the door and the smoke from the fire, but by leaning back on his bench, Maddyn could keep an eye on the dais and the sleeping king. In only a few minutes, Prince Cadlew, heir to the throne, mounted the dais and hesitantly went over to his father. A lean man, his face positively gaunt, Cadlew was tight-muscled and hard from long years in the saddle. His raven-dark hair was heavily streaked with gray, and his cornflower-blue eyes were webbed with crow's-foot wrinkles, yet he could still swing a sword with the best of them. Cadlew caught the king's arm and shook him awake. Surrounded by guards, with the pages trailing uncertainly behind, the prince led his father away. The entire hall sighed in relief. Caradoc leaned over to whisper to Maddyn.

"I'll wager there's plenty of men who'd rather see our prince sitting on that fancy chair."

"It'd be a safe wager, sure enough. Here, I've been stewing with curiosity. What did the prince say when he called you to his chamber this afternoon?"

"Offered to take us into his warband. I turned him down."

"You what?!"

"Turned him down." Caradoc paused for a calm sip of mead. "Thanked him for the honor, mind, but I'd rather negotiate our wages summer to summer than swear fealty."

"Ah, curse you to the ninth hell!"

"Listen, Maddo. I know it sounds splendid to think of being honorable men again and all that, but a silver dagger's got to be free to change sides if he doesn't want to hang after a defeat."

"Well, true-spoken. We've changed sides too often before to be treated honorably, no matter what a prince says about us."

"Just that. Not a word of this to the others, mind."

"I wouldn't worry about it. You should know that we'd all follow you to the death."

Caradoc looked away, tears in his eyes. Maddyn was too embarrassed to do more than leave him his silence.

While he sipped his mead, Maddyn considered the troop, seventy-five strong, and everyone of them a blood-besotted man who fought like a demon from hell. It had taken Caradoc three years, but he'd scraped and scrounged and bargained until he had a troop so valuable that the prince would consider taking them into his own warband. Every one of them, too, had one of Otho's mysterious daggers at his belt. Some of the best smiths in the king's court had gone down on their knees to beg the dwarf for the secret of that metal, but not even the offer of whole sacks of gold coins and jewels would have softened Otho's stance. Once he had remarked to Maddyn that someday, when he found a deserving lad, he'd pass the secret on, but so far, no such paragon of smithly virtue had ever appeared.

After a hard summer's fighting, the men of Eldidd, paid and pledged alike, were back in winter quarters in the king's palace at Abernaudd. They'd fought late, that autumn, skirmishing in the hills with Cerrmor troops, or riding raids up to the borders of Pyrdon, which the people of Eldidd still insisted on calling a rebellious province. The rumors were going round that in the spring they'd make a proper attack on Pyrdon, but those rumors went round every winter. The truth was that Eldidd couldn't afford to drain off men and supplies to conquer Pyrdon when it had two bigger enemies at its eastern borders. Maddyn frankly didn't care where they rode in the spring. All that mattered was that for the winter they'd be well fed and warm.

To avoid drunken brawls between his men and the king's, Caradoc led the silver daggers back to their own barracks before the great feast was truly over. As they crossed the ward, Maddyn lingered to walk with Caudyr, whose clubfoot slowed him down. With the clatter of hooves and a jingle of tack, a squad of the king's personal guard came through the gates. Back from a cold, long patrol, they were hungry and eager to get to the warm feast inside. Even though there was plenty of room to pass, they started cursing and yelling at Maddyn and Caudyr to move aside. They were both willing, but Caudyr had no choice but to lurch slowly along. One of the horsemen leaned over in his saddle.

"Move your cursed ass, rabbit! They should have drowned a lame runt like you at birth."

When most of the squad laughed, Maddyn swirled around, reaching for his sword, but Caudyr grabbed his arm.

"It's not worth it. I'm used to being the butt of a jest."

As they went on, Caudyr tried to hurry.

"Look at him hop!" called another guardsman. "You were right enough about the rabbits."

At that, the squad leader, who'd drifted on ahead, turned his horse and trotted back.

"Hold your tongues, you bastards!" It was young Owaen, and he was furious. "Who are you to mock a man for a trouble that the gods gave him?"

"Oh, listen to you, lad!"

Like a bow shot, Owaen was out of his saddle. He ran over to the guardsman and grabbed, pulling him down and dumping him on the cobbles before the startled fellow could react. With an oath, the man leapt up and swung at him, but Owaen dropped him with one punch. The laughter and catcalls abruptly stopped.

"I don't want to hear anyone else mock a man for a trouble he can't help."

Except for the nervous horses, stamping restless hooves, the ward was dead silent. Puzzled as much as pleased, Maddyn kept his eyes on Owaen, who was barely seventeen, for all that he'd been riding to war for the past three years. Normally he was the most arrogant man Maddyn had ever met. Wearing the Eldidd dragons on his shirt wasn't enough for Owaen, who had his own device of a striking falcon marked on his shirt, his dagger, his saddle—on every piece of gear he owned, from the look of it. He was also the best swordsman in the guard, if not the entire kingdom, and his fellow riders knew it. When the squad dismounted, it was only to pick up the unconscious man and sling him over his saddle to carry him away. With a small, friendly nod in Caudyr's direction, Owaen followed them.

"Now that's a puzzle and a half," Caudyr said. "Owaen's the last man I ever thought would do such a thing."

"No more did I. I know that Caradoc thinks highly of the lad. Maybe he's right, after all."

In the barracks a couple of the men were building a fire in the stone hearth. Others sat on the line of bunks and talked of dice games. Pale, mousy Argyn, who was one of the most cold-blooded and vicious killers in the warband, was already asleep, but for all that he was snoring like a summer storm, no one disturbed him to shut him up. The long room smelled of sweat, woodsmoke, and horses, especially of horses, since the troop's mounts were stabled directly below the slatted floor. To Maddyn, it was a comfortable kind of smell that said home to him after all these years of riding in one warband or another. He sat down on his bunk and took his harp out of its padded leather bag.

"Here, Maddo!" Aethan called out. "For the love of every god in the Otherlands, don't sing that same blasted song about King Bran's cattle raid, will you?"

"Ah, hold your tongue. I'm trying to learn it."

"And don't we all know it?" Caradoc broke in. "I'm as sick as I can be of you missing that stanza in the middle and going back over it."

"As the captain orders. But don't be taking my head off, then, for never knowing a new song."

In sheer annoyance he put the harp away and stomped out of the barracks, followed by a small crowd of disappointed Wildfolk, who tugged at his sleeve and his brigga leg to try to get him to go back and sing. When he ignored them, they disappeared, a few at a time, but all of them with reproachful looks on their tiny faces. He went straight to the kitchen hut, where there was a scullery lass, Clwna, who liked him well enough to sneak out to the hayloft with him every now and then. By his reckoning, she should have been done with her work. The kitchen hut's door was open to let a cheerful spill of light fall across the cobbles, and clustered around it were the king's hunting dogs, waiting hopefully for scraps. Maddyn kicked his way through the pack and stood in the doorway. The scullery boys were washing the last of the kettles at the hearth, and the cook herself, a gray-haired woman with enormous muscular arms, was perched on a tall stool and eating her own dinner out of a wooden bowl.

"I know what you're after, silver dagger. Clwna's gone already, and no doubt with another of you lads."

"No doubt. With my lady's gracious permission, I'll wait here for a bit to see if she comes back."

The cook snorted and pushed a strand of hair back from her forehead with her little finger.

"You silver daggers are a strange lot. Most men would be howling with rage if their wench slipped out with another lad."

"We share what we get when we can get it. I'm just glad that Clwna's a sensible lass."

"Sensible, hah! If you call it sensible to get yourself known as one of the silver daggers' women. I'm fair minded to beat some sense into the lass, I am."

"Oh, now here! How could you be so cruel to deny us a bit of comfort when we're fighting for the very honor of Eldidd?"

"Listen to him!" The cook rolled her eyes heavenward to invoke the gods. "Out of my kitchen, bard! You're giving the scullery lads wrong ideas."

Maddyn made her a mocking bow and left, shoving his way through the dogs. As he crossed the ward, it occurred to him that the entire troop had been in the barracks when he'd left it. While he was willing to share Clwna with other silver daggers, the thought of sharing her with an outsider griped his soul. He ducked inside the back door of the great hall and snagged himself a torch from one of the sconces, then searched through the ward with a growing sense of righteous irritation. In the aftermath of the feast there were lots of people about: servants bringing firewood and barrels of ale, glutted riders strolling slowly back to barracks or privy, serving lasses intent on flirtations of their own or running similar errands for their noble mistresses. About halfway to the stables he saw his prey—Clwna walking along arm in arm with one of the king's guard. From the disarray of her dresses and the bit of straw in her hair, Maddyn knew that his suspicions were justified. Clwna herself settled any lingering doubt by screaming the moment she saw him.

"So!" Maddyn held the torch up like a householder apprehending a thief. "And what's all this, lass?"

Clwna made a miserable little shriek and stuffed her knuckles into her mouth. With his hand on his sword hilt, Owaen stepped forward into the pool of light. Maddyn realized that the situation could easily go beyond irritation to danger.

"What's it to you, you little dog?" Owaen snapped. "The lady happens to prefer a real man instead of a bondsman with a sword."

It took every scrap of will that Maddyn possessed to stop himself from hitting Owaen in the face with the flaming torch. In his rage he was only dimly aware that they were gathering a crowd, but he did hear Clwna nattering on and on to some sympathetic listener. Owaen stood smiling at him, his mouth a twist of utter smugness.

"Well, come on, old man," he said at last. "Don't you have a word to say to me?"

"Oh, I'll have plenty of words, little lad. You forget that you're talking to a bard. I haven't made a good flyting song in a long, long time."

"You wouldn't dare!" Owaen's voice was a childlike howl of indignation. "That's not fair!"

At that the ring of onlookers burst out laughing; for all his swordcraft, he looked such an outraged boy standing there that Maddyn had to chuckle himself, thinking that in truth it hardly mattered who tumbled Clwna around in the hay. He was just about to say something conciliatory to the lad when Owaen, his face blushing red, unbuckled his sword belt and threw it onto the cobbles.

"Well and good, then, bard!" he snarled. "It's breaking geis to draw on you, but hand that torch to someone, and I'll grind your face in the stones for you!"

"Oh, for the sake of every god in the sky, Owaen," Maddyn said wearily. "She's hardly worth—"

Owaen swung at him, an open-handed slap that he dodged barely in time. At that there were yells, and a couple of men in the

crowd leaped forward and grabbed the lad. Howling and swearing, he tried to break free, but they dragged him back and held
him. By the blazons on their shirts Maddyn could tell that they
were guardsmen, too. The reason for this unexpected civility
pushed his way through the onlookers.

"Now, what's all this?" said Wevryl, captain of the king's guard.
"Owaen, by the black hairy ass of the Lord of Hell! I swear that
Trouble was your dam and Twice Trouble your grandam! What
was he doing to you, bard?"

"Naught, truly, but making a fool of himself."

"My apologies!" Clwna broke in with a wail. "I never meant to
cause trouble, Maddo." She paused for a couple of moist sobs.
"Truly I didn't."

"Oh, over a lass, was it?" The captain looked profoundly annoyed. "The same tedious old horse dung, is it? Ye gods, it's only
fall! What are you lads going to be like when the winter sets in, eh?
Very well, bard. Take the lass away, will you? Owaen, as for you,
it'll be a couple of lashes out in the ward tomorrow morn. I'll not
be having trouble over a kitchen slut."

Owaen's face drained dead white. In the crowd, a couple of men
snickered.

"Oh, here, Captain," Maddyn said. "If you're flogging him for my
sake, there's no need."

"Not for your sake—for the sake of peace in the dun. You might
pass that on to that troop you ride with, too. I won't tolerate this
sort of fighting. Save the bloodlust for spring and our enemies."

In the morning, when they dragged Owaen out to the ward for
his lashes, Maddyn refused to go watch, although most of the
other silver daggers and half the dun did. It was entertainment of
a sort. With his blue sprite and a couple of gnomes for company,
he wandered around to the back of the stables and lounged on a
bale of straw in the warm sun. Caradoc eventually found him
there.

"Is it over?" Maddyn said.

"It is. Wevryl tells me that Owaen's been naught but trouble ever
since he rode his first battle, bragging and swaggering around, so
he decided it was time to show the lad his place. Aches my heart.
Look, they put this young hothead in the king's guard because he's
the best swordsman they've ever seen, and so what does he do? Sit
around most of the year and watch the old king sleep. No wonder

he's as hot as summer tinder. He'd be better off in the silver daggers."

"You keep saying that. Well, if he keeps on being so cursed arrogant, you might have your chance to recruit him yet."

They always say that bards have a touch of prophecy. For close to a week, Maddyn saw no sign of Owaen, not even in the great hall at meals. He was apparently keeping strictly to himself and letting his wounds heal, and as painful as two stripes were, it would be the shame that would be paining him the more, Maddyn assumed. Since every silver dagger knew what shame tasted like, when Owaen did reappear, they went out of their way to treat him as if nothing had happened. The young handpicked riders in the king's guard had no such hard-earned compassion. When a stiff-backed Owaen took his place at table for the first time, he was greeted with a chorus of catcalls and a couple of truly vicious remarks about whipped dogs and kennels. Since Wevryl was nowhere in sight, Caradoc stood on his position as a captain and went over and broke it up. His face bright red, Owaen gulped ale from his tankard and stared down at the tabletop.

When Caradoc came back, he sat down next to Maddyn.

"Little pusboils," the captain remarked. "Now that's a truly stupid way to treat a man when your life might depend on him someday in a scrap."

"Even stupider when he's a man who could cut you into pieces without half trying."

"Now that, alas, is true-spoken."

Later that morning Maddyn was grooming his horse in front of the stable when Clwna, all nervous smile and sidelong glance, came sidling up to him. If she hadn't been so thin and pale, she would have been a lovely lass, but as it was, her blond hair always smelled of roast meat and there was always grease under her fingernails.

"Have you forgiven me yet, Maddo?"

"Oh, easily. Going to meet me out in the hayloft tonight?"

She giggled, hiding her mouth behind her hand like a court lady, a gesture that was somehow pathetic.

"Here, I'll be riding to town today," Maddyn said. "I'll buy you some ribands from the tailor. What colors would you like?"

"Oh, blue and green, and my thanks. You're so sweet, Maddo. I like you the best of anybody."

"Oh huh! And how many of the lads do you say that to?"

"Only you. And maybe Aethan but only sometimes. Sometimes he frightens me." Unconsciously she brought her hand to her throat. "Sometimes he looks at me, and I think he's going to hit me, but then he only says some mean thing and walks away."

"When he does that, he's thinking of another woman, lass, not of you. Stay away from him when he's in that mood."

"I will, then." She went suddenly tense, looking over his shoulder. "Oh ye gods!"

Maddyn turned to see a gaggle of guardsmen strolling their way with Owaen among them. At the sight of Clwna, they began nudging each other and snickering.

"There's the fair maiden, Owaen. Oh, she doesn't look half so tasty in the daylight. Was she worth it, Owaen? Was she? As hot as Bardek spices, then."

Owaen walked away fast, his head up high, his mouth set tight. Clwna burst out weeping and ran. Maddyn thought of following her, then decided that she'd have to learn her lessons, too.

That night the first of the long slashing winter rains came in from the Southern Sea. Penned inside with no more amusements than dice and ale, the king's guard kept up their relentless teasing. It seemed to Maddyn that no matter when he saw Owaen, the lad was being mocked by his fellows. There were jests about Clwna, jests about whipping dogs into shape, jests about a man stupid enough to challenge a bard—on and on, over and over, and each more tired and feeble than the last. Maddyn could only assume that Owaen's arrogance had irked his fellow guardsmen for years; doubtless they envied him, too. Maddyn also noticed Caradoc keeping a careful eye on the situation. Often the captain stepped in when the teasing turned vicious and stopped it.

Finally, on the fourth solid day of rain, things came to a head. After dinner that night, Caradoc lingered in the great hall and kept Maddyn there with him after the rest of the silver daggers went to the barracks. They collared a couple of tankards of dark ale from a serving lass and moved to a table in the curve of the wall, where they were barely noticeable in the shadows but had a good view of Owaen, who was sitting at the end of a table of guardsmen.

"Tomorrow this demon-get storm will blow over," Caradoc remarked. "I hope that someone else does somewhat stupid and soon. Give them a new butt for their jokes."

They lounged there for about half an hour while the prince's bard sang manfully over the laughter and talk. Because of all the noise, Maddyn never heard what started the fight. All at once, Owaen and another lad were on their feet and yelling at each other in inarticulate rage. Caradoc leapt up and ran, but too late. The other lad grabbed his sword and drew. Maddyn hardly saw Owaen move. There was a flash of steel in torchlight; his opponent staggered back, blood running down his face. Caradoc caught him by the shoulders and laid him down in the straw just as Maddyn reached them. The hall broke out in screaming and shouting. Owaen threw his bloody sword down on the table and stared, his mouth open in shock. When men grabbed him from behind, he went limp in their hands. Maddyn knelt beside Caradoc and the bleeding victim.

"How badly is he cut?"

"Cut? He's dead."

Half disbelieving it, Maddyn stared at the corpse on the floor. Owaen had struck twice in that blur of motion, slashing the lad's face half open, then catching his throat on the backswing. Shouting and swearing, men clustered round; Caradoc and Maddyn left the corpse to them and worked their way free of the mob just in time to see the guard marching Owaen out of the hall. The lad was weeping.

"Ah, horseshit!" Caradoc growled. "He's just too blasted good with that blade. I could have stopped it in time if it'd been anyone else. Ah, horseshit!"

"And a stinking heap of it. What'll you wager he didn't even realize he'd killed the lad until he heard you say it?"

Caradoc muttered an inaudible oath under his breath, then went in search of their tankards.

For a long hour, Maddyn and Caradoc waited in the nervous crowd for news of Prince Cadlew's judgment. Finally two pages, young eyes bright with excitement, came running in to announce that the prince was going to have Owaen hanged on the morrow. Since the other lad had drawn first, no one thought the sentence just, but no one could argue with the prince, either. The very same lads who'd driven Owaen to his fit of temper spoke contritely and defended him to everyone else, while serving lasses wept and said how handsome he was to die so young. Caradoc drank steadily, then suddenly slammed his tankard onto the table.

"I'm not going to stand for it! What do you think, Maddo? Shall I pull the lad's neck out of the noose?"

"By all means, but how?"

"Just watch. Find me one of those wretched pages."

Suitably bribed, a page was quite willing to take the prince a message asking for an audience. After some minutes' wait, the boy returned and took them to one of the royal reception chambers, a sumptuous room with carved oak furniture, thick Bardek carpets in blue and green, and real glass in the windows. Cadlew was standing by the hearth with a golden goblet of mead in his hand. When Maddyn and Caradoc knelt at his feet, he nodded pleasantly to them.

"Rise. You have our leave to speak."

"My humble thanks, Your Highness," Caradoc said. "A long time ago, in the middle of summer, you made me promise of a boon, whenever I should ask for it."

"And so I did. I remember the charge you led very well indeed. I've plenty of fine horses for a reward, or a jeweled sheath, perhaps, for that dagger you carry. Or here, there are those new swords from Bardek. The steel is particularly fine."

"Well, my liege, I want somewhat of far less value than that, and cursed if I don't think I'm daft for wasting a boon on it."

"Indeed?" The prince smiled briefly. "It's pleasant to see that even silver daggers have whims. Ask away."

"Then, my liege, give me young Owaen's life. Don't hang the lad."

Honestly startled, the prince raised his goblet and had a small sip, then made a courtly, indifferent shrug.

"Done, then, on one condition: you take him into your warband and out of mine. I want no more of this trouble."

"My humble thanks, Your Highness. Don't worry your royal heart. I'll beat the lad into shape sooner or later."

"I've no doubt, Captain, that you could beat the Lord of Hell into shape, and sooner rather than later. Let me summon a guard. I've no idea where they put the lad."

Guards with torches took Maddyn and Caradoc around to the back of the ward, where a cluster of round, stone storage sheds stood by the outer wall. Another guard was lounging against a tiny shed with no windows and an iron-barred door. At the news, he stepped aside gladly.

"Didn't truly seem fair. Glad you changed our liege's mind, Captain."

With a shrug, Caradoc lifted the bar and opened the door. Inside Owaen was sitting on a pile of dirty straw, his arms clasped around his knees, his face stained with tears. At the sight of them he scrambled to his feet and stood at stiff attention, head held high.

"Come to hang me already?" Owaen's voice was perfectly level. "I'll be glad to have it over and done with."

"You're not going to hang at all, you young dolt," Caradoc said. "I've bought your pardon. Now get out here."

Staring at the captain all the while, Owaen took a few slow, cautious steps to the door, as if he were afraid of waking himself from this wonderful dream. Caradoc grabbed his arm with one hand and slapped him across the face with the other.

"That's for forgetting you were in the king's hall." Caradoc slapped him again, even harder. "And that's for striking twice. One more slip like this, and I'll slit your throat, not twist it. Understand me?"

"I do." Owaen could barely whisper; doubtless his mouth was stinging from the slap. "But why pardon me?"

"I want you in my troop. You'll have a short enough life anyway as a silver dagger."

Owaen nodded, trembling, turning to stare at the ward as if it were the most beautiful sight in the world. He rode close enough to the Otherlands, Maddyn thought, and it wouldn't have been a pretty way to die.

"Now listen," Caradoc went on. "I gave up a chance at one of those Bardek blades for you, so you'd blasted well better fight like a son of a bitch and earn your hire. Now come along. I'll send someone else to get your gear from the guardsmen's barracks. I don't want your behind anywhere near your old companions."

Owaen nodded again, still trembling; words were beyond him, apparently. Maddyn laid a hand on his shoulder.

"There isn't a man in the troop who hasn't disgraced himself as badly as you have," Maddyn said. "Lots of us are a cursed sight worse. Come along, lad. You're better off among your own kind."

Owaen started to laugh, a low hysterical chuckle, and he kept it up all the way across the ward to the barracks.

The sky was low and slate gray, and a chill wind rustled in the branches of the leafless trees that stood like sentinels on the shores of the wide artificial lake. A stone causeway ran about half a mile through the rippled gray water to the island where the dun stood, the palace of Casyl, king of Pyrdon. By rising in his stirrups Nevyn could just see the high broch above the stone walls. He paused his horse and reined his pack mule up beside it while he studied the place that, if all went well, would be his home for some years ahead. Drwloc certainly fitted the description of the oracle of Wmm. All around the island clustered stands of water reeds, and at the sandy landing were little leather coracles drawn up against the coming storm.

He rode on to the end of the causeway, where two guards were lounging against the gate. At the sight of him, they straightened up and came to attention. Much to his annoyance, Nevyn was dressed the part of an important personage in brand-new clothes, a pair of fine gray brigga, a shirt of the whitest linen, a dark blue cloak with a splendid jeweled ring brooch to clasp it. He was no longer an herbman, but a wandering scholar, with letters of introduction from several very important priests of several major gods.

"Good morrow, sir," a guard said with a bow. "May I ask your business in the palace?"

"My name is Nevyn, and I've been sent by Retyc, high priest of Bel in Lughcarn, to inquire about a position as tutor for the young prince."

At that, both guards bowed.

"Of course, sir. We were told that the king expected you. Ride on, but please watch the footing. We've got some slippery spots— moss and suchlike."

For safety's sake, Nevyn dismounted and led his beasts along the causeway. Just wide enough for four horses abreast, it was a splendid bit of defensive planning; ten good men could hold it against an army all day if they had to, but then, Pyrdon's freedom had been won and held by military genius and little else. The causeway ended on a tiny strip of bare ground before the iron-bound double gates of the dun itself. There, more guards greeted Nevyn and ushered him into the cobbled ward, which was crammed with storage sheds, stables, and barracks. It was plain that the dun was organized with a long siege in mind. Pages came to take his horse and mule, and another lad escorted him into the tall broch itself.

Although the royal crest of a rearing stallion was stamped or carved everywhere, on the chairs, on the hearth, on the red-and-silver banners on the walls, the furnishings were sparse and made of roughly cut dark wood. At the table of honor the king himself was sitting in an ordinary low, half-round chair and drinking ale from a plain pewter tankard. At thirty-one, Casyl was a tall, slender man with thinning pale blond hair and deep-set blue eyes. His heavy hands were scarred here and there, small nicks from battle. When Nevyn began to kneel before him, the king stopped him with a wave of his hand and a good-humored smile.

"You may dispense with the usual groveling, good sir, at your age. Sit down. Page, fetch the scholar some ale."

Nevyn took a chair at the king's right, then brought out the letters of introduction from his shirt, where he'd been carrying them for safekeeping. The king looked at the seals on the message tubes, nodded his recognition, then tossed them onto the table.

"Later I'll have my scribe read them to me. Unfortunately, my father was an old-fashioned man, and I was never taught a single letter when I was a lad. Now I don't have the time for such luxuries, but I don't intend to repeat the same mistake with my son."

"So the priests of Wmm told me, Your Highness. I admire a man who shows respect for learning."

"No doubt you would, given your calling in life. Now, my scribe has started teaching the lad how to letter, but I want someone who can tell him about history, the laws, that sort of thing. In his last letter, Pedraddyn of Wmmglaedd said you'd bring books with you."

"I have them on my pack mule, Your Highness. In case you shouldn't require my services, I'll leave them behind for the next candidate."

"Oh, you can take it for granted that you're staying. It's all been passing strange. When I first sent to the temples for a tutor, I was expecting to get a priest. That's who they usually send to a king's dun. But they told me that they just didn't have the right man available. It didn't matter where I sent, and I asked at more than one holy place."

"Indeed? How very peculiar, Your Highness."

"So I was cursed glad when Pedraddyn wrote to say that you'd turned up. No doubt it's Wyrd, and who can question that?"

Nevyn smiled politely and said not a word in answer. Yet for all his talk of Wyrd, Casyl spent the good part of an hour asking shrewd questions about the education he had in mind for the prince. Like most illiterate men, the king had a prodigious memory, and he dredged up references to every book or author he'd heard mentioned over the years just to see if Nevyn knew them, too. They were just beginning to discuss Nevyn's maintenance and recompense when there was a bustle and confusion at the door: maidservants shrieked, guards swore and shouted. An enormous gray-and-black boarhound raced into the great hall with a very dead chicken in its mouth. Right behind ran a young boy, as blond and pale as Casyl. Yelling at the top of his lungs, he chased the panicked hound right under the royal chair, so suddenly that the dog nearly dumped the king on the floor. Swearing, Casyl jumped clear as the lad flung himself down and grabbed the hound's collar.

"Give it back, Spider! Bad dog!"

"Maryn, by the fat rump of Epona's steed! Can't you see I'm talking with an important guest?"

"My apologies, Father." The prince went on hauling the hound out from the chair. "But he stole it, and I told Cook I'd get it back, because he's my dog."

With a dramatic sigh the king stood back out of the way and let the prince pry the by now much ill-used and doubtless inedible chicken out of the boarhound's jaws. Nevyn watched in bemused fascination: so this was the future king of all Deverry and Eldidd. As was necessary for the plan, he was a handsome child, with large, solemn gray eyes in a rosy-cheeked oval face and neatly cropped golden hair.

"Get that bleeding fowl out of the great hall, will you?" Casyl snarled. "Here, I'll call a page."

"Please, Father, I'd best take it back myself, because I promised Cook I would."

"Well and good, then. Come back when you're done." The king aimed a vague kick at the dog. "Begone, hound!"

Boarhound and marked prince alike scurried out of the royal presence. With a sigh, Casyl sat back down and took his tankard from the table.

"He's a wild lad, good scholar, and this is a rough sort of court, as you've doubtless noticed."

"Well, Your Highness, there is much virtue in a simple life under less than easy conditions."

"Nicely put. I can see that you'll be able to teach the prince tact, if naught else. I see no reason to pretend to pomp that I can't afford. The glory of my kingdom has always lain in her soldiers, not her fine manners."

"And young Maryn had best learn that, my liege, if he wants to have a kingdom to govern when his turn comes."

It took Nevyn some time to fit into the life of the palace. In the mornings he gave Maryn his lessons, but in the afternoon the prince went to the captain of the warband for training in riding and swordcraft. Nevyn spent much time alone at first, in his large, wedge-shaped chamber at the very top of the broch. It was nicely furnished with a bed, a writing desk, and a heavily carved chest for his clothing, but its best feature was the view, a vast sweep of the lake below and the rolling farmland beyond. At meals, he ate with the other high-ranked servitors and their families: the bard, the chamberlain, the equerry, and the king's chirurgeon. At first they regarded him warily with an eye to keeping the king's special favor for themselves, but since he cared naught for privilege and petty signs of rank, they soon accepted him.

For Maryn's studies Nevyn had brought a number of important books, among them a general précis of the laws for beginners and several volumes of history, starting with the Dawntime and continuing through the annals of the various Deverrian and Eldidd kings. Eventually he would send to Aberwyn for copies of Prince Mael's books, particularly the treatise on nobility, but they would have been hard slogging for a beginner. Every morning he would let the lad read aloud for a while, stumbling often but always pushing on, then take the book and finish the passage himself. Together they would discuss what they had read. Once Maryn realized that history was full of battles and scandal in equal parts, his interest in his studies picked up enormously.

Once he'd become a well-known figure in the palace, Nevyn took to spending some time with the queen, who was glad to have someone new and well educated in the dun. Seryan had been born of the line of Cantrae pretenders to the throne and was a distant cousin of the current king, Slwmar the Second. At nineteen she'd been married off to Casyl—much against her will, because not only was the king five years her junior but his kingdom was a rough, wild place compared to her home in Lughcarn. Now, some seventeen years later, she'd made her peace with her life. She had her two elder daughters and her young son to occupy her, and as she admitted one day to Nevyn, she'd grown fond of Casyl with time.

"If an old man may speak frankly," Nevyn said. "He's a much better man than any of that pack of ferrets around the throne in Cantrae."

"Oh, I agree with you *now*, but what does a lass of nineteen know? All I could think of was that he was such a young lad, and that I'd never get to attend any of my mother's splendid feasts again."

And with a sigh, the queen changed the subject away from such personal matters to a particular song the bard had sung in hall the night before.

Not long after Nevyn's arrival, the first snows came. The lake froze to a solid glitter of white, and the farmlands lay shrouded, with only the distant trails of smoke to mark where the houses stood. Life in the dun settled into a slow routine centered on the huge hearths in the great hall, where the noble-born sat close to the fire and the servants lay in the warm straw with the dogs. As the drowsy weeks slipped past, Nevyn began to grow honestly fond of Maryn. He was a hard child to dislike—always happy, always courteous, supremely confident because of his position as marked prince yet honestly concerned with the welfare of others. Nevyn knew that if his work were successful and Maryn did indeed take the throne of Deverry, everyone would look back on his childhood and say that obviously the lad had been born to be king. No doubt little legends about a gallantry beyond his years would spring up, and the ordinary events of childhood would be viewed as mighty omens. That his mother was a highly intelligent woman and his father an unusually honorable man would never enter into that kind of thinking. Nevyn was quite willing to have things that way. After all, he was there to create a myth, not write history.

And the myth seemed determined to get itself created. Shortly before the Feast of the Sun, which would also mark Maryn's tenth birthday, the prince came to his tutor's chamber for his lessons in an unusually thoughtful mood. Since the lad's mind wandered all through the reading, Nevyn finally asked him what was wrong.

"Oh, naught, truly. But, sir, you're a wise man. Do you know what dreams mean?"

"Sometimes, but some dreams only mean that you ate too much before you went to bed."

Maryn giggled, then cocked his head to one side in thought.

"I don't think this was that sort of dream. It seemed ever so real while I was sleeping, but then I woke up, and it seemed daft." He squirmed on his chair and looked away in embarrassment. "Father says a real prince never gives himself airs."

"Your father's right, but no one can blame you for what you do in dreams. Tell me about it, if you'd like."

"I dreamt I was king of all Deverry. It was ever so real. I was leading my army, you see, and I could smell the horses and everything. We were in Cantrae and we were winning. You were there, too, sir. You were my royal councillor. I was all sweaty and dirty, because I'd been fighting, but the men were cheering and calling me the king."

For a moment Nevyn found it hard to breathe. It was possible that the prince had only picked up the images from his tutor's mind, in the uncanny way that children can sometimes read the minds of adults they want to please, but the detail, such as the smell of horses, was so exact that he doubted it.

"You think it's daft, don't you?" the prince said.

"I don't. How good are you at keeping secrets?"

"Truly good, and I'll swear a vow if you like."

Nevyn stared into the boy's eyes, where his soul lay, like a fire ready in a hearth, waiting for a spark in the tinder.

"Swear to me you'll never repeat what I say, not to your father or your mother, to priest or peddler, not to anyone."

"I swear it, on the honor of my clan, my royal line, and the gods of my people."

"Well and good. You *will* be king someday, king of all Deverry. The great god Wmm has marked you out in his oracle and sent me here to aid Your Highness."

When Maryn looked away, his face pale, his soft boy's mouth was slack, but his eyes were those of the king to come.

"You're dweomer, aren't you, sir, just like in the tales? But oh, Father says there's no such thing as dweomer anymore, that it was all in the Dawntime."

"Indeed, my liege? Watch the hearth."

Nevyn summoned the Wildfolk, who first obligingly put the fire out cold, then lit it again with a great gust of flame when Nevyn snapped his fingers. Maryn jumped up and grinned.

"Oh, that's splendid! Then my dream was truly, truly true?"

"It was, but not a word to any living soul until I tell you that the time is ripe."

"I won't. I'd die first."

He spoke so solemnly that he seemed more a man than a child, caught in one of those rare moments when the levels of the soul blend and let something of its Wyrd slip through to the conscious mind. Then the moment vanished.

"Well, if I'm going to be king, I guess I'd better know all these wretched laws, but oh, they're so boring! Can't we read about battles and stuff for a while?"

"Very well, Your Highness. As the prince wishes."

That night, Nevyn had to admit to himself that he was well pleased by the way things were going. He could only hope that he'd have enough time to train the lad properly, at least five more years. Although he'd never leave Maryn's side again until the long wars were over and the land at peace, he wanted to put, not a puppet on the throne, but a king.

FOUR

The year 842. While he was walking down by the riverbank, Retyc the high priest saw this omen. A flock of sparrows was pecking in the grass. Suddenly a raven flew by. All the sparrows flew up and followed the raven, just as if he were another sparrow and the leader of their flock. Someday, His Holiness said, a man from another people will come to lead Deverry men to war . . .

—The Holy Chronicles of Lughcarn

Late on a warm autumn day the silver daggers made their camp on the grassy banks of the Trebycaver. It was an organized chaos: ninety men tending a hundred and fifty horses, the fifteen women who followed the camp pitching tents and getting supplies out of the pair of wagons, the handful of bastard children running around and shouting, free at last after a long day behind one saddle or another. While the others worked, Maddyn and Caradoc strolled through, shouting an order here, a jest there. By a pile of saddles a weary Clwna was nursing her fussy new daughter, Pomyan. Clwna looked so pale and faint that Maddyn hunkered down beside her.

"How do you fare, lass? You shouldn't have ridden so soon after having the babe."

"Oh, I'm as well as I need to be. It was better than never catching up to you again."

"We could have waited a few days."

"Huh. I'm sure the captain would have waited for the likes of me."

When she moved the baby to her other breast, the tiny lass raised her head and looked cloudy-eyed at Maddyn. He smiled at her and wondered who her father was, a perennial question about every child born to the camp followers, although he was the only man who seemed to care one way or the other. When Caradoc called him to come walk on, he mentioned to the captain that he thought Clwna looked ill.

"Well, she'll have a couple of days to rest now," Caradoc said. "I think we'll leave this ragtag piss-poor excuse for a troop here while you and I ride to see this so-called King Casyl."

"Very well. I'll admit we're not much to look at these days."

"Never were, and all these wretched women and barracks brats don't help us give ourselves fine military airs."

"You could have ordered us to leave them behind when we left Eldidd."

"Horseshit. Believe it or not, there's a bit of honor left in your old captain's heart, lad. They're a bunch of sluts, but it was my men who swelled their bellies, wasn't it? Besides, there was enough grumbling about leaving Eldidd as it was. Didn't want open mutiny." Caradoc sighed in profound melancholy. "We got soft there. That's the trouble with staying in one place too long. Should've left Eldidd long ago."

"I still don't see why we left it now."

Caradoc shot him a sour glance and led the way out of the camp to the riverbank. In the slanting sun, the water ran rippled gold through banks soft with wild grass.

"Don't repeat this to anyone, or I'll smash your face for you," Caradoc said. "But I moved us out because of this dream I had."

Maddyn stared, frankly speechless.

"In the dream someone was telling me that it was time. Don't ask me why or time for what, but I heard this voice, like, and it sounded like a king's voice, all arrogant and commanding, telling me that it was time to leave and ride north. If we starve in Pyrdon, then I'll know the dream came from the demons, but by the gods, I've never had a dream like that before. Tried to ignore it for a blasted eightnight. Kept coming back. Call me daft if you want."

"Naught of the sort. But I've got to say that I'm surprised to the bottom of my heart."

"Not half as surprised as I was. I'm getting old. Daft. Soon I'll be drooling in a chair by a tavern fire." Caradoc sighed again and shook his head in mock sadness. "But we're about ten miles from this King Casyl's dun. Tomorrow we'll ride up there and see just how daft I was. Let's get back to camp now. I'll be leaving Owaen in charge, and I want to give him his orders."

On the morrow, Maddyn and Caradoc left the camp early and followed the river up to the town of Drwloc. After the splendors of Abernaudd, the town wasn't much as royal cities went, about two thousand houses crammed inside a timber-laced stone wall. As they led their horses along streets paved with half-buried logs for want of cobbles, Maddyn began to wonder if Caradoc was indeed going daft. If this was the jewel of the kingdom, it seemed that the king wouldn't be able to afford the silver daggers. They found a tavern over by the north gate, got themselves ale, then asked casual questions about the king and his holdings. When the tavernman held forth upon his liege's honor, bravery, and farseeing mind without ever mentioning luxuries or reserves of cash, Caradoc grew positively gloomy.

"Tell me somewhat," the captain said at last. "Does His Highness keep a large standing army?"

"As large a one as he can feed. You never know what those Eldidd dogs are going to do."

This news made him a good bit more cheerful. They took their ale outside to sit on a small wooden bench in front of the tavern. In the warm hazy day, the townsfolk hurried past on assorted errands, an old peasant leading a mule laden with cabbages, a young merchant in much mended checked brigga, a pretty lass who ignored them both in the most pointed fashion.

"We should have ridden north earlier," Caradoc said. "His Highness isn't going to want to feed extra men all winter when the summer's fighting is done. Ah, curse that dream! May the demon who sent it to me drown in a tub of horse piss."

"Well, there's no harm in riding out to ask."

With a gloomy nod, Caradoc sipped his ale. Down the twisting street, a silver horn rang out; a squad of horsemen appeared, walking their mounts at a stately pace. At their head were two riders with rearing stallions blazoned on their shirts, and a guard of four more rode behind. In the middle, on a splendid bay gelding, rode a handsome blond lad of about fourteen. His white, red, and gold plaid cloak was thrown back and pinned at one shoulder with an enormous ring brooch of gold set with rubies. Beside him on a matched bay was an old man with a thick shock of white hair and piercing blue eyes. Maddyn stared briefly, then jumped up with a shout.

"Nevyn! By all the gods!"

Grinning broadly, the old man turned his horse out of line and waved, paused to say something to the lad, then rode over, dismounting as Maddyn ran up to greet him. Maddyn clasped his outstretched hand and shook it hard.

"By the hells, it gladdens my heart to see you, sir."

"And mine to see you," Nevyn said with a somewhat sly smile. "See, I told you that our paths would cross again."

"And right you were. What are you doing in Pyrdon?"

"Tutoring the marked prince. Are the rest of the silver daggers with you?"

"Not far, just camped down the river. Wait—how do you know about them?"

"How do you think? Has your captain had any strange dreams lately?"

Maddyn turned cold with an awe that ran down his back like melting snow. Tankard in hand, a puzzled Caradoc strolled over to join them as the young prince dismounted and led his horse over to join his tutor. When Maddyn and Caradoc knelt to him, the prince gave them a courteous nod of acknowledgment, but the gesture was splendidly firm for one so young. Maddyn was instantly struck by how noble the young prince was, the gallant way he stood, the proud set to his head, the easy way his hand rested on his sword hilt, as if he'd seen many a battle beyond his years. A prince indeed, he thought, born to be king. At the thought, his cold awe grew stronger, and he wondered just why Nevyn the sorcerer was here in this obscure kingdom.

"Your Highness," the old man said. "Allow me to present Maddyn the silver dagger, and the captain of the troop, Caradoc of Cerrmor. Men, you kneel before Maryn, marked prince of Pyrdon."

At the casual mention of his name by one he didn't know, Caradoc glared at Nevyn, who ignored him with a bland smile.

"Silver daggers, are you?" Maryn said with an engaging, boyish smile. "Pyrdon may be at the ends of the earth, but I've heard of your troop. How many of you are there?"

"Ninety, Your Highness," Caradoc said. "And we have our own smith, chirurgeon, and bard."

Maryn glanced at Nevyn for advice.

"It would pay to look them over, Your Highness, but you'll have to consult with your father the king first, of course."

"Well and good, then. Men, you may rise and stand in our presence." The prince glanced Nevyn's way again. "I don't suppose I could go look them over right now."

"Not with the king expecting you back. Have the captain bring them to you on the morrow."

"Oh, very well. Captain Caradoc, assemble your troop before the gates of the royal palace on the morrow. Send me word through the guards on the causeway."

"Well and good, Your Highness. We'll arrive around noon."

With a laugh of excitement, the young prince strode back to his men. Nevyn winked at Maddyn, then rejoined his lord. As the royal escort rode on, Caradoc stared openmouthed until they were out of sight. He retrieved his ale from the street and led the way back to the bench, where he sat down with an exaggerated heavy sigh.

"Very well, Maddo. Who *is* that old man?"

"The herbman who saved my life up in Cantrae. Remember me telling you about Brin Toraedic? And he's the same one who tipped Caudyr off to leave Dun Deverry."

"An herbman for a prince's tutor? Horseshit."

"Oh, by the gods, can't you see what's been stuck under your face? The old man's dweomer."

Caradoc choked on his ale.

"Well, he's the one who sent you the dream," Maddyn said after he'd recovered. "He admitted as much to me."

"Ah well, if we get this hire, it cursed well won't be dull, will it now? Dweomermen, impressive young princes—it all sounds like one of your songs."

"Oh, it's stranger than any song I know. If Nevyn's come to live in Pyrdon, I'll wager he's got grave things afoot, and the gods only know what they are."

"Now here," Casyl snapped. "When I spoke of getting you a personal guard, I was thinking of twenty men, not ninety."

"But, Father, there's bound to be fighting next summer. It would be splendid if I could lead close to a hundred men."

"Lead? Listen, you young cub, I've told you a thousand times that you're staying in the rear for your first campaign."

"Well, if you're so worried, then the more men I have, the safer I'll be."

Casyl growled under his breath, but it was a fond exasperation.

"My liege the king?" Nevyn said. "If I may interject a word?"

"By all means."

"Although I doubt the prince's motives, he does speak the truth. The larger the guard, the better. The time might well come soon when he'll need many men around him."

Casyl turned and looked at him with narrowed eyes. They were sitting in the shabby council chamber at a round table, set with only a pair of wobbly bronze candelabra.

"Father." Maryn leaned across the table. "You know that Nevyn's omens always come true."

"It's not a matter of his prediction, but of the coin. How are we going to pay and shelter ninety mercenaries?"

"I've got the taxes from that bit of land in my own name. They'll help provision the troop. I get two whole cows this fall, just for starters."

"And how long will it take hungry men to dispatch that much beef?"

"But, Father! You've heard all those tales about the silver daggers. If even half of them are true, why, they fight like demons from hell!"

Casyl leaned back in his chair and idly rubbed his chin with the back of his hand while he thought it over. Nevyn waited silently, knowing that Maryn was bound to get his own way in the end.

"Well," Casyl said at last. "I haven't even gotten a look at them yet. I'll review them when they arrive tomorrow, and then we'll see."

"My thanks, Father. You know that the prince will always put himself under the king's orders."

"Out, you little hypocrite! Go talk to your mother. She told me earlier that she wanted a word with you."

Maryn made him a formal bow, nodded to Nevyn, then ran out of the chamber, slamming the door behind him and breaking into a loud whistle as he trotted down the hall.

"Ah ye gods, next summer my son rides to war! Tonight, Nevyn, I feel as old as you."

"No doubt, Your Highness, but I still hear a lad, not a man, when he talks of the glories of war."

"Of course, but he'll learn. I only pray that our next campaign is an easy one. Here, *have* you had some kind of omen?"

"Of sorts. Your Highness, the king in Cerrmor is fated to die soon, I think before the winter's out."

Casyl went very still, his hands tight on the arms of the chair.

"His only son is dead," Nevyn went on. "His three daughters are too young to have sons yet. Tell me, Your Highness, have you ever fancied yourself as king in Deverry? When Glyn dies, you're the heir."

"Ah, by the hells, it can't be! He's just a young man."

"Fevers and suchlike come to the young as well as the old. Your Highness had best think carefully, because with a Cantrae wife he won't be terribly popular with his new vassals."

Casyl sat so still, his eyes so heavy-lidded, that he seemed asleep. Nevyn waited for a few minutes to let him think before he went on.

"And about the silver daggers, Your Highness? You'll need men like that if you're going to have a chance to claim the Cerrmor throne."

"Chance? Don't be a dolt, man! Even if I had an army twice the size of the one I do, my chance is about as good as a flea's in a soap bath, and I think me you know it."

"If the Cerrmor lords accept you, then you have a very good chance, my liege."

Casyl rose and paced to the open window, where the cold night air came in with a heavy scent of damp.

"If I strip my kingdom of men to march on Cerrmor, Eldidd will march north. It's a question of trading one kingdom for another, isn't it? Throwing away the land I have in a bid to gain land I've never seen. There are men in Cerrmor who have claims as good as mine. Somewhere back in my family line is a bastard son, and the other factions could easily use that against me. And while we all squabble over Cerrmor, the Cantrae line will be taking over the rest of the kingdom. Does it sound like a fair bargain to you?"

"It doesn't, my liege, especially since I know a man who has a better claim to the throne of all Deverry than any other man alive."

"Indeed?" Casyl turned, leaning back casually on the window frame, smiling a little in academic interest. "And who might that be?"

"Does His Highness truly have no idea?"

Casyl froze, only his mouth working in a twist of pain.

"I think me he does." Nevyn was inexorable. "Your son, my liege. While a Cantrae wife would be held against you, a Cantrae mother strengthens Maryn's position a hundredfold. He has ties to every royal line, even Eldidd, strong ties."

"So he does." Casyl's voice was a whisper. "Oh ye gods! I never gave a moment's thought to it before, truly. I never dreamt the Cerrmor line would fail like this. Do you think that Maryn has a chance at acceptance, or will he have to fight for his throne?"

"I think me Cerrmor will welcome him. Will they want a Can-trae king on the throne instead?"

"Of course not." Casyl began pacing back and forth. "It's going to be a hard and dangerous road to the throne, but how can I deny my son's claim to his Wyrd?"

"There's more at stake than Maryn's Wyrd. This is a matter of grave import for the entire kingdom. Truly, I know that I've talked of strange omens and suchlike without a shred of proof, but you'll know that I've spoken the truth when news comes of Glyn's death. In the meantime, it might be politic to hire Maryn as large a guard as possible."

"Politic indeed if he's the heir to two thrones. Done, then. I'll have a look at those silver daggers on the morrow."

On the morrow morning, Maryn was restless beyond a simple excitement at the chance to acquire a personal guard. When Nevyn suggested that they have a talk, the prince insisted on leav-ing the dun and going down to the narrow sandy beach of the island where they could be completely private. Although it was unseasonably warm still, thin cirrus clouds mackereled the sky, and the leaves on the birches were a sickly yellow.

"Very well, Your Highness," Nevyn said once they were settled on an outcrop of rock. "What grave matter is troubling you?"

"Maybe it's naught. Maybe I'm going daft or suchlike."

"Indeed? Out with it."

"Well, when I met those silver daggers yesterday, I got the strangest feeling. This is the beginning, the feeling said. You hear about men's Wyrds talking to them, but I never truly understood before. I do now, because I heard my Wyrd say that to me. Or am I daft?"

"Not daft at all, truly. Your Wyrd is gathering, sure enough."

Slack-mouthed, the prince stared out over the lake, rippling as the wind rose in a gust that shook the birches.

"Are you afraid, Your Highness?"

"Not for myself. I just thought of somewhat. Nevyn, if I'm meant to be king, then men are going to die for me. There'll have to be a war before I can claim the throne."

"That's true."

He was silent for a long while more, looking so young, so ab-surdly smooth-faced and wide-eyed, that it seemed impossible that here sat the true king of all Deverry. For all that Maryn had taken his training well, at fourteen he was far from ready for the work ahead, but then, Nevyn doubted if any man, no matter how old and wise, would ever be truly ready.

"I don't want all those deaths on my head." He spoke abruptly, with the ring of command in his voice.

"Your Highness has no choice. If you refuse to take your Wyrd upon you, then more men will die fighting to put some false king on your throne."

Tears welled in his eyes; he brushed them irritably away on his sleeve before he answered.

"Then I'll follow my Wyrd." He rose, and suddenly he looked older. "Let no man bar me from my rightful place."

Just at noon the message came that the silver daggers had arrived. Nevyn rode out with Maryn and the king to conduct something of a test of his plans. Out in the meadow at the end of the causeway, the men sat on horseback in orderly ranks with Caradoc, Maddyn, and a young man that Nevyn didn't recognize front and center. Behind them was a disorderly mob of pack horses, wagons, women, and even a few children.

"That's a surprise," Maryn remarked. "I didn't think men like this would have wives."

"I wouldn't exactly call them wives," Casyl said. "There's still a few things you have to learn, lad."

Nevyn and Maryn rode behind the king as he trotted over to Caradoc. Nevyn was not impressed with the troop at first sight. Although they were reasonably clean and their weapons were in good repair, they were a hard-bitten, scruffy lot, slouching in their saddles, watching the royalty with barely concealed insolence. At every man's belt, the silver hilt of the dagger gleamed like a warning. Caradoc, however, bowed low from the saddle at the king's approach.

"Greetings, Your Highness. I've brought my men as the young prince ordered. I most humbly hope Your Highness will find them acceptable."

"We shall see, but if I should offer you shelter, then you'll be riding at the prince's orders, not mine."

Caradoc glanced at Maryn with a slight, skeptical smile, as if he were reckoning up the lad's age. In his mind Nevyn called upon the High Lords of Air and Fire, who promptly answered the prearranged signal and came to cluster around the lad. Their force enveloped him, giving him a faint glow, an aura of power. A light wind sprang up to ruffle his hair and swell his plaid, and it seemed that the very sunlight was brighter where it fell upon him. Caradoc started to speak, then bowed again, dipping as low as he could.

"I think me it would be a great honor to ride for you, my prince. Would you care to review my men?"

"I would, but let me warn you, Captain. If you take this hire, you'll be riding with me on a long road indeed. Of course, only the hard roads lead to true glory."

Caradoc bowed again, visibly shaken to hear the lad talk like the hero of a bard's tale. The silver daggers came to a stiff-backed attention in a sudden respect, and the young lieutenant beside Maddyn caught his breath sharply. When Nevyn glanced his way, he nearly swore aloud: Gerraent, with the falcon mark on shirt and sword hilt just as it always seemed to be.

"This is Owaen, good councillor." Caradoc noticed his interest. "Second-in-command in battle. Maddyn's our bard, and also second-in-command in peaceful doings."

"You seem to keep things well in hand, Captain," Maryn said.

"I do my best, my prince."

Owaen was looking Nevyn over with more curiosity than he showed for either the prince or the king. In those hard blue eyes Nevyn saw the barest trace of recognition, a spark of their old, mutual hatred, that lasted only briefly before it was replaced by bewilderment. Doubtless Owaen was wondering how he could feel so strongly about an unarmed old man that he'd only just met. Nevyn gave him a small smile and looked away again. He was seething with a personal excitement; here were Gerraent and Blaen, now called Owaen and Maddyn, and there was Caradoc, who in a former life had been king himself in Cerrmor under the name of Glyn the First. Glyn had been such a good king that Nevyn was shocked to find him as an outcast man and a silver dagger until he reminded himself that just such a man was essential now to the well-being of the kingdom. A mercenary like Caradoc fought for only one thing: victory. Not for him the niceties and snares of honor; he would stoop to any ruse or low trick if he had to in order to win. The members of his charmed circle of Wyrd were all gathering for the work, and that meant that somewhere soon Brangwen's soul would join them. Soon he would have another chance to untangle his snarl of Wyrd.

All at once he remembered the camp followers, hovering at a respectful distance behind their men. He felt sick, wondering if she were among them. Could she have fallen so low in this life?

For a moment, he was honestly afraid to look; then he steeled himself. When Casyl and Caradoc began discussing the terms of the hire, Nevyn left the prince in the care of the lords of the elements and jogged his horse along the ranks, as if the prince's councillor were having one last good look at the men his liege wished to take into his guard. Maddyn broke ranks to join him.

"Let's leave the horse trading to Carro and your king. By the hells, Nevyn, it gladdens my heart to think we'll be spending the winter in the same dun. I know Caudyr will want to talk with you, too."

"Caudyr?" It took him a moment to remember the young chirurgeon of Dun Deverry. "Well, now, is that young cub the chirurgeon Caradoc spoke of? I take it he followed my advice, all those years ago."

"So he did, and I'll wager it saved his life when Slwmar died, too."

"Good. It seems he took my advice about abortions as well, judging from the pack of children I see over there. How many lasses have you picked up along the road, Maddo? I seem to remember that you've always had luck with women."

"Oh, these are hardly all mine. We share what we can get when we can, you see."

Nevyn did see, entirely too well. The thought of Brangwen living passed from man to man was like a bitter taste of poison in his mouth. Most of the women were riding astride, their skirts hitched up around them, some with a small child behind them, but all of them, mothers or not, were as hard-eyed and suspicious as their men. At the very rear, a pale blond woman was sitting in a mule cart, cushioned by blankets as she nursed a baby.

"That's Clwna," Maddyn said, gesturing at her. "When we're back at the dun, I'd be ever so grateful if you or some other herbman would have a look at her. She hasn't been well since the babe was born, and Caudyr can't seem to mend her. She's as much my woman as any of them are."

"Oh, let's talk to her right now." Nevyn's heart sank with dread. "The king and your captain will doubtless be a while yet."

When they rode over, Clwna glanced up indifferently. There were dark circles like bruises under her blue eyes, and her skin was far too pale. Nevyn almost gasped in relief when he realized that she was not his Brangwen at all.

"This is Nevyn, the best herbman in the kingdom," Maddyn said with forced cheer. "He'll have you right as rain straightaway, my sweet."

Clwna merely smiled as if she doubted it.

"Well, it's a simple enough diagnosis, truly," Nevyn said. "A good midwife would have spotted it in a minute, but the only women Caudyr's ever tended were rich and well fed. Here, lass, your blood is weak because you just birthed a babe, and I'll wager you haven't been eating right. Get an apple, put an iron nail in it, and leave it there overnight. Then take it out and eat the apple. You'll see the red streak of the sanguine humor, which is what you need. Do that every night for a fortnight, and then we'll see."

"My thanks," Clwna was stammering in surprise. "It's good of a courtly man like you to give advice to a silver dagger's wench."

"Oh, I'm not as courtly as I seem. Here, your babe is a pretty little thing. Who's the father?"

"And how would I know, my lord?" She shrugged in sincere indifference. "Maddyn's or Aethan's, most like, but she could be the captain's, too."

In return for their winter's keep and a silver piece a man if they should see any fighting, Caradoc pledged his loyalty to Prince Maryn through the spring, with terms to be renegotiated at Beltane. Getting so large a troop quartered in the cramped island dun was something of a problem. The chamberlain and the captain of Casyl's warband conferred for an hour, then sent servants running all over the ward until at last the mercenaries had a barracks of their own, a stable for their horses, and a shed for their wagons and extra gear. The chamberlain was an old man with an amazing mind for details and a scrupulous sense of propriety. He was quite outraged, he told Nevyn, to find that the silver daggers found nothing wrong with keeping the women right in the same barracks with them.

"Well, why not?" Nevyn said. "It'll keep the lasses safe from the king's riders. Or do you want fights all winter long?"

"But what of those innocent children?"

"Let us profoundly hope that they're sound sleepers."

After the evening meal Nevyn went out to visit Maddyn in the barracks. When he came into the long room, dimly lit by firelight, he had to pause for a moment and catch his breath at the combined reek of horse, man sweat, and smoke. Most of the men were playing dice; the women huddled at the far end to gossip among themselves while the babies slept nearby. At the hearth Maddyn,

Caradoc, and Caudyr sat on the floor and talked, while Owaen lay nearby, stretched out on his stomach with his head pillowed on his arms. Although he seemed asleep, he looked up briefly when Maddyn introduced him to Nevyn, then went back to watching the fire.

"Come sit down," Caudyr said, sliding over a bit to make room. "It gladdens my heart to see you again. I thought that a sorcerer like you would have more important work at hand than selling herbs."

"Oh, the herbs are important in their own way, too, lad. Now tell me, how did you end up with that silver dagger in your belt?"

For a long while Caudyr, Maddyn, and Nevyn talked of old times, while Caradoc listened with close attention and Owaen fell asleep. At length the talk turned inevitably to Nevyn's strange employment in the king's palace. Nevyn put them off with vague questions until Caradoc joined in.

"Here, good sorcerer, what's the dweomer doing hiring a piss-poor bunch of men like us? I think me we've got a right to know, since you're asking us to die for the prince as like as not."

"Now here, Captain, I'm not asking a thing of you. The prince is the one who gives you meat and mead."

"Horseshit. The prince does what you tell him, at least when somewhat important's at stake." He exchanged a glance with Maddyn. "I was impressed with the lad, very impressed, you might say."

"Indeed?"

When Caradoc hesitated, Maddyn leaned forward.

"You've found the true king, haven't you? Admit it, Nevyn. That lad has to be the true king, or no one on earth ever will be."

Although he wanted to whoop and dance in triumph, Nevyn restrained himself to a small, cryptic smile.

"Tell me, Captain," he said casually. "How would you feel about leading your men all the way to Dun Deverry someday?"

Caradoc pulled his silver dagger and held it point up to catch the wink and glint of firelight.

"This is the only honor any of us have left, and I'll swear you an oath on it. Either I see the king on his throne, or I die over the prince's body."

"And you're willing to die for a man you saw for the first time today?"

"Why not? Better than dying for some little pusboil of an arrogant minor lord." With a laugh, he sheathed the dagger. "And when does the war begin?"

"Soon, Captain. Very soon."

Smiling to himself, Caradoc nodded. Nevyn felt like weeping. He could see in the captain's berserker eyes the bloody price they would all pay for victory.

Since everyone in Eldidd knew about the silver daggers, the news that they'd left for Pyrdon spread fast. It was just his luck, Branoic decided, that they'd move on just when he needed to find them. Even though a single rider could travel faster than a troop with a baggage train, they had a head start of some ten nights, and he never caught them on the road. After one last cold night of sleeping outside because he couldn't afford an inn, he rode into Drwloc around noon and found a cheap tavern, where he spent his last two coppers on a tankard of ale and a chunk of bread. He ate standing up with his back to the wall while he kept an eye on the other patrons, who were a scruffy lot to his way of thinking. As soon as the trade would allow, the serving lass minced over to him with a suggestive little smile. Unwashed and skinny, she appealed to him about as much as the flea-bitten hounds by the hearth, but he decided that he might as well get some information out of her.

"How far is it to King Casyl's dun, lass?"

"About two miles on the west-running road. You must be from a long way away if you don't know that."

"I am, truly. Now tell me, has a troop of mercenaries been through here? They hail from Eldidd, the lads I want, and they all carry daggers with silver pommels."

"Oh, they were, sure enough, and a nasty lot they looked. I don't know why the king took them on."

"Because they're some of the best fighting men in the three kingdoms, no doubt."

He strode away before she could flirt with him further. Out in the tavern yard his chestnut gelding stood waiting, laden with everything he owned in the world: a bedroll, a pair of mostly empty saddlebags, and a shield, nicked and battered under its coat of dirty whitewash. He hoped that Caradoc wouldn't hold his lack of mail against him, but he had a good sword at least, and he knew how to use it.

When Branoic rode up to the causeway leading to Casyl's dun, the guards refused to let him pass, and no more would they take in a message for a dirty and dangerous-looking stranger. Since he had no money for a bribe, Branoic tried first courtesy, then arguing, but neither worked. The guards only laughed and told him that if he wanted to see Caradoc, he'd have to camp there until the captain rode out. By then Branoic was so furious that he was tempted to draw his sword and force the issue, but common sense prevailed. He hadn't ridden all the way from Eldidd only to get himself hanged by some petty king.

"Well and good, then," he said. "I'll sit at your gates and starve until you're shamed enough to let me in."

As he strode away, leading his horse, he glanced back to see the guards looking apprehensive, as if they believed him capable of it. In truth, since he had neither coin nor food, he had little choice in the matter. In the meadow across the road he slacked the chestnut's bit and let it graze, then sat down where he could glare at the guards and be easily seen. As the morning crept by, they kept giving him nervous looks that might have been inspired by guilt, but of course, they may have been merely afraid of his temper. Although he was only twenty, Branoic was six foot four, broad in the shoulders, with the long arms of a born swordsman and a warrior's stance. Down his left cheek was a thick, puckered scar, a souvenir of the death duel that had gotten him exiled from his father's dun in Belglaedd. Better men than Casyl's guards had found him nerve-wracking before.

He'd been waiting by the road about two hours when he heard the blare of silver horns. As the farther gates opened, the guards by the road snapped to smart attention. Walking their horses down the causeway rode the silver daggers, sitting with the easy, arrogant slump in their saddles that he remembered. At their head was a lad of about fourteen, with a red, gold, and white plaid slung from his shoulder. When Branoic started forward, one of the guards yelled at him.

"You! Get back! That's the marked prince, Maryn, and don't you go bothering the captain when he's riding with him."

Although it griped his soul, Branoic retreated without arguing. The affairs of a prince were bound to take precedence over those of a commoner. He was just about to sit back down when he heard himself being hailed, but this time by the prince himself. He hurried back over and clasped the lad's stirrup as a sign of humility.

"Any man who asks has access to me." Maryn shot a pointed glance at the guards. "A prince is the shepherd of his people, not

one of the wolves. Remember that from now on." He turned back
to Branoic with a distant but gracious smile. "Now. What matter
do you have to lay before me?"

"My humble thanks, Your Highness." Branoic was practically
stammering in amazement. "But truly, all I wanted was a word
with Caradoc."

"Well, that's an easily granted boon. Get your horse and ride
with us a ways."

Branoic ran to follow his order. When he fell into line beside
Caradoc, the captain gave him an oddly sly smile.

"Branoic of Belglaedd, is it? What are you doing on the long
road north?"

"Looking for you. Do you remember when last we met? You told
me you'd take me on if I wanted to ride with you. Was that just a
jest?"

"It was a jest only because I didn't think you'd want to leave
your noble father's court, not because I wouldn't be glad to have
you in my troop."

"Thanks be to the gods, then. A bastard son's got a shorter welcome than a silver dagger unless he minds every courtesy. I've
been exiled. It was over an honor duel."

Caradoc's eyebrows shot up.

"I heard about that. You killed the youngest son of the gwerbret
of Elrydd, wasn't it? But why would your father turn you out over
that? I heard it was a fair fight."

"It was, and judged so by a priest of Bel, too." For a moment
Branoic had trouble speaking; he felt as if he could physically
choke on the injustice. "But it made my father a powerful enemy,
and so he kicked me out to appease the misbegotten gwerbret. The
whole way north, I was afraid for my life, thinking that Elrydd
would have me murdered on the road. But either I've thought ill of
him unjustly, or else I gave his men the slip."

"I'd say the latter, from what I remember of His Grace. Well and
good, lad, you're on, but you have to earn this dagger. If we see
fighting, you'll get a full share of the pay, mind, but you'll have to
prove yourself before I have Otho the smith make you a blade.
Agreed?"

"Agreed. And my thanks—there's not a soul in the world to take
me in but you."

For a few minutes they rode in silence. Branoic studied the
young prince riding some few yards ahead and wondered what it

was that made him seem so unusual. He was a handsome boy, but there were plenty of good-looking men in the kingdom, and none of them had his aura of glamour and power. There were other princes, too, who had his straight-backed self-confidence and gracious ways, but none that seemed to have ridden straight out of an old epic like Maryn. At times, it seemed as if the very air around him crackled and snapped with some unseen force.

"And what do you think of our lord?" Caradoc said quietly.

"Well, he makes me remember some odd gossip I heard down in Eldidd."

"Gossip?"

"Well, omens and suchlike."

"Omens of what?"

In a fit of embarrassment Branoic merely shrugged.

"Out with it, lad."

"Well, about the one true king of Deverry."

Caradoc laughed under his breath.

"If you stick with this troop, lad, you'll be leaving Eldidd and Pyrdon far behind. Can you stomach that?"

"Easily. Oh, here—what are you telling me? Will we be riding all the way to Dun Deverry some fine day?"

"We will, at that, but I can promise you a long bloody road to the Holy City." Caradoc turned in his saddle. "Maddyn, get up here! We've got a new recruit."

Somehow or other, Branoic had missed meeting the bard in his previous encounters with the silver daggers. About thirty-three, he was a slender but hard-muscled man with a mop of curly blond hair, streaked with gray at the temples, and world-weary blue eyes. Branoic liked him from the moment he met him. He felt in some odd way that they must have known each other before, even though he couldn't remember when or how. All that afternoon, Maddyn introduced him around, explained the rules of the troops, found him a stall for his horse and a bunk when they returned to the dun, and generally went out of his way to make him feel at ease. At the evening meal they sat together, and Branoic found it easy to let the bard do most of the talking.

The other lieutenant in the troop, Owaen, was a different matter altogether. They had barely finished eating when he strode over, his tankard in hand, and Branoic found himself hating him. There was just something about the way that the arrogant son of a bitch stood, he decided, all posturing with his head tossed back, his free hand on the hilt of his silver dagger.

"You!" Owaen snapped. "I see by your blazon that you used to ride for the Eagle clan of Belglaedd."

"I did. What's it to you?"

"Naught, except for one small thing." Owaen paused for an insolent sip of ale. "You've got the clan device all over your gear. I want it taken off."

"What!?"

"You heard me." Owaen touched the yoke of his shirt, which sported an embroidered falcon. "Those eagles look too much like my device. I want them gone."

"Oh, do you now?" Slowly and carefully Branoic swung free of the bench and stood up to face him. Dimly he was aware that the hall had fallen silent. "I was born into that clan, you piss-proud little mongrel. I've got every right to wear that device if I want, and want it I do."

Like dweomer Caradoc materialized in between them and laid a restraining hand on Branoic's sword arm.

"Listen, Owaen," the captain said. "The lad's gear will get lost or broken soon enough, and the eagles fly away of their own accord."

"That's not soon enough."

"I won't have fighting in our prince's hall."

"Then let's go out in the ward," Branoic broke in. "Let's settle it, Owaen, with a fistfight between the two of us, and the winner gets the device."

"For a new man, you're an insolent little bastard." Then Owaen caught the grim look on Caradoc's face. "Oh, very well, then. You're on."

Nearly everyone in the great hall trooped after them to watch when they went out. While a couple of pages ran off for torches, the combatants took off their sword belts and handed them to Maddyn. Wagers went back and forth between the onlookers. When the torches arrived, Branoic and Owaen faced off and began circling, sizing each other up. Since Branoic had won every fistfight he'd ever fought, he was confident—too confident. He plunged straight in, swung, and felt Owaen block his punch at the same moment that a fist jammed into stomach. Gasping, he dodged back, but Owaen was right there, dancing in from the side, clipping him on the side of the jaw. Although the blow stung more than hurt, Branoic went into a berserker rage, swinging back, closing, punching, feeling nothing but a swelling dizziness as Owaen blocked and danced and hit in return.

"Enough!" Caradoc's voice sliced through the red haze surrounding him. "I said hold and stand, by the Lord of Hell's balls!"

Arms grabbed him and pulled him back. With a gasp for breath Branoic tossed his head and saw blood scatter from a cut over his left eye. Owaen was standing in front of him, his nose running blood. He smiled as Branoic took a step back and felt his knees buckle under him. When the men holding him lowered him gently to the cobbles, all he could do was sit there, gasping for breath, feeling his face and stomach throb with pain and the blood run down his cheek.

"This had better end it," Caradoc said. "Owaen gets the little chickens since he's so fond of them, but I don't want anyone mocking Branoic for this, either. Hear me?"

There were mutters of agreement from the other silver daggers. In a flood of good-natured laughter the crowd broke up, settling wagers as they drifted back to the great hall. Branoic stayed outside; he felt so humiliated that he was sure he could never look another man in the face again. Maddyn caught his arm and helped him stand.

"Now look, lad, I've never seen a man before who could give Owaen a bloody nose."

"You don't need to lie to spare my feelings."

"I'm not. If you can keep Owaen from knocking you out cold on the cobbles, then you've won a victory of sorts."

It was so sincerely said that Branoic felt his shame lift. Stumbling and staggering, he had to lean on Maddyn as they headed for the barracks. About halfway there they were stopped by the old man whom Maddyn had pointed out earlier as the prince's councillor. Nevyn held up the lantern he was carrying and peered into Branoic's bleeding face.

"I'll tell Caudyr to get out to the barracks. This lad needs a couple of stitches in that cut over his eye. Make sure you get him to lie down, Maddo."

"Oh, I'll wager he won't be wanting to dance the night away."

Although Branoic tried to smile at the jest, his mouth hurt too badly. Suddenly Nevyn looked straight into his eyes, and the gaze caught him like a spear, impaling deep into his soul. In his muddled state, he felt as if he'd been trying to find this man all his life for some reason that he should remember, that he absolutely had to remember. Then the insight vanished in a flood of nausea.

"He's going to heave," Nevyn said calmly. "That's all right, lad. Get it all out."

Branoic dropped to his knees and vomited, his stomach burning from Owaen's fist. Never in his life had he felt so humiliated, that Nevyn would see him like this, but when he was finally done and looked up to apologize, the old man was gone.

Nevyn returned to his chamber, lit the ready-laid fire with a wave of his hand, and sat down in a comfortable chair to think about this blond, young Eldidd man that Caradoc had brought in from the road like a stray dog. Nevyn had recognized him the moment he'd seen him, or rather, he knew perfectly well that he should recognize the soul looking out through those cornflower-blue eyes. Unfortunately, he couldn't quite remember who he'd been in former lives. While Maddyn felt well disposed to the lad, Owaen had hated him on sight, a mutual feeling, it seemed. Logically, then, in his last life Branoic might have been a loyal member of Gweniver's warband, still bearing his old grudge against the man who had tried to rape a holy priestess. Since Nevyn had never paid any particular attention to the warband, it was also logical that he wouldn't remember all its members. On the other hand, he'd felt such a strong dweomer touch at the sight of the lad that surely he had to be someone more important than one of Gwyn and Ricyn's riders.

"Maybe her brother-in-law?" he said aloud. "What was his name, anyway? Ye gods, I can't remember that either! I must be getting old."

Over the next few days, his mind at odd moments worried over the problem of Branoic's identity like a terrier in front of a rat cage—it growled and snapped but couldn't get the rat out. He did decide, however, that the lad's arrival was an omen of sorts, a true one rather than another faked and theatrical glamour such as those that he and the priests were spreading about the coming of the king. One or two at a time, men he had trusted in lives past were coming to help him bring peace to the kingdom.

Soon enough he had news of an ominous kind to occupy his attention. Some weeks past, he had sent to the temple of Bel at Hendyr for copies of two important works on Deverry common law, and when the messenger returned, he also brought a letter from Dannyr, the high priest down in Cerrmor, a letter that was sealed twice and written in the ancient tongue of the Homeland that few could read.

"King Glyn has fallen ill," Dannyr wrote. "Everyone whispers of poison, although such seems doubtful to me. The king's chirurgeons have diagnosed a congestion of the liver, and truly, it is no secret that the king has indulged himself with mead in unseemly quantities ever since he was old enough to drink. Yet I thought it wise to inform you of these rumors nonetheless, for we cannot have it said that the true king poisoned one of his rivals. Any counsel you might send would be appreciated, but for the love of every god, write only in the ancient tongue."

When he finished, Nevyn swore aloud with vile oaths in both the ancient and the modern tongues. Dannyr was exactly right; no one would believe Maryn the true king if they thought he'd used poison to gain a throne. All the blame—if, indeed, blame there were— had to be cast onto the other claimant up in Dun Deverry, or rather, onto the various minions of the Boar clan that surrounded the eighteen-year-old king. At that point Nevyn remembered Caudyr, and he thanked the Lords of Light with all his soul for giving him the weapons he needed to win this battle. The chirurgeon's evidence about the circumstances surrounding the death of the last king would no doubt throw any suspicion firmly where it belonged. Smiling grimly to himself, Nevyn went to his writing desk and drafted a letter to Dannyr straightaway.

Yet when he was done, and the letter safely sealed against the off chance that there was someone around who could read it, he sat at his desk for a long time and considered this matter of poison. Even though it seemed that Glyn was dying of self-induced natural causes, there was no doubt that poison had become available in the torn kingdoms. Who was brewing it? What if there were followers of the dark dweomer around, waiting their chance to plunge the country deeper into chaos? And did they know about Maryn? He went cold all over, cursing himself for a fool, for a proud, stupid dolt to think he could keep such a crucial secret from those who made it their business to ferret out secrets. He would have to see if his suspicions were correct, and if they were, mere scrying through a fire would be useless.

He barred the door to his chamber, then lay down on his bed, lying on his back with his arms crossed over his chest. First he calmed his breathing, then summoned the body of light, seeing the glowing man shape first in his mind, then pouring his will into it until it seemed to stand beside him in the chamber. He transferred his consciousness over, heard a rushy click, and floated in the air, looking down at his inert body. Slipping out a window, he flew up high until he could look down on the dun, a black, dead lump in the throbbing silver mist of elemental force arising from the lake. Although the mist made it difficult for him to hold his place—he was forced to fight against some truly dangerous currents—still he was glad to see it, because its presence would make scrying into the dun difficult indeed. The lake had turned the dun into a safe fortress on more planes than one.

Navigating carefully, Nevyn got clear of the lake's aura and flew over the sleeping countryside, a dull red-brown now that autumn was sapping the energies of the plant life. In their true forms, beautiful, ever-changing crystalline structures of colored light, the Wildfolk swarmed around and accompanied him on his flight. About five miles from the dun he had his first warning of evil when the spirits paused, shuddering, then disappeared in silver flashes and long winking-outs of light. He stopped and waited, hovering above a patch of woodland to take imperfect shelter in its ebbing glow. None of the Wildfolk returned. Whatever had frightened them had done so badly. He flew up higher until the blue light was as thick as fog, ever swirling and drifting, hiding the landscape below. When he visualized light flowing from his finger-tips, light appeared, the volatile mind-stuff responding instantly to the form he imposed upon it. With glowing lines of light he drew an enormous sigil of protection in front of him. Since it would be visible for a great distance, it was the perfect bait to draw the attention of any other travelers on the etheric that night.

For a long while he waited there like a hunter near a snare until at last he saw another human-shaped body of light far off from him in the blue mists. He drew another sigil, this one of greeting and friendship, and was rewarded by seeing his fellow traveler first go stock-still, then turn and flee at top speed. Instinctively Nevyn started after, only to stop himself before he'd gone far. He had no idea of how strong the enemy was or even if he were alone. He was certain, however, that an enemy it was. Any servant of the Light would have answered that sigil with a similar one and then come to meet him.

Rather than risk some foolhardy battle, Nevyn returned to the dun and his physical body. Stretching, he sat up on the bed and looked into the fire on the hearth.

"Bad news. I think me that someone's spying on us."

In alarm the spirits of fire flared up, sending a shower of sparks up the chimney.

"If you see anything the least bit unusual, tell me."

Within the flames the gleaming salamanders nodded their agreement. Nevyn got up, took his heavy cloak, and left the chamber. He went up the spiral staircase to the last landing of the broch, where a trapdoor gave access to the roof. After a quick glance round to make sure that no servants were there to see this eccentric behavior on the part of the learned councillor, he pried it up and climbed out onto the roof. He had a strange sort of guard to post.

First he raised his arms high and called upon the power of the Holy Light that stands behind all the gods. Its visible symbol came to him in a glowing spear that pierced him from head to foot. For a moment he stood motionless, paying it homage, then stretched his arms out shoulder high, bringing the light with them to form a shaft across his chest. As he stood within the cross, the light swelled, strengthening him, then slowly faded of its own will. When it was gone, he lowered his arms, then visualized a sword of glowing light in his right hand. Once the image lived apart from his will, he circled the roof, walking deosil, and used the sword to draw a huge ring of golden light in the sky. As the ring settled to earth, it sheeted out, forming a burning wall around the entire dun. Three times around he went, until the wall lived on the etheric of its own will.

At each ordinal point, he put a seal in the shape of a five-pointed star made of blue fire. Once the four directions were sealed, he spread the light until it was not a ring but a hemisphere over the dun like a canopy. He made two last seals at zenith and nadir, then withdrew the force from the astral sword until it vanished. To signify the end of the working, he stamped three times on the roof. The dome, however, remained visible—that is, visible to someone with dweomer sight. Although he would have to renew the seals five times a day, whenever the astral tides changed, everyone within the dome would be safe from evil, prying eyes.

Wrapping his cloak tightly around him, for the air nipped with the promise of winter, he went to the wall and idly looked down into the ward. Someone was walking there, and the way he moved was suspicious: taking a few steps, pausing to look carefully round, then walking slowly on again. With his mind full of thoughts of spies, Nevyn left the roof and rushed down the inside staircase so fast that he nearly ended his physical existence there and then. When he ran out into the ward, the mysterious figure was no longer in sight. Muttering under his breath, he summoned Wildfolk, among them a large mottled gnome who had indeed seen the prowler. The gnome led him straight around the main broch and toward the stables with absolutely no sign of fear, which made Nevyn think he'd been overly dramatic to assume that the dark dweomer had a spy right in the dun. Sure enough, when he saw his quarry, he realized it was Branoic. Even in the dark the lad's sheer size and the straight-backed way he stood were recognizable.

"Good eve, lad. Taking the air?"

"In a way, Councillor. I . . . uh well . . . I thought I saw a fire."

"Ye gods! Where?"

"Well, I was wrong about it, you see." The lad sounded profoundly embarrassed. "I'm cursed glad now that I didn't go waking everyone up. I must have just been having a bad dream."

"Indeed? Tell me about it."

"Well, since I'm the new man, I got the bunk right by the drafty window in our barracks. I dreamt I was awake and looking out, and the dun walls were blazing with fire. So I started to shout the alarm, but then I remembered that this dun has stone walls, not a wooden palisade or suchlike. Right then I must have woken up. But I lay there thinking about it, and it nagged at me, so I grabbed my boots and came to look around. And as soon as I did, I realized that it had to be a dream, but it was a demon-sent vivid one, good sir."

Nevyn was taken completely aback. Obviously this young lout of a warrior had a touch of the dweomer, and in his dream state had seen Nevyn sealing the walls. Yet none of the men in the charmed circle of his Wyrd had ever shown such talents. By the hells, he thought, and irritably; just who is he?

"Tell me, do you often have dreams like that?"

"Well, sometimes. I mean, I've never dreamt about fires before, but at times I have these dreams that seem so real I'd swear I was wide awake. Every now and then . . ." He let his voice trail away.

"Every now and again you dream somewhat that turns out to be true."

With a gulp of breath, Branoic stepped sharply back.

"If my lordship will excuse me," he stammered. "I'd best be gone. It's freezing out here."

He turned and frankly ran from the man who'd discovered his secret. Young dolt! Nevyn thought, but with some affection. He would have to talk some more with Branoic, no matter who he . . . and then he saw it, what had been right under his nose but so unwelcome that he'd kept it at bay for days.

"It can't be! The Lords of Wyrd wouldn't do this to me! Would they?"

And yet he was remembering his Brangwen's last incarnation, when as Gweniver she'd dreamt of becoming the best warrior in all Deverry. In this life, the Lords of Wyrd had given her a body fit to fulfill that dream and then, or so he hoped, finally put it to rest. While every soul is at root of one polarity, which translates into the sex of the physical body, each spends part of its lifetimes in bodies of the opposite sex in order to have a full experience of the worlds of form. Nevyn had simply been refusing to see that such a time had come for Brangwen, his lovely, delicate, little Gwennie as he still thought of her. For all he knew, she was working out part of her Wyrd that had nothing to do with him personally. Whatever the reason, she'd returned to him just as he'd known she would, but as Branoic of Belglaedd.

As he paced back and forth in the dark, silent ward, Nevyn was sick with weariness. He could see a dark message for himself in her soul's choice of a body. Deep in his heart he'd been hoping that she would love him again, that they would have a warm, human relationship, not merely the cold discipline of apprentice and master. Apparently such a love was forbidden; he saw Branoic as a warning, that he was to teach the dweomer to the inner soul and forget about the outer form and its emotions. As much as it ached his heart, he would accept the will of the Great Ones, just as he had accepted so much else in the long years since he'd sworn his rash vow.

And after all, he had work on hand so important that his own feelings, even his own Wyrd, seemed utterly insignificant. Thinking about the battle ahead he could lay aside his personal griefs and feel hope kindling in his heart. Danger lay ahead, and great griefs, but afterward the Light would prevail again in the shattered kingdom.

On the morrow, a cool but sunny day, Maddyn went for a stroll round the edge of the lake. He found a warm spot in the shelter of a leafless willow tree and sat down to tune his harp. It had never been an expensive instrument, and now it was battered and nicked from its long years of riding behind his saddle, yet it had the sweetest tone of any harp in the kingdom. Although many a bard in many a great lord's hall had offered him gold for it, he would rather have parted with a leg, and although those same bards had begged him to tell them his secret, he never had. After all, would they have believed him if he'd told the truth, that the Wildfolk had enchanted it for him? He often saw them touching it, stroking it all over like a beloved cat, and every time they did, it sang with a renewed, heart-aching sweetness.

As he tuned the strings that day by the lake, the Wildfolk came to listen, appearing out of the air, rising out of the water, sylph and sprite and gnome, clustering round the man that they considered their own personal bard.

"I think it's time I made up a song about Prince Maryn. I take it you think he's the true king, too. I've seen you riding on his saddle and clustering round him in the hall."

They all nodded, turning as solemn as he'd ever seen them until an undine could stand the quiet no longer. Dripping with illusionary water, she reached over and pinched a green gnome as hard as she could. He slapped her, and they tussled, kicking and biting, until Maddyn yelled at them to stop. All sulks, they sat down again as far apart from each other as they could.

"That's better. Maybe I'll sing about Dilly Blind first. Shall I?"

With little nods and grins, they crowded close. Over the years Maddyn had elaborated the simple folk songs about Dilly Blind and the Wildfolk into something of an epic, adding verse after verse and clarifying the various stories. He had taught his mock-saga to bards in dun where there were noble children until half of Eldidd knew the song. At moments like these, when the wars seemed far away, it amused him to think that a children's song would outlive him, passed down from bard to bard when he was long since in his warrior's grave.

When the song was done—and it was a good twenty minutes long—most of the Wildfolk slipped away, but a few lingered, his blue sprite among them, sitting close beside him as he watched the ripples in the lake, the harp silent in his hands. He remembered that other lake up in Cantrae, ten years or so ago now, that had tormented his thirst as he rode dying. It had been about the same time of day, he decided, because the sun had rippled it with gold flecks just as it was doing to Drwloc in front of him. He could see in his mind the dark reeds and the white heron, and he could feel, too, the burning thirst and the pain, the sickening buzz of the flies and his dark despair.

"It was worth it," he remarked to the sprite. "It brought me to Nevyn, after all."

She nodded and patted him gently on the knee. Maddyn smiled, thinking of what lay ahead. There was not the least doubt in his mind that Nevyn had found the man born to be king of all Deverry. He believed with his heart and soul that the young prince had been handpicked by the gods to reunite the kingdom. Soon he and the other silver daggers would ride behind Maryn when he set out to claim his birthright. The only thing Maddyn wondered about was when the time would come. As the sunlight faded from the lake, and the night wind began to pick up, it seemed to him that his entire life had led to this point, when he, Caradoc, Owaen, and all the rest of the men in his troop were poised and ready, like arrows nocked in the bows of a line of archers. Soon would come the order to draw and loose. Soon, he told himself, truly, soon enough.

He jumped to his feet and called out, a peal of his berserk laughter ringing across the lake toward the sunset. The strings of his harp sounded softly in answer, trembling in the wind. Grinning to himself, he slung the harp over his shoulder and started back to the dun, glowing with warm firelight and torchlight in the gathering night.

Part Two

Summer, 1065

The Lords of Wyrd do not make a man's life as neatly as a master potter turns out bowls, each perfectly shaped and suitable to its purpose. In the ebb and flow of birth and death are strange currents, eddies, and vortices, most of which are beyond the power of the Great Ones to control.

—The Secret Book of Cadwallon the Druid

The sound of rain drumming on the ward outside echoed pleasantly in the great hall. In her chair by the fire, Aunt Gwerna was drowsing over her needlework. Occasionally she would look up and answer a dutiful "true-spoken" to one of her husband's rhetorical questions. Perryn's uncle, Benoic, Tieryn Pren Cludan, was in one of his expostulatory moods. He sat straight in his chair, one heavy hand gripping a tankard, the other emphasizing his points by slamming the chair arm. Benoic was going quite heavily gray, but he was still as strong-muscled as many a younger man, and as strong in the lungs, too.

"It's these worm-riddled pikemen," he bellowed. "Battle's not the same with common-born men fighting in it. They should be guarding the carts and naught else. Cursed near blasphemous, if you ask me."

"True-spoken," Perryn said dutifully.

"Hah! More of this wretched courtly mincing around, that's all it is. Trust the blasted southerners to come up with somewhat like this. It's no wonder the kingdom's not what it was."

While Benoic soothed his feelings with a long swallow of ale, Perryn tried to unravel the connection between spearing a man off his horse and the fine manners of the king's court.

"You young lads nowadays!" his uncle went on. "Now, if you'd only ridden in some of the battles I did at your age, then you'd understand what life here in Cerrgonney means. Look at you, lad, riding around without a copper to your name. Ye gods! You should be getting yourself a place in a warband and working at rising to captain."

"Now here, Perro," Gwerna broke in. "You're welcome at our table anytime you pass by."

"Course he is, woman!" Benoic snapped. "That's not the point. He should be making somewhat of himself, that's all. I don't know what's wrong with you, lad, and your cursed cousin Nedd is even worse. At least there's some excuse for you."

"Oh, er, my thanks."

"But Nedd's got dun and demesne both, and all he does is ride around hunting all day. By the Lord of Hell's balls!"

"Now, my love," Gwerna interceded again. "He and Perryn are both young yet."

"Twenty, both of them! Old enough to marry and settle down."

"Well, here, Uncle, I can hardly take a wife when I don't even have a house to put her in."

"That's what I mean. There's some excuse for you."

Perryn smiled feebly. Although he was a member of the northern branch of the ancient and conjoint Wolf clan and was thus entitled to be called a lord, he was also the fifth son of a land-poor family, which meant that he owned naught but the title and a long string of relatives to play unwilling host when he turned up at their gates.

"Are you riding Nedd's way when you leave us?" Benoic asked.

"I am. On the morrow, I was thinking."

"Then tell him I want to hear of him marrying, and soon."

The next morning, Perryn rose at dawn and went to the stable long before the dun came awake. He brought out his dapple-gray gelding, a fine horse with some Western Hunter blood in him, and began saddling up. On his travels he packed an amazing amount of gear: two pairs of saddlebags, a bulging bedroll, a small iron kettle, and at his saddle peak a woodcutter's ax slung where most lords carried a shield. Just as he was finishing, Benoic came out to look the laden horse over.

"By the asses of the gods, you look like a misbegotten peddler! Why don't you take a pack horse if you're going to live on the roads this way?"

"Oh, er, good idea."

With a snort, Benoic ran his hand down the gray's neck.

"Splendid creature. Where did a young cub like you scrape up the coin for him?"

"Oh, er, ah, well." Perryn needed a lie fast. "Won him in a dice game."

"Might have known! Ye gods, you and your blasted cousin are going to drive me to the Otherlands before my time."

When he left the dun, Perryn set off down the west-running road in search of a pack horse. Around him stretched the fields of Benoic's demesne, pale green with young barley. Here and there farmers trotted through the crops to shoo away the crows, who rose with indignant caws and a clatter of wings. Soon, though, the fields gave way as the road rose into the rocky hills, dark with pines. Perryn turned off the muddy track that passed for a road and worked his way through the widely spaced silent trees. Once he was in wild country, he had no need of roads to find his way.

Early in the afternoon, he reached his goal, a mountain meadow in a long valley that belonged to a certain Lord Nertyn, one of his uncle's vassals but a man Perryn particularly disliked. Out in the tall grass twenty head of Nertyn's horses grazed peacefully, guarded by the stallion of the herd, a sturdy chestnut who stood a good sixteen hands high. When Perryn walked toward the herd, the stallion swung his way with a vicious snort, and the others threw up their heads and watched, poised to run. Perryn began talking to the stallion, a soft clucking noise, a little murmur of meaningless sound until the horse relaxed and allowed Perryn to stroke his neck. At that, the rest of the herd returned to their feed.

"I need to borrow one of your friends," Perryn said. "I hope you don't mind. I'll take splendid care of him."

As if he agreed, the stallion tossed his head, then ambled away. Perryn picked out a bay gelding and began patting its neck and combing its mane with his fingers.

"Aren't you sick of that fat lord who owns you? Come along and see somewhat of the road."

When the gelding turned its head, Perryn smiled at it in a particular way he had, a deep smile that made him feel slightly cool, as some of his warmth was flowing out to the recipient of the smile. With a soft snort, the bay leaned its head against his chest. He patted it for a few more minutes, then walked away, the bay following close behind. Although Perryn honestly didn't understand why, once he got a few minutes alone with a horse, the animal would follow him anywhere without halter or rope. It was a useful trick. Whenever his coin ran low, he would simply take a horse from someone he disliked and sell it to one of the dishonest traders he knew. Because of his noble blood, no one ever suspected him of being the worst horse thief in the northern provinces. He'd often stolen a horse from a cousin one week, then ridden back the next to express surprise and sympathy at the loss. Only Benoic and Nedd were safe from his raiding.

That night, Perryn and the two horses made a comfortable camp in a forest clearing, but the next day they had to return to the road or go miles out of their way around a steep hill. They had barely reached the track when it began to rain. Perryn kept riding until the mud made traveling difficult for the horses, then turned a little way into the forest and dismounted. In the imperfect shelter of the pines he crouched down between the horses and waited for the storm to slack. It was uncomfortable, of course, with his clothes stuck to him and water running into his boots, but he ignored the discomfort, the way forest deer ignored the rain, browsing in the wet when they were hungry. If someone had asked him what he thought about during those two cold hours, he wouldn't have been able to say. He was merely aware of things: the rain, the smell of pine, the slick-wet trunks and pale green ferns. Every sound brought a message: a squirrel scuttling into its hole, a deer moving cautiously far away, a stream running close by. Eventually the rain stopped. By the time he reached Nedd's dun, he was dry again. Indeed, he'd quite forgotten that he'd been caught by the storm.

The dun stood on a muddy hillock behind a crumbling stone wall and a pair of rusty iron-bound gates that squeaked like a demon when Perryn shoved them open. Instead of a broch, Nedd had a stone round house with a roof that leaked all round the edge and two hearths that smoked badly. Although there were the usual barracks over the stables for a warband, the roof there was so bad that Nedd had simply moved his ten men into the half round of a room that passed for his great hall. They slept on straw mattresses, laid any which way in the dry spots out in the middle of the room. Nedd, as befitted his rank, had an actual bed by one hearth. Scattered through this disorder of moldy straw were also two tables, benches, a collection of leather buckets for drips, and one elegant chair, carved with the Wolf blazon. When Perryn came in after stabling his horses, he found his cousin sitting in the chair with his feet on one of the tables.

"By the gods," Nedd said with a grin. "You've come like an omen, cousin. Here, fetch yourself some ale. There's an open barrel by the other hearth."

Since their mothers were sisters, the cousins looked much alike. They both had flaming red hair, freckles, and bright blue eyes, but while Nedd was a good-looking man, the most charitable description of Perryn would have been "nondescript." Tankard in hand, he joined Nedd at his table. At the other, the warband were drinking and dicing.

"Why have I come like an omen?"

"You're just in time to ride to war with me." Nedd smiled as if he were offering a splendid gift. "I've got this ally to the west, Tieryn Graemyn—you've met him, haven't you—and he's sent out a call for aid. I'm supposed to bring him twelve men, but I've only got ten, so I've got to scrape up the other two somewhere. Come along, cousin! It'll be good sport, and you can spare me the cost of a silver dagger."

Seeing no way out of it, Perryn sighed. Nedd had fed him for many a winter, and besides, a noble lord was supposed to respond joyously to the call for war. He forced out a smile.

"Oh, gladly," he said. "And what's the war about?"

"Cursed if I know. I just got the message today."

"Can you spare me a shield?"

"Of course. Ye gods, Perro, don't tell me you ride without one?"

"Er, ah, well, I do at that. They take up too much space on your saddle."

"You should have been born a woodcutter, I swear it!"

Perryn rubbed his chin and considered the suggestion.

"Just jesting," Nedd said hurriedly. "Well, I hope a silver dagger turns up soon. There's always a lot of them in Cerrgonney. We'll wait a couple of days, then ride, even if we're one short. Better that than riding in after the fighting's over."

The gods, however, apparently decided that if Lord Nedd was going to march to war, it might as well be straightaway. On the morrow, not long after breakfast, the kitchen gardener ambled in to announce that there was a silver dagger at the gates.

"And he's got a woman with him, too," the old man said. "I feel cursed sorry for her kin."

"Is she pretty?" Nedd said.

"She is."

Nedd and Perryn shared a small smile.

"Splendid," Nedd said. "Send them in, will you?"

In a few minutes the silver dagger and his woman came in, both of them travel-stained and roughly dressed, the lass in men's clothing with a sword and silver dagger of her own. Although her blond hair was cropped short like a lad's, she was not merely pretty but beautiful, with wide blue eyes and a delicate mouth.

"Good morrow, my lords." The silver dagger made them a courtly bow. "My name's Rhodry of Aberwyn, and I heard in your village that you've got a hire for the likes of me."

"I do," Nedd said. "I can't offer you more than a silver piece a week, but if you serve me well in the war, I'll shelter you and your lass all winter."

Rhodry glanced up at the roof, where sunlight broke through in long shafts, then down at the floor, where Nedd's dogs snored in mildewed straw.

"Winter's a long way away, my lord. We'll be riding on."

"Oh well," Nedd said hastily. "I can squeeze out two silver pieces a week, and there'll be battle loot, too."

"Done then. His lordship is to be praised for his generosity."

For Jill's sake, Lord Nedd gave his silver dagger an actual chamber to sleep in instead of a mattress out in the great hall. Although the wickerwork walls were filthy, it did have a door. Rather than sit on the straw of the floor, which seemed to be inhabited, Jill perched on top of an unsteady wooden chest and watched as Rhodry cleaned his chain mail. As he ran an old rag through the rings to wipe away the rust, he was frowning in the candlelight.

"What are you thinking about?" she said.

"That old saying: as poor as a Cerrgonney lord."

"Lord Nedd's a marvel and a half, isn't he? Are we actually going to stay here all summer and the winter, too?"

"Of course not. I'd rather sleep beside the roads. Are you sure you'll fare well enough when I leave you behind?"

"Oh, no doubt the kennel will be comfortable enough when the dogs are all out of it. How long do you think the war will last?"

"War?" He looked up with a grin. "I wouldn't dignify it with the word, my love. If Nedd's allies are anything like him, no doubt there'll be a lot of shouting and skirmishing, and then an end to it."

"I hope you're right. I feel danger coming in this."

His smile gone, he laid the mail aside.

"More of your wretched dweomer?"

"Just that, but it's not battle danger, exactly. I'm not even sure what I do mean. Forgive me. I shouldn't have said anything at all."

"I wish you hadn't, truly." He hesitated for a long moment, staring down at the straw. "I . . . ah, by the black ass of the Lord of Hell, let's just forget it."

"I know what you want to know. I don't see your death coming. Ah ye gods, if ever I did, don't you think I'd beg you not to ride to war?"

"And what good would that do? When my Wyrd comes upon me,

I'll die as easily from a fever or a fall from a horse as from a sword cut. Let me beg a boon from you, my love. If ever you see my death, say not a word about it."

"I won't, then. I promise."

With a nod of thanks, he got up, stretching, and looked down at the mail glittering in the candlelight. He was so beautiful that she felt like weeping, that he would have to risk his life in the petty feuds of men like Lord Nedd. As she always did on the nights before he was about to ride to war, she wondered if he would live to ride back to her.

"Let's lie down together, my love," he said. "It's going to be a long while before I sleep in your bed again."

Once she was lying in his arms, Jill felt the wondering grow to a cold stab, closer and closer to fear. She held him tight and let his kisses drown it away.

Early on the morrow, the warband made a sloppy muster out in the ward. Jill stood in the doorway and watched as the men drew their horses up in a straggling line behind the two lords. The four men at the rear, including Rhodry, led pack horses laden with provisions because Nedd didn't own an oxcart and couldn't have spared the farmers to drive it if he had. Just as it seemed the line was finally formed, someone would yell that he'd forgotten something and dash back to the house or the stables. At the very last moment, Nedd discovered that Perryn didn't own a pot helm. A servant was dispatched to the stables, which apparently did double duty as an armory, to look for one.

Perryn stood rubbing the back of his neck with one hand while Nedd berated him for a woodcutter and worse. When Jill caught Rhodry's eye, he sighed and glanced heavenward to call the gods to witness Perryn's eccentricity. She had never seen a noble lord like Perryn, and she didn't know whether to laugh or cry over him. He was tall, but slender and ill proportioned, with narrow shoulders, long arms, and big, heavy hands out of scale to the rest of him. Although his face wasn't truly ugly, his eyes were enormous, his mouth thin, and his nose on the flat side. When he walked, he had all the grace of a stork strutting.

When the servant came back with a rusty helm, Nedd announced that if anyone had forgotten anything else, he'd cursed well have to do without it. Jill gave Rhodry one last kiss, then ran to the gates to wave the warband out. In a disorderly line they trotted down the hill, then into the road, disappearing to the west in a spatter of mud. With a prayer to the Goddess to keep her man safe, Jill turned back to the dun and the long tedium of waiting for news.

The small demesne of Tieryn Graemyn lay three days' ride to the west of Nedd's dun. The road ran narrow through sharp hills and scrubby pine, mostly uninhabited, until some ten miles from the tieryn's dun the warband came to a small village, Spaebrwn, one of three that paid Graemyn allegiance. As the warband watered their horses at the village well, Perryn noticed the townsfolk watching with frightened eyes. A Cerrgonney war was like a Cerrgonney storm, blowing the thatch from cottage and lord's manor alike.

Late in the afternoon they reached Graemyn's dun, set up on a low hill out in the middle of a stretch of fairly flat pastureland bordered by trees. The big gates swung open to admit them into a ward crowded with men and horses. As Nedd's warband dismounted, stableboys ran to take their horses and lead them away into the general confusion. The tieryn himself strolled out to greet these reinforcements. A grizzled dark-haired man, he bulged with muscles under his linen shirt.

"I'm truly glad to see you, Nedd," he remarked. "Your twelve brings us up to what strength we're going to have."

Under the tieryn's firm voice there was an anxious edge that made Perryn apprehensive, and for good reason, as it turned out at the council of war in the great hall. Even with Nedd and three other allies, Graemyn had only some two hundred men. Ranged against them were Tieryn Naddryc and his allies with close to three hundred. The dispute concerned two square miles of borderland between their demesnes, but it had grown far beyond the land at stake. Although Graemyn was willing to submit the matter to the arbitration of the high king, Naddryc had refused the offer some weeks past. In a subsequent skirmish between mounted patrols, Naddryc's only son had been killed.

"So he wants my blood," Graemyn finished up. "I've stripped the countryside to provision the dun. You never know what's going to happen when a man gets it into his head to start a blood feud."

The other lords all nodded sagely, while Perryn devoutly wished that he *had* been born a woodcutter. A feud could rage for years, and here he was, honor-bound to ride in it for Nedd's sake.

After the meal, the lords gathered round the honor table and studied a rough map of eastern Cerrgonney. They drank over it, argued over it, and yelled at each other while Perryn merely listened. He was part of the council only by courtesy to his birth; since he had no warband, he had no right of decision. He stayed until the lords adopted Nedd's plan of making a surprise attack on the enemy's line of march, then slipped away, getting a candle lantern from a page and taking it out to the stables. When he found his dapple gray, he hung the lantern on a nail in the wall of the stall and sat up on the manger. The gray leaned his face into Perryn's chest with a small snort. He gently scratched its ears.

"Well, my friend, I wonder if I'll live to see the winter, I truly do."

Blissfully unaware that there was such a thing as a future to consider, the gray nibbled on his shirt.

"At least you'll be safe and out of it. That's somewhat to be glad about."

If Cerrgonney men had fought on horseback, as warriors did in most of Deverry, no amount of honor or obligation would have induced Perryn to ride to war, but since up in that grain-poor province horses were too valuable to slaughter, Cerrgonney men rode to battle but dismounted to fight. Yet even though he knew his friend would be safe, Perryn's heart ached at the thought of battle. As he did every time he was forced to ride to war, he wondered if he were simply a coward. Doubtless every lord in the province would have considered him one if they'd discovered his true feelings about honor and battle glory, which seemed far less important to him than fishing in a mountain stream or sitting in a meadow and watching the deer graze. At times like these, the old proverb haunted him: what does a man have worth having but his honor? A good bit more, to Perryn's way of thinking, but he could never voice that thought to anyone, not even Nedd, no matter how much he simply wanted to ride away from killing men he didn't know in a war that never should have happened in the first place.

"Ah well, my friend, my Wyrd will come when it comes, I suppose. I wonder if horses have Wyrds? It's a pity you can't talk. We could have a splendid chat about that, couldn't we?"

Suddenly he fell silent, hearing someone open the stable door. His silver dagger gleaming in the lantern light, Rhodry strode briskly down the line of stalls.

"Oh, it's you, my lord. The tieryn's captain detailed me to keep

an eye on the stables, you see, and I heard someone talking."
Rhodry glanced around puzzled. "Isn't someone else here?"

"Oh, er, ah, well, I was just talking to my horse."

Rhodry's eyes glazed with a suppressed mockery that Perryn
was used to seeing on men's faces.

"I see. My lord, can I ask you if we're riding out tomorrow?"

"We are. Going to make a flank attack, give them a bit of a
surprise."

Rhodry smiled in honest pleasure at the news. He was handsome, strong, and eager for battle, just the sort of man that Perryn
was supposed to be and the type who always despised him. Perryn
wasn't sure if he envied or hated the silver dagger—both, he decided later.

On the morrow, the army mustered before dawn in a ward
bright with flaring torchlight. The men were silent, the lords grim,
the horses restless, stamping, tossing their heads at every wink of
light on helm and sword. As usual, Nedd's warband was the last to
take their place in line, shouting at each other and squabbling over
who would ride with whom. As he took his place beside his cousin,
Perryn noticed Rhodry, smiling to himself as if he were gloating
over a beautiful woman.

"We're going to cut straight across country," Nedd said. "We'll
need you to scout, Perro."

"No doubt. None of you could find your way through a copse to
a mountain, I swear it."

"Even woodcutters have their uses."

Perryn merely shrugged. The restlessness of the horses was
making him wonder if disaster lay ahead of them; sometimes animals could tell such things, in his experience. At last Graemyn
blew his silver horn. As the first dawn silvered the sky, the gates
swung open. With his sword raised high, the tieryn rode out, his
personal warband clattering behind him, four abreast, the line
snaking out and down the hill. Suddenly Perryn heard distant war
cries, as if someone were racing to meet Graemyn beyond the
walls. The men nearest the gates screamed in rage; the horns rang
out to arm and charge. Naddryc had prepared a surprise of his
own.

The ward turned into a shoving, shouting chaos as men dismounted, grabbing shields and helms, and rushed out the gates.
Perryn swung down, then gave the gray one last pat.

"Farewell, and pray to Epona that we meet again."

Then he ran after Nedd and out the gates. The battle was sweeping halfway up the hill, a raging, ragged swirl of men and riderless horses as Naddryc's men struggled up while Graemyn's tried to shove them back. In the dust pluming upward Perryn lost sight of Nedd almost at once. A burly fellow with an enemy blazon of blue and yellow on his shield charged him and swung in hard from the right. Perryn flung up his shield, caught the blow and thrust it away, then swung back, slapping his opponent hard on the thigh. Cursing, the man stumbled; Perryn got a hard cut on his sword arm. Bleeding, the man withdrew, feinting, parrying more than he swung. As he followed, Perryn realized that the enemy tide was ebbing back down the hill. Screaming war cries, Graemyn's men swept after. We should hold this higher ground, Perryn thought. But it was too late, and no one would have taken orders from him, even if he'd tried to give them.

Down on the flat the battle re-formed itself into random knots and mobs of fighting. As Perryn ran toward the closest one, he suddenly heard laughter off to one side, a bubbling sort of chuckle that rose now and then to a howl over the smack and clang of swords striking shield and mail. It was such an eerie sound that for a moment he paused, looking this way and that to try to find the source. That brief curiosity cost him dear. At a shout behind him he turned to see three men running straight for him, and they all carried the blue-and-yellow shield. With a yelp of terror, Perryn flung up his shield and sword barely in time to parry the two hard blows that swung in on him.

Although the third man dodged past and ran on, the other two enemies closed in for a quick if dishonorable kill. As he desperately dodged and parried, Perryn heard the laughter again, shrieking, sobbing, ever louder, until all at once Rhodry lunged at the man attacking from the right and killed him with two quick slashes, back and forth with a gesture like waving away a fly. Gasping for breath, Perryn took a wild swing at the other blue-and-yellow, missed, nearly tripped, and regained his balance just in time to see the man fall, spitted in the back through the joining of his mail. Rhodry jerked his sword free with a shake to scatter the drops of blood.

"My thanks, silver dagger," Perryn gasped.

For an answer Rhodry merely laughed, and his eyes were so glittering-wild that for a moment Perryn was afraid he'd turn on him. Yelling at the top of their lungs, five men from Nedd's warband ran up and swept Rhodry and Perryn along toward a hard knot of fighting around Graemyn himself. Although Perryn tried to keep up, the entire line was swirling and breaking, falling back around him as Naddryc's superior numbers began to tell. He got cut off as two of his allies shoved past him, running for their lives. When he ran for a man he thought was one of Nedd's, the fellow swung his way and raised a shield marked with the red acorns of another enemy warband. Swearing, Perryn charged, but something struck him from behind.

Fire stabbed, then spread down his shoulder. All at once, his fingers were loosening on the sword's hilt of their own will. He swirled around and caught a strike on his shield, but when he tried to raise his right arm, his fingers dropped the sword. Then he felt the blood, sheeting down his arm and pouring into his gauntlet. As the enemy pressed in, Perryn brought up the shield like a weapon and swung hard as he dodged back, stumbling over uncertain ground. Yet there were enemies behind him.

With a shout of desperation, Perryn charged and rammed the shield full strength into the enemy in front of him. Taken utterly off guard by this suicidal manoeuvre, the man slipped and fell backward. A startled Perryn fell on top of him, with his shield caught between them and his whole weight slamming it down. The enemy's head jerked back, and he lay still, whether dead or merely stunned Perryn neither knew nor cared. He scrambled up, shamelessly threw his shield, and ran for the dun—but only for a few yards. Suddenly he realized that the battle was lost, that the field belonged to the enemy, that the last of his comrades were fleeing through the gates just ahead of a line of blue-and-yellow shields. He fell to his knees and watched as the gates swung shut. Enemies ran past, shouting to one another.

"They're going to stand a siege—whoreson bastards—get to the postern!"

No one even looked at the half-dead warrior slumped on the ground. It occurred to Perryn that without his shield no one would even recognize him as an enemy in this confusion. His head spinning, he staggered to his feet and grabbed a sword with his left hand from a nearby corpse, then took off, trotting after the others and yelling, "To the postern!" While he didn't give a pig's fart about Graemyn, Nedd was trapped in the dun in a half-provisioned siege with no one to lift it. Graemyn had called in every ally he had for this battle.

In the dust-smeared, milling mob, the ruse worked well. He kept up with them for about twenty yards, then fell back and ran for the trees edging the battlefield. If anyone even saw him go, they had no time to chase after. Among the pines, neatly tethered, were Naddryc's horses with only a couple of servants to guard them. Perryn charged the nearest horse handler, who promptly broke and ran. In one smooth slash Perryn cut a tether rope, threw the sword away, and grabbed the reins of a solid chestnut gelding.

"Good horse. Please help me."

The chestnut stood patiently as Perryn hauled himself into the saddle. Keeping to the trees, he rode away from the battle. Although every step the horse took made the world swim in front of him and his dangling right arm throb, he bit his lower lip until it bled and kept riding. He had to get news to Benoic. That was the only thought he allowed himself to have. When he reached the road, he kicked the horse to a gallop and stayed on by sheer force of will. Gallop, trot, gallop, trot, walk—on and on he went, reminding himself that he could get help in Spaebrwn. Although he wondered at times if he'd live to reach the village, the blood was drying on his arm, not welling up fresh.

Just before noon, he crested the last hill above Spaebrwn and pulled the horse to a halt. For a long time he stared down at the glowing spread of ashes and charred timbers, half hidden under a drift of smoke. The breeze brought with it a sickening smell, too much like roasted pork. Some of the villagers had waited too long to flee.

"Ah ye gods, our Naddryc takes his revenge a bit too seriously, if you ask me."

The gelding snorted and tossed its head, spooked by the smell of burning. Perryn urged him on, skirted the ruins, and turned back into the pine forest. Even though he could neither raise his arm nor move his fingers, he was going to have to try to ride back to Nedd's dun on his own. By taking side trails through wild country, he could shorten the distance to some forty miles. Once they were well among the trees, he paused the horse again and thought of the dun, pictured it clearly in his mind, and remembered all the warm, safe times he'd enjoyed Nedd's company there. Then he went on, heading straight for it. Every time he started drifting from the most direct path, he felt a deep discomfort, something like a fear or anxiety, pricking at him. As soon as he turned the right way, the discomfort vanished. Although he didn't understand it in the least, this trick had led him back to places he thought of as home many a time in the past.

Perryn picked his way through the forest until sundown, then dismounted and led his horse through the dark for a few miles more, stumbling only to force himself up again, until they reached a small stream. Slacking the horse's bit with his left hand seemed to take an eternity. Finally he got it free and let the gelding drink.

"My apologies, but there's no oats."

In a golden mist the forest was spinning slowly around him. He sat down just before he fainted.

Like sheep in a snowstorm, the remains of the army huddled in Graemyn's great hall that night, eighty-odd men in decent shape, twenty-some badly wounded. Rhodry sat on the floor with the last six men of Nedd's warband. No one spoke as they watched the table of honor across the hall, where Graemyn and his allies talked, heads together, faces drawn and tight-lipped in the torchlight. Frightened serving lasses crept through the warband and doled out scant rations of watered ale. By the servants' hearth a young page sat weeping, wondering, most like, if he'd ever see his mother again. Finally Nedd left the honor table and limped back to his own men. He slid down the wall rather than sat until he could slump half upright in the straw.

"You should be lying down, my lord," Rhodry said.

"The blasted cut's not that bad." Nedd laid his hand on his thigh as if trying to hide the bloody bandage.

"My apologies, my lord."

"Oh, and you have mine. We're all going to have to watch our cursed tempers."

Everyone nodded, looking at the floor, out into space, anywhere rather than at each other.

"We've got provisions for a good six weeks," the lord went on. "Longer if we start eating horses."

"Is there any chance for a parley?" Rhodry asked.

"There's always a chance. Graemyn's sending a herald out on the morrow."

Rhodry watched the parley from a distance, because at dawn he drew a turn on guard up on the ramparts. Outside, Naddryc's men had cleared the battlefield of corpses, leaving a torn, bloodstained stretch of bare ground for about three hundred yards. Beyond that were the tents and horses of the besiegers. Around the dun, well beyond javelin range, trotted a mounted patrol. In a rough count, Rhodry estimated that Naddryc had at least a hundred and thirty men left. When the sun was about an hour's worth up in the sky, the gates opened, and Graemyn's chamberlain, carrying a long staff wound with red ribbons, slipped out. The patrol trotted over to him, made honorable half-bows from their saddles, then escorted him over to the camp. Rhodry leaned onto the ramparts and waited. When a flutter of crows flew past cawing and dodging, he envied them their wings.

Although the herald returned in about half an hour, Rhodry had to wait to hear the news until he was relieved from watch. He scrambled down the ladder and hurried into the great hall, where the warbands were eating in an ominous silence. Although the other lords were gone, Nedd was eating with his men. Rhodry sat down and helped himself to a chunk of bread from a basket, but he looked expectantly at the lord.

"Naddryc won't parley," Nedd said quietly. "He's made Graemyn one offer. If we surrender without a fight, he'll spare the women and children. Otherwise, he'll raze the dun and kill every living thing in it."

When Rhodry swore under his breath, the other men nodded in stunned agreement.

"He's a hard man, Naddryc," Nedd went on. "And he's sworn a vow of blood feud."

"And if we surrender, what then?" Rhodry said. "Will he hang every man in the dun?"

"Just that, silver dagger."

Rhodry laid the chunk of bread back down. For a moment he wished that they'd sally, die fighting, die clean, instead of swinging like a horse thief, but there was the tieryn's lady, her serving women, his daughters and little son.

"Ah well," Rhodry said. "A rope's a better death than a fever. They say you jerk once and there's an end to it."

"For all your silver dagger, you're a decent man, Rhodry of Aberwyn. I only hope that my noble allies are as honorable as you."

"Oh, here, my lord! You don't mean they're arguing about it?"

"They are. Well, by the hells, we'll hold out for a while before we do anything at all. The bastard can wait for a few days while he savors his piss-poor victory."

"Why not wait until he starves us out?"

"What if he changes his terms? I wouldn't put it past the whoreson to demand prompt surrender if we're going to save one woman's life."

Perryn woke to sunlight streaming down between the trees, like golden spears of light to his dazed sight. When he sat up, he shrieked at the pulse of pain in his arm. On his knees he crawled to the stream and drank, cupping the water in his left hand. Then he realized that his horse was gone. He staggered up, took a few steps, and knew that he would never be able to walk the remaining twenty miles to the dun. Fortunately, there was no reason that he'd have to. He walked another couple of yards, then went very still, waiting, barely thinking, until he felt the odd sensation, a quivering alertness, a certain knowledge that somewhere close was, if not that horse, then another. Following its lead, he angled away, ignoring the discomfort that told him he was no longer heading straight for the dun, and worked his slow way through the trees until at last he saw the brightening light ahead that meant a mountain meadow. The pull of a horse was so strong that he forgot himself, hurried, and banged his injured arm against a tree. When he yelped aloud, he heard an answering whicker just ahead. More cautiously this time he went on and broke free of the forest into a little grassy valley, where the chestnut was grazing, the reins tangling in the grass. When Perryn staggered over, the horse raised its head and nuzzled his good arm.

"Let's get that bridle off, my friend. If I die along the way, you'll starve if you get those reins wrapped around a bush or suchlike."

Taking the bridle off with only one hand was a long agony of effort, but at last he got it done. Leaning against the gelding for support, he went through the saddlebags and found the horse's previous owner's spare shirt and a chunk of venison jerky. He managed to tear the shirt into strips by using his teeth and made himself a rough sling, then ate the jerky while he rode on, guiding the horse with his knees. All afternoon they rode slowly, dodging through the widely spaced trees, climbing up and down the hills, until by sunset they'd made another ten miles. When they found another meadow, he let the horse graze and envied him the grass with his stomach clenching in hunger. Although he was only intending to rest for a few moments, as soon as he sat down, sleep took him.

When he woke, moonlight flooded the meadow. Nearby the

chestnut stood, head down and asleep. The night was unnaturally silent; not the cry of an owl, not the song of a cricket, nothing. As he sat up, wondering at the silence, he saw something—someone —standing at the edge of the meadow. With a whispered oath, he rose, wishing for the sword he'd left behind on the battlefield. The figure took one step forward, tall, towering in the moonlight—or was it moonlight? He seemed to drip pale light as palpable as water, running down the strong naked arms, glittering on the gold torc around his neck, shimmering on the massive antlers that sprang from a head mostly cervine, though human eyes looked out of it. Perryn began to weep in a fierce, aching joy.

"Kerun," he whispered. "My most holy lord."

The great head swung his way. The liquid dark eyes considered him not unkindly, but merely distantly; the god raised his hands in blessing to the man who was perhaps his last true worshipper in all of Deverry. Then he vanished, leaving Perryn wrapped in a shuddering awe that wiped all his pain and exhaustion away. With tears running down his face, he went to the place where the god had appeared and knelt on the grass, now god-touched and holy.

Eventually the chestnut raised its head with a drowsy nicker and broke the spell. Perryn mounted and rode on, guiding the horse instinctively through the dark forest. Although he rode for the rest of the night and on into the morning, he felt no hunger, no pain, his wound only a distant ache like a bee sting. About an hour after dawn, they came out of the trees just a mile from Nedd's dun. He trotted up to the hill, then dismounted and led the tired horse up to the gates. He heard shouts and people running, but all at once, it was very hard to see. He concentrated on keeping his feet as Jill raced toward him.

"Lord Perryn! Are they all lost, then?"

"Cursed near. Besieged."

Then he fainted into a merciful darkness, where it seemed a great stag came to meet him.

Between them, Jill and a servant named Saebyn got Perryn up onto a table in the great hall. As she soaked the blood-crusted shirt away from his wound, Jill found herself trying to remember every small thing Nevyn had ever told her about herbcraft, but the memories did her little good, because she had no proper tools and precious few herbs. The only thing Saebyn could turn up for a vulnerary was rosemary from the kitchen garden. At least Nevyn had

always said that any green herb was better than none. When she
finally loosened the shirt from the wound, she sent Saebyn off for
more hot water and some mead, then carefully peeled the crusted
linen away. Her gray gnome popped into reality and hunkered
down on the table for a look.

"It's not as bad as I feared," Jill said to him. "See? It just sliced
the muscle and missed those big blood vessels in the armpit."

With a solemn nod, the gnome tilted his head to one side and
considered the unconscious man. All at once it leapt up and hissed
like a cat, its skinny mouth gaping to show every fang, its arms
extended and its hands curled like claws. Jill was so surprised at
hearing it make a sound that she caught it barely in time when it
launched itself at Perryn and tried to bite him.

"Stop that!" She gave the gnome a little shake. "What's so
wrong?"

Its face screwed up in hatred, the gnome went limp in her
hands.

"You can't bite Lord Perryn. He's ill already, and he's never done
anything to you, either."

The gnome shook its head yes as if to say he had.

"What? Here, little brother, why don't you come back later, and
try to explain."

It vanished just as Saebyn returned with the stableboy behind
him. Jill washed the wound with water, then had Saebyn hold
Perryn's arms down and the stableboy his feet. Gritting her teeth,
she poured the mead directly into the open wound. With a howl of
pain, Perryn roused from his faint and twisted round. It was all
the two men could do to keep him lying there.

"My apologies, my lord," Jill said firmly. "But we've got to disperse the foul humors in this wound."

For a moment he merely gasped for breath; then he turned his
head to look at her.

"Forgot where I was," he mumbled. "Go ahead."

Jill wadded up a bit of rag and made him bite on it, then washed
the wound again. He trembled once, then lay so still that she
thought he'd fainted again, but his eyes were open in a stubborn
resistance to pain that she had to admire. Mercifully, the worst
was over. She made a poultice of the rosemary leaves, laid it in the
wound, then bound it up with clean linen.

"Benoic," he said at last. "I've got to ride to Benoic."

"You can't. You could bleed to death if you try. Tell me the message, and I'll take it on."

"Ride to my uncle. Tell him Nedd's trapped in Graemyn's dun." His voice fell into a whisper. "Your Rhodry was still alive, last I saw of him."

"My thanks." Although she nearly broke, she forced her voice steady. "I'll pray that he still is."

While Saebyn told her who Benoic was and what road to take to Pren Cludan, Jill cut one of the embroidered wolves from Perryn's bloody shirt to take as a token. When she rode out, she took two horses. By switching her weight back and forth, she would be able to ride at close to a courier's speed. As soon as she was well away from the dun, she called to her gnome, which promptly appeared on the saddle peak.

"Can you find Rhodry? Can you tell me if he's still alive?"

It nodded yes, patted her hand, then disappeared. Out on the road, where no one could see her, Jill allowed herself to cry.

A little after dawn on the next day, Rhodry climbed the ramparts and looked out over the dun wall. In the misty morning the enemy camp was coming awake; cooking fires blossomed among the dirty canvas tents, and men strolled around, yawning as they tended their horses. Just beyond the camp was the beginning of a circle of earthworks, about twenty feet, so far, of packed mound edged with a ditch that would soon close them round and block any attempts at escape. It was also an unnecessary effort on Naddryc's part. The decision had been made. Soon the lords would surrender and hang to spare the women and children. All that Rhodry wanted was for it to be very soon to end the waiting. When he was fourteen years old, he'd begun learning how to live prepared to die; at twenty-three, he was a master at that part of the warrior's craft. Now the day was upon him, but his Wyrd would come at the end of a rope.

To die by hanging, to be thrown into a ditch with a hundred men who'd met the same priest-cursed end, to lie far from Eldidd, unmarked, unmourned, nothing but a silver dagger who'd had the ill luck to take the wrong hire—that was his Wyrd, was it? Rhodry shook his head in sheer disbelief, that all his berserk battle glory, that strange dweomer prophecies and magical battles had led him to this, a thing so numbing that he felt no fear and very little grief, only a dark hiraedd that he'd never see Jill again. What if he'd only

ridden east instead of west and been hired by Naddryc instead of
Nedd? That would have been worse, he decided, to be party to this
dishonorable scheme. He would die and Naddryc live, but at least,
he would have his honor, while the lord had thrown his away for
hatred's sake.

Rhodry was so wrapped in his brooding that when something
tweaked his sleeve, he spun around, his sword out of its scabbard
before he was aware of drawing. Jill's gray gnome stood on the
rampart, grinning at him while it jigged up and down in excitement. Rhodry felt a flare of hope. If only he could make the little
creature understand, if only it could tell Jill—but what was she
supposed to do then? Run to some great lord and say that the
Wildfolk had told her the tale? The hope died again.

"It's cursed good to see you, little brother, but do you realize
what kind of evil has befallen me?"

Much to his surprise it nodded yes, then held up one long finger
as a sign to pay attention. Suddenly there were Wildfolk all
around it, little blue sprites, fat yellow gnomes, strange gray fellows, and parti-colored ugly little lasses. Never had Rhodry seen
so many, a vast crowd along the rampart.

"What is all this?"

When the gray gnome snapped his fingers, the Wildfolk lined up
in pairs, then began to bob up and down with a rhythmic motion,
each with one hand held out before it. The gray gnome stood at the
head of the line with one hand out like the others, but the left
raised as if holding a sword. Rhodry finally understood.

"An army! Oh, by great Bel himself, do you mean that someone's
riding to relieve this siege?"

The gnome leapt up and danced while it nodded yes. With a
rushy sound the rest of the pack disappeared. When Rhodry's eyes
filled with tears, he wiped them away, swallowing hard before he
could speak.

"Did you tell Jill I was trapped here?"

This time the answer was no. The gnome sucked one finger for a
moment, then began to walk back and forth while it imitated a
stiff, clumsy, bowlegged gait.

"Lord Perryn? He escaped the battle?"

Although the gnome nodded yes, its expression was peculiarly
sour. It shrugged, as if dismissing something, then leapt to
Rhodry's shoulder and kissed him on the cheek before it vanished.
Rhodry tossed his head back and laughed—until it occurred to

him that now he had to convince the noble lords that rescue was on the way, that there was no need to surrender, without, of course, mentioning the Wildfolk.

"Oh, horsedung and a pile of it!"

All morning, while he watched the mounted patrols ride round and round the dun, he went over and over the problem, trying out phrases, rejecting them, trying some more. Eventually Lord Nedd climbed awkwardly up the ladder onto the catwalk and limped over.

"Just thought I'd have a look at the bastards." Nedd leaned onto the wall and stared down, his red hair oddly dull in the sunlight, as if he were ill. "Ah well, at least we'll hang soon and get it over with."

"Er, well, my lord, I was just thinking about that, and . . ."

"At least I don't have a widow to mourn me." The lord went on as if he hadn't heard Rhodry's tentative words. "By the Lord of Hell's balls, I'd always wanted my land to revert to Perryn if I died, and now he's died before me."

Nedd was close to tears over his cousin's death, a surprising thing to Rhodry, who considered him no great loss. Or had considered him lost, until just a few hours ago.

"Here, my lord, what if he escaped from the field?"

"Oh, indeed! What if a crow sang like a little finch, too? Perryn wasn't much of a swordsman, silver dagger, and Naddryc's bastards were slaughtering the wounded after the battle."

"True-spoken, but . . ."

"I know what you're thinking," Nedd snarled. "Why mourn poor Perryn? He's better off dead."

"I wasn't, my lord. Naught of the sort!"

"My apologies. I forget you didn't know him well. By the asses of the gods, I got so blasted sick of all the chatter. What's wrong with your wretched cousin, how can you stand him in your dun, he's daft, he's a half-wit, he's this or he's that. He wasn't daft at all, by the hells! A little . . . well, eccentric, maybe, but not daft." He sighed heavily. "Well, it doesn't matter, anyway. I'll see him in the Otherlands tomorrow morn."

"My lord, he's not dead."

Nedd looked at him as if he were thinking that Rhodry was daft himself. Here was the crux, and Rhodry steadied himself with a deep breath before he went on.

"My lord, you must have heard the old saw, that Eldidd men

often have a touch of the second sight? It's true, and I'll swear to you that I know deep in my heart that Perryn's alive, and that he's bringing an army back to relieve the siege."

The lord's eyes narrowed.

"Look at me, a misbegotten silver dagger. I've been in more battles and tavern brawls than most men even hear of. I've faced hanging before, too, for that matter. Am I the kind of man to turn to fancies because he can't face death? Didn't you praise me for my courage on the field?"

"So I did." The lord looked away, thinking. "I've seen you go berserk, too. Why wouldn't you have a touch of the sight as well, for all I know? But—"

"I know it sounds daft, but I beg you, believe me. I know it's true. It comes to me in dreams, like. I know there's a relieving army on the way."

"But who—oh ye gods, my uncle!" Suddenly Nedd grinned. "Of course Perryn would ride straight to Benoic—well, if he's truly alive."

"I know he is, my lord. I'll swear it to you on my silver dagger."

"And that's the holiest oath a man like you can swear. Ah, by the black hairy ass of the Lord of Hell, what does it matter if we hang tomorrow or in an eightnight, anyway? Come along, silver dagger. We've got to convince my allies of this, but I'll wager they'll grab at any shred of hope they can see."

Four days after she left Nedd's dun, Jill rode back with an army of two hundred twenty men, every last rider that Tieryn Benoic could scrape up, whether by calling in old alliances or by outright threats. As the warband filed into the ward, Saebyn ran out, clutched the tieryn's stirrup as a sign of fealty, and began telling the lord everything that Perryn had told him over the past few days. Jill threw her reins to the stableboy and hurried into the great hall, where Perryn lay propped up on Nedd's bed with a pair of boarhounds on either side of him and three of those sleek little hounds known as gwertraeion at his feet. She shoved a dog to one side and perched on the edge of the bed to look over her patient, whose eyes were clear and alert, and his cheeks unfevered.

"Is the wound healing well?" she said.

"It is. You must have brought my uncle with you from all the noise outside. I knew he'd come. If he didn't have me and Nedd to complain about, his life would be cursed dull."

At that, Benoic himself strode in, slapping his pair of gauntlets impatiently against his thigh.

"You dolt, Perro! And Nedd's twice a dolt! But Naddryc's a whoreson bastard, having the gall to besiege my kin. Well and good, we'll wipe him off the battlefield for it. Are you riding with us?"

"I am. A wolf can run on three legs."

"Now wait a moment, my lord," Jill broke in. "If you ride, that cut could start bleeding again."

"Let it. I've got to go with them. I can lead the army through the forest, you see. We'll save twenty miles and a night that way."

"Splendid," Benoic said. "Glad to see you're finally showing some spirit, lad. Don't worry, Jill. We'll have your man out of that worm-riddled dun as fast as ever we can."

"Your Grace is most honorable and gracious. If I were a bard, I'd praise your name for this."

With a small bow she retired and left them alone. Out in the ward a pair of Benoic's vassals were conferring with their captains while the men unsaddled and tethered their horses outside for want of room in the stables. She went out the gates and walked about halfway down the hill, then sat down where she could be alone and called to the gray gnome, who appeared promptly.

"Is Rhodry still all right?"

It nodded yes, then hunkered down in front of her and began picking its teeth with one fingernail.

"You still haven't told me why you hate Lord Perryn."

It paused to screw its face up in irritation, then went on picking until it'd finally gotten its fangs clean enough to suit it.

"Come on now, little brother. You could at least tell me why. Or is it too hard to explain?"

Rather reluctantly, he nodded his agreement to this last.

"Well, let's see. Did he hurt you or some other Wildfolk?"

No, he hadn't done that.

"Can he even see you?"

Apparently not, since it nodded a no.

"Is he an evil man?"

Frowning in concentration, the gnome waggled its hands as if to say: not exactly that, either.

"You know, I'm having a hard time thinking up more questions."

It smiled, pressed its hands to its temples as if it had a headache, then disappeared. Jill supposed that she'd never find out the reason, but as long as the gnome behaved itself and didn't pinch the lord or tie knots in his hair, it didn't particularly matter at the moment, not when she had Rhodry's safety to worry about. She decided that she couldn't bear to sit here in Nedd's moldering dun and wait for news.

Since she had a mail shirt and a shield of her own, on the morrow Jill rose and armed when the warband did. Once the army was mustered outside the gates, she led her horse into line at the very rear. Since these men had been hastily assembled from Benoic's various allies and vassals, everyone who noticed her at all seemed to assume that she was a silver dagger hired by some other lord. All that counted to them, truly, was that she was another sword.

By keeping strictly to herself and speaking to no one, Jill escaped discovery all that day, because Perryn led the army off the road into the forest on a track so narrow that they had to ride single file. All day they wound around hills and through the trees by such confusing paths that she prayed Perryn actually knew what he was doing. She also understood why all the provisions were on pack mules, not in carts; apparently Benoic knew his nephew's daft ways very well. That night, however, they made camp in a mountain meadow, and there Jill was caught out. Like the excellent commander he was, Benoic made a point of walking through the camp and speaking to his men personally. When he came to Jill, he stared for a moment, then roared with laughter.

"Have all my men gone blind? Mail or no, Jill, you don't look like a lad to me. What are you doing with the army?"

"Well, Your Grace, my man's all I have in the world. I've got to see him with my own eyes as soon as ever I can."

"Huh. Well, we can't be sending you back now. You'd only get lost trying to follow Perro's wretched deer trails. You'd best come camp with me. You can keep your eye on Perryn's wound, and everyone will know you're under my protection."

When Jill shifted her gear over to the tieryn's campfire, she found Perryn there, slumped against his saddle. Although he was pale with exhaustion, he looked up and smiled at her.

"I thought you'd find a way to come along," he said.

"Why, my lord?"

"Oh, er, ah, just rather thought you were that sort of lass. I hope Rhodry's worthy of you."

"I hold him so, my lord."

Nodding absently, he stared into the fire. She was struck by how sad he looked, a perpetual melancholy that was beginning to wear lines in a face too young to have them, rather as if he were in exile from some far country rather than among his kin. A puzzle, that one, she thought to herself.

On the morrow, Jill saw yet another puzzling thing about the lord. Since she was riding right behind him, she could watch how he managed his leading. When they came to a spot where two trails joined or one petered out, he would wave the army to a halt, then ride a few steps ahead to sit on his horse and stare blankly around him, his head tilted as if sniffing the wind. For a moment he would look profoundly uncomfortable, then suddenly smile and lead the men on with perfect confidence. She was also impressed with his riding. Most of the time he left the reins wrapped around the saddle peak and guided the horse with his knees, while he swayed in a perfect balance in spite of having one arm in a sling. On horseback he looked much more graceful, as if his peculiar proportions had been designed to make him and a horse fit together in an artistic whole.

About two hours before sunset, Perryn found the army a large meadow in which to camp and announced that they were a scant six miles from Graemyn's dun. After the horses were tended, Jill put a clean bandage on Perryn's wound, which was oozing blood and lymph, and tied up his sling again. Although he pleaded that he was too weary to eat, she badgered him into downing some cheese.

"We'll reach the dun tomorrow," he remarked. "I can rest then, after the battle, I mean."

"Now listen, my lord. You can't fight. Trying to swing a sword would open that wound up again."

"Oh, don't trouble your heart about that. I'll just trot around the edge of things. See what I can see."

It was such a daft remark that Jill couldn't answer.

"Oh, er, ah, well, I heard my uncle talking with the other lords, and they're thinking of riding right into battle." He looked sincerely distressed. "There's bound to be wounded horses, and maybe I can get them to safety."

"Oh. I keep forgetting how valuable horses are up here."

He nodded, staring into the fire, as if he were working out some elaborate line of thought. It was some minutes before he spoke again.

"I cursed well hope that Nedd and Rhodry are still alive."

Although she knew that they were, she had no way of telling him.

"So do I," she said instead. "You seem to honor your cousin highly, my lord."

"I don't, because he's not truly honorable. But I love him. We were pages together in Benoic's dun. I think I would have gone mad if it weren't for Nedd."

"Was the tieryn as harsh as all that?"

"He wasn't, not truly. It was me, you see. I just . . . well, oh, ah, er."

As she waited for him to finish, Jill wondered if Nedd's efforts to keep him sane had all gone for naught. Finally he got up and went to his blankets without another word.

"You're certain it will be today?" Graemyn said.

"As certain as the sun is shining," Rhodry said. "Your Grace, I know it sounds daft, but I swear to you that the relief army's close by. We'd best be ready to arm and sally. If they don't come, then Your Grace will know I'm daft, and we can all surrender and be done with it."

For a long moment Graemyn considered him with an expression that wavered between doubt and awe. Perched on Rhodry's shoulder, the gray gnome squirmed impatiently until at last the tieryn nodded his agreement.

"True enough, silver dagger." He turned to his captain. "Have the men arm. One way or another, today sees the end of this."

The gnome grabbed Rhodry's hair and gave it a tug, then vanished.

The warband drew up behind the gates; watchmen climbed to the ramparts. As the waiting dragged on in the hot sun, the men ended up sitting down on the cobbles. No one spoke; every now and then someone would look Rhodry's way with a puzzled frown, as if thinking they were daft to trust this silver dagger's words. All at once, a watchman yelled with a whoop of joy.

"Horsemen coming out of the forest! I see the Wolf blazon! It's Benoic, by the gods!"

Laughing, cheering, the men leapt to their feet. Nedd threw an arm around Rhodry's shoulders and hugged him; half a dozen men slapped him on the back. At the tieryn's order, two servants lifted down the latch beam at the gates and rushed to man the winches. From outside, the battle noise broke over them; men yelling, horns blowing, horses neighing in panic, and through it all was the strike of sword on shield and mail. Rhodry started to laugh, a little cold mutter under his breath; he felt so light on his feet that it seemed he hovered over the cobbles.

"Remember!" Nedd hissed. "We're going after Naddryc."

Although he nodded agreement, Rhodry went on laughing.

With a groan and creak the gates swung back. Screaming and jostling, the warband rushed out, just as when leaves and sticks dam a stream, which worries at them, nudges them, and at last breaks free in a churn of white water. Down the hill, the enemy camp was a screaming, shoving, bloody madness. Half of Naddryc's men had had no time to arm; those wearing mail were trying to hold the breach in the earthworks against a full cavalry charge, and they were doing it with swords, not pikes. Horses went down; others screamed and reared; but for every horse lost, three or four of the enemy were trampled. All at once the cry went up: the sally to our rear! the sally to our rear! Rhodry's laugh rose like a wail as the horsemen drove through. The defenders broke, swirling and running to face the new threat as Graemyn led his men downhill.

"There he is!" Nedd shrieked. "With the trimmed shield."

A burly man with mail but no helm was racing across the battlefield in retreat, the silver edging on his shield winking in the sunlight. At an angle Rhodry went after him, his laugh gone as he thought only of running, and soon he'd left the wounded Nedd behind. Naddryc was slowing, panting, gasping for breath. Then he stumbled, and Rhodry dodged round to cut him off. For a moment they merely stared at each other, panting while they got their breath back, Naddryc's mouth working under his blond mustache.

"So," Rhodry said. "Here's the man who was going to kill women and children."

Then the cold, mad chuckle took over his voice. As he lunged, Naddryc dodged back, flinging up his sword and shield. He parried gracefully, his shield a little high to protect his bare head, and made a quick thrust that Rhodry easily turned aside. Suddenly light flared in a drift of black smoke; someone had fired the tents. Rhodry feinted in from the side, then struck; Naddryc parried barely in time, jumped back, and began to circle. As Rhodry swung to face him, the murk reached them, smoke, dust, thicker than a sea fog. They both checked, coughing for a moment, but the smell of burning drove Rhodry mad.

With a choking, gasping howl he charged, as wild as an injured lion, striking, parrying, cursing, and coughing while Naddryc desperately tried to fend him off, rarely getting in a blow of his own as he parried with both sword and shield. Yet even in his madness Rhodry saw that the lord was tiring. He feinted to the side again, dodged fast to the other, and then back as Naddryc tried to follow —too slowly. Rhodry's blow caught him hard on the side of the neck. With a ghastly bubbling scream he fell to his knees, then buckled as his life's blood pumped out the artery.

Rhodry's berserker fit left him, dropped away like a wind-caught cloak, but he was possessed by an even madder panic. Somewhere Jill was lying dead or wounded, somewhere in the burning. He knew it, even as he knew that he was being irrational. He heard Nedd yell his name, but he turned and ran toward the blazing tents in the same blind way that he'd charged Naddryc. All at once he heard hoofbeats and saw a horse emerging from the murk. Even flecked with soot, Sunrise's pale gold coat still shone.

"Rhoddo!" Jill yelled. "Get up behind me! Naddryc's horses are about to stampede."

Rhodry sheathed his sword and swung up behind her. He was barely settled when she kicked Sunrise to a trot.

"What are you doing here?"

"Rescuing you. I could hear you laughing and rode straight for the sound. Look behind us. Are they coming?"

When he glanced back, he could see little in the smoke and dust, but he did make out an orderly procession of horselike objects moving away from the burning camp.

"By all the gods! Someone's gotten them out of there."

"It must be Epona herself, then. When I rode by a few minutes ago, they were screaming and pulling at their tethers."

She paused the horse and turned in the saddle to give him a puzzled look. He grabbed her and kissed her, remembered his irrational panic, and kissed her again. With a laugh she pushed him away.

"You're breaking my neck, twisted around like this. Wait till we're alone, my love."

At that Rhodry remembered that they were in the middle of a battle, but as he looked around, somewhat dazed as he always was when the fit left him, he realized that the fighting was over. Naddryc had been so outnumbered that most of his men had been slaughtered and the fortunate few remaining taken prisoner. As they dismounted and walked on, leading the horse over the uncertain ground, he saw Nedd talking to Graemyn over Naddryc's corpse.

"Come here, silver dagger." Nedd hailed him with a shout. "Your Grace, this is the man who killed this bastard."

"You'll be well rewarded for this, silver dagger," Graemyn said. "Indeed, well rewarded for everything you've done for me."

The tieryn knelt beside the corpse, then took his sword two-handed and severed Naddryc's neck in one swift blow. Rhodry's stomach churned; it was an impious thing that he was seeing. Graemyn grabbed the head by the hair and stood up, looking at every man nearby as if challenging them to say one wrong word, then strode away, the head dangling in his hand. Even though the priests had long since banned the taking of trophy heads with mighty curses, the sight of Graemyn with his enemy's head touched something deep in Rhodry, as one string of a harp will sound when another is plucked. Although Jill and Nedd were watching the tieryn in honest revulsion, he felt a certain dark satisfaction.

"I'd do no less to a man who threatened my wife and kin," Rhodry said.

"Well." Nedd considered this briefly. "He had provocation, sure enough."

Before he went back to the dun, Rhodry knelt beside the headless corpse and methodically looted it of every small and valuable thing, coin, ring brooch, a gold-trimmed scabbard, and a silver belt buckle. This hire had drawn to an end, and a silver dagger had to think of eating on the long road.

When the fire broke out in the tents, Perryn was riding around the edge of the actual battle, rounding up wounded horses and leading them to safety outside the earthworks. The meaning of the spread of smoke didn't quite register on him until the chestnut he was riding snorted nervously and danced. Then he remembered Naddryc's horses, tethered behind the tents. With an oath he turned the chestnut and galloped straight for the camp. At first the horse balked, but Perryn talked to him, patted him, soothed him until at last he picked up courage and allowed himself to be ridden near to the fire.

Between the burning and the earthwork, horses were rearing, screaming with that ugly half-human sound a horse makes only in terror, kicking out at the grooms trying to save them as they pulled desperately at their tether ropes. Perryn wrapped his reins around the saddle peak and guided the chestnut with his knees as he rode right into the panic. Although the chestnut trembled and threatened now and then to buck, he kept moving as Perryn talked, pouring out the words, smiling his special smile, reaching out with his one good hand, patting a horse here, slapping one there, as if he were the stallion of a herd, who asserts his control with nips and kicks as much as affectionate nuzzles. The panic began to ebb. Although the horses were dancing and sweating with gray fear-foam, they fell in behind and around him in the swirling smoke. At last the grooms cut the last tether.

"Take them out!" one yelled. "And may the gods bless you!"

With a wave and a yell, Perryn led the herd forward at a calm jog. Circling around the inner earthwork, they swept free of the burning camp just as a rain of sparks and glowing bits of canvas began to fall. Perryn called out wordlessly, and they galloped out of the breach to the safety of the meadow beyond. When he looked back, he could barely see the dun, rising half hidden in the murk. With the horses huddled around him, he waited for a good half hour until the smoke diminished to a few wisps. As he was leading the herd back, Nedd came out on horseback to meet him.

"I was looking for you," Nedd said. "I figured that you were the only man on earth who could have saved Naddryc's horses."

"Oh, er, ah, well, they trust me, you see."

For a moment they merely stared at one another.

"Er, well," Perryn said at last. "Did you think me slain in that first scrap?"

"I did, but now I see that I wasn't so lucky."

"I'm not rid of you, either."

Leaning from their saddles, they clasped hands, and they were both grinning as if they could never stop.

Back at the dun, the cousins turned the horses over to the servants, then went into the great hall, where a conference of sorts was in progress at the table of honor. While the lesser lords and allies merely listened, Benoic and Graemyn were arguing, both red-faced and shouting.

"Now listen here!" Benoic bellowed. "You've made it cursed hard for Naddryc's brother to settle this peacefully. What's he going to say when he gets his brother's body back in two pieces?"

"Anything he blasted well wants to say! What's he going to fight me with? Ghost riders from the Otherlands?"

"And what about Naddryc's allies? Were their mothers all so barren that they only had one son apiece? Don't they have uncles to ride to their nephew's vengeance?"

At that, Graemyn paused and began to stroke his mustache.

"If you want this thing over and done with," Benoic went on in a normal tone, "you'd best send messengers down to Dun Deverry straightaway to plead for the high king's intervention. If you do, I'll back you in this war, for my misbegotten nephew's sake if naught else. If you don't, I'm pulling my men and Nedd's out right now."

Benoic had always had a splendid talent for blackmail.

"Done, then," Graemyn said. "I'll get the messengers on the road today."

With a nod of satisfaction, Benoic rose and gestured for Nedd and Perryn to follow.

"Come along, lads. We've got wounded men to look in on and that silver dagger deserves some praise. He's the one who slew Naddryc, eh? Hah! Just what the bastard deserved—cut down by a wretched silver dagger."

Although his head was swimming with exhaustion, Perryn went along with them because he was afraid to tell his uncle how weak he felt. They found Rhodry standing by the door and drinking ale down like water while Jill smiled at him as if she were thinking he'd won the battle all by himself. Perryn sighed at the cruel injustice, that she would honestly love her arrogant berserker. He found her appealing, a lovely lass, half wild and wandering, with her golden horse that suited her so well, but she was also attached to the best swordsman he'd ever seen. Although he hated to admit it, Perryn was terrified of Rhodry.

"Well, silver dagger," Benoic said, "you've earned your hire twice over. You always hear about people with the second sight seeing deaths, or shipwrecks, that sort of evil thing, but your touch of it has come in cursed handy."

"So it has, Your Grace. We Eldidd men can be a peculiar lot."

Although the others laughed at the jest, it made Perryn's unease deepen. There was something odd about the silver dagger that he couldn't put into words but that pricked at him, a discomfort much like the one that warned him he was straying from a true path. Rhodry was more than a danger to him; he was a reproach, or part of a curse, or—something. Perryn felt so baffled that he shook his head, a gesture that was a mistake. All at once the room seemed to spin around him, and a crackling golden fog rose out of nowhere. He heard Nedd call out, then fainted. Although he woke briefly when Nedd and Benoic laid him on a bed, he was asleep before they left the chamber. All that day he slept, and he dreamt of Jill.

On the morrow, every unwounded man in the dun rode out with the noble-born, ostensibly in honorable escort as they returned the bodies of Naddryc and his allies, but in reality as a warband in case Naddryc's kin decided to continue the blood feud. Jill spent a long morning helping Graemyn's wife, Camma, tend the wounded, a job that usually fell to the wives of Cerrgonney lords for want of enough chirurgeons in the province. When noon came, they were both glad of the chance for a wash and the time to sit down over a light meal of bread and cheese.

"My thanks for your aid, Jill. You know quite a bit about chirurgery."

"My lady is most welcome. I've seen a lot of bloodshed in my life."

"So you must have, following your silver dagger around like this. He's certainly a handsome man, isn't he? I can see how he'd turn the head of a young lass, I truly do, but do you ever regret riding with him? You must have left a great deal behind for your Rhodry."

"I didn't, my lady. All I've ever known in my life is poverty. Rhodry has never let me starve, and well, that's good enough for me."

Camma stared, caught her rudeness, then gave Jill a small smile of apology. Jill decided that it was time to change the subject.

"Lord Perryn's wound seems to be healing well. I'm awfully glad. After all, Rhodry owes his life to him."

"So do we all." For a moment, Camma's face turned haggard. "Well, his clan breeds stubborn men, the stubbornest in all Cerrgonney, I swear, and that's saying a great deal."

"It is. Do you know his clan well?"

"I do. His aunt and mother are both cousins of mine, or I should say, his mother was, poor lamb. She died some years ago, you see, but Perryn's Aunt Gwerna and I often meet. Gwerna had the raising of him, truly. He was the last of seven children, you see, and his mother was never truly well again after his birth. She had a hard time carrying him, some bleeding and bad pains, and then he was in her womb only seven months, not nine."

"By the Goddess herself! I'm surprised the babe lived!"

"So were Gwerna and I. He was such a scrawny little thing, but healthier than any other early babe I've ever seen. Since his mother was so ill, Gwerna found a wet nurse, and she made the lass carry Perro in a kind of sling right against her breasts and under her dresses day and night for the warmth, you see, and the lass sat by the fire all day and slept by it at night, too. I think that's what saved him, constantly being kept warm for a couple of months." She paused, considering. "Maybe it was his hard start in life that made him so odd, the poor lad. Gwerna always called him the changeling. He made you think of all those old tales where the Wildfolk steal a human babe and leave one of their own in its stead."

Jill felt an odd wondering whether, if in Perryn's case, the old superstition might be true, but the gray gnome materialized on the table and gave Camma such a nasty sneer that it seemed to be heaping scorn on the very thought. It sat down by the trencher of cheese and rested its chin on its hands to listen as Camma went on.

"It's naughty of me to be telling tales on him, now that he's a man and grown, but if you'd seen him, you'd understand, Jill. Such a skinny little lad, and that red hair of his was always like a thrush's nest, no matter how much Gwerna combed it." Camma smiled, taking a sincere pleasure in these memories of better times. "And he was always out in the hills or the woods, every chance he got. He used to sob every autumn when the snows came, because he'd have to stay indoors for months. And then, there was the time he ran away. He couldn't have been more than eight. Graemyn and I rode to pay Gwerna and Benoic a visit, and one day Perryn got caught stealing honey cake from the kitchen. Well, every lad does that now and again, but Benoic got into one of his tempers. He was going to beat the lad, but little Nedd begged and begged his uncle to spare him, so Benoic relented. Well, the next morning, there was no sign of Perryn. Gwerna had every man in the dun searching for him, but the whole two weeks we were there, no one ever found him, and Gwerna was in tears, sure he was starved or drowned. I thought so myself. But then, when it was almost winter, Gwerna sent me a message. When the snows came, Perryn turned up at the gates, dirty and tattered, but well fed. He'd lived in the hills on his own for three months."

"Ye gods! And what did he have to say for himself?"

"Well, he'd heard everyone calling him the changeling, and so he got it into his head that he should go live with the Wildfolk where he belonged. But I never found any, he says, the poor little lad. Poor Gwerna, she wept over that, and even Benoic stopped being so hard on him—well, for a while, anyway."

Jill would have liked to hear more, but the object of these reminiscences came strolling over to the table. The gnome snarled at him, then disappeared.

"Perro, you should be in your bed," Camma said. "One of the servants can bring you a meal."

"It's cursed dull, lying abed. I'll be fine."

Cradling his sling-supported arm, Perryn sat down across the table from Jill. Under his eyes were dark shadows like smears of soot.

"My lord," Jill said, "you truly should be resting."

"I'll never mend shut up like a hog in a pen. I want to go out to the woods, sit out there for a while."

Coupled with Camma's tale, his request made an odd sort of sense. Out of duty to the man who'd saved Rhodry's life, Jill saddled up his gray gelding, helped him mount, then led the horse out of the dun. Out in the fields, only part of the earthwork still stood; the day before, Benoic's men had dumped the bodies of the slain into the ditch and filled it in with the mound above. They walked beyond this grim scar on the earth to the edge of the forest and found a spot among the scattered pines where the ground was cushioned with needles and the sunlight came down in shafts. With a sigh of pleasure, Perryn sat down, his back to a tree. He actually did seem stronger now that he was outside, with color in his face and life in his eyes.

"It's splendid of you to trouble yourself over me, Jill."

"Oh, hardly! I owe you many an honor for saving Rhodry."

"You don't, at that. I made that ride for Nedd's sake and my own. What was I to do? Lie there and let them kill me? I wasn't even thinking of Rhodry, so there's no need for thanks."

"I've never known anyone who thinks like you. You're as scrupulous as a priest."

"Everyone says that. I wanted to be a priest, you know. My uncle got into a temper over it, and my father just laughed."

"Well, I can't see Benoic allowing one of his kinsmen to serve Bel instead of the sword."

"Oh, not Bel. I wanted to be a priest of Kerun, but I couldn't even find a temple of his."

Jill was quite surprised. She knew little of Kerun's worship, except that he was one of the dark gods of the Dawntime who had been displaced as the temples of Bel and Nudd grew in power. The stag god was lord of the hunt, while Bel presided over the settled life of the growing grain. Vaguely she remembered that you were supposed to give the first deer taken in a new year to Kerun, but she doubted if anyone bothered anymore.

"He's a splendid god," Perryn remarked.

"So are all the gods," Jill said, in case any were listening.

"Oh, truly, but Kerun's the only one who . . . oh, er, ah, well, who seemed to suit me, I suppose I mean." He thought for a long moment. "Or, er, I should say, he's the only god that I'm suited for. Or somewhat like that. I've always felt that if I prayed to the others, they'd take it as an affront."

"What? Oh, come now, don't be so harsh with yourself. The Goddess of the Moon is mother of us all, and she and the Three Mothers will listen to anyone's prayer."

"Not to mine. And the Moon's not my mother, either."

Although Jill supposed that this statement bordered on blasphemy, she neither knew nor cared enough about the worship of the gods to refute it.

"It's not that I like being this way, mind," Perryn went on. "It's just that I know it in my heart. Kerun's the only god who'll have me. I would have liked being his priest, living out in the wilderness somewhere and doing whatever his rites are. I couldn't even find anyone who knew much about that, you see."

"Well, here, maybe you should go to Dun Deverry. I've been told there are ancient temples there where the priests know everything there is to know. I'll wager there's a book or suchlike, and you could maybe hire someone to read it to you."

"Now there's a thought!" He smiled at her. "You're actually taking me seriously, aren't you?"

"Of course. My father always said that if a man wants to be a priest, the gods will favor those who help him."

"Your father sounds like a splendid fellow. But it's just that no one ever takes me seriously, not even Nedd. I mean, he cares about me and defends me and suchlike, but he thinks I'm daft, you see, even though he won't admit he does."

"Well, I don't think you're daft."

"Truly?"

"Truly. I'll be honest with you. I think you're a truly eccentric man, but I've met stranger fellows than you along the long road. Compared to some of them—why, you're perfectly ordinary."

With a toss of his head, he laughed. She was surprised at his laughter, deep, smooth, genuinely humorous, and realized that she'd been expecting it would be as halting and strange as his way of speaking.

"Well, then, maybe I should ride to Dun Deverry and see more of the world," he said at last. "I could scrape up some coin from my brothers. They'd probably give me a bit, you see, just to be rid of me for a while. My thanks, Jill. I never thought of that. I hate cities, and it never occurred to me that there'd be anything worth having in one."

"Well, I like them myself. They stink, but there's always so much to see among the smells."

He smiled, watching her so warmly that she went on her guard, mindful that they were alone and hidden. Since she could have bested him easily in any sort of fight, she wasn't afraid of him, but she refused to give him the slightest encouragement that might cause trouble with Rhodry. She had no desire to see poor Perryn dead at the hands of her jealous man. Aware that her mood had changed, he sighed and looked away.

"Oh, er, ah, well, I might have made a good priest. I'm certainly not much of a warrior."

"Oh, now, don't smear mud on your name."

He nodded absently. She waited for him to go on and waited and waited, until in some twenty minutes she realized that he was capable of sitting silently for hours. Although she felt no interest in him as a man, as a puzzle he was fascinating.

That night, the army made camp about twenty miles north and east of Graemyn's dun, on the very spot of land that was the cause of the war, where they would remain while a messenger went ahead to Naddryc's brother. Since the weather was warm, the cart containing the noble remains was stowed a good bit downwind of the camp itself. As Nedd remarked to Rhodry, it was possible that

Aegwyc wouldn't even unwrap his brother's corpse to see how it had been mutilated.

"So we can hope, my lord," Rhodry said. "How far away is it to Lord Aegwyc's dun?"

"Just ten miles. With luck, he'll come by sunset tomorrow."

Together they walked back to the camp, sprawled over a meadow. Although the dust was thickening to a velvet gray, Rhodry, of course, could see quite well with his half-elven eyesight. As they passed a clump of scrubby bushes, he saw something move within it and stopped for a better look, as it was unlikely that a rabbit or other animal would come this close to so many human beings. Cowering among the twisted trunks was one of the Wildfolk, but he'd never seen one like it: a blackish, deformed gnome with long fangs, bulging eyes, and red claws. For a moment it stared at him in terror, then vanished.

"Somewhat wrong?" Nedd said.

"Naught, my lord. It just looked like . . . oh, like someone had dropped a bit of gear in there, but it was only a rock."

Later, as they sat by the campfire, Rhodry had the distinct feeling that he was being watched, but although he looked carefully around him, he never caught either man or spirit looking his way.

"Using the Wildfolk to spy could be cursed dangerous," said the man who was calling himself Gwin.

"I know that, but there's naught else I can do until I get a look at Rhodry in the flesh." His companion looked up from the scrying mirror, laid out on a square of black velvet on the table in front of him. "At least he's got out of that siege. That stinking little feud could have been the ruin of all our plans."

Gwin merely nodded, well aware how close they'd come to losing their prey to a warrior's Wyrd. The man who was using the name Merryc carefully wrapped up the mirror and put it back into the secret pocket of his saddlebags. Although they were both Bardek men, they'd been chosen for this hunt because there was Deverry blood in their families. Both had straight, dark brown hair and skin light enough to go unremarked in the kingdom, especially in the northern provinces, where men of their homeland were rarely seen. Gwin's mother, in fact, had been a Deverry girl, sold by her impoverished clan to a Bardek merchant as a concubine. As he vaguely remembered, his father had been fairly pale by Bardek standards, too, but then he'd only seen the man a handful

of times before they'd sold him off as an unwanted slave child at
the age of four. He knew nothing about Merryc's background nor,
in fact, his true name. Men who were chosen for the Hawks of the
Brotherhood kept their own secrets and allowed others theirs.

"Do you know where he is now?"

"I do," Merryc said, buckling the saddlebag. "It's not far. I think
it'll be perfectly safe for us to ride by on the morrow. We can stop
and gawk at the army for a few minutes. No one will think much
of it. What traveler wouldn't stop and stare at the doings of the
noble-born?"

"True-spoken. And then?"

"We watch. Naught more. Remember that well. All we do is
watch from a distance until Rhodry and the lass are out on the
road alone. Then we can summon the others and make our move."

"Well and good, then, but there's somewhat about this plan that
vexes me. It's too complex, all twisted like a bit of those interlaced
decorations they favor here."

"Well, and I have to admit I feel the same, but who are we to
argue with our officers?"

"No one, of course."

"That jest wasn't funny in the least."

"I didn't mean it to be a jest."

Gwin felt a sudden shudder of fear, as if by saying the ordinary
phrase "nev yn" he might have summoned Nevyn into their inn
chamber like a demon rising at the very sound of its name. Then
he brushed the irrational thought aside. It was only a symptom of
his unease with the convoluted scheme which his superiors in the
blood guild had laid upon them. It was all very well for them,
safely back in the islands, to talk of kidnapping Rhodry unharmed
without attracting the attention of the dweomer of light.

"Has anyone told you what we're supposed to do about that lass
of his?" Merryc said.

"They have. Kill her. If there's time, we're allowed to have a bit
of sport with her first."

"Splendid. By all accounts, she's lovely."

"But only if it's safe. She's not important at all to whatever the
point of all this is, or so I was told. She just needs to be gotten out
of the way."

Merryc nodded, considering this new bit of information. They
were both too low in the Hawks' guild to have been given more
than what they absolutely needed to know. Although he accepted

his ignorance as part of the discipline, privately Gwin wondered just what the blood guilds intended to do with Rhodry once they had him safely back in Bardek. Naught that was pleasant, no doubt, but that was no affair of his. In fact, neither he nor Merryc had any idea of who had hired their guild and sent them on this errand. The blood guilds took work from whoever could pay their high price, and there were men in Deverry as well as Bardek who knew it.

On the morrow they rode out of Bobyr, the village in which they'd been staying, and headed northeast. Some two hours after noon, they came to a wide meadow and the army camp, a sprawl of tents thirty feet off the road, with the horses grazing beyond them. Although most of the men were sitting on the ground, most of them dicing, there were guards spaced at regular intervals around the encampment.

"Let's hope Rhodry isn't off beyond the horses," Merryc muttered.

In a moment they had worse things to worry about than where Rhodry might be. As they walked their horses slowly along, stopping now and then to stare in feigned amazement, they heard someone yell in the camp. A mounted squad of ten galloped out from behind the tents, split into two, and surrounded them before they could think of running. Trying to escape, in any case, would have been a mistake. The leader of the squad, a gray-haired man in the plaid brigga of the noble-born, guided his horse up to them.

"No need for trouble, lads," he said. "I just want to know who you are, and who you ride for."

"My name's Gwin, and this is Merryc, my lord, and we don't ride for any noble lord. We work for the merchant guild down in Lyn Ebon, mostly as caravan guards, but they sent us up here with letters and suchlike for the new guild in Dun Pyr."

"Got some proof of that, lad? There's a war on, and for all I know, you're spies."

Gwin reached into his shirt and pulled off a thin chain with a stolen seal ring of the guild in question. The lord examined it, grunted in approval, and handed it back.

"My apologies, then. Ride on, but be careful on the road. Most like, you won't meet any trouble, but it pays a man to keep his eyes open."

"It does, my lord, and my thanks."

When the lord waved his arm, the squad parted and let them

through, directly by a man who had to be Rhodry from his description. Luck and twice luck, Gwin thought, but he let nothing show on his face but a careful indifference as he casually glanced the silver dagger's way. With the same indifference, Rhodry looked back, then turned his horse and followed the squad back to camp. Neither Gwin nor Merryc spoke until they had gone another mile or so; then Merryc laughed, a dark chuckle under his breath.

"Well and good, then. I won't need to be ordering the Wildfolk about from now on."

"Have the others seen him yet?"

"They haven't. I talked to Briddyn through the fire last night, and they're still too far south. They won't need to do their own scrying, anyway, unless somewhat happens to me."

"It won't. That's why I'm along."

"Arrogant, aren't you?" Merryc turned in the saddle and smiled at him. "But I won't deny that you're the best swordsman in the Brotherhood. Let's hope you can best Rhodry if things come to that."

"Let's hope they don't. Remember, they want him alive."

During the first days after the army rode out, while the dun waited tensely for news, Jill spent a fair amount of time with Perryn, usually out in the woods. The cure, if such it was, of sun and open air was doing him far more good than bed rest. Soon the dark circles were gone, and he could spend a whole day awake. Yet no matter how much time she spent with him, she never felt that she was getting to know him, because he was as guarded and private as one of the wild animals he loved so much. After that first day he never mentioned his longing for Kerun's priesthood again. When she tried to talk about his kin or the life of the dun, he always drifted into saying some daft thing that put an end to the conversation. Although he seemed to be glad of her company, at times she wondered if he would prefer to be alone. On the third day, however, she had a disturbing revelation of his feelings.

In the afternoon they went out for their usual walk, but this time he told her to lead the horse a little farther into the forest, where there was a tiny stream bordered by ferns that he wanted her to see. After she watered his gray, Jill dutifully admired the ferns, then sat down next to him in the cool shade.

"We should be getting news of the army soon," he remarked. "If there was a battle, they'd send messages."

"Let's pray they're on their way home, and without another army chasing them."

"True-spoken. Though . . . ah, er, oh, well . . ."

Jill waited patiently while he collected his thoughts. She was beginning to get used to his lapses.

"Er, ah, it's been splendid sitting out in the woods with you. No doubt we won't be able to when Rhodry rides home."

"Of course not. Rhodry can turn rotten jealous, even though he's got no reason to be."

"Oh. Er, ah, he doesn't have any reason to be?"

"None, my lord."

She went on guard, waiting to see how he would take her firm dismissal. For a moment, he considered the ferns sadly.

"None, is it?" he said at last. "Truly?"

He turned his head and smiled at her, a peculiar sort of smile, open and intense, that seemed to reach out and wrap round, troubling her will with a warmth as palpable as a touch of a hand. When she wrenched her eyes away, he laid a gentle hand on her cheek. She twisted away and knocked his hand off, but he smiled again in a way that made him seem to glow. She stared at him, because for a moment she was incapable of moving. When he kissed her, his mouth was soft, gentle, but sensual with a thousand promises.

"You truly are beautiful," he whispered.

With a wrench of will, she shoved him away.

"Now, here," she snapped. "There can't be any more of this between us."

"And why not?"

His smile was so disturbing that Jill scrambled up and stepped back as if he were an enemy with a sword. He made no effort to follow, merely watched her with his head tilted in a childlike, questioning way. When she stepped back a few more feet, she felt the spell break.

"I'm going back to the dun," she snarled. "Obviously you've got the strength to ride back alone."

As she jogged back to the dun, she was debating the problem. He can't be dweomer—he must be dweomer—where would he even have learned it—but what else could that be? Now that she was away from him, the incident was oddly blurred in her mind, as if it had never truly been registered in her rational memory. She decided that, dweomer or not, she was going to avoid being alone with Perryn from now on. When he returned, late in the afternoon, she saw him from across the great hall. He was so bland, so vague and awkward, that she found herself wondering if she'd dreamt the incident by the stream.

Hunkered down in the middle of the field, the lords were parleying, Aegwyc with ten of his men for an escort, Graemyn with ten of his, one of whom was Rhodry. Since he was the man who'd killed Aegwyc's brother, he had to be there to admit it if the lord demanded. He profoundly hoped that he wouldn't, even though Graemyn assured him that he would pay the lwdd himself. So far, Graemyn had had little chance to say anything, because Benoic was doing most of the talking.

"So it's settled, then?" Benoic said at last.

"It is." Aegwyc sounded very tired. "I'll abide by the high king's arbitration—provided I feel it's fairly run."

"And I'll do the same," Graemyn broke in before Benoic could agree for him. "I swear it on the honor of my clan."

"And I on mine." With a sigh, Aegwyc rose, staring past them to the full army. Rhodry supposed that he was counting up the odds against the few men he could muster. "Send me a herald when the king's men arrive."

"I will." Benoic got to his feet and waved the rest of the men up. "You have my hand on that."

Solemnly they shook hands. For a moment Aegwyc lingered, looking over the ten men around the tieryn. He would know that one of them had to be his brother's killer, and he looked each one full in the face, pausing a little longer when he came to Rhodry. Rhodry looked boldly back and saw the lord's mouth tighten in bitterness. There was only one reason that a silver dagger would be part of this parley, after all. With a sudden wrench, Aegwyc turned and led his men away. Rhodry let out his breath in a long sigh of relief.

"Ah, you killed the bastard fairly, silver dagger," Benoic said.

"So I did, but still, it's a hard thing to look a man's kin in the face when you've brought him his Wyrd."

As he mounted his horse for the ride back to camp, Rhodry had the feeling that someone was staring at him. He twisted in the saddle to look, but everyone around him was busy mounting up.

No one would be staring at me, anyway, he thought, unless Aegwyc can send the evil eye from far away.

Yet the feeling persisted for a moment before it faded. During the long ride back to Graemyn's dun, he would feel it every now and then, that someone, somehow, and for some strange reason, was spying on him.

"I'm cursed glad to see your arm out of that sling," Nedd remarked.

"So am I," Perryn said.

He picked up a leather ball, hard-packed with straw, and began squeezing it repeatedly to exercise his hand. Soon he would have to start working his arm, too, but it ached so much that he wanted to wait a day or so. Nedd paced back and forth across the small bedchamber and watched with a worried frown.

"Will that heal up properly?" he said.

"Don't know yet. I never was much good with a sword anyway. It's not like I've got fine-honed skills to lose."

"Well, the war's over, if you ask me. Aegwyc can't cause much trouble. His brother bled the demesne white for his war with Graemyn."

"So is our uncle going to pull out?"

"Not him. He's having a fine time bullying Graemyn and doing his talking for him. But I know it aches your heart to be shut up inside a dun like this. You could just ride on if you like."

"My thanks, but I'll stay. Just in case . . . oh, ah, er, well, somewhat happens."

"Even if the fighting did break out again, you wouldn't be able to join us with your arm so weak."

"I know. Not the point, you see."

"And what is the point?"

"Oh, er, ah, Jill."

"What? You're daft! Rhodry could cut you into shreds, and I mean no insult, because he could do the same to me—easily."

"No reason it has to come to an open fight, is there?"

"Oh, none at all. There's no reason that the sun has to rise every morning, either, but somehow it always does."

His hands on his hips, Nedd considered Perryn as if he were thinking of drowning him.

"I'll wager I can get Jill away from him," Perryn said.

"Of course. That's why I'm so blasted worried. Ye gods, I've never known a man with your luck for the lasses. How do you do it, anyway?"

"Just smile at them a lot and flatter them. It can't be any different than what most men do."

"Indeed? It's never worked that well for me."

"Oh, you're probably not smiling the right way. You've got to . . . oh, er, let some warmth flow out with it. Easy, once you get the knack."

"Then you'll have to tell me how. But here, if you lay a snare for Jill, you'll likely catch a wolf in it."

"The wolf's going to be following my beloved cousin's orders and riding with him all over Cerrgonney."

"I can't do that. It's dishonorable."

"What about all those times I lied to our uncle for your sake? That was dishonorable, too."

"So it was. Do you want a night in Jill's bed as badly as all this?"

"I've never wanted anything in my life as much as I do her."

"Ah, curse you, you bastard! Well and good, then. Rhodry and I will find somewhere to ride together."

"My thanks, cousin. My most humble thanks."

They had a long wait ahead of them while the speeded courier traveled the two hundred-odd miles to Dun Deverry. Although he could buy a swift passage on one of the many barges that sailed down from the mountain mines on the Camyn Yraen, he would have to ride back. In other parts of the kingdom, of course, there would have been local gwerbrets to hear their appeal, but the various gwerbrets who had once ruled in Cerrgonney warred so incessantly among themselves that King Maryn the Second had abolished the rank in the summer of 962. After a bloody rebellion, his son, Casyl the Second, made the decree of abolishment stick in 984. From then on, the kings personally took the fealty of every Cerrgonney lord and judged the various squabbles among them.

During the wait, Perryn stalked Jill, but from a wary distance, always watching for those rare times when Rhodry left her alone. The moments were hard to catch, because she was doing her best to avoid him. Since she was the first woman who'd ever resisted his strange appeal, he was puzzled, but the resistance only made her the more desirable. Finally his chance came to make his move. At sunset on the tenth day, Graemyn's courier returned with the news that the king would most graciously take this matter under his regal judgment. In fact, a herald and a legal councillor were coming directly behind him on the road.

"Splendid!" Benoic said. "Now, here, Graemyn, you've got to send an honor guard along to meet them."

"I was just about to say exactly that. If one of my noble allies would care to take his warband on this errand, I'd be most grateful."

Perryn shot Nedd a pointed glance. Nedd sighed.

"I'll do it gladly, Your Grace," Nedd said. "I have six men left as well as my silver dagger. Will that be the proper size for the escort?"

"Exactly right. If the warband's too large, Aegwyc might claim intimidation. My thanks, Lord Nedd."

Nedd scowled Perryn's way with a face as sour as if he'd bitten into a Bardek citron. Perryn merely smiled in return.

"Well, my love, we'll be riding out at dawn."

Jill went cold with fear.

"Oh here, what's so wrong?" Rhodry went on. "We won't be in the slightest danger."

"I know." She found it very hard to speak. "It's just that we've been apart so much."

"I know, but I've got plenty of battle loot, and the reward from Tieryn Graemyn, so once this hire's over, we'll settle into a decent inn for a while."

With a nod, she turned away, tempted to tell him the truth, that she was afraid of being left in the same dun as Perryn, but the truth might lead to bloodshed. Although she would have been pleased by the sight of Perryn lying dead, his kin would only cut Rhodry down in turn. He put his arms around her and drew her close.

"I'll be back soon, my love."

"I hope so." She reached up and kissed him. "Rhoddo, oh, Rhoddo, I love you more than I love my life."

As it turned out, the warband left a good hour after dawn, because Nedd and his men could never leave a place simply and easily. When they were finally on their way, Jill stood at the gates for a long time, wishing she could ride with them, feeling the dweomer cold run down her back in warning. When she turned back, she found Perryn watching her. She brushed past him without so much as a "good morrow" and hurried to the safe company of Lady Camma and her serving women. All day she avoided him, and that night, she barred her chamber door from the inside.

On the morrow, however, Perryn caught her alone. Jill had gone down to the stables to tend Sunrise, as she never left him to the slipshod attentions of stableboys. She was just leading him back to his clean stall when Perryn strolled over.

"Good morrow," he said. "I was thinking of going riding. Won't you come with me?"

"I won't, my lord."

"Please don't call me 'lord' all the time."

Then he smiled his warm bewitchment, coiling round her heart. "I love you, Jill."

"I don't give a pig's fart. Leave me alone!"

When she stepped back, she found herself against the stall door. With another smile, he laid his hand on her cheek, a touch that flooded her with warmth. Dweomer, she thought, it has to be dweomer. When he kissed her, she knew in a nightmarish way that she was weakening, that she was sorely tempted to betray Rhodry for this skinny, daft, nondescript man.

"We could ride into the meadow," he whispered. "It's lovely out in the sun."

His words—the very rational act of speaking—broke the spell. She shoved him so hard that he nearly fell and twisted free.

"Leave me alone!" she snarled. "Love me all you want, but I belong to Rhodry."

As soon as she was back in the great hall, her fear turned to hatred, a blind murderous thing because he'd made her feel helpless, her, who could fight with the best of men and fend for herself on the long road. If she could have murdered him and escaped scot-free, she would have. All day her fury grew as she watched him stalk her. Finally, early in the evening she noticed that he'd left the hall. A servant told her that he'd gone to bed because his wound was bothering him. Good, she thought, may it burn like fire! As she sipped a last tankard of ale in the company of the other women, she barely listened to their talk. She would have to do something about Lord Perryn, she decided, and then finally thought of the obvious place to turn for help. Nevyn. Of course! He'd understand, he'd tell her what to do. She got a candle lantern, then went up to her chamber. Using the candle flame, she could contact him, wherever he might be.

She went into the chamber, set the lantern down, then barred the door. As she turned round, she saw Perryn, sitting so quietly in the curve of the wall that she'd never noticed him, her mind full of dweomer thought. When she swore at him, he grinned at her, but it was only an ordinary sort of triumphant smile.

"Get out! Get out right now, or I'll throw you out bodily."

"What a nasty tongue you have, my love."

"Don't you call me that."

"Jill, please." He gave her one of those entrancing smiles. "Let me stay with you tonight."

"I won't." But she heard her voice waver.

Smiling, always smiling, he walked toward her. She felt mead-muddled, her thoughts hard to form, harder yet to voice, and she tried to move away, she staggered. He caught her by the shoulders, then kissed her, his mouth so warm and inviting on hers that she returned the kiss before she could stop herself. Her body was as out of control as a river in full spate. When he wrapped his arms around her and kissed her again, she wondered if she'd ever truly wanted a man before or merely been like a young lass, flirting without even knowing what she's offering.

"You know you want me to stay," he whispered. "I'll leave early. No one has to know or see a thing."

When she forced herself to think of Rhodry, she had just enough strength to shove him away, but he caught her wrists and pulled her back. Although she struggled, her knees seemed to have turned to lead and her arms to water. Still with his ensorceling smile, he pulled her back and kissed her. She felt herself give in with one last muddled thought that Rhodry would never have to know. The pleasure she felt came from her surrender as much as his caresses. She could hardly let go of him long enough for them to get into bed, and once they were lying down, she was trembling. Yet Perryn himself was in no hurry, kissing her, caressing her, taking off their clothing one piece at a time, then caressing her for a while more. When he finally lost his patient reserve, his passion for her was frightening. She could only surrender to her own, let it match his and carry her where it willed.

Afterward, she lay in his arms and clung to him while the candlelight cast a pale, dancing glow on a world gone strange. The stone walls seemed alive, swelling and shrinking rhythmically as if they breathed. The light itself broke up and flared as if it came from a great fire to fall on shards of glass. If Perryn hadn't kissed her again, she would have been frightened, but his lovemaking was too engrossing for her to think of anything else. When they were finished she fell asleep in his arms.

She woke suddenly a few hours later to find him asleep beside her. In the lantern the candle stub guttered in a spill of wax. For a moment she was so confused that she wondered what he was doing there, but an odd bit at a time, she remembered. She nearly wept in shame. How could she have betrayed her Rhodry? How could she have played the slut with a man she hated? She sat up, waking him.

"Get out of here," Jill said. "I never want to see you again."

He merely smiled and reached for her, but the candle went out with a last dancing flare. A red eye in the dark, the wick slowly faded. In the darkness she was freed from his smile, and she got up before he could grab her.

"Get out, or I'll find my sword and cut you in pieces."

Without a word of argument he got up and began searching for his clothes. She leaned against the wall, because the room seemed to be spinning around her. Every little scuffle or rustle Perryn made was unnaturally loud, as if the noise echoed in a chamber ten times the size. Finally he was done.

"I truly do love you," he said meekly. "I'd never just trifle with you once and then desert you."

"Get out! Get out *now!*"

With a dramatic sigh he slipped out, shutting the door behind him. Jill fell onto the bed, clutched her pillow, and sobbed into it until finally she'd cried herself to sleep. When she woke, sunlight poured into her chamber window as thickly as a flood of honey. For a long time she lay there, wondering at light made solid. The dented pewter candle lantern shone like the finest silver, and even the gray stone of the walls seemed to pulse within this splendid light. With some difficulty she dressed, because the patterns of stains and pulled threads on her clothing were as engrossing as fine needlework. When she went to the window, she thought she'd never seen such a fine summer day, the sky so bright it was like sapphire. Down below in the ward stableboys were tending horses, and the sound of hooves on cobbles drifted up like the chime of bells. Her gray gnome appeared on the windowsill.

"Do you know how I've shamed myself?"

It gave her a look of utter incomprehension.

"Good. Oh ye gods, I might be able to live with myself over this, and then again, I might not. Pray that Rhodry never finds out."

Puzzled, the little creature hunkered down and began picking its toes. She realized that its skin, instead of being the uniform gray she'd always thought it, was made up of colors, many different ones in minute specks, that merely blended to gray from a distance. She was so busy examining it that she didn't hear the door opening until it was too late. She spun around to find Perryn, his hands full of wild roses, smiling at her.

"I picked these out in the meadow for you."

Jill was tempted to throw the lot right in his face, but their color caught her. She had to take them, to study them, roses more lovely than she'd ever seen, their petals the color of iridescent blood, always shifting and gleaming, their centers a fiery gold.

"We've got to talk," he said. "And we don't have much time. We've got to make a plan."

"What? Plans for what?"

"Well, we can't be here when Rhodry rides back."

"I'm not going anywhere with you. I never want you in my bed again."

But he smiled, and this time, after their lovemaking, she felt the bewitchment a hundredfold. Even as her thoughts grew muddled, she knew that somehow he'd linked himself to her, that some strange force was flowing through the link. Then he took her shoulders and kissed her, the flowers crushed between them with a waft of scent.

"I love you so much," he said. "I'll never let you go. Come with me, my love, come to the hills with me. That's where we belong. We'll ride free together, all summer long."

Jill had one last coherent thought, that he wasn't daft: he was downright mad. Then he kissed her again, and it was too difficult to think.

Lord Nedd's warband met the king's herald a day and a half's ride from the dun. Rhodry was riding next to his lordship when they crested a small hill and saw, down below them on the road, the royal emissaries, all mounted on white horses with red trappings set with gilded buckles. At the head came the herald, carrying a polished ebony staff with a gold finial strung with satin ribands. Behind him rode an elderly man in the long dark tunic and gray cloak of a legal councillor, with a page on a white pony at the old man's side. Bringing up the rear were four of the king's own

warband, wearing purple cloaks and carrying gold-trimmed scab-
bards. Nedd stared slack-mouthed.

"Ye gods," he said feebly. "I should have made the men put on
clean shirts."

The two parties met in the road. When Nedd announced himself, the herald, a blond young man with a long upper lip made
longer by pride, looked him over for a moment stretched to the
limit of courtesy.

"My humble thanks for the honor, Your Lordship," he said at
last. "It gladdens my heart that Tieryn Graemyn takes our mission
with serious intent and grave heart."

"Well, of course he does," Nedd said. "Why else would he have
sent the wretched message in the first place?"

The herald allowed himself a small, icy smile. Rhodry urged his
horse forward, made a graceful half-bow in the saddle, and addressed himself to the herald.

"O honored voice of the king, we give you greetings and pledge
our very lives as surety for your safe passage."

The herald bowed, visibly relieved to find someone who knew
the ritual salutations, even if that someone was a silver dagger.

"My humble thanks," he said. "And who are you?"

"A man who loves our liege more than his own life."

"Then we shall be honored to ride beside you on our journey to
justice."

"May the king's justice live forever in the land."

Rhodry had to tell Nedd how to dispose his men: his lordship to
ride with the herald, his warband to fall in behind the king's men.
Rhodry himself was planning on taking the humblest place at the
very rear, but as he rode down the line, the councillor caught his
eye and beckoned him to fall in beside him.

"So, Rhodry Maelwaedd," he said. "You're still alive. I'll tell your
honored mother that when next we meet at court."

"I'd be most grateful, good sir, but have I had the honor of meeting you? Wretch that I am, I fear me I've forgotten your name."

"Oh, I doubt if you ever knew it. It's Cunvelyn, and I know your
lady mother fairly well." He considered Rhodry shrewdly for a
moment. "It truly does gladden my heart to see you alive and well.
Doubtless you haven't heard the news from Aberwyn."

"None, good sir, except what scraps the occasional traveler gives
me."

"Ah. Well, your brother's second wife appears to be barren, while his cast-off lady was delivered of a fine healthy son."

Rhodry swore under his breath with a most uncourtly oath, but the councillor merely smiled. It was a moment he'd remember all his life, a moment as unlikely as the sun rising suddenly in a midnight sky, changing night magically into day. When Rhys died, he would be Aberwyn's heir, and he allowed himself to hope for the thing that he'd long since given up hoping for: recall. Aberwyn was such an important rhan that the king himself might well take a hand in bringing home its heir from the dangers of the long road.

"I would advise you to keep yourself as safe as possible," Cunvelyn said. "Are you short up for coin?"

"Not in the least."

"Good. Perhaps then you can avoid hiring out your sword straightaway."

"I will, good sir."

Although Rhodry's heart ached to ask more, he knew that the old man's court training would allow no more answers. For a few moments they rode in silence; then Cunvelyn turned to him.

"Your little daughter's well, by the by. Your lady mother keeps her always by her side."

Rhodry had to think for a moment before he remembered the bastard he'd sired on a common-born lass. How many years ago was it? he wondered. Three, I think.

"That's most kind of my lady mother," he said hurriedly. "And what is she named?"

"Rhodda, to keep her father's memory alive."

"I see. Mother always did know how to badger Rhys."

The councillor allowed himself the briefest of smiles.

Rhodry spent the rest of the journey in a fury of impatience to tell Jill the councillor's news. If he were reading the hints aright, soon they would be back in Eldidd, living in the comfort and splendor he assumed that she wanted. And this time, she would be more than just his mistress. He was no longer a spoiled younger son who needed a strong wife to keep him in rein; he was a man they needed, a man in a position to make demands. He would get her a title, settle land upon her as a dower gift, and marry her, no matter what his mother and the king thought of it.

Late on a splendid sunny day, the herald and his escort rode up to Graemyn's dun. As they clattered through the gates, Rhodry was looking around for Jill. The ward was full of riders, standing in a reasonable excuse for a formation, while the two tieryns stood at the door of the broch to greet their honored guest. In the confusion, he saw no sign of her, nor did she come to meet him while he stabled his horse and Nedd's. Although he was rather hurt, he thought little of it, assuming that Lady Camma had kept her at her side for some reason, until Nedd came hurrying into the stable.

"My lord?" Rhodry said. "Is Jill in the great hall?"

"She's not. Is Perryn in here?"

"He's not. Isn't he with the other noble-born?"

Nedd went a little pale about the mouth.

"Oh, by the black balls of the Lord of Hell!" Nedd snarled. "He wouldn't have—the rotten little weasel—oh, curse him for a pig's ballock!"

"My lord, what is all this?"

"I don't know yet. Come with me."

Rhodry tagged after as Nedd searched the great hall for Camma, finally finding her as she gave orders to the servants about the feast to come. When Nedd caught her arm, she saw Rhodry and gasped, a little puff of breath.

"Oh, by the gods," she said. "But you've got to know, and it best be sooner than later, I suppose. Nedd, if I ever get my hands on your misbegotten wretch of a cousin, I'll beat him black and blue."

"I'll hold him down while you do it. What's he done with Jill?"

Camma laid a maternal hand on Rhodry's arm, her large dark eyes full of sincere apology.

"Rhodry, your Jill's gone. All I can think is that she rode off with Perryn, because he disappeared not an hour after she did. My heart truly aches for you."

Rhodry opened his mouth and shut it again, then clasped his sword hilt so hard that the leather bindings bit into his palm. Nedd had gone dead white.

"Did you know somewhat about this?" Rhodry growled.

"Oh, er, ah, well, not truly. I mean, ye gods! I knew he fancied your lass, but I never thought anything would come of it."

With a great effort of will, Rhodry reminded himself that it would be dishonorable to kill him in front of a lady. Camma gave his arm a little shake.

"Oh, come now," she said. "Who in their right mind would ever have thought that Jill would leave a man like you for one like Perryn?"

His pride was sopped just enough to make him let go the hilt.

"Now, here," Nedd said to the lady. "Did my uncle know of this? I can't believe he'd let Perro do such a dishonorable thing."

"And why do you think your wretched cousin slipped out like a weasel? Benoic chased him with some of his men, but Perryn went off through the forest. They never found a trace of him."

Nedd started to answer, then simply stared at Rhodry. They were in a terrible position, and they both knew it. If Rhodry swore bloody vengeance where the lord could hear, he would be honor-bound to stop Rhodry from riding—if he could. The fear in Nedd's eyes was satisfying to see.

"Now, here!" came Benoic's bellow. "What's all this?"

Hands on hips, the tieryn strode over and shoved himself between them.

"I take it Rhodry's found out the truth?"

"He has," Camma said.

"Humph! Now listen, Nedd, your worm-riddled cousin's in the wrong, and you know it as well as I do. On the other hand, silver dagger, she wasn't legally your wife, so you've no right to kill him. Beat him black and blue, decidedly, but not to kill him. Will you make me a solemn oath that you won't kill or maim him? If you do, you ride out of here with my blessing and a bit of extra coin. If you won't, then you're not leaving at all."

Rhodry glanced around at the hall, filled with armed men.

"Now, now, come to your senses, lad," Benoic went on. "I know cursed well that the first thing a man thinks of in times like this is spilling blood. But ask yourself this: if you cut your Jill's throat, wouldn't you be weeping over her not five minutes later?"

"Well, Your Grace, so I would."

"Good. I feel the shame my nephew laid upon his clan. Do you want her back or not? If not, then I'll pay you a bride price, just as if she'd been your wife. If you do, then swear me that vow, and ride with my aid."

Faced with this scrupulous fairness, Rhodry felt his rage slip away. In its place came a cold realization that nearly made him weep: Jill didn't love him anymore.

"Well, Your Grace, call me a fool if you want, but I do want her back. I've got a thing or two to say to her, and by every god in the Otherlands, I'll find her if I search all summer long."

"This is a bit of luck," Merryc said.

"Well, in a way," Gwin said. "We won't have to bother with the lass, sure enough, but Rhodry's going to be following her, not moving in the direction we want him to."

"Oh, indeed? Think, young one. From everything I've been able to see, this Perryn fellow knows the woods like his mother's tit. What does a man like Rhodry know of woodcraft? When he was a lord, he had foresters and game wardens to worry about such things, and silver daggers stick to the roads." He smiled gently. "I'll talk to Briddyn through the fire about this, but I think we've found the perfect bait to lure our bird down to the seacoast. The only clues he'll find are the ones we throw in his path."

All summer long Salamander, or Ebañy Salomonderiel, to give him his full Elvish name, had been riding through Deverry and tracking his brother down, but he'd done it slowly by a long, winding road, because the People never hurried anywhere, and for all his human blood, he'd been raised among the elves. Right at first, just over the Eldidd border, he'd found a pretty lass who'd taken to more than his songs; he idled in Cernmetyn with her for a pair of pleasant weeks. Then, once he was up in Pyrdon, a noble lord paid him well for entertaining the guests at his daughter's wedding—six merry days of feasting. After that, he wandered through Deverry, always heading north to Cerrgonney, but sometimes lingering in an interesting town for a few days here, a lord's dun for an eightnight there. When he'd scried Rhodry out and found him besieged, he'd put on a good burst of speed, but only until he saw the siege lifted. Then it had seemed that his brother would be perfectly safe for a good long time, so he'd dallied again with another lass who'd been faithfully waiting for him since the summer before. It had seemed terribly dishonorable, after all, to just ride out quickly after she'd waited for such a long time.

And so it was that he was some hundred miles to the east of Graemyn's dun on the sunny afternoon when Rhodry escorted the herald and the councillor there. He'd made an early camp by a stream, early simply because he was tired of riding, and tethered his horses out in a tiny meadow before he went down to the running water to scry. He saw Rhodry trembling as Camma told him her news, and with so much emotion behind it, the vision was strong enough so that he actually could hear—though not with his physical ears—something of what was said. It seemed, indeed, that he stood beside his brother as Benoic took the matter in hand. Then the vision vanished abruptly, banished by his own flood of feeling. He leapt to his feet and swore aloud.

"By the gods!" He shook his head in amazement. "Who ever would have thought it, indeed? I can't believe Jill would desert him, I quite simply can't."

Kneeling again, he stared at the sun-dancing water and thought of Jill. Her image built up slowly, and when it came, it was oddly wavering and blurred. She was sitting in a mountain meadow and watching while Perryn tethered out three horses, including her Sunrise. His first thought was that she was ill, because she sat so quietly, her mouth slack like a half-wit's, yet it was hard to see, because the vision was so misty. With a toss of his head, he dismissed it.

"Now, this looks most dire, peculiar, and puzzling. I think me I'd best try for a better look."

When he called aloud in Elvish for Wildfolk, four gnomes and a sylph materialized in front of him.

"Listen carefully, little brothers. I've got a task for you, and if you do it, I'll sing you a song when you're done. I want to go to sleep, and I want you to stand here and watch for danger. If anyone or any animal comes toward me, pinch me and wake me up."

The gnomes nodded solemnly, while the sylph dipped and hovered in the air. Salamander lay down on his back, crossed his arms over his chest, and slowed his breathing until he felt that his body was melding with the sun-warmed earth. Then he closed his eyes and summoned his body of light. Unlike human dweomer-masters, who use a solid, bluish form shaped like their own body, the elven thought form is much like an enormous flickering flame, yet with an ever-shifting face peering out of the silver light. Once Salamander's form lived steady in his imagination, he transferred his consciousness over to it, at first only pretending to look out of its eyes at his body lying below, then seeing the world in the bluish etheric light. He heard a sound like a sharp click; he was out on the etheric plane, looking down from the flame shape at his sleeping body, guarded by the Wildfolk, and joined to him by a long silver cord.

Slowly he rose up, orienting himself to the valleys, bright red and glowing with the dull auras of plants, and to the stream, which exhaled elemental force in a rushy silver curtain that rose high above the water. Getting entangled in that curtain could tear him apart. Carefully he moved away from it before going higher, then thought of Jill. He felt a certain tug pulling him in her direction, and set off to follow it. For a long ways, impossible to measure on the etheric, he sped over the dull-red forests, broken here and there by brighter patches of farmlands, tended by the peasants whose auras gleamed around them, pale yellows and greens, mostly, in the bluish light of the plane. As he traveled he became more and more aware of Jill's presence, pulling him forward.

Yet in the end he had a guide. He had just flown high over a small stream when he saw one of the Wildfolk coming toward him. In its proper sphere the creature was a beautiful nexus of glowing lines and colors, a deep olive, citrine, and russet with a spark here and there of black, but it was obviously in distress, swelling up twice its size, then shrinking and trembling.

"Here, here, little brother," Salamander thought to it. "What's so wrong?"

For an answer it spun and danced, but dimly he could feel its emotions: rage and despair for something it loved. He remembered then Jill's gray gnome.

"Do you know Jill?"

It bobbed and swelled with joy.

"I'm her friend. Take me to her."

The gnome swept on ahead of him like a hunting dog. As he flew after, dodging round the curves of a hill, Salamander saw far below him the mountain valley, a red-glowing bowl of grass, dotted with the dim silvery auras of the horses, and two human auras, Perryn's a strange green and gray that Salamander had never seen before, Jill's pale gold—but enormous, swelling up around her, sending off billows, then shrinking again but to a size far too large for any human being. When he dropped down toward her, he saw Perryn turn and say something. From the young lord's aura came a light-shot surge, spilling over Jill like an ocean wave. In response, her aura billowed and sucked the magnetic effluent up.

Salamander hovered, trembling with shock. At that moment, Jill looked up, straight at him, and screamed aloud. She had seen his body of light.

"Jill, I'm a friend!"

Yet although she could see him, she couldn't seem to hear his thought. She flung herself to her feet and pointed at him, yelling all the while at Perryn, who merely looked puzzled. Salamander swooped away, following the silver cord as fast as he dared back to his body, which lay safely where he'd left it with the Wildfolk still on guard. He swooped down until he hovered over it, then let himself go. Again the click, and he felt flesh wrap him round, warm and painfully heavy for a moment. He dismissed his body of light, then sat up, slapping his hand thrice on the ground to seal the end of the working. The gnomes looked at him expectantly.

"My thanks, my friends. Come travel along with me for a while. I'll sing you the song I promised, but I've got to make speed. A good friend of mine has been well and truly ensorceled."

In a flood of silver light the dawn climbed up purple mountains and washed over the meadow, a green torrent of grass that swirled in the summer wind. Jill sat on their blankets and watched Perryn, crouched down by the fire, where he was heating water in a little iron kettle. He took his razor, a bit of soap, and a cracked mirror out of his saddlebags and began to shave, as calmly and efficiently as if he were in a bedchamber. Jill had a vague thought of slitting his throat with the long, sharp steel razor, or perhaps her silver dagger, but thinking was very difficult.

"You'd best eat somewhat," he remarked.

"In a bit." Speaking was difficult, too. "I'm not truly hungry."

Idly she looked away, only to see her gray gnome, hunkered down some yards beyond Perryn. She was so glad to see the little creature that she jumped up and ran over, but just as she bent down to pick it up, it snarled, swiped at her with its claws, and vanished. Very slowly she sat down right where she was, wondering why the gnome was so angry at her. It seemed that she should know, but the memory wouldn't return. She picked up a pebble from the grass and stared at it, a constant wavering flow of crystalline structure made visible, until Perryn came to fetch her away.

All that morning they rode through the forest, following long, roundabout trails. Every tree was a living presence, leaning over the trail and reaching down to her with brushy fingers. Some frightened her; others seemed perfectly harmless; still others, a definite few, seemed to be asking her to befriend them with a trembling outreach of leafy hands. When she looked away from the trail, the forest changed into a maze of solid walls, broken only by shafts of sunlight as heavy as stone. Although at times Jill considered simply riding away from Perryn, she was hopelessly lost. Every now and then, she thought of Rhodry and wondered if he was trying to follow them. She doubted that he'd believe her when she told him that she hadn't ridden away of her own free will—if, indeed, he ever caught them. How could he find her, when the whole world had changed?

Every color, even the somber gray of the rocks, seemed as bright and glowing as a jewel. Whenever they came to a clearing or a mountain meadow, the sun poured over her like water; she could swear that she felt it dripping and running down her arms. The sky was a solid dome of lapis lazuli, and for the first time in her life she truly believed that the gods traveled across the sky the way we travel across the earth, just because the color truly did seem fit for divinities. Under the heavy burden of all this beauty, she felt as if she were reeling in her saddle, and at times tears ran down her face, just from the loveliness. Once as they rode through a meadow, a pair of larks broke cover and flew, singing their heart-breaking trill as they went up and up into the azure, crystalline sky, their wings rushing and beating in a tiny thunder. Jill saw then that whatever else might happen, that moment, that beating of wings, that stripe of sound would all endure eternally, as indeed would every moment, a clear note in the unfolding music of the universe. When she tried to tell Perryn of the insight, he only stared at her and told her she was daft. She laughed, agreeing with him.

That afternoon, they camped early near a good-sized stream. Perryn took a line and hook from his gear, remarked that he was after fish, and wandered away upstream. For a long time Jill lay on the bank and stared into the water, watching the Wildfolk in the eddies, a white foam of little faces, traces of sleek bodies, little voices and lives, melding and blending into each other. It seemed that there was something that they wanted of her, and finally she stripped off her clothes and joined them. Giggling, laughing, she ducked and splashed in the water with the undines, tried to catch them as they swam away from her, and for the first time she heard them clearly, giggling in return, calling out her name, Jill, Jill, Jill, over and over again. Then suddenly they shrieked and disappeared. Jill turned in the water and looked up to see Perryn, standing on the bank with a string of three trout in one hand. Her heart sank, just as when a pupil looks up from a game to find her tutor glaring with a piece of unfinished work in his hand.

Yet when she clambered up onto the bank, he was far from angry with her, catching her, kissing her, wrapping her round with his desire until she wanted him, too, and lay down willingly with him in the grass. Afterward, he got up, dressed, and methodically began cleaning the fish, but she lay naked in the soft grass and tried to remember the name of the man she once had loved and who, or so she suspected, still loved her. Although she could see his face in her mind, her memory refused to give up his name. Puzzling over it, she got up and dressed, then chanced to look down at the stream. The Wildfolk were back, staring at her reproachfully.

"Rhodry, Jill," they whispered. "How could you have forgotten your Rhodry?"

She doubled over and wept, sobbing aloud. When Perryn came rushing to comfort her, she shoved him away so hard that he tripped and fell. Like a frightened animal she ran, racing through the long grass of the clearing, plunging into the forest, only to catch an ankle on a root and sprawl headlong. For a moment she lay there panting, seeing how dark the trees were, how menacingly they reached down to grab her. Now they looked like a line of armed guards, raising weapons high. When he came to fetch her back, she went without arguing.

That evening he built a fire and skewered the trout on green sticks to roast them. Jill ate a few bites, but the food seemed to stick in her mouth, the fish suddenly as cloying as pure honey. Perryn, however, wolfed down his share as if he were starving, then fell asleep by the fire. She watched him for a long time. Although it would have been ridiculously easy to kill him, the memory of the forest stopped her. If he died, she would be alone, trapped out there, starving, wandering in circles, growing more and more panicked—with the last of her will she wrenched her mind away from the thoughts that were threatening to turn her hysterical. Shaking, suddenly cold, she stared into the fire, where the spirits were forming and falling in the flames, dancing along the wood that this pair of humans had so thoughtfully provided. Jill could almost hear them talking in the hiss and crackle. Then a log burned through and fell with a shower of golden sparks. In the rushy dance of flame, a proper face appeared, golden and shifting. When it spoke, it was in a true voice, and one with authority.

"What is this, child? What's so wrong?"

"Wrong?" She could barely stammer. "Is it?"

For a moment the face regarded her; then it was gone. Somewhat bewildered, unable to think, Jill lay down next to Perryn and fell asleep.

As formless as water, the days slipped into one another. Jill couldn't count them; she'd lost the very idea of counting, as if the part of her mind that dealt with things like nights and coins had fallen out of her saddlebags and gotten lost in the grass. Whenever he spoke to her, it was hard to answer, because her words became lost in the splendor of the forest. Fortunately he rarely spoke, apparently contented with her silent presence near him. At night, when they made camp, he was an eager lover, wanting her in their blankets often before they'd eaten, then bringing her dinner like a page as she lay drowsily by the fire. His slow hesitance, his shuffling walk, his vague smiles and stumbling words—all were gone. He was all laughter and calm efficiency, all strength and life as he strode through the wild country. She supposed that his daft mousiness was simply a shield he put up when he was forced to live in the lands of men.

She was proven right when they rode into a village to buy food at the open market. Perryn became his old self, looking aimlessly this way and that, stumbling through every simple sentence as he haggled for cheese and peaches, for loaves of bread from the baker. Since Jill could speak no more clearly than he could, she was of no help to him. Once she saw a farmer's wife watching them in puzzlement, as if she were wondering how a pair of half-wits like they could survive on the road.

With the shopping done, they went to a tiny tavern for ale. After nothing but spring water to drink, the ale tasted so good that Jill savored every sip. Although the little room had dirty straw on the floor, an unswept hearth, and battered tables, she was happy there. It was good to see other people, her own kind, good to listen to human voices instead of the endless wind through the forest and the chatter of streams. A balding stout fellow, wearing the checked brigga of a merchant, gave her a friendly smile.

"Here, lass," he said. "Why do you carry a silver dagger?"

"Oh, ah, er, well," Jill said. "My father was a silver dagger, you see. It's a reminder of him."

"A pious gesture, truly."

Jill had the sudden startling experience of hearing him think: A pretty lass, but stupid; ah well, wits don't matter in a lass. The thought was as clear in her mind as if he'd spoken aloud, but she decided that she was only deluding herself. When it was time to leave the tavern, she wept, simply because they were going back to the lonely wilderness.

That afternoon they rode through low rolling hills, where the pine forest thinned, and farms appeared in sheltered valleys. Jill had no idea of where they were; all she knew was that the sun rose in the east and set in the west. They made camp, however, in a place Perryn knew well, or so he said, a tiny vale, along a stream, and bordered with white birches. Before he lit the fire, he gave Jill a kiss.

"Let's lie down," he said.

All at once, the thought of making love with him filled her with revulsion. When she shoved him away, he caught her by the shoulders and pulled her to him. Although she tried to wrestle free, his superior strength told against her. He grabbed her, lifted her, and laid her struggling on the ground. She fought against him, but even as she did, she knew that she was slowly, inexorably giving in to him, fighting with only half her strength, letting him steal a kiss here and there, then a caress, then finally surrendering, letting him take her, press her down, and turn her world to a fire of pleasure. When he lay down next to her, he started to speak, then fell asleep in openmouthed exhaustion.

Jill lay next to him and watched the sunset coming through the branches like a shower of gold coins. The white birches glowed with an inner fire, as if they were watching them and blessing them in silent presences. She could hear the stream running nearby in little voices, the aimless chatter of the Wildfolk. Just as the sunset was fading into twilight, Perryn sat up with a yawn and a gasp. She saw dark circles under his eyes, two livid pools of shadow. For a moment he stared at her as if he hardly knew where they were.

"Are you all right?" Jill said.

"Oh, er, well, just tired."

Yet as the evening wore on, she realized that things went far beyond his being tired. When they ate, he gobbled the food, then fell asleep again. She sat by the fire and watched the birches glowing, bending close, it seemed, to study this pair of intruders in the grove. For one moment she thought she saw someone standing among the trees and watching her, but when she got up for a closer look, the shadowy form disappeared. In a bit Perryn woke again and stumbled over to the fire. A leap of flame washed his face with light and seemed to cover it with blood; his eyes seemed great hollow rents in a mask. Jill cried out at the sight.

"What's wrong?" he said.

Yet she had no words to tell him what she instinctively knew, that their afternoon's lovemaking had driven them to a crisis point, just as when a warrior rides a charge, thinking of naught but the flash of steel around him, only to find himself behind the enemy line, cut off and alone when it's too late to ride back.

When he left Graemyn's dun, Rhodry had no idea of which way to ride. For the first day, he went west, but at sunset the gray gnome appeared at his camp and threw itself into his arms to cling to him like a frightened child.

"There you are! Here, my friend, where's Jill?"

The gnome considered, pointed east, then disappeared. I've wasted a whole blasted day, he thought. Then, even in the midst of his despair, he felt that strange sensation of being watched.

For three days more, he rode east. He felt more like a storm than a man, his rage and desperation mingling to drive his mind this way and that, tearing his reason to shreds as he swept down the forest road. At times, he wanted to find her only to slit her throat; at others, he swore to himself that if only he could have her back, he would never ask a single question about what she'd done with Perryn. Gradually he felt more hopelessness than rage. Perryn could have taken her any way at all, slipping deep into the forest where he'd never find them. His one hope was the gnome, who came to him at odd moments. Always it pointed east, and it was filled with fury, gnashing its teeth and clutching its head at any mention of Perryn. Sooner or later, or so Rhodry hoped, it would lead him back to Jill.

Late on a day when white clouds piled in the sky and threatened rain, Rhodry was riding along a narrow track when he came to a clearing. Beside the road was a small wooden round house with two oaks growing in front of the door. He dismounted, led his horse over, and called out a halloo. In a few moments an aged man with the shaved head and golden torc of a priest of Bel came out.

"Good morrow, Your Holiness," Rhodry said.

"May the gods bless you, lad. What troubles your heart so badly?"

"Oh, by the hells, do I look as wretched as that?"

The priest merely smiled, his dark eyes nearly lost in wrinkled folds of pouched eyelids. He was as thin as a stick, his ragged tunic hanging loose, his fingers like gnarled twigs.

"I'm looking for someone, you see," Rhodry went on. "And I've about given up hope of ever finding her. A blond lass, beautiful, but she always dresses like a lad, and she carries a silver dagger. She'd be riding with a skinny red-haired fellow."

"Your wife left you for another man?"

"Well, she did, but how did you know?"

"It's a common enough tale, lad, though I've no doubt it pains you as if you were the first man ever deserted by a woman." He sighed with a shake of his head. "I haven't seen her, but come in and ask the gods to help you."

More to please the lonely old hermit than in any real hope of getting an omen, Rhodry followed him into the dim, musty-smelling shrine, which took up half the round house. On the flat side stood the stone altar, covered with a rough linen cloth to hide the bloodstains from the sacrifices. Behind it rose a massive statue of Bel, carved from a tree trunk, the body roughly shaped, the arms distinguished by mere cuts in the wood and the tunic indicated only by scratches. The face, however, was beautifully modeled, large eyes staring out as if they saw, the mouth so mobile it seemed that it would speak. Rhodry made a formal bow to the king of the world, then knelt before him while the priest stood to one side. In the shadowy light it seemed that the god's eyes turned his worshipper's way.

"O most holy lord, where's my Jill? Will I ever see her again?"

For a moment silence lay thick in the temple; then the priest spoke in a hollow, booming voice utterly unlike his normal tone.

"She rides down dark roads. Judge her not harshly when you meet again. One who holds no fealty to me holds her in thrall."

Rhodry felt a cold shudder of awe laced with fear. The god's eyes considered him, and the voice spoke again.

"You have a strange Wyrd, man from Eldidd, you who are not truly a man like other men. Someday you'll die serving the kingdom, but it's not the death you would ever have dreamt for yourself. Men will remember your name down the long years, though your blood run over rock and be gone. Truly, they'll remember it twice over, for twice over will you die."

Suddenly the priest threw up his hands and clapped them together hard. Dazed, Rhodry looked around. The statue was only a piece of wood, cleverly carved. The god had gone.

All that day, while he traveled fast along, Rhodry puzzled over the omen. What did it mean, that Jill rode down dark roads? He desperately wanted it to mean that Perryn had somehow forced her to come with him rather than her going willingly, but it was hard to convince himself of that, because Jill could have slain the lord easily if he had tried violence. Still, he clung to the first bit of hope he had that she still loved him. His heart was so torn for love of and fear for her that he never remembered the rest of the omen until years later, that, contrary to all nature and all sense, he would die twice over.

On the morrow, the meaning of the part of the omen that dealt with Jill came clearer when he reached a small village. In the tiny tavern he got his first hot meal and tankard of ale in days. As he was eating mutton stew by the unswept hearth, the tavernman strolled over to gossip.

"You're the second silver dagger we've seen in here lately," he said. "Or, well, I don't suppose this lass was truly a silver dagger."

"A blond lass?" Rhodry's heart was pounding even as he spoke casually. "Beautiful, but dressed like a lad?"

"Just that! Do you know her?"

"I do. How long ago were she and her red-haired lad in here? I'd like to see Jill and Perryn again."

The tavernman considered, scratching his bald spot.

"Not more than four nights ago, I'd say. Friends of yours, are they? Neither of them are much for words, I must say."

"Oh, Perryn never says much, truly." Rhodry tried to sound cheerfully friendly. "But usually his lass is good for a bit of hatter."

"Indeed? Then she must be ill or suchlike, because it was hard for her to say two words together. One of those thick-headed lasses, think I, all pretty face with nothing between her two ears."

"Here, I hope she wasn't ill. She's usually as bright as a lark and twice as merry."

The tavernman considered a long moment.

"Well, maybe she and that man of hers had a bit of a scrap. From the way she looked at him, I'd say he beats her a good bit. Fair terrified, she looked."

Rhodry's hand tightened on the tankard so hard that his knuckles went white. Riding down dark roads, he thought, I see.

"But be that as it may, lad, they went south when they left here. She said she was riding south, to find her grandfather."

For a moment Rhodry was puzzled. Nevyn! he thought. Of course that's how she'd describe him.

"Well and good, then, and my thanks." He tossed the man a piece of Benoic's silver.

Leaving the tankard unfinished, Rhodry rode out fast, heading for the crossroads and the track that would take him south.

The tavernman watched, rubbing Rhodry's coin, until the silver dagger was out of sight. All at once he felt both guilty and frightened. Why had he lied like that, and all for the couple of coins that the strange fellow had given him? He hated to lie. Dimly he remembered arguing with the fellow, but here, after all he'd said, he'd gone and done it. He wished he had a horse, so that he could ride after the silver dagger and tell him the truth. He shook himself and looked up. The village idiot, poor old Marro, was shuffling along the street. The tavernman flung him Rhodry's coin.

"Here, lad, take that home to your mother, and tell her I said she's to buy you cloth for a new shirt."

Grinning from ear to ear, Marro ran off. The tavernman went back to his customers.

"South?" Salamander said aloud. "How by every boil on the Lord of Hell's balls did Rhodry know to turn south?"

The Wildfolk clustered around his campfire seemed to be pondering the question.

"My apologies, little brothers. Just a rhetorical question."

Stretching, Salamander got up and frowned at the night sky while he wished he'd scried Rhodry out earlier. Since he was not much more than an apprentice at dweomer, it was difficult for him to scry without a focus of some sort and impossible when he was occupied with something else, such as riding horseback. As he thought about it, he supposed that Rhodry was riding south out of a simple desperation that had brought him a silver dagger's luck. Without dweomer, he himself would never have been able to track Jill down, because that strange man of hers knew the woods as well as a wild deer did. As it was, of course, he knew exactly where they were, just ten miles to the northeast of him, so that, indeed, Rhodry was to the north of them and on the right road by heading south. The question was, how did Rhodry know it?

"Tomorrow, little brothers, tomorrow we track this bear to his den."

In unease the Wildfolk rustled around him, shoving and pinching each other, opening their mouths in gaping expressions of despair and hatred. Salamander shuddered in honest fear. For all he knew, the man that had stolen Jill was a dweomermaster of great power, and he was riding to his doom.

"You know, I suppose I really should contact Nevyn and tell him about all this."

The Wildfolk all nodded a vigorous yes.

"But on the other hand, suppose I do, and he tells me that I should leave this nasty mess strictly alone. How then could I redeem myself for my dilatory ways this summer? I think me I'd best just continue on."

The Wildfolk threw their hands in the air, stuck out their tongues at him, and disappeared in a wave of pure disgust.

In the morning, the dark circles under Perryn's eyes looked as purple as fresh bruises against his unnaturally pale skin. His red hair no longer flamed; rather it was as dull and matted as the fur of a sick cat. He worked slowly, taking things out of his saddlebags, staring at them for a moment, then putting them back while Jill sat nearby and watched him.

"You truly do look ill," she said.

"Just tired."

She wondered why she cared if he were ill or not, but in truth, she was coming to see him as much a victim of his strange powers as she was. The thought came to her only intermittently, however; thoughts of any sort were rare these days. The pieces of gear in Perryn's hands seemed to be changing size constantly, sometimes swelling, sometimes shrinking, and they had no edges in any proper sense, just lines of shimmering force that marked where they met the air. Finally he pulled out a plain rod of iron, about a finger thick, set in a wooden handle.

"Thank every god," he said. "Here I thought I'd lost it."

"What is it?"

"A rambling scribe. Never tell anyone I've got one, will you? You can get hanged for carrying one in Cerrgonney."

None of this made any sense at all. She forced herself to pick it apart, a little at a time.

"We're still in Cerrgonney?" she asked at last.

"We are, but in the southern part. Nearly to Gwaentaer."

"Oh. And what's that thing for?"

"Changing a horse's brand."

"And why will they hang you for having one?"

"Because only a horse thief would carry one."

"Then why are you carrying one?"

"Because I'm a horse thief."

Jill stared openmouthed at him.

"Where do you think I get the coin we've been spending?" He

was grinning in amusement. "I take a horse from some noble lord, sell it to one of the men I know, and well, there we are."

Somewhere, deep in her mind, Jill remembered that thievery was a wrong thing. She thought about it while she watched him repack the saddlebags. Thieving was wrong, and being a horse thief was the worst of all. If you took a man's horse, he could die out in the wilderness. Da always said so. Da was always right.

"You shouldn't take horses," she said.

"Oh, I only take them from men who can afford the loss."

"It's still wrong."

"Why? I need them, and they don't."

Although she knew that there was a counter to this argument, she couldn't remember it. She leaned back and watched the sylphs playing in the light breeze, winged forms of brilliant crystal, darting and dodging after each other in long swoops and glides.

"I'll be leaving you here later," Perryn said in a moment. "We're low on coin, and I've got to take a horse."

"You will come back, won't you?" Suddenly she was terrified, sure that she would be hopelessly lost without him. "You won't just leave me here?"

"What? Of course not. I love you more than I love my life. I'll never leave you."

He drew her into his arms and kissed her, then held her close. She was unsure of how long they sat together in the warm sun, but when he let her go, the sun was close to zenith. She wandered over the stream and lay down to watch the Wildfolk sporting there until she fell asleep.

Late that same afternoon, Rhodry came to Leryn, one of the biggest towns in Cerrgonney with about five hundred houses huddled behind a low stone wall on the banks of the Camyn Yraen. Since Leryn was an important port for the river barges that brought the mountain iron down into Deverry, he was planning on buying a passage downriver for a ways to save himself some time and to give himself and his horse a much-needed rest. First, though, he went to the market square and asked around about Jill and Perryn. Quite a few of the locals knew the eccentric Lord Perryn well.

"He's daft," said the cheese seller. "And if that lass is riding with the likes of him, she's even dafter than he."

"A bit more than daft he is," snorted the blacksmith. "I've wondered many a time where he gets all those horses."

"Ah, he's noble-born," chimed in the cloth merchant. "The noble-born have horses to spare, they do. But I haven't seen him in many a long week now, silver dagger, and I've never seen a lass like you described."

"No more have I," said the cheese seller. "She sounds a bit of a hard case, she does."

As he went back to the cheap tavern he'd marked earlier, Rhodry was wondering if Jill and Perryn had taken a different road south. If so, he'd have to abandon his plans for the river, in case he passed them by. As he was stabling his horse, a fellow came out to join him, a rather nondescript man with the bent back of a wandering peddler.

"You the silver dagger who was asking for Lord Perryn?"

"I am, and what's it to you?"

"Naught, but I might have a bit of information for you for the right price."

Rhodry took two silver pieces from his pouch and held them between his fingers. The peddler grinned.

"I came up this way from the southeast. I stayed one night in a little village inn, oh, some thirty miles from here, it was. I was trying to get my sleep about dawn that night when I heard someone yelling out in the stable yard. So I sticks my head out the window, and I see our Perryn arguing with this blond lass. Seems like she was leaving him, and he was yelling at her not to go."

Rhodry handed over the first silver.

" 'I'm going to find no one,' she says," the peddler went on. "Seemed like a cursed strange thing to say, so it's stuck in my mind, like."

"So it would. Did she say where 'nev yn' was?"

"Not truly. But she did say to his lordship that if he tried to follow her to Cerrmor, she'd take his balls off with her silver dagger."

With a laugh, Rhodry handed him the second coin, then dug out a third for good measure.

"My thanks, peddler, and it gladdens my wretched heart that you lost that hour's sleep."

When Rhodry left the stable, Merryc laughed quietly under his breath. It was a good jest, to make the silver dagger pay for the false rumors that were going to mean his doom.

Jill woke suddenly at the sound of horses coming. She sat up, wondering why she hadn't tried to escape before Perryn returned. Now it was too late. She stood up, very slowly, because the ground seemed unsteady under her feet. As she walked back to camp, the grass swelled and billowed, as if she trod on a huge feather mattress.

"Jill! Fear not! Rescue is at hand, though truly, as a shining avenger one could want better than I."

Startled, she spun around and stared openmouthed at the man dismounting from his horse on the other side of the clearing. For a moment she thought he was Rhodry, but the voice and the pale hair were all wrong. Then she remembered him.

"Salamander! Oh ye gods!"

Suddenly she was weeping, doubling over as she sobbed, throwing herself from side to side until he ran over and grabbed her tight.

"Whist, whist, little one. All's well, more or less, anyway. You've been ensorceled, but it's over now."

The tears stopped, and she looked up at him.

"It was true, then? He has the dweomer?"

"I'm not so sure of that, but you were ensorceled well and truly. Where is he?"

"Off stealing a horse from someone."

"And the horse dung, too, no doubt. This lad sounds stranger and stranger."

"You might well say that and twice. Please, we've got to get away before he gets back."

"Not that, because I've got a thing or two to say to him."

"But he's dweomer!"

Salamander smiled lazily.

"It is time for all truths to be known. So am I."

She pulled away, staring at him.

"How else did I know you'd been ensorceled, and how else would I have found you? Now come along. Let's get your gear on your horse. I want to curse this fellow to the three hells, and then we've got to be on our way. Rhodry's got a long head start on us."

At the mention of Rhodry's name, she began to sob again. Salamander pulled her close into his arms.

"Na, na, na, little one. Remember you're a warrior's daughter. There'll be time enough for tears later, when we're well away from here. We'll find your Rhodry for you."

"Oh ye gods, I don't know if your brother will even want me back."

"My . . . here! How did you find out?"

The urgency in his voice stopped her tears.

"I . . . well, I had a true dream. I saw your father."

"Gods! If you have that kind of power, and this fellow still . . . well, he may be a bit more powerful than I thought, but cursed if I'll run until I get a look at him. Let me saddle your horse for you, and you tell me the tale."

As best she could, Jill told him about Perryn and the events of the last few days, but it was difficult for her to find words to put things in any sort of order, or indeed to remember exactly how long she'd been traveling with Perryn. At times it seemed a few years, at others months. She was shocked when Salamander told her that it had been at most a fortnight. While he listened, he grew angry, until finally he cut short one last stumbling sentence with a wave of his hand.

"I've heard enough, little one. This ugly bastard should be flogged and hanged, if you ask me. I wonder if I can get him to a lord's justice."

"Not here. All the lords are his kin."

"And who will believe me when I come to them talking of dweomer, besides? Well, there's other kinds of justice in the kingdom."

When she looked at him, she saw his anger like ghostly flames burning over his face and looked away again. Yet the vision jogged her memory.

"Was it you I saw a while back? I saw an elf all covered with silver fire in the sky."

"It was, true enough. But you were seeing only a well . . . call it an image of me."

She nodded, the thought and the memory slipping away again. She wondered why he was so angry with Perryn, but it seemed that somehow she should know the answer.

Salamander was just finishing tying her bedroll behind the saddle when he paused, cocking his head to listen. It was several minutes before she heard the sound of hoofbeats, three horses coming fast. Ducking and dodging among the trees, Perryn rode up with two chestnut colts following him along. As Salamander walked to meet him, Perryn dismounted and ran the last few yards.

"Who are you?" Perryn shouted. "Jill, what are you doing?"

Although she was shaking too hard to speak, her saddled and loaded horse was an obvious answer. When Perryn started to run to her, Salamander stepped in between. Perryn swung at him flat-handed. All at once Wildfolk swarmed into existence and mobbed him, a good hundred of them biting pinching kicking punching as they fell upon him like dogs on a tossed bone. Perryn screamed and yelped, hitting blindly at an enemy he couldn't see, and finally went down under them, a tossing, heaving mound.

"Enough!" Salamander yelled.

The Wildfolk disappeared, leaving Perryn trembling and whimpering on the ground.

"That's better, dog," Salamander snarled. "A fine scion of the Wolf clan are you, a horse thief and a wife stealer both!"

He flung up one hand and chanted a long string of Elvish words under his breath. Suddenly Jill saw a green-and-gray glow streaming around Perryn—no, it was emanating from him in a cloud of light. From it stretched long smoky tendrils that tangled her round. She suddenly realized that she too stood in a similar cloud, but that hers was pale gold.

"Do you see that, *Lord* Perryn? Do you see what you've been doing?"

Perryn looked from her to himself and back to Salamander, then suddenly moaned and hid his eyes with his hands. The gerthddyn said a few more Elvish words, then snapped his fingers. A golden sword made of what seemed to be solid light appeared in his hand. He swept it back and forth, slashing at every tendril that bound her to Perryn. The light lines snapped like cut tether ropes and slapped back to him. Perryn screamed, but she felt her mind and her will come back to her, and with them, a revulsion, a burning hatred for this man who'd broken her like a wild horse. When Salamander chanted again, the glowing clouds and the sword vanished. Perryn raised his head.

"Don't look at me that way, my love," he whispered. "Oh, by Kerun himself, you're not going to leave me, are you?"

"Of course I am, you bastard! I never want to see you again in my god-cursed life."

"Jill, Jill, I beg you, don't go! I love you!"

"Love?" She felt her hatred burning in her mouth. "I spit on your idea of love!"

When Perryn began to weep, the sound was beautiful to her. Salamander looked as if he was thinking of kicking him, then restrained himself.

"Listen, you!" he snarled. "Out of sheer pity I'll tell you one thing: you've got to stop stealing women and horses this way, or it'll kill you. Do you hear me?"

Slowly Perryn got to his feet to face the gerthddyn, and his face worked as if he was desperately trying to summon some dignity.

"I don't know who you are," he whispered. "But I don't have to stay here and have you pour vinegar in my wounds. I can't stop you from taking Jill away, so go. You hear me! Get out!" His voice rose to a shriek. "Go away! Both of you!"

Then he fell sobbing to his knees again.

"Very well." Salamander turned to Jill. "Let us leave this whimpering dolt to whatever justice the gods have in store for him."

"Gladly."

In a swirl of joyous Wildfolk, they mounted their horses. A big black gnome with purple splotches threw the lead rope of the pack horse up to Salamander, then disappeared as they rode away. Jill glanced back once to see Perryn stretched out on the grass, still weeping in a sea of swelling emerald, with his gray nuzzling his shoulder in concern. Nothing had ever pleased her as much as his pain.

For about a mile they rode in silence, until they came free of the trees to one of the muddy tracks that passed for a Cerrgonney road. There Salamander paused his horse, waved at her to do the same, and turned in his saddle to look her over in sincere concern. She could only stare blankly back at him.

"How do you feel, Jill?"

"Exhausted."

"No doubt, but you'll get your strength back in a bit."

"Good. Will the world ever hold still again?"

"What? What's it doing at the moment?"

"Well, everything's all . . . not hazy, exactly, but nothing will hold still, and these colors . . . everything's so bright and glowy." She hesitated, struggling with the unfamiliar task of forming sentences. "Nothing has edges, you see. It all sparkles and runs together. And there's no Time anymore. Wait, that's not right. But it is."

"Oh ye gods! What did that lout do to you?"

"I don't know."

"My apologies, just a rhetorical question. Jill, this is blasted serious."

"I could figure that out myself, my thanks. Will I ever see the world like it really is again?"

"You mean, will you ever see it as you used to, because as for the world as it really is, my turtledove, that's what you're seeing right now. Before, you've only seen the dull, dead, dark, and deceiving surface, as most people do."

"But here! These colors, and the way everything moves—"

"Are real enough. But, truly, most inconvenient withal. The gods are kind, turtledove. They let most men see only what they need to see, and hide the beauty away. If they didn't, we'd all starve, because even a simple act like picking an apple from a tree would be a momentous and ominous event."

"I can't believe that."

"No need for you to believe it, actually. Belief has no bearing whatsoever on your current and most dire condition. Belief is an illusion, and truly, all that men see is illusion as well, because the universe is naught but a rushy net of pure power."

"That can't be true."

"It is, but this is no time for us to argue recondite matters like a pair of Bardek sages. That little round-ear bastard has hurt you worse than I feared, Jill." He paused for a long, troubled silence. "I'm not truly sure what to do about this. Fortunately, our esteemed Nevyn will."

"Salamander, you're babbling! What did Perryn do to me?"

"Well, look, you saw those lines of light, didn't you? What he was doing was pouring life force into you, more than you could possibly use or handle. Look, every time you two lay down together, he gave off a tremendous amount of life force. It's not solid like water but it's more solid than a thought, and it can be transferred back and forth. Normally, whenever a man and woman are together, they each give some out and get some back, all in balance. Now, I doubt me if this truly makes sense to you."

"Oh, but it does." Her disarranged mind was casting up images, of Sarcyn and Alastyr, of the dark dweomer that had touched and tainted her life the summer before. For a moment she nearly vomited. When she spoke again, it was only in a whisper. "Go on. I have to know."

"Well, then, somewhat's wrong with Perryn. He was pouring the force out like mead at a lord's feast, more than you could ever possibly replace in the ordinary course of things. And all that extra power was running free in your mind, free to be used in any way you wished, but since, alas, you had no idea of what to wish for, or indeed that it was even there, then it took the first channel it found to run in, like water again, if we may expand and polish our image, my turtledove, that escapes from a river only to follow a ditch. You can't lie and say you've no dweomer talent, you know."

"I don't care! I never wanted to have anything of the sort."

"Oh, of course not, you lackwit! That's not what I'm saying. Listen, these are dark and dangerous matters indeed, and the source of many a strange thing. No one who studies the dweomer of Light would fool with them carelessly, the way Perryn seems to have done."

"Are you telling me he follows the dark path?"

"I'm not, because that poor, weak, bumbling idiot obviously could do naught of the sort. I know not what Lord Perryn may be, my little robin, but I do know that we've got to get you far, far away from him. Let's ride. We'll reach some safe spot, and then I'll see what Nevyn thinks of all this."

After Jill rode away, Perryn had just enough strength to unsaddle his horse and send him out to graze. He lay down on his blankets and fell asleep, waking for a few moments at sunset, then sleeping the night away. When he woke in the morning, he rolled over, automatically reaching for Jill, and wept when he remembered that she was gone.

"How could you leave me? I loved you so much."

He forced himself to stop crying, then sat up and looked around the camp. In spite of his long sleep, he was still tired, his body aching as if he'd been in a fight. When he remembered the man who'd taken her away, he turned cold all over. Dweomer. What else would have shown him that peculiar vision of clouds of light and golden swords? *See what you've been doing, Lord Perryn.* But he'd done nothing at all, only loved her. What did ropes of mystic light have to do with love? And she'd said that she hated him. He shook his head, refusing to cry again.

At last he forced himself up and began packing his gear. He'd already placed himself in danger by staying so long; the lord who once had owned these colts might come looking for them. As he worked, he wondered which way to ride. He couldn't go back to Nedd, not for a long time, not with Benoic's wrath waiting for him. You're twice a dolt, he told himself, first taking another man's woman—and then losing her. Benoic would heap scorn on him for years over this, he knew. After the splendor of having had someone to love, of having had someone who had loved him—he refused to believe that Jill had never loved him—his life stretched ahead like a bleak, foggy road. It seemed to take him forever to leave the spot. He would just get some small task done, like rolling up his blankets, when something would make him think of Jill, and he would weep again. The dapple gray stayed close to him, nuzzling his shoulder or nudging him in the back as if to say that he should cheer up.

"At least you love me, don't you?" Perryn whispered. "But a horse is a wretchedly easy thing to please."

Finally he was ready to set out, with his gray saddled and his pack horse and the two new colts on lead ropes. He mounted, then merely sat in the saddle for a long time and stared at the place that would hold his last memories of Jill. Where to go next? The question seemed insuperable. At last, when the gray was beginning to dance in irritable restlessness under him, he turned back northwest. Not far away was the town of Leryn, where he knew a dishonest trader who would take the colts and ask no questions. All that day he rode slowly, and the tears came and went of their own accord.

Rhodry might have taken a barge passage immediately if it hadn't been for the gray gnome, who came to him early on the same morning that Salamander caught up with Jill. The little creature was ecstatic, dancing around and grinning so broadly that it exposed all its long pointed teeth.

"Well, little brother, I take it you know that Jill's left Perryn."

The gnome nodded, then pointed to the southeast.

"Is that where Jill is?"

The gnome shook its head no, then pantomimed Perryn's graceless walk.

"Oho! How far away is our dear Lord Perryn?"

The gnome shrugged and waved its hands as if to say not very far at all. Rhodry debated for a long while. On the one hand, he wanted to be after Jill; on the other, his desire for revenge was like a lust. Finally the vengeance won.

"Well and good, little brother. I'll saddle up my horse, and you lead me to him."

The gnome grinned and jigged, pointing always off to the south and east.

It was late in the afternoon when Rhodry came to a scrappy little village, a huddle of houses at the top of a hill without even a proper wall around it. Although there was no tavern, the blacksmith's wife kept a few barrels of ale in her kitchen for thirsty travelers, but she refused to have a silver dagger in her house. She did, however, let him buy a tankard and drink it out in the muddy yard, where chickens scratched near a small sty that held a pair of half-grown pigs. The woman, a stout sort with wispy gray hair, set her hands on her hips and glared at him the whole time as if she thought he would steal the tankard. When he was done, Rhodry handed it back with an exaggerated bow.

"My thanks, fair lady. I don't suppose you get many travelers through here."

"Why do you want to know?"

"I'm looking for a friend of mine, that's all, a tall, skinny fellow with red hair and—"

"You'd best go over to the baker's then. A fellow like that bought a tankard from me not half an hour ago, and he said he needed to buy bread."

"Oh, indeed? He didn't have a lass with him, did he?"

"He didn't, just a couple of extra horses. Too many horses, if you ask me. Didn't like the look of him, I didn't."

Following her directions, Rhodry hurried along the twisting street. When he reached the house with the big beehive clay ovens in the front yard he saw Perryn's dapple gray, his pack horse, and a pair of colts tied up nearby. He laughed aloud, just a quick snatch of a berserker's chuckle, and thanked Great Bel in his heart. As he tied up his horse, he could see Perryn through the open door, handing over some coppers to a fellow in a cloth apron. Rhodry strode in. His hands full of loaves, Perryn turned and yelped, a satisfying gulp of pure terror.

"You bastard," Rhodry snarled. "Where's my wife?"

"Oh, er, ah, well, I don't know."

His face pale, the baker began edging for the door. Rhodry ignored him and went for Perryn. He grabbed him by the shirt and slammed him against the stone wall so hard that Perryn dropped the bread. Rhodry kicked it out of the way and slammed him again.

"Where's Jill?"

"I don't know." Perryn was gasping for breath. "She left me. I swear it. She left me on the road."

"I know that, dolt! Where?"

When Perryn smirked at him, Rhodry hit him in the stomach. He doubled over, choking, but Rhodry straightened him up and hit him again.

"Where did she leave you?"

Half blind from tears in his eyes, Perryn raised his head. Rhodry slapped him across the face.

"I know you're going to kill me," Perryn gasped. "Not going to tell you one rotten thing."

Rhodry saw no reason to admit that he'd sworn a vow to leave him alive. He grabbed him by the shoulders, hauled him forward, and slammed into the stone again.

"Where is she? If you tell me, you live."

"I don't know, by the gods!"

Rhodry was about to hit him in the stomach a second time when he heard noises behind him. He glanced over his shoulder and saw the white-faced baker, flanked by the blacksmith carrying an iron bar and two other men with threshing flails at the ready.

"Now what's all this, silver dagger? You can't ride in and just murder someone."

"I'm not going to murder anyone. This whoreson piss-pot little bastard stole my wife away, and now he won't tell me where she is."

The four villagers considered, glancing at one another and at the sword at Rhodry's side. Even though the four of them would have had more than a good chance against one man, no matter how skilled with a sword, it seemed they were the prudent sort.

"Ah well," the blacksmith said. "Then it's no affair of ours, if he's been meddling with your woman."

"Just get him out of my house," the baker moaned.

"Gladly. Rats don't belong in a granary."

Rhodry twisted Perryn's right arm behind his back and shoved him out of the bakery. When his victim struggled, Rhodry swung him sideways and knocked him against the wall of the next house so hard that he screamed.

"Where's Jill?"

"I don't know, and I wouldn't tell you if I did."

Rhodry hit him in the stomach so hard he vomited, falling to his knees. When he was done, Rhodry hauled him up, twisted his arm again, and then marched him round the bakery to a big stone shed. He threw him face forward against the wall, peeled him off and turned him round, then shoved him back again. By then Perryn could barely stand up.

"For the last time, where is she?"

Gasping, Perryn wiped feebly at the blood pouring from his nose and from a cut over his eye. Rhodry unbuckled his sword belt and let it drop.

"Come on, coward! Draw on me, if you dare."

Perryn merely gasped and sniveled. Rhodry's stomach tightened in sheer contempt.

"You base-born little half-gelded swine!"

Rhodry jumped him, grabbed him with one hand, and began hitting him as hard as he could with the other. The pleasure of beating Perryn filled his entire mind, just as when a sheet of flame races through the forest and sweeps everything before it. Suddenly he remembered the holy vow he'd sworn to Benoic. He let Perryn go and leaned him back against the wall. Fortunately, the lord was still breathing. He looked at Rhodry for a moment with glazed eyes, one of which was already swelling shut, tried to speak, gasped, then crumpled, sliding slowly down the wall to the ground. Rhodry gave him one last kick and turned to find the four villagers, standing as solemnly as judges, and three small boys, wide-eyed with excitement. Nearby was the gray gnome, clapping its hands and grinning while it did a little victory dance. Rhodry retrieved his sword belt and buckled it on while he caught his breath.

"There. I didn't murder him, did I now?"

They all shook their heads in agreement.

"I thought silver daggers didn't have wives," said one of the boys.

"I did. Let me tell you somewhat. If ever you find another silver dagger with a wife, then you keep your blasted little paws off her."

The lads looked at Perryn, then nodded again. When Rhodry walked toward them, they all parted to give him plenty of room and fell in behind him like an honor guard while he fetched his horse. He mounted and rode out, heading northwest to return to the river. His hands were bloody, bruised, and aching, but he'd

never enjoyed a pain more in his life. As soon as he was out of
sight of the village, the gnome appeared on his saddle peak.

"That was a splendid bit of fun, wasn't it, little brother?"

With an evil grin the gnome nodded a yes.

"Now, am I going the right way? Is Jill heading for the river?"

Again, it nodded yes.

"Is she going to Cerrmor?"

It waggled its hands and shrugged its shoulders to show that it
didn't truly know. It occurred to Rhodry that place names would
mean nothing at all to the Wildfolk.

"Well, if she's on the river, I'll catch her up, sure enough. My
thanks, little brother. You'd best get back to Jill and keep an eye on
her."

Out of compassion on the one hand and a sense of having seen
justice done on the other, the blacksmith and the baker picked
Perryn up and carried him into the baker's cow shed, where they
laid him down on a heap of straw. Perryn could barely see them
out of his swollen eyes. His chest ached so badly that he was sure
Rhodry had broken a couple of his ribs, and his lower lip was split
and bleeding. The baker's wife brought out a bowl of water, gave
him a drink, then washed his face for him.

"Didn't like the look of that silver dagger, I didn't. Here, did you
really take his wife?"

Perryn mumbled out a sound that passed for "I did."

"Huh. I don't see why any lass would take you over him, but
then, lasses is flighty sometimes. Ah well, you can stay here for a
day or two, lad, if you'll give me a couple of coppers for horse
feed."

Perryn nodded a yes, then fainted.

Irritated to the point of rage, Nevyn sat in his chamber and
glared at Salamander's image as it danced over the glowing coals
in the charcoal brazier. The gerthddyn seemed honestly bewildered.

"But I couldn't leave Jill with that lout—"

"Of course not, you dolt! That isn't the point. The point is this
Perryn himself. You've left behind a gravely ill man—"

"Who repeatedly raped my brother's woman."

"I know that, and I'm furious about it, but what I'm trying to tell
you is that he's deathly ill."

"And if he dies, what loss will it be?"

"Hold your tongue, you chattering elf!"

Salamander's image shrank back and turned pale. Nevyn took a deep breath and controlled himself.

"Now listen, Ebañy. If Perryn continues on this way, he's going to pour out his life force until there's precious little left. Then he'll get some illness—most likely a consumption of the lungs—and die, just as you've guessed. But in the meantime, he'll also be harming other women because he can't help himself. He's like a man with a plague, spreading foul humors and contagion over the countryside even though he doesn't wish another soul harm. Now do you see?"

"I do at that, and my apologies." Salamander did look sincerely chastened. "But what could I have done? Ensorceled him? Roped him like one of his horses and dragged him along with us? Jill can't bear the sight of him, and in her state—"

"Well, true enough. Let me think . . . the nearest dweomerworker is Liddyn of Cantrae. He can possibly find our Perryn and corral him. Truly, your first concern has to be Jill. Form a link with her aura and then—slowly, mind you—draw off some of that excess magnetism. The process should take some days, because you'll have to absorb it yourself. Or, here, expend it. Do some of your wretched little tricks with it. It might amuse her."

"I doubt me if any show of dweomer will do more than terrify her now."

"Maybe so. Ah ye gods! What a nasty mess you've dropped in our laps!"

"So they have. Here, one more strange thing about Perryn. When I first saw him, I opened up my sight and looked into his soul. I was thinking perhaps that he was some man linked to Jill by his Wyrd or suchlike."

"Was he?"

"I couldn't tell you that. I couldn't read his soul." All at once Salamander looked rueful. "Truly, I must have let my rage, wrath, and righteousness override my reason. I kept seeing him as some kind of half-human monster, not as a man at all."

"Valandario's been telling you and I have been telling you that dweomer demands that a man keep his feelings under control. Do you see now what we mean? Ye gods!"

"You have my true and humble apologies, O master. Here, since

I've seen Perryn, I can scry him out whenever you or Liddyn need my aid."

"And doubtless we will. He's got to be caught.

"True enough. I wasn't thinking. It was just seeing our Jill so . . . well, so broken and so shamed. It ached my heart."

"It aches mine, too." Nevyn realized then that part of his anger at Salamander was only a spillover from his rage at what had happened. "I only wish I could come join you. If you're riding south, maybe I will. It depends on how things go here."

"Where are you, by the by?"

Nevyn managed a laugh.

"My turn for the apologies. I'm in the gwerbret's dun in Aberwyn."

"Ye gods! I'm surprised Rhys will let you cross his threshold."

"Oh, he bears me no particular ill will. Lady Lovyan asked me to come with her and pretend to be a legal councillor. She's going to try one last time to get Rhys to recall Rhodry."

"No doubt the hells will melt first."

"No doubt. On the other hand, Rhys loves Aberwyn, and he might do what's best for her in the end."

When Salamander looked profoundly skeptical, Nevyn sighed in agreement. Being stubborn was a crucial part of a noble-born man's honor, and Rhys, like all Maelwaedds, would never betray his.

After finishing his talk with Salamander, Nevyn went to the open window and leaned on the sill to look out. From his chamber high up in the broch, he could see the gardens, a long reach of lawn lit with a hundred tiny oil lamps, where the ladies of the court were having an evening entertainment. Minstrels played, and the noble-born danced among the flickering lights. He could hear them laughing, half out of breath, as they circled round, stamping and slapping their feet in time to the harps and wooden flutes. Ah, my poor Jill, he thought, will you ever be as happy as they again?

His anger came close to choking him, a cold fury with Perryn, with Rhys, stubborn men who insisted on having what they wanted no matter what the cost to anyone else. Rhys was the worse, he decided, because his refusal to recall his brother could plunge Eldidd into open war. And then all those noble lords below would ride in a circling dance of death, this entertainment long forgotten. He pulled the shutters closed so hard that they banged like thunder in the chamber and turned away to pace back and forth. Finally he shook the mood away and turned to the brazier again.

When he thought of Rhodry the image appeared in an instant. He was standing, his back to the wall, in a crowded tavern and watching a dice game while he sipped from a tankard. At times, when Rhodry was in a particular melancholy mood, Nevyn could reach his mind and send him thoughts, but tonight he was preoccupied and oddly enough, not at all unhappy. At times he smiled to himself as if remembering a triumph. Most odd, Nevyn thought. Why isn't he brooding over Jill?

When someone knocked on his door, he canceled the vision. Lady Lovyan came in, her plaid cloak caught at the shoulder with a ring brooch set with rubies winking in the candlelight.

"Have you had enough of the dancing, my lady?"

"More than enough, but I came to see you for another reason. A speeded courier just rode in from Dun Deverry." She handed him a piece of parchment, tightly rolled from its long sojourn inside a message tube. "This is supposedly for my eyes alone, but I doubt if Blaen would mind you reading it."

After the long ritual salutations, the letter itself was brief: "I am in Dun Deverry in attendance upon the king. He tells me only that he's most interested in talking with a certain silver dagger known to you. Would the dragon roar if our liege usurped one of his privileges? By the by, Lord Talidd seems to have found a friend in Savyl of Camynwaen. Blaen, Gwerbret Cwm Pecl."

"Humph," Nevyn snorted. "Blaen isn't much of a man at subterfuge."

"Rhys would have understood that message in an instant if he'd read it." Lovyan took the letter back and dropped it into the glowing charcoal. The smell of burning leather drifted into the room, and Nevyn hurried to open the shutters. "The news about Savyl of Camynwaen's troubling. I do *not* like the idea of Talidd's finding another gwerbret to plead his case with our liege."

"No more do I. Ye gods, this is all getting vexed!"

"Do you think Rhys would rebel if the king overrode his decree of exile?"

"Not on his own, but he might be persuaded by men who think they have a chance at the rhan if he died childless."

"Just so. They'd try to push him into it, anyway. On the other

hand, if the king does intervene, then Rhys could stop my nagging
tongue without losing any face."

"True enough. He could bluster about the decree all he wanted
in front of the other lords but accept it privately."

"So I hope. Well, we don't even know if the king truly plans to
recall Rhodry." She looked at the twisted sheet of parchment ash
in the brazier, then picked up the poker and knocked it into dust.
"Let us hope that Blaen sends us more news soon."

Rhodry had no trouble buying passage on a barge that was making the run down to Lughcarn. His horse shared the stern with the
barge mules that would pull the boat upriver again; he had a place
to sleep in the bow with the four crewmen, who spoke to him as
little as possible. The rest of the barge's hundred feet were laden
with rough-shaped iron ingots from the smelters of Ladotyn up in
the high mountains. Although the barge rode low in the water, the
river current was smooth and steady, and for three days they
glided south, while Rhodry amused himself by watching the countryside go by. Once the hills were behind them, the grassy meadows and rich grain fields of Gwaentaer province spread out, green
and gold in the late summer sun, flat and seemingly endless.

On the fourth day they crossed the border into Deverry proper,
though Rhodry didn't see much change in the countryside to mark
it. Toward noon, the bargemaster told him that they'd make Lughcarn that night.

"It's the end of our run, silver dagger, but I'll wager you can find
another barge going down into Dun Deverry."

"Splendid. This is a cursed sight faster than riding, and I've got
to reach Cerrmor as soon as ever I can."

The bargemaster scratched his beard thoughtfully.

"Don't know much about the river traffic south out of the king's
city, but I'll wager there's some." He shrugged his massive shoulders. "Well, whether there is or not, you'll be only about a week's
ride from Cerrmor then."

By late afternoon Rhodry saw the first sign that they were coming close to the city. At first he thought he was seeing clouds on the
southern horizon, but the steersman enlightened him. A dark pall
of smoke hung in the air, smoke from the charcoal ovens, smoke
from the charcoal itself as it fed the forges to turn rough iron into
Lughcarn steel. By the time they turned into the docks just outside
the walled city, his linen shirt was flecked with soot. The docks

themselves and the warehouses just beyond were grimy gray. As he rode through the gate in the soot-blackened city walls, Rhodry was thinking that he'd be very glad to leave Lughcarn behind.

Yet it was a rich city under the soot. As he searched for a tavern poor enough to take in a silver dagger, Rhodry passed fine houses, some of them as tall as a poor lord's broch, with carved plaques over the doors proclaiming the name of one great merchant clan or another. There were temples all over the city, too, some to obscure gods usually relegated to a tiny shrine in the corner of a temple of Bel, some, like the great temple of Bel itself, as large as duns, with gardens and outbuildings of their own. Until he finally found the poor section of town, down by the river on the southern bank, he saw very few beggars, and even among the wooden huts of the longshoremen and charcoal burners he saw almost no one in rags and not a child who looked in danger of starving.

He found a shabby tavern whose owner agreed to let him sleep in the hayloft of the stable out back for a couple of coppers. After he stabled his horse, he went back in and got the best dinner the place offered—mutton stew lensed with grease and served with stale bread to sop up the gravy. He took it to a table where he could keep his back to the wall and looked over the other patrons while he ate. Most of them looked like honest workingmen, gathered there to have a tankard while they chewed over the local gossip, but one of them might have been a traveler like himself, a tall fellow with straight dark hair and skin colored like a walnut shell that bespoke some Bardek blood in his veins. Once or twice, Rhodry caught the fellow looking at him curiously, and when he'd finished eating, the fellow strolled over to him with a tankard in his hand.

"Have you come from the north, silver dagger?"

"I have at that. Why?"

"That's the way I'm heading. I was wondering what the roads are like up in Gwaentaer."

"Now, that I can't tell you, because I came down on a barge."

"A good way to travel when you're coming downriver, but not so good going up. Well, my thanks, anyway." Yet he lingered for a moment, as if wondering about something, then finally sat down. "You know, a silver dagger did me a favor once, a while back, and I wouldn't mind returning it to a fellow member of his band." He dropped his voice to a murmur. "You look like you hail from Eldidd."

"I do."

"You wouldn't be Rhodry of Aberwyn, would you?"

"I am. Here, where did you hear my name?"

"Oh, it's all over the south. That's what I mean about returning a favor. Let me give you a tip, like. It seems that every misbegotten gwerbret has riders out looking for you. I'd head west if I were you."

"What? By the black ass of the Lord of Hell, what are they looking for me for?"

The fellow leaned closer.

"There's been a charge laid against you by a Tieryn Aegwyc up in Cerrgonney. He claims you took his brother's head in battle."

Instantly, Rhodry understood—or thought he did. No doubt Graemyn had put the blame on him in order to reach a settlement in the peace treaty. After all, who would believe a silver dagger's word against that of a lord?

"Ye gods! I did no such thing!"

"It's of no matter to me. But like I say, you'd best be careful which way you ride."

"You have my thanks from the bottom of my heart."

All that evening, Rhodry kept one eye on the tavern door. If that charge stood up in a gwerbretal court, he would be beheaded as the holy laws demanded. Fortunately, his years on the long road had taught him many a thing about avoiding trouble. He could no longer ride the barges south, not when they could be called to the bank at any point by the king's guard and searched. He would have to slip south on back roads and, of course, lie about his name. Cerrmor itself was big enough so that he'd be able to stay unknown for at least a day or two. Once he found Jill, he'd have a witness on his side. Besides, he reminded himself, Nevyn's there too. Even a gwerbret would listen when the old man spoke.

In the morning, he rode out the east gate to plant a false trail. Much later, when it was too late, he realized that Tieryn Benoic would never have been party to such a falsehood.

"Someone worked you over good and proper, lad," said Gwel the leech. "Who was it?"

"Oh, er, ah, well," Perryn mumbled. "A silver dagger."

"Indeed? Well, it's a foolish man who earns a silver dagger's wrath."

"I . . . er . . . know that now."

In the polished mirror hanging on the wall of the leech's shop, Perryn could see his face, still blue, green, and swollen.

"You should have had this broken tooth out long before this," Gwel said.

"True-spoken, but I couldn't ride until a couple of days ago. He broke some of my ribs, too."

"I see. Well, you give silver daggers a wide berth after this."

"You have my sworn word on that."

Having the tooth pulled was more painful than having it broken, since it took much longer, and the only painkilller the leech could offer him was a goblet of strong mead. It was some hours before Perryn could leave the leech's shop and stagger back to his inn on the outskirts of Leryn. He flopped down on the bed in his chamber and stared miserably at the ceiling while his mind circled endlessly round and round like a donkey tied to a mill wheel: what was he going to do? The thought of returning to Cerrgonney to face his uncle's scorn made him feel physically sick to his stomach. And there was Jill. It seemed as the days went by that he loved her more than ever, that he'd never appreciated what he had until he'd lost it. Thinking that most men were no different about those they loved was no consolation. If only he could talk to her, beg her to let him explain, tell her how much he loved her—he was sure she would listen, if only he could get her alone, if only he could get her away from that fellow with the terrifying stare and the even more terrifying dweomer. If only. He didn't even know which way they'd gone.

Or could he find her? In his muddled state, half mad with pain and the aftermath of the leech's mead, he found himself thinking of her as his heart's true home, and with the thought came the pull, the sharp tug at his mind that had always shown him the way to other homes. Slowly, minding his aching jaw, he sat up on the bed and went very still. Truly, he could feel it: south. She'd gone south. He wept, but this time in rising hope, that he could track her down, follow her along until he had a chance alone with her, and somehow—oh, by great Kerun himself—steal her back again.

"Now this is passing strange," Salamander announced. "Rhodry's still heading south, but by the ears of Epona's steed, why is he taking every rotten cow path and village lane instead of riding on the king's good roads?"

Jill turned to look at him. They were sitting on the bow of a river barge, and Salamander was using the foaming, sun-flecked waters as a focus for scrying. Since she still was seeing with power, the water seemed like solid, carved silver, but she could remind herself now that what she was seeing was only illusionary. She refused to believe that she was seeing a hidden reality no matter how often Salamander insisted on it.

"Does he seem to be looking for a hire?"

"Not in the least, and I've been watching him for two days now. It seems that he knows where he's going, but he's being cursed careful on the way." With an irritable toss of his head, he looked away from the river. "Well, I'll spy out the esteemed brother again later. How are you feeling this morn?"

"A lot better. At least things are holding still most of the time."

"Good. Then my unpracticed cure is actually working."

"You have my heartfelt thanks, truly."

For a while she idly watched the southern horizon, where Lughcarn's smoke hung like a tiny cloud. She wished that she could simply forget about Perryn, that Salamander had some magic that would wipe her mind clean of his memory, but she knew that the shame she felt would nag at her for years. She felt as unclean as a priestess who'd broken her vows and was somehow to blame, too, for her abduction. If she'd only told Rhodry, or called to Nevyn earlier, or—the "If only's" ran on and on.

"From the hiraedd in your eyes," Salamander said abruptly, "I think me you're brooding again."

"Oh, how can I not brood? It's all well and good to chase after Rhodry, but I imagine he'll only curse me to my face when we find him."

"Why? You were no more at fault than one of the horses Perryn stole."

She merely shook her head to keep tears away.

"Now, here, Jill, my turtledove. Your mind's back, you can think again. Let me tell you somewhat. I've been thinking about our horse-stealing lord, and I've talked with Nevyn, too. There's somewhat cursed peculiar about that lad. He has what you might call a wound of the soul, the way he pours out his life at will."

"But I'm the one who fell right into his wretched arms. Ah ye gods, I never dreamt that I was as weak-willed as some slut of a tavern lass."

Salamander growled under his breath.

"Haven't you listened to one blasted word I said? It's not a question of weak will. You were ensorceled, dweomer-bound and dweomer-muddled. Once his life force swept over you, you had no will of your own, only his will. All his lust ran to you like water through a ditch."

For a moment she wanted to vomit as she remembered how it felt to have him smile at her in his particular way.

"Why do you call it a wound?" she said.

"Because it's going to kill him, sooner or later."

"Good. I only wish I could be there to watch."

"And no one expects you to feel differently, my delicate little lass. But can't you see, Jill? You're as blameless as if he'd tied you down and raped you by force."

"Ah ye gods, and that's what I hate most. I felt so beastly helpless!"

"You *were* helpless."

"Oh, true enough. It's a cursed hard thing to admit."

"Boils need lancing, on the other hand."

When she threw a fake punch his way, he smiled.

"Truly, you're coming back to your old self. But don't you see the curious thing? Given that Perryn has no true dweomer, then where by all the hells does this power come from? What gave him the wound?"

"As much as I hate to talk about the worm-rotted bastard, I'll admit the question's of some interest."

"Of great interest, especially to Nevyn. Unfortunately, at the moment, there is no answer."

"Well, if anyone can find it, it's Nevyn."

"Precisely. Especially once he gets his hands on him."

"Is he planning on hunting Perryn down?"

"Not truly. I've been waiting to tell you this until you were stronger, but I think you can bear it now. Perryn's been following us."

She felt the blood drain from her face. Salamander caught her hand and held it between both of his.

"You're in no danger now, none at all."

"Not now, maybe, but what about when we're out on the roads again, following Rhodry?"

"By then Perryn will be on his way to Eldidd under armed guard. Here, there's a dweomerman at court named Lord Madoc. He'll have Perryn arrested as soon as he enters the city, then send him to Nevyn. From what you told me, that rambling scribe in our lordling's saddlebags is more than enough reason for the king's wardens to take him under arrest."

"So we're going to Dun Deverry?"

"We are. And we may not have to leave it, either. Do you know Rhodry's cousin Blaen of Cwm Pecl?"

"I do."

"The good gwerbret's at court at the moment. Nevyn wants us to speak with him. It seems that the king's sent out the word that he wants to see Rhodry. Apparently the various gwerbrets are keeping watch for him, and when they find him, they'll send him straight to Dun Deverry."

"The king? What—"

"I don't know, but I think me we can guess. The king knows Rhys won't be getting any more heirs for Aberwyn."

"Recall."

"Just that. So soon enough, Jill, you'll be having a splendid wedding."

"Oh, will I now? You sound like a village idiot. Think! They're never going to let the heir to the most important rhan in Eldidd marry a silver dagger's bastard. The best I could hope for is being his wretched mistress again, living in his court and hating his wife. Well, if he even wants me anymore. What do you think this is, one of your tales?"

"I have the distinct and revolting feeling that I was thinking just that. Jill, please, forgive me."

She merely shrugged and watched the farmland gliding by. A herd of white cattle with rusty-red ears were drinking from the river, watched over by a lad and two dogs.

"Do you forgive me?" he said at last.

"I do, and my apologies, too. I'm all to pieces still."

"So you are. After you've baited our trap for Perryn, you could just ride away without seeing Rhodry, if you wanted."

"Never. Maybe he'll curse me to my face, but I want to tell him that I always loved him."

Salamander started to speak, but she covered her face with her hands and wept.

The king's palace in Dun Deverry was enormous, six broch towers joined by a sprawling complex of half-brochs, surrounded by outbuildings, and protected by a double ring of curtain walls. As an honored guest, Blaen, Gwerbret Cwm Pecl, had a luxurious suite high up in one of the outer towers, so that he had a good view of the gardens that lay between the pair of walls. In his reception chamber were four chairs with cushions of purple Bardek velvet as well as a table and a hearth of its own. Although Blaen cared little for such luxuries as things in themselves, he appreciated them as marks of the king's favor. Besides, his wife, Canyffa, was accompanying him on this trip, and he liked to see her surrounded by comfort. A tall woman with dark hair and doelike brown eyes, Canyffa was as calm as he was excitable. Although their marriage had been of the usual arranged sort, Blaen privately considered that he'd been exceptionally lucky in his wife. At moments, he could even admit to her that he loved her.

This particular morning Canyffa had been called to wait upon the queen in Her Majesty's private chamber—a signal honor, but one that had come her way before. Blaen perched on the window-sill in their bedchamber and watched as she dressed with special care. After one of her serving women laid out several dresses on the bed, she sent the lass away and studied the choices, finally picking a modest one of dove-gray Bardek silk, a color that showed off the reds and whites of her husband's clan's plaid to advantage.

"I think Gwerbret Savyl's wife is going to be attending the queen this morning as well," she remarked. "I assume that my lord would like me to keep my ears open."

"Your lord would like naught better, truly. What's the wife like, anyway?"

Canyffa considered before answering.

"A weasel, but a lovely one. I gather that they're well suited."

"In weaselhood, perhaps. No one would call Savyl lovely. Cursed if I know why he's sticking his oar in this particular stream! Camynwaen's a long way from Belglaedd. What use can Talidd possibly be to him?"

"I believe they've got blood kin in common, but still, the point's well taken, my lord. I shall see if I can cultivate the lovely Lady Braeffa." She paused for a quick smile. "But if I'm going to sacrifice myself this way, I shall expect a handsome present from our Rhodry when he's recalled."

"Some of the finest Bardek silver, no doubt. I'll make sure he honors you properly. Well—if we can get him recalled, anyway."

While Canyffa was off with the queen, Blaen had a guest of his own, a powerful man who was worth another sort of cultivation.

He had his page fetch a silver flagon of mead and two glass goblets, then sent the lad away. The gwerbret filled the glasses with his own hands and gave one to his guest, who took an appreciative sip. The recently ennobled Lord Madoc, third equerry to the king, was a slender man of about forty, with neatly trimmed blond hair barely touched with gray, and humorous blue eyes. He was also, or so it was said, Nevyn's nephew. Indeed? Blaen thought to himself. But I'll wager he's another sorcerer, nephew or not. Since he'd been a successful horse breeder in Cantrae province before his recent court appointment, Madoc certainly did his job well, and he had a plain yet decent sort of manners that allowed him to fit into the court as smoothly as any minor lord—if not more so. Yet, every now and then, there was something about the way he looked or smiled that implied that the power and pomp of the court failed to impress him.

"My thanks for the invitation to visit you, Your Grace," Madoc said. "To what do I owe the honor?"

"Simple hospitality, in a way. I know your uncle well."

"Of course. I had a letter from him recently. He's quite well."

"Splendid. Is he still in Eldidd?"

"He is, Your Grace. Lovyan, Tieryn Dun Gwerbyn, has taken him into her service."

I'll just wager, Blaen thought to himself. More like he's taken her into his, whether she knows it or not.

"That's good news," he said aloud. "Our Nevyn's getting a bit old to travel the roads with a mule."

"His health's a marvel, isn't it, Your Grace? But then my mother is still alive and sharp as a sword, and her past seventy."

"Let's hope the gods grant that you inherit their stamina, then." Blaen gave him a friendly grin. "Lovyan's kin to me, of course, my mother's sister."

"So I'd heard, Your Grace, but then, there's been quite a bit of talk of late of your cousin Rhodry."

"No doubt. Trying to keep a secret at court is generally a waste of time. The gossip started buzzing, I'll wager, the moment our liege summoned me here."

"A bit sooner than that, truly." Madoc shook his head in mock sadness. "The first rumors, Your Grace, were that the king might summon you."

"I'll wager you know, then, that our liege is looking for my scapegrace cousin."

"I do, at that, and the gossip is that the king means to override his sentence of exile."

"Well, I can't really tell you if that's true or not. I haven't been sworn to any secrets, mind—our liege hasn't told me, that's all. I'll guess that he's not sure yet."

"Most like, Your Grace. Overriding a gwerbret's decree is naught to be done lightly."

"Just so." Blaen paused for a long swallow of mead. "But curse it all, the king can't do one thing or the other until Rhodry's been found."

"Still no news, Your Grace?"

"Not a shred. By every god and his wife, what's wrong with those packs of idiots that the gwerbrets call riders? The kingdom's big, sure enough, but they should have found one silver dagger by now."

"So you'd think, Your Grace." For the briefest of moments, Madoc looked troubled. "I truly thought they would have tracked him down quite quickly."

"So did I." Here was the crux, and Blaen paused briefly. "In fact, I was wondering if perhaps you'd help with the hunt."

"Me, Your Grace? Well, I'd certainly do anything that my duties here allow, but I'm not sure what I could do."

"I'm not truly sure either, but I suspect a man known as Nevyn's nephew might see things hidden from others."

Madoc blinked twice, then smiled.

"Ah, Your Grace. You know about the old man's dweomer, then."

"I do. He went out of his way to let me know, last summer, it was. He seemed to find it strangely easy to see things a long way away."

"So he can, Your Grace. Let me be blunt. If I could scry Rhodry out, I would, but I've never seen him in the flesh, and so I can't."

Blaen had a gulp of mead to hide his surprise. He'd been expecting a lot of fencing before Madoc admitted the truth, but here the man had just spat it out.

"I see," Blaen said at last. "Pity."

"It is. I may be able to get you news some other way. His Grace is right. Things are growing worrisome. Rhodry really should have been found by now."

"Just so. Do you know what my worst fear is? That some of the men whose clans stand to inherit Aberwyn when Rhys dies may have taken steps to have the legitimate heir removed."

"Ye gods! Would they stoop so low?"

"Aberwyn is one of the richest rhans in the kingdom, and it's going to grow richer. Just a year ago the king gave the city a more liberal charter. One of the terms was that Aberwyn would have a share in the royal monopoly on trade with Bardek."

Madoc nodded, a grim little smile twisting his mouth.

"His Grace's point is well taken. Well and good, then. If His Grace will excuse me for a moment?"

"Of course."

Blaen was expecting Madoc to leave the chamber, but instead he went to the window and looked up at the sky, where white clouds billowed and tore on the edge of a summer storm. He stood there while Blaen downed two more goblets of mead and wondered what the man was doing; finally he turned back, looking troubled.

"Rhodry's almost to Drauddbry, and he seems to be traveling south. He's bought himself a second horse to make speed. It would appear that he's heading for Cerrmor."

"I wonder what they want in Cerrmor."

"They, Your Grace?"

"Well, isn't Jill with him?"

"My apologies, Your Grace. I forgot you wouldn't know. He and Jill were separated by an unfortunate turn of events. She's following along after him with a friend, a gerthddyn who gallantly offered to escort her. The last I heard, they were coming to Dun Deverry to beg your aid."

"Which they'll have, of course." Blaen considered for a moment. "Have you ever met my cousin or his woman?"

"I've not, Your Grace."

"They match each other like a pair of fine boots. If Rhodry's going to inherit Aberwyn, I'd rather see Jill beside him than the noble-born sheep his mother would pick for him."

"But isn't she common-born?"

"She is, but details like that have been arranged away before. I'll have to think on it."

Several hours later, it occurred to Blaen that he implicitly believed what Madoc had told him. I've seen dweomer before, he reminded himself, but still he shuddered. What had Madoc been reading in the cloudy sky?

Thanks to the rain, the bargemen had hung canvas across the bow of the barge, an imperfect shelter but better than none at all.

Jill wrapped her cloak around her tightly and watched Salamander staring at the foaming water rushing by. Every now and then his mouth would frame a silent word or two. By then, her sight was nearly back to normal. The water was merely water; Salamander no longer changed color to reflect what he was feeling. There was only a certain vividness to colors, a certain urgency to patterns of line and shape, to remind her of the splendors she had seen when she'd been bathed in forbidden power. With a grudging self-mockery, she had to admit that in a way she was sorry to lose that dangerous beauty. Finally Salamander turned to her to whisper.

"I've just been talking with Lord Madoc. He wanted to know where I'd last scried Rhodry out so he could tell Blaen. Not that it'll do much good, truly. A speeded courier still couldn't catch up with him."

"True enough, but the courier could tell the gwerbret in Cerrmor to watch out for him."

"If he stays in Cerrmor."

Jill raised her hands in a gesture of frustration. She was wishing that she hadn't taught Rhodry the ways of the long road so well. For days now he'd slipped through the net of riders looking for him like a fox through a hedgerow.

"Well, we'll be in Dun Deverry tomorrow," Salamander said. "And we can talk with Blaen directly."

"Good. You know, in spite of everything, I'm really looking forward to seeing the king's city. I've wandered over this kingdom since I was eight years old, but I've never been there. There aren't any hires for silver daggers in the king's own lands."

All at once the gray gnome popped into being, not a foot away from her. When she held out her hands to it, it hesitated, screwing up its face at her.

"Oh, here, little one! What have I done to make you so angry with me?"

It held out for only a moment longer, then threw itself into her arms. She hugged it tight.

"I'm so glad you've forgiven me. I've missed you."

Smiling, it reached up to pat her cheek.

"We'll be back with Rhodry soon, with any luck. Have you visited him? Is he well?"

It nodded yes to both questions, snuggling against her like a cat.

"I wish I knew where he was going."

The gnome looked up and pointed at her.

"He's following me?"

Again it nodded yes, but so indifferently that she wasn't sure if it had truly understood. Salamander had been watching all of this closely.

"Interesting and twice interesting," he pronounced. "But I wonder what it means."

Although the leech advised Perryn to stay in Leryn for at least five days to recover from the beating, he left town as soon as he could possibly ride. Once he'd tuned his mind to Jill, her presence ached him like another wound, drawing him after her. Yet his longing was tempered with fear, of the strange fellow with the moonbeam pale hair who had taken her away. As he thought things over, he wondered if he had somehow dreamt that terrifying scene where he'd seen clouds of colored light and glowing swords. Every time he tried to convince himself that he'd been dreaming, he came up against the inescapable fact that Jill was gone. He simply refused to admit that she ever would have left him of her own free will; there had to be another man involved, and him a powerful one. Although most people in the kingdom dismissed tales of dweomer, Perryn had always instinctively believed they were true, that indeed there was a thing called dweomer and that with it men could work marvels. Now, to his very cold comfort, he'd been proven right. His one consolation in all this was that if he didn't have Jill, neither did Rhodry.

Three days' ride brought him to Gaddmyr, a large, prosperous town behind a double ring of stone walls. Although he would have preferred to avoid the town entirely, he was too low on provisions. Normally he hated being in towns, packed in with a lot of smelly, sweaty people, bound up in their petty human concerns like pigs in a sty, but that night he found it a certain comfort to sit in the tavern room of a shabby inn with human beings around him to distract him from his constant, aching longing for Jill. Out in the forest, he would have missed her constantly; there, he could drink down strong ale and try to forget her. When the tavernman came by to ask him if he'd be spending the night, on impulse he said that he would.

"But, er, ah, I don't truly want to share a chamber with someone. Could I, oh, ah, sleep out in the hayloft?"

"No reason why not. Plenty of room out there."

Perryn got himself another tankard of ale and found a seat in an out-of-the-way corner. Although he was planning on simply drinking himself so blind that he'd be unable to think, the tavern lass changed his mind. She was a round-faced little thing, with dark hair and knowing dark eyes, and a smile that promised a few interesting hours if not much more. Perryn decided that she was a much better way to distract himself from thoughts of Jill than a hangover would be. He chatted with her for a few minutes, asked her name, which was Alaidda, and found, as he'd expected, that she was utterly cold to him. When she turned to go, he gave her one of his smiles. Although he'd never understood what he was doing the smile worked as it always did. Alaidda stared at him, her lips half parted, her eyes stunned as she lingered beside him. When he smiled again, she cast a nervous glance at the tavernman, then came much closer.

"And is the innkeep going to mind if you talk a bit with a customer?"

"Oh, he won't, as long as it's just talk."

"What are you, then? His daughter?"

"Hah! Far from it."

"Indeed?" Perryn paused for another longing smile. "So—part of your hire is keeping his bed warm."

Alaidda blushed, but she moved closer still, until her full breasts were brushing his arm. He smiled yet again and was rewarded by seeing her eyes go all dreamy as she smiled in return. When Perryn saw that the tavernman was engrossed in conversation with a pair of merchants, he risked laying his hand on her cheek.

"He doesn't look like much of a man to me. A lass like you could use a little better company of a night. I'm sleeping out in the hayloft, you see. Out of . . . er, well . . . out of the way. I could go out there right now."

"I could follow in a bit, but I can't stay long." She giggled in an oddly drunken way. "But then, it won't take long."

With another giggle, Alaidda hurried away to the kitchen. Perryn lingered long enough to finish his ale and allay the tavernman's suspicions, then slipped out to the hayloft. Since the lass had something to hide, he didn't take a candle lantern. He found his gear in his horse's stall, hauled it up the ladder, and stumbled around in the dark until he got the blankets laid out and his boots off. As he sat waiting in the mounded hay, he began to wonder why he was even bothering with this seduction. No woman would ever match his Jill. The thought of her brought him close to tears, but in a few minutes he was distracted by the sound of Alaidda climbing the ladder. He went to meet her and kissed her before she got any thoughts of changing her mind.

"Oh ye gods!" She sounded honestly troubled. "I hardly know what's wrong with me, running after you like this."

"Naught's wrong. Come lie down with me, and I'll show you why you did."

Meekly she let him take her to his blankets. At first she was shy in his arms, but with every kiss he gave her, he could feel not only a growing sexual tension, but a power, a strange dark feeling that rose from deep within and flooded him until it was almost more demanding than the sexual force. As the power grew, she responded to it, whimpering in his arms at every caress. Finally she caught his hand.

"I don't have time to take my dress off. Just pull it up, and now. Please?"

As soon as they were finished, she gave him one last kiss and a sincere confession that she wished she could stay all night, then hurried back to her jealous man. By then, Perryn was so exhausted that he was glad she was gone. He fell onto his blankets and stared up into a strange light-shot darkness that revolved slowly around him. When he tried to close his eyes, the feeling of motion persisted, so strong that he wanted to vomit; he opened his eyes in a hurry. He could feel cold sweat running down his back and chest, and his trembling lips felt bloodless and cold. Although he wanted to get up and go ask for help in the tavern, he knew that he could never climb down the ladder without breaking his neck. He could only lie there, gripping the straw under him, and pray that he wasn't dying.

Panic hit him like waves slapping a pier in a storm. He found himself remembering the dweomerman who'd taken Jill away, the fellow taunting him, then adding one last insult: you've got to stop stealing women and horses, or it'll kill you. At the time, Perryn had assumed the fellow meant that some outraged husband would murder him or suchlike, but now he realized the truth. Something was wrong, very gravely wrong, and he didn't know what it was. Did the dweomerman know? Would he help if he did? Not likely, from the hate-filled things the fellow had thrown into his face. In a confused babble, his thoughts went round and round until at last he slept, tumbling into a darkness without dreams.

About two hours before noon on the morrow, Jill finally got her first view of Dun Deverry when the barge tied up at the riverside piers about a half mile to the north. For a long while she stared at the massive walls that curved around the city, rising high above them on its seven hills. Even from their distance she could just pick out the roofs of the king's palace. Floating high above the towers and snapping in the wind were tiny flecks of yellow that had to be the cloth-of-gold banners of the Wyvern throne.

"Quite a sight, isn't it?" Salamander said. "Let's get those horses unloaded and get on our way. Just wait until you see the gates."

The gates were easily twelve feet high and twenty broad, and they were carved all over with panels of key patterns set round with bands of interlace. The iron banding was stamped as well with rows of interwoven spirals and rosettes. Since the walls were a good twenty feet thick, they walked through a sort of a tunnel and found yet another set of gates at the other end, just as elaborately decorated as the first. Beyond them was a wide public space, planted with oak trees around a central fountain, where a marble wyvern rose from the spray. From this park the narrow streets unwound, spiraling through the houses and up the hills, or twisting down through shops and taverns toward the lake to the west. Everywhere Jill looked she saw people hurrying about on some business or another, or here and there the splendidly dressed riders of the king's own guard.

Salamander led her to the inn he had in mind, a three-story broch rising in the midst of a grassy garden. She looked at the roof, covered with fine slate, and noticed that the windows glinted with glass.

"We can't stay here! It'll cost a fortune!"

"Jill, my miserly turtledove." The gerthddyn shook his head in mock sadness. "If so, I shall earn a fortune in the tavern room to pay for it. I cannot stand cheap inns. They stink, and the mattresses are crawling with bugs. If I wanted to sleep on a floor, I would have been born a hound."

"Well, but there's plenty of decent inns that cost less."

"Why cavil over a few silvers? Besides, someone is meeting us here."

As they led their horses up to the gates, a burly young man strolled out. He glanced with some appreciation at Salamander's beautifully woven cloak and gold-trimmed horse gear, then bowed.

"Is this silver dagger with you, sir?"

"He is. My bodyguard. Have you a chamber on the second floor?"

"We do. I'll just call the lad to tend to your horses, sir."

"Splendid. The first things we shall want are baths."

But they had to postpone this by now necessary luxury for some time. When Jill followed Salamander into the tavern room, which had Bardek carpets on the floor and silver sconces on the walls, she saw a tall man in the plaid brigga of the noble-born pacing back and forth near the hearth. The sight of him wrung her heart, because Blaen looked so much like her Rhodry.

"That's Gwerbret Blaen!" she said.

"Of course. He's the one who's meeting us here."

"He doesn't know about . . . well, about Perryn, does he?"

"Of course not! Don't you think I have any respect for your honor? Leave that part of this to me."

As they walked over, Blaen saw them and strode to meet them. Although Salamander made him a courtly bow, he barely returned it, instead catching Jill's hand and giving it a hard squeeze.

"It gladdens my heart to see you, Jill, though it'd gladden it more if Rhodry were with you." He looked around and found the tavernman staring gape-mouthed at the sight of the gwerbret greeting a silver dagger as an old friend. "Innkeep! Send up a flagon of your best mead to their chambers! And a plate of cold meats, too."

The chambers justified Jill's worst fears about expense. Not only were they carpeted, but all the furniture was beautifully polished wood, as heavily carved with interlace as anything in a lord's dun. The flagon and the plate, both silver, arrived promptly. Blaen handed the servant lass coins worth twice what the refreshments cost and dismissed her peremptorily.

"Now," said the gwerbret, pouring himself a gobletful. "Lord Madoc's told me, gerthddyn, that you know how to do more things than spin tales, so you can speak freely. Do you know where Rhodry is?"

"Almost to Cerrmor. In fact . . ." He paused to glance out the window to check the sun. "I'd say he's in Cerrmor at the moment. But why is he there? That, alas, I cannot say, Your Grace."

"No more can anyone, apparently, curse them all." Blaen

glanced at Jill. "Pour yourself some mead, silver dagger. You've had quite a journey. By the way, Jill, how did Rhodry come to leave you behind?"

"Ah, Your Grace, that's a strange tale indeed." Salamander broke in smoothly. "Rhodry was on a hire in Cerrgonney, you see."

"I'd heard somewhat about Benoic and his unlovely kin."

"Well and good, then. Well, Rhodry had left Jill at the dun of a certain Lord Nedd, the man he rode for, but he never came back for her. Fortunately I came along—I'd been looking for her for reasons of my own, you see. I scried Rhodry out and found him riding south. I refuse to believe that he simply deserted her."

"No more do I." Blaen pledged her with his goblet. "Don't think that for a moment, lass."

Jill forced out a brave smile.

"So, after much thought, brooding, and ratiocination, I arrived at the conclusion that someone, for reasons most recondite and unknown, was luring Rhodry south. We have a hint or two that he was told that Jill had left him and was coming after her. Be that as it may, he's been acting like a hunted man all the way south from Lughcarn, while before that he traveled openly. Either somewhat happened to him in Lughcarn, or someone told him a falsehood of some sort."

"That would stand to reason, truly." Blaen sighed and drank heavily. "I'll wager this has somewhat to do with the situation in Aberwyn. You know Rhodry has enemies, don't you?"

"We do, Your Grace. Has the king made a decision as yet about a recall?"

Jill turned away and busied herself with pouring a goblet of mead. She wished that she could simply drink herself into forgetting that Rhodry was being taken away from her.

"Jill," Blaen said. "You look heartsick."

"Why shouldn't I be, Your Grace? I'm losing my man. Do you think they'll let Rhodry marry a woman like me?"

"I see no reason why not, once I've done ennobling you. I'm settling land in your name over in Cwm Pecl. The gods all know that there's plenty to spare in my province."

"Your Grace!" Jill could barely speak. "You're far too generous! How can I—"

"Hush. Listen, Jill, Rhodry's no weak younger son any longer. Once we get him recalled, he'll be Aberwyn's only heir, and that means he'll be the gwerbret when his black-hearted brother dies.

He'll be in a position to demand the wife he wants, no matter what his mother or the rest of the noble-born think of it."

Salamander laughed.

"And there you are, my turtledove—an ending exactly like one of my tales."

"So it seems."

Jill smiled, because they both wanted her to be pleased, but she felt the dweomer cold down her back. When Blaen launched into a monologue on Eldidd politics, she wandered away to the window and looked down on the garden below. Salamander had told Blaen a pretty tale, sure enough; she could see how it would protect her. If Rhodry wanted nothing more to do with her, everyone would assume that he'd merely tired of her and left, as men so often did to their women. And if he forgave her . . . the thought staggered her, that she, of all lowly commoners, might someday be the wife of a great gwerbret. For a moment she was terrified, thinking of the responsibilities, the power that could be hers. Lovyan would teach me, she thought, if Rhodry even wants me anymore, that is.

But as the thought came to her, so did another . . . or not precisely a thought, a feeling, rather, a sudden urgency. Rhodry was in danger. She knew it with complete clarity, that he was in the worst danger of his life and that in this moment of danger he was thinking only of her. She shut her eyes and thought back to him, tried desperately to reach him, to warn him. Images flickered in her mind, as hazy as those seen when a person is first falling asleep, ever-changing glimpses: Rhodry on a narrow street, Rhodry ducking down an alley when some of the city wardens strolled by. Although the images flickered, the feeling of danger grew until she could barely breathe. He was talking with someone —he was asking about Nevyn, asking about her—they were lying, saying that she was in Cerrmor, giving him friendly directions—

"Rhodry, don't go!"

She heard a crash, looked around dazed, and realized that she'd dropped the goblet she was holding. Blaen and Salamander had whirled round to look at her. She had screamed her warning aloud.

"What by the gods?" Blaen said.

"Rhodry's in Cerrmor. He's in danger. I know he is. I saw—I felt it. I tried to warn him." She tossed back her head and sobbed, because she knew that the warning had never reached him. "We've got to get to Cerrmor. We've got to leave now."

Blaen set down his goblet and hurried over to pat her shoulder awkwardly as she wept, as if he thought her mind turned weak and childish by grief, but Salamander was taking her warning in dead seriousness. Through her tears she saw him snap his fingers over the charcoal brazier in the corner, then stare intently into the lambent flames. She forced the tears back and wiped her face on her sleeve.

"Ah ye gods!" There was panic in his voice. "I can't find him! Jill, I can't scry him out!"

The chamber seemed to swell around her, and the light grew painfully bright. The silver flagon on the table threw off sparks like a fire.

"Call to Nevyn," she said.

Then Blaen grabbed her and half led, half shoved her into a chair. She slumped back and watched Salamander, bending over the brazier. His tunic seemed to ripple around him as if he stood in a breeze. She was afraid to look at the intricate carpets.

"Jill, do you need a chirurgeon?" Blaen said.

"I don't, my thanks. It's just the fear." She forced herself to raise her head and look him in the face. "Your Grace, don't you see what this means? Remember Alastyr? If Salamander can't scry Rhodry out, someone's hiding him—with dweomer."

As it danced over the flames, Salamander's image looked close to tears. Nevyn himself felt a weary sort of rage, cursing himself because he should have seen this danger coming. Had the Lords of Light sent some omen that he'd overlooked? He quite simply didn't know.

"I can't find him either," Nevyn thought.

"Is he dead, then?"

"He can't be, because Jill would know if he were. When you consider how much she saw of his danger, I think we can trust that she'd feel his death. How soon can you get to Cerrmor?"

"We should arrive tomorrow."

"Ye gods! What are you going to do, turn into birds and fly?"

"Naught of the sort, truly." Salamander managed a faint smile. "The king has placed one of the royal riverboats at Blaen's disposal. We'll leave soon, and not only will the current be running our way, but we'll have a crew of rowers. The Belaver runs cursed fast from here to Drauddbry, I'm told."

"Splendid. Is Blaen going with you?"

"He's not. The intrigue at court would gripe your very soul, and he doesn't dare leave. We have letters from him, though, for the gwerbret in Cerrmor. Are you going to join us there?"

"I'll leave at once. I never dreamt they would go as far as this. Can't you see what must have happened? Rhodry's rivals must have hired one of the Bardek blood guilds to dispose of him."

Salamander's image, floating above the fire, looked intensely puzzled.

"How would petty lords from Eldidd even know those guilds exist?"

"Well, some merchant or other must have told them, or . . . I see what you mean. It sounds very farfetched once I say it aloud."

"Then what's happened?"

"What indeed? Be very careful until I reach Cerrmor. Ye gods, I'll have to take a ship! I can't leave until I've spoken with Lovyan, of course, but I can start packing. Her Grace is out hunting with the gwerbret at the moment."

Down on the Eldidd coast, it was a bright sunny day, although the wind that whipped the silver-and-blue banners of Aberwyn was chilly and the shadows that lay in the great ward of the gwerbret's dun were positively cold. As she stood beside her horse, Lady Lovyan glanced doubtfully at the sky.

"It might be a bit windy to fly the falcons."

"Oh, let's try our luck, Mother," Rhys said.

He spoke with such forced cheer that she knew this hunting party was merely an excuse to speak with her alone.

"By all means, then. We'll have a good ride if naught else."

They mounted and rode out of the dun into the streets of Aberwyn. Behind them came the falconers, with the hooded birds on their wrists, and four men from Rhys's warband as an escort. As they wound their way through the curving streets, the common folk bowed to their overlord, who acknowledged the gesture with an upraised hand. Occasionally—and quite spontaneously—boys and young men cheered him. For all his stubbornness, Rhys was a good ruler, scrupulously fair in his judgments over everyone but his younger brother, and his townsfolk appreciated him for it.

When they left the city, they turned north on the river road that followed the Gwyn, sparkling and full from the summer's heavy rains. Among the willows and hazels that grew along the water, Lovyan saw a tree or two that were turning yellow.

"It seems that autumn's coming quite fast this year," she remarked.

"It does. Well, we've had a wretchedly cold summer." Rhys turned in his saddle to make sure that his men were following at a respectfully far distance behind, then turned her way. "Here, Mother, I've got somewhat to ask you. It's about little Rhodda."

"Indeed?"

"I was thinking that I might formally adopt the child and legitimize her."

Lovyan was caught with nothing to say. Rhys gave her an ironic smile that must have cost him dear.

"It's time I faced the harsh truth of things. I'll never give Aberwyn an heir."

"The gwerbretrhyn can't pass down in the female line."

"Of course not, but she'll marry someday, won't she? Have a husband, maybe a son or two. At least they'll have some Maelwaedd blood in them."

"If the Council of Electors accepted her husband as your successor, anyway."

"There's precedent for it, hundreds of years of precedent." He tossed his head in anger. "Besides, at least it'll give my vassals pause. Ye gods, don't you think it aches my heart? I know cursed well that every tieryn in Eldidd is already scheming and politicking to get my lands for their son when I die."

"True-spoken, alas. But you know, my sweet, there's a much easier solution—"

"I will not recall Rhodry."

His mouth settled into the tight line she knew so well.

"As His Grace decides, of course, but how can you adopt the child without her father's permission?"

"Rhodry's an outlaw. Under the laws she has no father."

"Very well, then. I'll think the matter over, since His Grace persists in being as stubborn as a wild boar."

He merely shrugged the insult away and went back to watching the road in front of him. Lovyan wondered why she even bothered to hint, scheme, and badger to get her youngest son home. Rhys simply couldn't bear to let Rhodry inherit, she thought. Now, if Rhodry would only get a son on that Jill of his, but there she is, poor lamb, riding all over with him and sleeping out in the rain on the ground, and the Goddess only knows what else. Doubtless her womanly humors are utterly disrupted and—

Suddenly Rhys's horse went mad. Lovyan could think of it no other way as the black neighed and bucked, then reared, striking out with its forehooves as if at an enemy. Rhys flew forward, caught himself on its neck, then slipped sideways as it bucked again. Although he was a splendid rider, the horse was rearing and pitching in utter panic, and he'd been taken off-guard. She heard his men shouting, heard other hoofbeats, but Rhys's black twisted, bucked, then slipped and went down, throwing Rhys hard and falling on top of him. She heard a woman screaming, then realized that the voice was hers.

Suddenly the escort was all around her. One man grabbed the bridle of her frightened palfrey and led her away; the others dismounted and rushed to their lord's side. Back under control, Lovyan gestured at the man holding her horse.

"Ride back to the dun! Bring Nevyn and a cart!"

"My lady." He made her a half-bow from the saddle, then galloped off.

Lovyan dismounted and hurried over just as the horse struggled to its feet, its off-fore dangling and broken. One of the riders blocked her way.

"My lady, you'd best not look."

"Don't speak nonsense! I've tended my share of wounds in my day."

She shoved him aside and knelt down beside Rhys. He lay so still that at first she thought him dead, but when she touched his cheek, his eyes fluttered open. His face twisted in agony as he tried to speak.

"Whist, whist, little one. We'll have Nevyn here soon."

He nodded, then stared up at the sky, his mouth working in pain. Blood ran down his face from a slash over his eye; she could see that his left leg was broken, probably in several places. Yet she knew that the worst damage might have been done internally, where no chirurgeon could heal, not even Nevyn. She could only pray to the Goddess until at last the old man rode up at the gallop, with a wagon rumbling after. Nevyn swung himself down from his horse and ran over.

"Does he live?"

"Barely."

Lovyan got out of the way and stood with the escort by the side of the road as Nevyn went to work, straightening the leg and roughly splinting it. As he ran his long graceful hands over Rhys's body, she saw him shaking his head and swearing under his breath, and her heart turned cold. At last Nevyn called the carter to help him lift the injured gwerbret into the wagon. By then, Rhys had mercifully fainted. Lovyan got in with him and cradled his bloody head in her lap. Nevyn watched, his ice-blue eyes unreadable.

"I want the cold truth," Lovyan said. "Will he die?"

"Well, my lady, I simply don't know. His Grace is a truly strong man, and he'll fight for his life, but it's very grave. A weaker man would be dead already."

To jostle the injured man as little as possible, they rode slowly back to Aberwyn. Over and over, Lovyan saw the accident in her mind. Why did the horse panic? There wasn't so much as a mouse running across the road. It had happened like dweomer. Suddenly she went cold all over and called out to Nevyn, who was riding a little behind. He urged his horse up to ride beside the cart.

"Nevyn, this accident was a most peculiar one."

"The man you sent to fetch me said as much, my lady. May I suggest that we discuss it privately?"

"Of course." She felt her fear like a hand at her throat. The old man apparently agreed with her sudden insight.

Rhys's wife, Madronna, met them at the gates. A willowy blond woman, she was pretty in a vacuous sort of way, but now her childlike face was composed by an iron will. Lovyan had to admire her daughter-in-law, who was sincerely fond of her husband.

"His chamber's prepared," Madronna said. "How bad is—"

"Bad, truly, but not the end. We'll nurse him through this between us."

While the men carried Rhys to the chamber, Lovyan went to her suite, took off her blood-soaked dress, and washed thoroughly. She put on a clean dress, a somber one of gray linen, then looked at herself in a mirror. The face that looked back seemed to have aged years since the morning. She was painfully aware of the deep wrinkles slashed across her cheeks and the numb, half-dead look of her eyes.

"Ah, Goddess, am I to bury another son?"

She laid the mirror down and turned away, knowing that she would do just that, for all Nevyn's skill with his herbs. Yet she could not cry. She found herself remembering the day her second son was brought home to her, her gentle Aedry, just sixteen that summer, brought home wrapped in a blanket and tied over his horse, killed riding with his father in a war. She stood in the ward and watched while they cut the ropes and brought him down, and she never allowed herself one tear, because she knew the warband was watching, and if she cried at all, she would start screaming like a madwoman. She felt the same now. No matter how furious Rhys made her, he was still her firstborn son.

With a toss of her head, she left the chamber and went down to the great hall. Over on the riders' side, the men were drinking steadily and saying little, even the ten men of her own that she'd brought as escort. As she walked past, she motioned to her captain, Cullyn of Cerrmor. He hurried over to the honor table and knelt at her side.

"Will he live, my lady?"

"I can only hope so, Captain. I need to send a speeded courier to Dun Deverry. The king has to be informed of this. Pick the man you think best and get him ready to go."

"Done, my lady, but it had best be one of Rhys's men."

"For the formality, I suppose you're right, but I can't command them."

"But, my lady, you're the regent here now."

"Oh by the gods, so I am! It's all happened so fast that I can barely think."

"It would take anyone that way, my lady." He hesitated, honestly sympathetic, but bound by considerations of rank. Finally he spoke again. "Your Grace, you know that I've had my differences with the gwerbret in the past, but it aches my heart to see your grief."

"My thanks."

When he looked up, she suddenly remembered Rhodry, and what Rhys's death might mean. The battle-grim warrior kneeling beside her loved Rhodry like a son, and she knew that Cullyn was as torn as she was. If Rhys died—even if he merely lay ill for months—the king would have the perfect reason to recall his brother, and Rhys would be unable to say a word in protest. She wanted Rhodry home with all her heart, but to have it take this?

"Ah gods." Her voice sounded like a moan, even to her, and she forced herself to stay in control of her rising tears. "Captain, fetch me a scribe and the captain of Rhys's warband. We've got to get that message to Dun Deverry as soon as ever we can."

For hours Nevyn worked on the injured gwerbret, but even as he set the broken leg and stitched the bad cut over the eye, he felt his hope receding. Sooner rather than later, Rhys would die. The fall had damaged one of his lungs—Nevyn could hear that by putting his ear to the gwerbret's chest—but how badly he couldn't know. The one good sign was that Rhys was not spitting up blood, which would mean that the lung had been punctured by a splinter from one of his many broken ribs. In time, it might heal, though he doubted it. What was worse was the damage to his kidneys. By opening up his second sight Nevyn could see the gwerbret's aura, and in it the centers of the various vortices of etheric force that correspond to the major organs of the body. Although such a diagnosis was rough, he could tell that something was severely wrong internally, centered on the kidneys. Just how severe, again, he couldn't say. He knew that time would make it all horribly clear.

Finally he'd done what he could do. Propped up on pillows, Rhys lay gasping for every breath he drew on the enormous bed, with its blue-and-silver hangings, worked all over with the dragon symbol of the rhan. His raven-dark hair was plastered to his forehead with sweat, and when he opened his eyes, they were cloudy.

"Will I live?"

"That depends on you to a large degree, Your Grace. Are you going to fight to live?"

Rhys smiled, as if saying that the question was superfluous, then fainted. With a sigh, Nevyn went to the chamber door to let in his wife, who had patiently waited all the long hours. She gave him a tremulous smile, then ran to her husband's side.

"If he looks the least bit worse, send a page for me immediately, my lady. I'm going down to the great hall to eat."

"I will, good herbman. My thanks."

Nevyn came into a somber hall. The warbands ate silently; the servants moved among them without saying a word. Alone at the head of the honor table, Lovyan was picking at a bit of roast fowl, eating a bite, then laying her table dagger down and staring into space. He sat down at her right hand.

"You should try to eat, Your Grace."

"Of course, but everything tastes like dirt from the stable yard.

I've sent a messenger off to Dun Gwerbyn to fetch my serving women. I rather feel the need of them."

"Just so. As regent you'll have much serious business to attend to."

A servant came with a trencher of fowl and cabbage, as well as a tankard of ale. Hoping he wouldn't offend Lovyan, Nevyn set to. He was hungry after his hard afternoon's work. She choked down a bit of bread like a dutiful child.

"I also sent a speeded courier to Dun Deverry," she remarked. "He'll go by ship to Cerrmor, then ride from there."

"Good, but truly, I think I'll send a message of my own. The king needs to know of this before . . . as soon as possible, and my messages travel faster than horses."

"No doubt." She shuddered like a wet dog. "Tell me the truth, my friend. When you slipped and said 'before,' you meant before Rhys dies, didn't you?"

"I'm afraid I did. My apologies. It may take weeks, but . . ."

She nodded, staring at her trencher, then suddenly pushed it away. Although she seemed on the verge of tears, she tossed her head and sat up straight, looking at him steadily.

"Let's lie to his poor little wife," she said. "Let her have a bit of hope. It's hard to be widowed when you've only been a wife for a year."

"So it is, and I agree. Besides, the gods may intervene and let him live. I've seen one or two cases where I'd given up hope, only to have the patient recover."

"Well and good, then." Yet her weary voice implied that such a hope was one that she would deny herself. "And what of that accident? There wasn't even a fly buzzing round his horse."

"So I thought, from what your messenger told me." He hesitated, wondering how much to say. "I'm not truly sure what happened, but I've made a few guesses. I suppose that poor beast was put out of its misery?"

"It was. The riders told me that it would have been in agony the whole way back to the dun, so they slit its throat and gave the meat to a nearby farmer."

"Well, I doubt if it could have told me much, anyway."

"Here, can you speak with animals?"

"Not in the least, my lady, I assure you. But I might have done a thing or two and judged its reactions. Well, as I say, doubtless naught would have come of it, anyway. Here's what I've been thinking. Most animals have what men call the second sight—that is, they can see the Wildfolk and a few kinds of apparitions. It's possible that the horse was frightened by malicious Wildfolk or by some sort of vision."

"A vision? A ghost or suchlike?"

"Or suchlike. There's never been a report of a ghost or banshee along the river road before, and they're generally tied to one place."

"I've never heard reports of any other sort of vision along that road either."

"Just so. I think we can conclude that the vision or the Wildfolk or whatever it was was deliberately sent there."

"Sent?" Her face went very pale.

"Just that, my lady. I'll wager that someone used dweomer to try and murder your son. When I find out who he is, then I swear to you, he'll rue the day he was born."

"My thanks." Although she spoke in a whisper, she was calm, the cold, bitter calm of a warrior surveying the field. "You told me that there was evil dweomer working behind Lord Corbyn when he rebelled. I never thought to see a blood feud worked by dweomer, but that's what this must be, isn't it? First they try to kill Rhodry, and now they've succeeded with Rhys. For some reason they hate the Maelwaedd clan."

"Ye gods, you're right enough! And Rhodry is . . ." He caught himself barely in time. There was no need to burden her with the truth at this particular moment. "Out somewhere on the roads. Well, doubtless the king's men will find him soon. The gods all know that they have more reason than ever to look for him."

Lovyan nodded, staring blindly down at her plate. Nevyn got up and went to the fire. He had to tell Salamander immediately that he could no longer come to Cerrmor. He would have to do his best to keep Rhys alive until the king made up his mind to recall Rhodry and instate him as Aberwyn's heir. He had another piece of information to pass along, too, the grim truth that Lovyan had seen, that the matter had gone far beyond the politicking of Eldidd lords. The dark dweomer was waging war on the Maelwaedd clan.

The king was having his hair bleached. In the midst of his private chamber, Lallyn the Second, high king of all Deverry and Eldidd, sat on a low bench carved with grappling wyverns while the royal barber draped towels around his liege's shoulders. As an honor to his high rank, Blaen was allowed to kneel at the king's side and hold the silver tray of implements. Ever since Madoc had come to him with the news, he'd been trying to have a private work with Lallyn, but in all the pomp that surrounded the king, private words were difficult to get. Even though the king sincerely wanted to hear what he had to say, this was the first chance they'd found all evening.

Carefully the barber began packing the king's wet hair with lime from a wooden bowl. Soon Lallyn would look like one of the great heroes of the Dawntime, with a lion's mane of stiff, swept-back hair to add further to his six feet of height. Such a hairstyle was a royal prerogative, and, as the king remarked, a royal nuisance, too.

"Blasted lucky, aren't you, Blaen? Look on our sufferings and be glad you were born a gwerbret's son."

"Glad I am, my liege."

The barber wrapped two steaming-wet towels around the king's head and fastened them with a circlet of fine gold.

"My liege, it will be some few minutes."

"It's always more than just a few. You may leave us."

Bowing, walking backward, the barber retreated to the corridor. Blaen sincerely hoped that the king was going to believe his strange tale.

"Now, Blaen, what's this urgent news?"

"Well, my liege, do you remember Lord Madoc?"

"The sorcerer's nephew? Of course."

"Here! You know that Nevyn's a sorcerer, my liege?"

Lallyn grinned at him while he adjusted a slipping towel.

"I do, at that. There's quite a tradition, passed down from king to marked prince, about sorcerers named Nevyn. The name's something of an honorific, or so my father told me, handed on like the kingship. In times of great need, one Nevyn or another will come to aid the king. I always thought it a peculiar tale and wondered why my father would tell me such a lie—until those gems were stolen, and lo and behold, a Nevyn appeared to return them to me. I prayed to my father in the Otherlands and made my apologies quite promptly, I tell you."

"I see. Well, then, I trust my liege will believe me when I tell him that Madoc has dweomer, too."

"Ah, I thought so, but I wasn't sure. I'm glad enough to know, but is this what you had to tell me?"

"Not at all, my liege. I've learned that dweomermen have ways of sending messages with their thoughts. Madoc came to me earlier with urgent news from Nevyn. He begged me to tell you, because he knew it would be difficult for a man of his rank to gain a private audience with the king, and this has to be kept private for as long as possible. Soon the whole court will know, because a speeded courier's on the way from Aberwyn, but Nevyn wanted Your Highness to get the news first."

"I see. And what is this grave matter?"

"Rhys of Aberwyn had a bad fall in a hunting accident today, my liege. They doubt if he'll live long—an eightnight, perhaps; at the most, a month."

The king stared at him for a moment, then swore in a way more fitting for a common-born rider than royalty.

"I agree, my liege. You can see why I thought it best that my liege heard this news straightaway."

"Just so." The king gingerly settled a slipping towel while he thought things over. "And I'm most grateful to you for it. Eldidd politics are always dangerous."

"So they are. No doubt my liege needs no reminding that the line of succession in Aberwyn will break as soon as Rhys dies."

"No doubt. I'm also quite aware how much your exiled cousin means to you, Your Grace. Rest assured that the matter is under my consideration."

Blaen felt the formal tone of voice like a slap across the face. He was being reminded that no matter how often they hunted or drank together, no matter how easily Lallyn would jest with him when the mood took him, the king was as far above him as he was above the common folk.

"My humble thanks, my liege. Your consideration is all that I'd ever ask for in this matter."

The king nodded with a glance away.

"Tell the barber that he can come back, will you? I want these towels off and now. I have some serious thinking to do."

In spite of the king's return to a more familiar tone, Blaen knew that he'd been dismissed. As he rose and bowed, he was wondering just what Talidd of Belglaedd and his allies had been telling their liege.

"I know Blaen will take good care of him, but I hate to leave Sunrise behind," Jill said.

"Oh, come now, my turtledove." Salamander was busy tying shut his saddlebags. "Every lad in the royal stables will be fussing over him, and with luck, we won't be gone long."

"I doubt me if we're going to have that kind of luck."

He paused, turning to look at her. They were in the inn chamber with their packed gear strewn around them.

"Well? Do you think—"

"I don't." He sighed elaborately. "I was merely trying to console."

There was a brief knocking at the door, and Blaen strode in without waiting for an invitation. With him were two serving lads, who immediately began gathering up the gear.

"The galley's ready," Blaen announced. "I'll accompany you down to the docks."

"His Grace is most kind." Salamander made him a bow. "And our liege the king as well."

"Indeed? I've found out—or, I should say, my lady found out—exactly why Savyl of Camynwaen is taking a hand in this affair. His younger brother has a slight claim to Aberwyn."

"Truly?" Jill said. "I never heard Lady Lovyan mention him."

"Well, it's not truly the sort of thing my aunt would dwell upon. You see, Rhodry's father had two bastard daughters with a mistress of his. Savyl's brother married one of them."

"Two daughters?" Salamander broke in. "Well, fancy that! Or . . . here, of course. You mean Gwerbret Tingyr."

"And who else would I be meaning?"

Jill gave Salamander a subtle sidewise kick.

"No one, Your Grace." Salamander covered smoothly. "I'd merely forgotten the gwerbret's name."

"Ah. Well, it's hard to keep all the noble bloodlines up in mind, truly. Here." Blaen tossed Salamander an embroidered cloth pouch. "Use this wisely."

Whistling under his breath, Salamander hefted the pouch and made it jingle.

"From the weight and the sound, Your Grace, there must be a cursed lot of gold in here."

"As much as I could raise. I intend to get it back from my scapegrace cousin once he's Aberwyn, mind."

Although he spoke casually, Jill could hear the tension in his voice, a wondering, perhaps, if he were bankrupting himself to little end. Once again she was overwhelmed by the sheer weight of ruling, the smothering web of obligations and intrigues that overlaid even something as fine as Blaen's and Rhodry's love for each other. Salamander made the gwerbret an exaggerated bow.

"We shall do our best to protect His Grace's investment." Then he flicked his long fingers and made the pouch disappear, seemingly into nothingness.

By then it was just sunset, and long shadows filled the curving streets. When they reached the wooden wharves to the south of the city, the sky had turned a velvet blue-gray with twilight. Over the grassy riverbanks bold swallows swooped and twisted. Riding low in the water some little way from the masses of barges and skiffs was the royal galley, about forty feet long and sleek as a ferret. There were red shields painted with the royal gold wyvern at every oarlock, and the men who lounged at the oars were wearing white shirts embroidered with the wyvern badge and long lines of interlace.

"The king's elite?" Salamander raised an eyebrow.

"The same," Blaen said. "I can't tell you, though, if our liege is doing this for Rhodry's sake or mine."

"Surely the king doesn't want to see Eldidd at war?" Salamander said. "Because if Rhodry doesn't return, war is what we'll have. Each clan will be accusing the others of murdering the rightful heir and claiming the rhan for themselves."

"I'm sure our liege knows that as well as you do." Yet Blaen sounded oddly stiff, a bit frightened, perhaps. "I'm not privy to all his thoughts, gerthddyn."

At the sight of Blaen, the galley's captain hopped to the pier and hurried over with a bow. While the servants loaded the gear aboard, Jill turned away and watched the smooth-flowing river. Desperately she tried to scry Rhodry out, but her untrained mind could show her nothing. All at once she felt another fear and involuntarily yelped aloud.

"What is it?" Salamander said.

"Perryn. He's close by. I know it."

She spun around, half expecting to see him in the crowd behind them, but there was no one there but curious passersby and a few longshoremen. Yet up in the velvet sky it seemed to her that she saw a long tendril of mist, reaching down toward her. Salamander saw it, too. When he threw up one hand and muttered a few words, the tendril vanished.

"He's in town, all right. Madoc will be taking care of that, Jill. Don't worry about a thing."

"Still, can't we get on that wretched boat and get out of here?"

"This very minute. There's the captain signaling us aboard."

Perryn paused just inside the south gate of the city. Just a moment ago he'd felt Jill's nearness; now the trail had suddenly gone cold. His dapple gray stamped impatiently and tossed its head. When they'd ridden into the vast city earlier that afternoon, the gray had nearly panicked. It had taken all of Perryn's horse empathy to calm it, and even so, it was still restless.

"Here, you! Are you going in or out? It's time to close the gates."

Perryn turned to see two city guards hurrying toward him, one of them carrying a torch. The cavernous gateway was already quite dark.

"Oh, er, ah, well . . . in, I think."

"Then don't just think—move, man!"

As Perryn obediently began to lead his horses toward the inner gate, the guard carrying the torch raised it high to shine the light full on his face.

"Your name wouldn't be Lord Perryn of Alobry, would it, now?"

"It is at that. Why?"

The torch bearer whistled sharply, three loud notes. The other guard grabbed Perryn's shoulder with his left hand and slammed his fist hard into his stomach, so quickly that Perryn had no time to dodge. He doubled over, retching, as two more guards ran up and grabbed his horses' reins from his helpless fingers.

"Good work! You've got the weasel Lord Madoc wanted, right enough."

"Talks like a simpleton, his lordship told me, and he must be one, too, to answer to his name like that."

Although the world still danced around him, Perryn forced himself to raise his head and look in time to see a guard rummaging through his saddlebags. With a bark of triumph, he held up the rambling scribe. When Perryn made a feeble grab at it, another guard slapped him across the face.

"None of that, horse thief. The only thing this scribe's going to write for you now is your death writ."

They disarmed him, bound his hands behind him, then pushed him along through the streets. Those few people still out at night stopped to stare and jeer when the guards announced that he was a horse thief. At one point they met a slender young man, wearing the plaid brigga of the noble-born, who was followed by a page with a torch.

"A horse thief, is he?" the young lord said. "When will you be hanging him?"

"Don't know, my lord. We've got to have the trial first."

"True enough. Well, no doubt I'll hear of it. My mistress is quite keen on hangings, you see." He gave the guard a conspiratorial wink. "She finds them quite . . . well, shall we say exciting? And so I take her to every single one."

At last they reached the guard station at the foot of the royal hill and turned Perryn over to the men there, though the man who'd first recognized him stayed to escort him into the royal compound itself. By then Perryn had recovered enough from the blows to feel the terror: they were going to hang him. There was no use lying to the king's officers; the rambling scribe would hang him on its own. Although at one point he did have a sentimental pang that he'd never see Jill again, at the root he was too terrified to care much about that one way or another. What counted was that he was going to die. No matter how hard he tried to pull himself together and face his death like a warrior, he kept trembling and sweating. When his guards noticed, they laughed.

"You should have thought about this rope when you were putting one on another man's horses, you cowardly little bastard."

"There must be a bit of fun to being hanged, lad. Why, a man gets hard, then spews all over himself when the noose jerks."

They kept up the jests the entire time that they were dragging him through the warren of sheds and outbuildings that surrounded the king's many-towered broch complex. In the flickering torchlight Perryn was completely disoriented. By the time that they shoved him into a tiny cell in a long stone building, he had no idea of which way north lay, much less of the layout of the palace grounds.

The cell was about eight feet on a side, with fairly clean straw on the floor and a leather bucket, swarming with flies, in one corner. In the door was a small barred opening that let in a bit of light from the corridor. Perryn stood next to it and tried to hear what the guards were saying, but they moved down along the corridor and out of earshot. He heard: "Of course Lord Madoc's interested in horse thieves; he's an equerry, isn't he?" before they were gone. All at once his legs went weak. He slumped down into the straw before he fell and covered his face with his hands. Somehow or other, he'd offended one of the powerful royal servitors. He was doomed.

Perryn had no idea of how long he'd sat there before the door opened. A guard handed him a trencher with half a loaf of bread and a couple of slices of cold meat on it.

"Pity that we had to take your dagger away, lad." His smile was not pleasant. "Just use your teeth like a wolf, eh? In the morning one of the undercouncillors will be along to see you."

"What for?"

"To tell you about your rights, of course. Here, they caught you red-handed, but you'll still get a trial, and you've got the right to have your kin by your side. Just tell the fellow, and he'll get a herald to them."

"I don't want them to know. Ah ye gods, I'd rather die slowly in pieces than look my uncle in the eye over this."

"Pity you didn't think of that before, eh? Well, I'm sure it can all be arranged. If you don't want your kin here, no need to waste the herald's time."

The warder handed in a tankard of ale, then locked the door. Perryn heard him whistling as he walked away.

Although the food and drink were unexpectedly decent, Perryn ate only to pass the time. The thought of Benoic and Nedd learning of his shame had taken his appetite away. Sooner or later they would, too, no matter whether they were there to watch him hang or not. He thought of the warder's words, that he might have thought of all this before, and wept a few tears for the truth of it.

"But I didn't really steal them. They followed me, didn't they?"

"Only in a manner of speaking."

He yelped and leapt to his feet, scattering the bread into the straw. There was a man standing on the other side of the door, a pleasant-looking fellow with blond hair and blue eyes. The sheer bulk of the elaborate embroidery on his shirt proclaimed him a member of the king's household.

"I'm Lord Madoc. Guards, bring him out."

"Are you going to hang me right now?"

"Naught of the sort. I want a few words with you, lad."

They bound his hands, then marched him along to the wardroom, a long, narrow chamber with an oppressively low ceiling. Down one wall was a row of sconces and lit torches; down the other, a narrow table spread with the tools of the torturer's trade.

"I'll confess," Perryn bleated. "You don't have to do anything to me."

"Splendid, but I wasn't planning on having you tortured. I want a look at you. Guards, tie him to the wall; then you can get back to your dinners."

"My thanks, Your Lordship." The guard captain made him a bow. "Do you have any idea of when he'll go to trial?"

"Oh, he won't be tried here. Our liege is remanding him to Rhys, Gwerbret Aberwyn. This little idiot raped the daughter of one of the gwerbret's highly regarded subjects, and under Eldidd law her father has the right to cut him to pieces."

Perryn's knees buckled. If he hadn't been tied to an iron ring attached to the wall, he would have fallen.

"Huh," the captain snorted. "A fine figure of a noble lord he is, raping women and stealing horses!"

Once the guards were gone, Madoc turned to Perryn and considered him with eyes so cold and distant that Perryn began to sweat again.

"Do you know who Jill's father is, lad?"

"I don't, my lord."

"Cullyn of Cerrmor, that's who."

Perryn yelped, a strangled little sob.

"Just so. They'll give him a sword and shield, hand you a dagger to defend yourself, then turn him loose on you. Think you'll win the ritual combat?"

Perryn shook his head no.

"I doubt me, as well. And even if you had all the gold in the world to offer as compensation, Cullyn wouldn't take it instead of your blood. So, are you going to face him, or are you going to do as I say instead?"

"Anything, my lord. I'll do anything. Please, I never raped her, I truly didn't. I thought she loved me, I truly did."

"I know, and your stupidity is the one thing that's saving you now. If I untie you, will you give me your word of honor that you won't try to escape?"

"Gladly. I doubt me if I could run, my lord, the way I feel."

"No doubt." He stepped back and considered him in a strange way, his eyes moving as if he were looking all around Perryn rather than at him. "Truly, you're halfway to being dead, aren't you?"

The lord's words seemed true enough. As soon as he was untied,

Perryn staggered and would have fallen if it weren't for Madoc's support. The equerry half led, half hauled him down the room to a low bench by a hearth, where some tinder and small sticks were laid ready for a fire. Madoc laid on a pair of logs, then snapped his fingers. Fire sprang out and danced along the wood. Perryn screamed. He clapped his hands over his mouth to force a second scream back, then swiveled around, crouching, to stare up at Madoc in terror.

"Well, you looked chilled, lad. Thought we'd have a bit of a blaze. Now, you young dolt, do you see what you've gotten yourself tangled up in? From now on, you're going to do exactly what I say, or . . ."

"I will. Anything at all, my lord. I swear to you on the honor of the Wolf clan and the gods of my people."

"Good. Remember that during your trip to Eldidd."

"I'm going there? You said you wouldn't . . ."

"I said I wouldn't let Cullyn get hold of you. There's another man there who very much wants a chat with you. My uncle."

THREE

In those days, Cerrmor had yet to expand to the place where the Gwarmael and the Bel rivers meet. A small village, Dei'ver, stood there, some forty houses and a pair of wooden docks, with a couple of inns to serve travelers who couldn't reach Cerrmor before nightfall. The royal galley put in there, ostensibly to buy ale, but in reality to set Jill ashore. Since Salamander had letters for the gwerbret, he would be marked at once as an important man in the city. Since she wanted to ask some questions of the kind of people who would have nothing to do with anyone associated with His Grace and his wardens, she needed to ride in alone.

Carrying the old saddle and bridle she'd brought from Dun Deverry for this purpose, and laden down with her gear, too, she made a great show of limping and cursing as she came into the village, as if she'd had to walk a long way in her riding boots. When she reached the dusty open space that did duty as a town square, she saw a couple of idlers sitting in the shade of a willow tree.

"What happened, silver dagger? Lose your horse?"

"I did. Broke his leg about five miles north of here. Is there anyone in town who can sell me another? By the love of every god, I hope I never walk that far again."

Since horses were a luxury beyond their reach, the villagers laughed in a nasty sort of way, but one of them waved his hand southward.

"Try the big inn by the Cerrmor road, lad. Old Mat sometimes has an extra horse or two in his stable."

"My thanks. By the way, have there been any other silver daggers through here recently? I'm looking for a friend of mine, an Eldidd man he is, but I wouldn't know what name he's traveling under."

The two of them exchanged a brief look.

"Well, seeing as how you're another silver dagger and all, I don't suppose there's any harm in telling you. An Eldidd man calling himself Adoryc came through here two days ago. He had the dagger in his belt."

"What's he wanted for?" the second man chimed in.

"Cursed if I know. The gwerbret's men don't tell the likes of me their business." Jill shrugged as best she could under all her burdens. "Well, I'll be getting along. My back's breaking."

As she limped away, Jill was thinking that Rhodry must have spread plenty of silver around on his ride south to keep local tongues mute. Even so, it was odd that no one who'd seen him had told the gwerbret's men the truth once the man who'd given them the coin had ridden on. It was probably the reputation of silver daggers that kept them honest, she supposed, the simple fear that Rhodry or someone else would come back to slit their throats if they failed to keep the bargain.

She found the big inn and Old Mat easily enough, and indeed, he did have a horse for sale, a decent gray gelding with a white off-fore and a white blaze. She haggled long enough to be convincing, then paid over some of Blaen's coin and saddled up the gelding. They left the village at a quick walk-trot pace, but once they were well on the road, she let the gelding canter.

In about an hour, not long before sunset, Jill reached the north gate of the city. Coming to Cerrmor always made her a bit melancholy. Since her parents had been born and raised there, she'd heard about it all her life, and it seemed that it should have been her home, too. Except that I have no home at all, she thought. Now she had even more reason to feel a total stranger, because dweomer was riding into town with her. With a bitter twist of her mouth, she realized that whether she fought against her own dweomer or not, it had already made her an alien among her people. It was also putting her in danger. As she led her horse down the narrow, twisting streets, through the packs of beggars and crowds of merchants and townsfolk, she was aware of how easy it would be for someone to slip up behind her and stick a dagger in her ribs. During her long walk down to the harbor, she constantly looked around and behind her.

That was probably why she saw the old woman at all. Just as Jill crossed the market square, a wagon filled with hay for the gwerbret's horses took a turn a little too sharply and tipped, blocking the street. Cursing, the carters picked themselves up off the cobbles as the strollers who had been right behind them milled in confusion and a noble on horseback began yelling at everyone to get out of his way that very instant. Jill turned her horse around and started working her way back along the edge of the square. All at once, she felt that she was being watched and spun around. Perched on a low wall with a market basket in her lap was a gray-haired woman wearing the black headscarf of a widow. Although much-mended, her plain blue dress was clean, caught in by a precisely folded kirtle. She was staring at Jill so intensely that Jill laid her hand on her sword hilt without thinking. The old woman shrank back.

"My apologies, lad. You just remind me of someone I used to know, like."

"No offense, good dame."

Up ahead the crowd cleared and began to disperse. Jill hurried through the opening, then stopped cold. That voice—the old woman's voice—by the gods, it had sounded familiar! But whose? Like her mother's. And the old woman had found her familiar in turn. Swearing under her breath, Jill got her horse turned around in the crowd and shoved her way back to the wall. The old woman was gone. Although she searched the area around the market square for some twenty minutes, she never caught another glimpse of the woman who might have been her grandmother. She felt her eyes fill with tears, irritably wiped them away, then headed down to the harbor. Rhodry—and the dweomer—had to come before her and her kin.

Immediately around the Cerrmor harbor, of course, was the area known as the Bilge, a tangle of narrow alleys, dirty shops, brothels, and taverns, all catering to the sailors, or perhaps preying upon them would be the better said. As much as Jill needed the kind of information the Bilge could give her, she had no intention of spending a night there. A safe distance upriver, in a bleak but decent district of warehouses and longshoremen's cottages, was an inn called the Capstan that had a good reputation among silver daggers, or at least, as good a reputation as any silver dagger inn could possibly have. Jill stabled her horse in a smelly split-roof shed, while the bald, squint-eyed innkeep scratched himself as he watched without a move to help her.

"You're cursed young to have the dagger."

"What's it to you?" Jill laid her hand on its hilt.

"Naught, naught. You can have a chamber to yourself if you like, lad. Custom's slow this time of year."

"Done, then."

The chamber was a tiny wedge of the second story, with warped shutters over the window and a mattress on the floor. When she kicked it out of the way, bedbugs swarmed and roiled. She dumped her gear in the corner, then left, padlocking the door behind her. The long narrow tavern room was dark and smoky, but the tabletops and the straw on the floor were reasonably clean. Jill swaggered in, trying to look as masculine as she could, and got herself a tankard of dark. Sooner or later someone was bound to realize that she was a lass, but she preferred it to be later. Since it was right at the dinner hour, the tavern was crowded with sailors spending their wages, a couple of wenches to help them at it, traveling peddlers, and a sprinkling of indifferently dressed men who were most likely thieves. The tavernman pointed to the hearth, where a stout woman fussed over a kettle.

"Beef stew tonight, silver dagger."

"Good."

Jill saluted him with her tankard and strolled away, to stand with her back to the wall. She'd had only a few sips of ale when she heard someone yelling out in the innyard. The tavernman ran to the window.

"Ye gods, it's some of the gwerbret's men! They're coming here."

Several of the customers melted away out the back as a man in mail threw open the front door. Three swordsmen, all dressed in dark red brigga, marched in and collared the innkeep.

"Any more customers upstairs?" the leader said.

"Not that I know of. Here, what is all this?"

"We're looking for someone, that's all." The swordsman turned to study the crowd. "We've already swept the Bilge. You can wager that we weren't entirely welcome, but sweep it we did. Here, you, silver dagger! Get over here."

Jill walked over as slowly and as insolently as she dared.

"What's your name, lad?"

"Gilyn. What's it to you?"

"Naught, scum, if that's the stance you're going to take. Do you know a man named Rhodry of Aberwyn? He's a member of your band."

"I do. Last time I saw him was up in Cerrgonney. What are you looking for him for?"

"Naught that concerns you." He started to turn away, then glanced back with a conciliatory smile. "Here, I'll tell you this, though. I swear on my honor that we mean him good, not ill. He's not wanted for a crime or suchlike. If you see him, tell him that, will you? It's worth gold in his hand if he'll just come to His Grace's dun."

"I will, then."

The gwerbret's men stomped out again, and the tavern's customers gave a unison sigh of relief. The tavernman turned to Jill.

"Do you believe what they said about your friend?"

"I do, at that, because Rhodry's a strange kind of man." She paused for a sip of ale. "He's never said a word about his past, and silver daggers don't pry into what a man may have done, but I'll wager he was noble-born."

"Indeed?" His eyes widened. "A lord with the dagger?"

She noticed that a number of people had paused to listen.

"Well, he wasn't a lord anymore, but he had the manners of the noble-born, all bows and courtesy, and he knew bard lore, too. And then there was the way he sat on a horse. You don't ride that splendidly unless your noble father's riding master put you on a pony when you were but three years old."

"I wonder what he did to be shamed?" a wench said with a melancholy sigh. "It sounds a sad tale. Was he handsome?"

"I suppose." Jill shrugged as if indifferent. "I was more interested in how well he fought."

"No doubt. Men!" She flounced off again to wait on a pair of staggering sailors in the corner.

Every one else smiled and drifted back to their tankards and talk. Jill was honestly startled at how well they accepted her as a lad. As she thought about it, she did have a dark voice for a woman in a country where a clear tenor was the most highly prized voice for a man, and no doubt they assumed her young, too, but she still was vaguely troubled when she realized just how much her years on the road had hardened her.

In a few minutes the tavernman and the wenches began passing out bowls of stew, which turned out to be surprisingly good, as was the bread served to sop it up with. When Jill found a place to sit down and eat, she was joined by a gray-haired man she judged to be a wandering peddler from his bent shoulders and the callus across his forehead from a pack strap.

"Tell me somewhat, silver dagger," he said, wasting no time in pleasantries. "Is this Rhodry a typical Eldidd man, with black hair and dark blue eyes?"

"He is, and built narrow from shoulder to hip."

"Hah. I think me I saw him two nights ago. He was in a tavern in the crafters' part of town. It stuck in my mind, like, because you don't often see a silver dagger doing his drinking among the potters and blacksmiths."

"True-spoken. Maybe you should tell that to one of the gwerbret's men."

"Maybe so. They might pay for it, like. Our Rhodry was calling himself Benoic, by the way. I wonder if he's lying ill somewhere, and that's why they can't find him."

"Ill? Did he look ill?"

"Not that I could see, but he was asking about herbmen. There seemed to be a particular old man he wanted, too. Not just any herbman would do. It had to be this one and his granddaughter."

"Nevyn."

"That was the name, truly. Strange sort of name, think I."

"It is. Well, the granddaughter's a pretty wench, you see."

"Ah." The peddler grinned and winked. "Well, maybe I'll step out after dinner and see if I can find one of the town wardens."

"I would if I were you. If they've got the warband out as well as the wardens, it must be important."

With a nod, the peddler devoted himself to his stew. Feeling close to despair, Jill ate mechanically, shoveling down food she no longer wanted just for the look of the thing. It was clear that Gwerbret Ladoic had ordered his men to search for Rhodry the moment he'd received the letters from the king. They hadn't found him yet, and she was beginning to doubt that they would, simply because the Bilge was the most logical place for him to be. For a moment she toyed with old tales of thieves having a vast system of tunnels under Cerrmor, then dismissed them as a gerthddyn's fancies. It also seemed clear that Rhodry had been certain that she and Nevyn were in Cerrmor. Someone had lied to him, lured him here—

All at once she broke off the thought and fixed her mind firmly on her meal. She concentrated on chasing a bit of meat through the gravy, forced herself to think of only that. For a moment, as she was thinking about Rhodry, she'd felt the touch of another mind on hers, just a light brush, but she could feel the cold, impersonal malice in it. In a few seconds the mind moved on, leaving hers. She laid the spoon down in her bowl. Appearances or not, she found it impossible to eat another bite.

"Just going out back," she said to the peddler.

He nodded and went on eating. No one else even looked up as she headed out the back door in the direction of the privy.

Directly behind the inn stood a horse trough, where the water caught the firelight spilling out the windows. She paused beside it, idly trailing one hand in the water as if washing it off, and using the dancing ripples to think of Salamander. Immediately she felt the touch of his mind, but it was some minutes before he answered her. She could see his image on the water only dimly.

"My apologies for taking so long. I was having dinner at the gwerbret's very table, and it took both some while and some fancy courtesies before I could leave."

"No matter. Some of the gwerbret's men were just in the Capstan. I take it that they haven't found Rhodry yet."

"They haven't, curse them. Are you still certain he's alive?"

"I am. It's the one thing I have to cling to. But here, I contacted you because I felt someone else touch my mind, someone who hated me."

"By the scaly underside of a dragon's balls! Say no more about this now, my turtledove. I'll see you on the morrow. There are times when words are safer than thoughts."

With that, his image disappeared.

When Jill returned to the tavern room, she found the peddler gone, but he came back in just a few minutes. With a broad grin he held up two silver pieces to show the crowd.

"From one of the town wardens. He's got a pouch of silver to pay for any information about Rhodry of Aberwyn, lads. I'd say that somewhat grand's afoot."

"Sounds like it'd be worth everyone's while to remember what they can about him," Jill remarked in what she hoped was a casual tone of voice. "My heart aches that I haven't seen him in months."

Everyone within earshot laughed their agreement and set to considering the question. Unfortunately, no one there had a scrap of information about Rhodry, and they agreed that lying to the gwerbret's men was unhealthy in the extreme. After a few hours Jill went up to her chamber. For all her grief, she was so weary from weeks of traveling that she fell asleep as soon as she lay down on her blankets. Yet she dreamt of Rhodry. It seemed she heard him calling out to her out of a desperate darkness.

Nevyn spent much of that night awake. He was sleeping on a cot in Rhys's chamber, where the slightest change in the gwerbret's labored breathing would wake him, because to a man as badly injured or ill as Rhys was, the hours right before dawn are always the most dangerous, when the astral tides of earth run low and sluggishly. Although Rhys spent a better night than anyone had a right to hope for, still Nevyn sat up, brooding over the low fire in the hearth and using it to talk with other dweomermasters. He had set men and women all over the kingdom to scrying, not for Rhodry, which was futile, but for odd breaks and discrepancies in their visions which might reveal an astral seal set over something that a dark master wanted hidden. So far, no one had found a thing. If Jill hadn't been certain that Rhodry lived, Nevyn would have despaired and thought him dead, but the sexual link between the pair was so strong that Jill would have felt his death like the loss of part of herself.

Toward dawn, when the tide of Aethyr came in, bringing fresh life to astral and etheric plane both, Nevyn fell asleep for a few hours, to be awakened by the servant come to help him bathe Rhys and turn him in the bed.

"Does His Grace still live, good sir?"

"He does." Nevyn got up and yawned, stretching like a cat. "Fill that kettle at the hearth, will you? I have to brew his various medicines fresh today."

Once Rhys was tended, Nevyn left him to his wife's care and went down to the great hall. So late in the morning, it was mostly empty, but a serving lass hurried out to the kitchen hut to fetch Nevyn some breakfast. He was eating porridge and ham at the honor table when Cullyn strode in, glanced around, and came over to join him. The serving lass brought Cullyn a tankard of ale, then retreated to the other side of the hall.

"Have you had any news of Jill?" Cullyn said.

"Not since last night. I heard from Salamander that he was staying with Gwerbret Ladoic, so I assume Jill is, too."

Cullyn nodded, frowned into his tankard for a moment, then flicked out a bit of straw with one finger and drank.

"I still don't understand how Jill and Rhodry got separated," Cullyn said.

"No more do I." Nevyn was thankful all over again that he'd refrained from swearing never to tell a lie—a vow that pleased the Lords of Wyrd, but which also made life unnecessarily difficult at times. "Although I do have a bit more information. It seems that Rhodry was asking around for me and Jill just before—well, before whatever it is that's happened to him. I'll make a guess that someone told him Jill had left him and headed to Cerrmor to find me or suchlike."

"It'd make sense. Then all they'd have to do was get him into the Bilge. No one there would look twice if they knocked him on the head or suchlike."

"Just so. Well, I'll be hearing from Salamander soon, I hope. I'll tell you the minute there's any news."

"My thanks. I'd be cursed grateful."

While he finished his ale, Cullyn stared idly across the hall, then suddenly smiled, just a quick twitch of his mouth that he hastily stifled. When Nevyn followed the captain's gaze, he saw Tevylla entering the hall, shepherding Rhodda ahead of her.

"Truly, Captain, the nursemaid's a good-looking woman."

Cullyn shot him a murderous glance and devoted himself to his ale until Tevylla had left the hall again.

As they sat together in a comfortable silence, Nevyn began to feel profoundly nervous about having Perryn brought to Aberwyn. If Cullyn ever found out what the young lord had done to his daughter, Perryn would die in a very unpleasant way no matter what Nevyn said about illnesses of the soul or suchlike. Yet lying about such a grave matter was beyond even him. For all that he didn't mind bending the truth on occasion, he refused to spin himself a web of half-truths that would choke him in the end. Since it would be a long while before Perryn arrived, he dismissed the problem in a fit of irritation. There were too many other troubles weighing on his mind for him to worry over that one.

"So you'll not be going to Cerrmor, then?" Cullyn said abruptly.

"I won't. I simply can't leave. Here's the gwerbret's life hanging by a thread and greedy lords circling round the rhan like hounds around a joint of meat on the table."

"But what of Rhodry?"

"That's the wound in our hearts, isn't it? What *of* Rhodry? I'm afraid we'll have to trust your daughter to pull him out of this particular trap. I think me she can do it, too, at least with Salamander there to help her. You trained her well, Cullyn."

"Did I, now? Well, we'll find out, won't we?"

"So we will, so we will. I only hope it's soon."

There was something else that he could never tell Cullyn. Deep in his mind, he knew that he was meant to stay in Aberwyn, not so much to nurse the gwerbret and aid Lovyan, but because staying where he was would undermine his enemies in a way that he could not foresee.

There was a silversmith in Cerrmor who did business with the silver daggers. Even though he couldn't make the daggers themselves, he was known for giving a fair price for battle loot and making decent repairs to ordinary weapons. His shop was the smallest and shabbiest on the street of the silversmiths, which ran down by the river but a good ways north of the Bilge; yet for all the squalor of the peeling wooden sign and filthy whitewash of the walls, when Jill pushed open the door, a string of beautifully crafted silver bells rang a sweet warning. She found herself in a narrow slice of the round house and faced with another door in a stout wooden wall. In a few moments, a stork-skinny bent-shouldered youngish man came out through it.

"And what can I do for you, silver dagger? Got somewhat to sell?"

"I don't, but I might be in the market to buy—information, that is. Have the gwerbret's men been in here, asking you about a man named Rhodry of Aberwyn?"

"They have, and of course I've told them I never laid eyes on him."

"You were lying, I take it."

"Of course. He was in here not more than two nights ago, asking me about herbmen. I recommended a good one that I know, and he slipped out the back way. He knew that the wardens were on the prowl after him."

Jill swore under her breath.

"Here, good smith, if you see Rhodry again, for the love of the gods, tell him to go to the gwerbret. He's not been accused of any crime, no matter what he thinks. Tell him that the woman he's looking for is under Ladoic's protection."

It was the smith's turn for oaths.

"I would've told His Grace's men if I'd known that! But Rhodry tells me that he's been accused of taking someone's head, and cursed if he'll lose his own over it, so of course I lied for him."

"Honorable of you." Jill meant it quite sincerely. "But that's torn it, then. Here, don't you think it's passing strange that every man in the rhan is looking for him and he hasn't turned up?"

"He must have left, I suppose."

"Maybe. Suppose you wanted to hire a couple of lads to get someone out of the way. Where would you go in the Bilge?"

"I see what you mean." The smith sucked his teeth for a few moments while he thought. "How come you're so interested in all of this?"

"He's a friend of mine. We rode on a couple of hires together. If somewhat's happened to him, I'll want vengeance for it—any silver dagger would." She took two silver pieces out of the pouch hanging from her belt. "I'll pay for the information."

"I won't take your coin, because I don't know anything for certain, but I've heard that there's a tavern in the Bilge called the Red Man. Supposedly if you ask the right questions there, you can hire anyone for anything."

"And if you ask the wrong ones?"

The smith smiled and pantomimed running a knife across his throat.

After she left the shop, Jill spent some time wandering the streets while she planned out her visit to the Bilge. Even without the smith's warning, she knew quite well that no one simply barged into the Bilge and started asking questions. She found a little open space around a public well and sat down on a wooden bench to think. Even the denizens of the Bilge were afraid of silver daggers, who avenged any murdered member of their band. On the other hand, if they thought her set to avenge Rhodry, they might well eliminate her first and worry about other silver daggers later. But of course Rhodry wasn't dead. Suddenly she realized that she had a move in this ugly game of gwyddbwcl: since he wasn't dead, the Bilge knew it, too. Once she let them know she knew, the rules would change.

When she started for the Bilge, she took a detour to a leatherworker's shop that she'd noticed earlier. She found the owner sitting cross-legged on a table, pieces of a saddlebag around him as he stitched. In the corner of the room a dirty child of three played with a pair of puppies, and from the back room came the smell of cooking and the sound of a crying baby. The craftsman glanced up.

"Ah, can I be of help to you, lad?"

"No doubt. I want to buy a jerkin."

"Very well. I'll measure you, and it'll be about three days."

"I need it now."

The craftsman laid aside the piece he was working on; then

slowly, carefully, as if he were afraid she would draw and swing at any moment, he got down from the table.

"I've no time to wait, hidesman."

"Er, well and good, then, if you don't demand a perfect fit. I've got one I was making for the miller's son, and he's about your size."

"Bring it out."

When the craftsman went to the back, he swept up the child and the puppies with him. In a few minutes he came back with the heavy leather vest, which had metal studs all down the sides. When she tried it on over her shirt, it was a little tight, but it would do. She threw six silver coins, about twice what it was worth, onto the table and strode out, leaving the craftsman shaking behind her. She took the jerkin to a public privy and put it on under her shirt this time, lacing it tight to flatten her breasts. Although it chafed, it would also protect her ribs against a casual knife. It was the best protection she could get, since the gwerbret's men frowned on civilians wearing mail in the city streets. Then she went on to the Bilge.

In the sunny morning the narrow, filthy streets were nearly deserted. A gaggle of ragged children played at hurley with a bent stick and a torn leather ball; a couple of women with market baskets hurried past her on their way to the fishmonger's down at the wharves. She saw one man, a white-haired beggar with no hands, sunning himself in a doorway. She strolled over to the ex-thief and dropped a silver piece in the wooden bowl beside him.

"Where's the Red Man tavern?"

"That's not a pleasant place, lad."

"Do I look like a pleasant sort of man?"

He laughed, revealing brown stumps of broken teeth.

"Well, then, keep going along this here street until you come to a tannery yard. The stink'll guide you. Then go around the tannery. You'll see the Red Man's sign down an alley to the left."

As she walked on, Jill kept on a close guard. Here and there, she saw a leather drape move at a window, or a figure appear briefly at an open door. She suspected that already the old thief had pressed some child into service as a messenger and sent it to the tavern with the news that a silver dagger was on his way. Even though she was sweating under the heavy jerkin, she appreciated it more than ever. If their enemies wanted to, they could murder her here in the street without anyone bothering to interfere. She wondered again about Rhodry, if perhaps the gwerbret's men had merely been led right past some place where he'd been hidden. In this tight-lipped little world, anything seemed possible.

To her surprise, the Red Man was clean, with newly white-washed walls and a well-swept cobbled yard around it. The sign hanging out front showed a bright red giant wearing naught but an enormous erection as he stood on top of a hill with an uprooted tree in each hand. The image was somehow annoying, a bawdry gone sour. When she went inside, she found that the half-round tavern room was also clean, with fresh straw on the floor and scrubbed tables. All the shutters were closed, leaving the room dark except for the firelight from the hearth, where a spitful of chickens were being turned by a ragged scullery lad. Half a dozen men sat at one table; the rest were empty. Near the hearth one fellow snored loudly in the straw with a pair of dogs cuddled at his back.

The tavernman who came to greet her was Bardekian, a fleshy black man whose face and arms were covered with old scars, all of them long, thin cuts from some sort of sharp knife.

"We don't get many silver daggers in here, lad."

"I suppose you're too good to be serving the likes of me."

"Not too good, too cautious. You're welcome to drink, but only a little. Listen, silver dagger, I know your kind. Two tankards, three —all is fine, no trouble. Then one more or suchlike, and somewhat snaps. There is the fight, there is the blood on my nice walls, there is the corpse on my clean floor. I serve you two tankards, no more. Done?"

Jill noticed the men at the table listening, and their hands were near their sword hilts. She gave them an insolent stare, then turned back to the tavernman.

"Done. Give me a tankard of dark."

Jill found a table where she could sit with her back to the wall and made a mental note of the position of every window and door. When the tavernman gave her the ale, she held up a silver piece.

"I'm looking for someone, someone who seems to have disappeared."

The tavernman's eyes flicked this way and that. The men at the other table leaned forward, listening.

"Someone else is looking for him, too," she went on. "I'll wager you can guess who I mean."

"Rhodry of Aberwyn?"

"Just that. I've got a score to settle with that lying little bastard. I don't give a pig's fart why the gwerbret wants him. His Grace can hang what's left after I'm done with him, for all I care."

The tavernman considered her shrewdly, then nodded, accepting her tale.

"I am glad I am not this Rhodry with the likes of you after me. What makes you think I know somewhat about him?"

"I'll wager you know naught but the name of a man who knows more."

"Here, they look for this Rhodry everywhere and never find him. I say he is dead. Forget him. You can't bring a man back from the dead to kill him a second time."

"Dead?" Here was the moment she'd been counting on, and she paused, giving him a twisted, ugly smile. "Come now, my friend. We both know better than that. Word gets around."

He hesitated, his dark face going a bit ashy in honest fear. A burly brown-haired fellow at the other table got up, swinging himself free of the bench, and strolled over, his narrowed eyes revealing nothing of what he might have been thinking. He had the biggest hands that Jill had ever seen on a man, enormous bear paws like clubs.

"Just how much is your hatred worth, silver dagger?"

"Hard coin."

Smiling a little, he sat down and took the silver piece she offered him.

"I had naught to do with getting him away, but I had a chance at the job, and I saw who was doing the hiring."

"I like a man who doesn't mince words." She got out two more coins and flipped him one. "You'll get the other at the end of the tale."

"Well and good, then. Now here, you're right enough. There never was any question of killing him, far as I could tell. I've got a friend who's made somewhat of himself, risen in the world, like. He's a footman for one of the rich merchants up on the cliffs, see, a man who doesn't fancy being jumped in the street one dark night, so my friend, he goes around with him. And his master's rich friends know that my friend is always useful for a bit of rough work, like convincing a man who owes them coin to pay up. So my friend comes in here, oh, three nights ago, it was, and saying that he's maybe got a job for us. A business acquaintance of his master's wants a word with a certain silver dagger, and he'll pay if we take this lad on the road and bring him somewhere."

"Where?"

"I don't know, because we never did it." He leaned closer in garlic-breathed sincerity. "If you'd have seen this Briddyn, you wouldn't have taken a copper from him, either. He was this big man, not paunchy, but all porky-like, and he had this smooth little face like a lad's, and this slick black hair and beard, like it was greased with lard, it was that slick."

"Indeed? Did you notice whether his hands were smooth, too?"

"I did, and they were. I can still see him, like, in my mind." He shuddered slightly. "In his beard he had this clip like lasses put in their hair, but it was a silver lizard with a butterfly in its mouth. There was somewhat about him that creeped my flesh, and it wasn't just his taste in jewelry, neither."

"Was he a Bardek man?"

"He might have been, but then again, he might have been a Deverry man with some Bardek blood in his clan. He was brownish, sort of, but it might have been just a lot of sun. So anyway, this Briddyn offers us a lot of coin, but it wasn't near half enough, not for meddling with a silver dagger. When we turned him down, I was blasted close to fouling my brigga. What if he takes it amiss, like? think I. I could tell my friend was thinking the same. Now, I don't know what he could've done to us, but he just took us that way. Creeped my flesh, he did."

Jill considered him and his story both over a sip of ale. Although she was inclined to think every inhabitant of the Bilge a liar, she doubted very much that a man like him had the imagination to think up so detailed and strange a description of this Briddyn fellow. When she looked at the other men, listening carefully at their table, she realized that her informant's little tale had made them uneasy, too. Yet, something simply smelled wrong. She slid over the last silver piece.

"My thanks. Now, this Briddyn was staying at the Golden Dragon Inn, but I'll wager he's long gone by now."

"No doubt."

In one fluid motion she drew her dagger with her right hand and grabbed his shirt with the left, dragging him half onto the table. Except for one slight shudder, he went perfectly still, staring into her eyes like a rat mesmerized by a ferret. He apparently could tell that she wanted to kill him just for the satisfaction of seeing blood run.

"Listen to me carefully, or you die. The first thing you said to me was this: 'I had naught to do with getting him away.' Getting him away where? You know more than you're telling."

He whimpered then, and threw a desperate look to the others sitting at their table. None of them moved; one even made an ostentatious show of drinking from his tankard, as if naught in the world troubled him at that moment.

"You whoreson scum," she went on. "I came here willing to pay good coin for what you know, and you hold out on me. Has the Bilge fallen on evil times? A man used to be able to buy what he wanted here." She laughed, a little mutter that was utterly crazed, and let him go with a shove that had him reeling in his chair. "Answer me. Get him away where?"

"I don't truly know." The fellow was whining like a child. "I don't. Please believe me. All I know is that Briddyn said that once we had him, he'd be taken away. So we didn't have to worry, like, about having to kill him or suchlike."

There was more—she knew it—but the others were beginning to get restless, and there were, after all, five of them as well as her informant. Jill rose, keeping the dagger in hand.

"You in the blue brigga! Get your hand away from that throwing dagger, or I'll nail you with mine."

With an oddly good-natured grin he complied, settling down again on the bench. The tavernman stepped forward.

"Get out, silver dagger. Get out of my tavern now. You have what answer you get. No one knows what happened to Rhodry. Briddyn must have gotten him, and after that, no one knows. Now get out."

"Well and good, then. I will. Oh, I believe you well enough. Who knows where the hawks fly, huh?"

She'd said it just as an idle chance, a random bit of bait, but the trap sprung closed fast. As the blood drained from his face, his dark skin turned as gray and sickly as dirty snow.

"I said get out." He could barely whisper. "Get out before you die."

The Deverry men watched in sincere puzzlement at his terror. Jill stepped closer, raising the dagger, and let herself laugh, that same crazed chortle, wailing higher and higher until he sank to his knees in the straw.

"Here!" One of the others rose to his feet. "What are you doing to our Araelo?"

"Leave him alone!" The tavernman was screaming now. "Leave him alone! Get out! All of you!" Then he burst into tears, dropping his face into his hands.

The men sat as if turned to stone. Jill stopped laughing cold, sheathed the dagger, and walked out. It took all her will, but she left slowly, calmly, and strolled down the middle of the street for about a hundred yards. When she glanced back, she saw that the door of the Red Man was closed—and bolted on the inside, too, she'd wager. She let out her breath in a long sigh and felt a fear-cold sweat running down her back and breasts under the leather jerkin. It was time to get out of the Bilge. Luck had brought her some important information, and she wanted to live long enough to tell Salamander.

Although her flesh creeped with nerves the whole way, Jill left the Bilge without incident and asked one of the town wardens the way to the Golden Dragon Inn. It turned out to be near the west gate, on the far side of the river, not far from the gwerbret's dun. Bold as brass, they are, she thought to herself. As she crossed the white stone bridge that arched over the river, she felt Salamander's mind tug at hers. She paused to lean over the rail and look down at the swift-flowing river. Although she failed to see his image, she could hear his thoughts in her mind and answer back.

"Jill, by the gods! I was trying to scry you out, and I saw you in the Bilge! You shouldn't have gone there alone."

"I did, and I lived, didn't I? I've got some horrible news, but I doubt me if I should tell you this way."

"It's time for me to 'hire' you anyway. I've moved into the Golden Dragon Inn."

"I'll be round straightaway."

As she went on, she was thinking that Briddyn must have a goodly amount of coin, if he shared Salamander's taste in inns. She turned out to be right, because the Golden Dragon was a splendid three-story building in the Bardekian style—that is, a long rectangular plan with a curved roof like a ship turned upside down. At either end, set into the curving roof beams, were enormous wooden statues of some god or other with his hands raised in blessing. Before she went in, Jill circled the place, noticing how the lovely garden in the front became a mucky innyard in back, with the dung heap and the well too close together for such an expensive place. As she loitered there, a young lass in a dirty apron came out the back with a pair of water buckets. When Jill went over, the lass wrinkled her nose.

"Get along, silver dagger. I'm not the kind of lass that would be interested in the likes of you."

"You're not to my taste anyway," Jill said, suppressing a smile. "All I want is a bit of information about one of the guests here, and I'll pay for it."

The lass considered, torn between greed and fear of her employer. When Jill held up a silver piece, the greed won.

"Who was this guest?"

"A merchant named Briddyn."

"Oh, him!" She wrinkled her nose again. "I remember him well enough, my thanks, and a nasty lot he was. Always complaining, naught suited him, not the sheets, not the ale, not the wretched pot to piss in, I swear it. Thanks be to the gods that he left! I'd have gone daft if I'd had to wait upon him any longer."

"I see." Jill handed over the coin. "Do you know what he trafficked in?"

"Cloth. He rode in with a big caravan, and I heard the stablemen talking, saying that it's a good thing his bales were light and easy to unload, because the bastard didn't tip. And he had one special bale of cloth in his chamber. He told me that if I touched it, he'd slap me about, as if I'd be interested in his nasty cloth."

"Did he have any visitors?"

"I never saw a one, but who would go visiting a nasty swine like that? When he left, he said he was going north to Dun Deverry. Huh—as if swine like that belonged in the king's own city!"

Quite puzzled, Jill went on her way. It was the most peculiar turn so far, she decided; mysterious strangers bent on doing harm to someone normally don't make such nuisances of themselves that every servant remembers them. As soon as she opened the front door of the inn, the innkeep and a beefy young man ran across the tavern room to bar her way.

"No silver daggers in my inn! Try the Capstan, lad."

"One of your guests summoned me here, pork gut. Salamander the gerthddyn said he had a hire for me."

When the innkeep snarled under his breath, she laid her hand on her sword hilt. He stepped back sharply.

"I'll send a lad up to ask, silver dagger." His voice shook badly.

"But you'd best be telling the truth, or I'll have the wardens on you."

Jill crossed her arms over her chest and scowled at him until the lad returned with the news that Salamander did indeed want a silver dagger for a bodyguard. Muttering under his breath about possible thievery, the innkeep took her up himself to the chamber, which was on the top floor, far above the stink of the streets. When Salamander opened the door, he was resplendent in a brigga of soft blue wool, a shirt stiff with floral embroidery, and a tooled belt of red leather.

"Ah, my thanks, good innkeep. You have brought me a most highly recommended silver dagger, who, though young, is known for deeds of derring-do and blood and guts, such as eating the livers out of bandits and the hearts out of thieves."

"You do go on so, sir! Will you be honoring us with a tale this evening?"

"Mayhap, mayhap. Come in, Gilyn. Let us discuss this hire."

It turned out that he'd rented not a chamber but an entire suite, paneled in dark wood and furnished with a cushioned chair, a carved table, and a long purple Bardek divan as well as a bed in a separate room.

"You don't stint yourself, do you?" Jill said.

"And why should I?" Salamander poured her a goblet of pale mead from a glass flagon. "Now, I'll wager that you can guess that the gwerbret hasn't found Rhodry."

"He's never going to."

Salamander glanced up, the mead glass still in his hand, his lips half parted as he stared at her in sudden fear.

"Rhodry's in the hands of the Hawks of the Brotherhood."

For a long moment the gerthddyn never moved or spoke. It seemed, indeed, that he'd stopped breathing until at last he whispered out his words.

"Oh ye gods, not that! Are you certain?"

"The man who was hunting for him had handled so much arsenic that his skin and hair were turned slick. When I just barely mentioned the work 'hawk,' the man I was talking to went all hysterical on me." She slammed her fist on the table so hard that the flagon jiggled and spilled. "I know what the Hawks do to men they get their hands on. If they've put Rhodry to torture, they're going to die. One man for every mark they give him. I swear it. I'll track them down like ferrets after rats. One man for every mark."

The she began to laugh, a maddened chuckle that took over her voice.

"Jill! Stop it! By the gods!"

She tossed her head and went on laughing. He grabbed her by the shoulders, shook her, yelled at her, then finally slammed her against the wall. The laughter stopped. When she saw the grief in his smoky-gray eyes, she wondered at herself for not being able to weep. She shook free of his hands and went to the window to look down at the narrow garden. It seemed painfully unjust that the sun should be so bright when her Rhodry was in the hands of darkness. Then she heard Salamander sob and spun around to see tears running down his face as he stood there limply, his hands at his sides. The contrast between his elegant clothing and his helpless pain made him look like a child in his father's finery. Unsure of what to say, she went over and laid a tentative hand on his shoulder.

"You forget he's my brother."

"I do, at that. Forgive me?"

He nodded, looked away, still weeping, his shoulders shaking, and yet he made no sound. Jill realized that she could say naught to him that would be a right thing.

"I'm going to the Capstan to get my gear."

He nodded to show that he'd heard, but he never looked at her.

During the long walk back to the Capstan, Jill felt as exhausted as if she'd fought a long battle, as drained as if she'd found Rhodry dead. She realized, then, that she was indeed thinking of him as being as good as dead, and that she could never mourn until she avenged him. If they did torture him to death, she swore that her vengeance would be a long thing, a slow, patient hunt with many a kill to its credit. So the Hawks had dweomer, did they? So did she, and she would use it to the full if she had to. When she looked up at the sky, it was a brilliant, swelling blue; the cobbles on the street seemed to glow from within. It was the power rising within her along the channel that Perryn's unwitting dweomer had carved out by accident, and she knew then that she could summon it when she needed it. Yet it would be dangerous: she was as untrained and unknowing as Perryn was; like him, she would be risking madness or even some slow death. She no longer cared. All that counted now was vengeance.

Once she collected her horse and gear, as a precaution she took the long way back to the Golden Dragon, sticking to the wider boulevards where she could ride rather than leading her horse down narrow streets. She took a turn by the harbor, where the merchantmen were drawn up at pier after pier to load the last of the summer's goods. In another month or so, the seas would be impassable, and already the water was a darker, colder blue. Here and there she saw Bardek men engrossed in conversations with the foremen of the longshore crews, while great bales of cargo marched down the gangplanks on the backs of men. You can get a cursed lot in one of those ships, she idly thought to herself.

"Gods!"

She kicked her horse to a jog and rushed back to the inn, caution forgotten.

She found Salamander perfectly calm, or rather, a little too calm, just as she was, his eye more steel than smoke, his voice brittle. He waved at a pair of full goblets on the table.

"We never drank the mead I poured. I suggest we do so. A pledge, I was thinking."

"Splendid idea. Tell me the elven word for vengeance, will you? We should swear in both our tongues."

"Anadelonbrin. Swift-striking hatred."

"Done, then. Anadelonbrin!"

"Vengeance!" And he tossed back his head and howled like a wolf on the coldest night in winter. "That's to summon the death wolves, my turtledove, the vengeance wolves of the goddess of the Dark Sun. Do you know Her? I think me you do, but by another name, because I can see Her eyes look out of yours at times. The elven seers teach that there are two suns, a pair of twin sisters. One is the bright sun that we see in the sky; the other is on the other side of the world. The bright sister gives life, and the dark, need I say, death."

"Then may Her wolves ever run before us."

They touched goblets and drank the mead together.

Salamander had, of course, contacted Nevyn through the fire and told him of Jill's discovery. For some hours that afternoon, Nevyn could do little but pace back and forth in the sickroom and let his rioting emotions spend themselves. Loathing, grief, fury—they all ran together and made him feel like screaming out curses on the gods and the Great Ones alike, that they would let such a thing happen. That Rhodry would die was horrible enough; that he would die slowly at the hands of perverted men was heart-wrenching. As always, he berated himself as well. Surely there must have been some warning he'd overlooked, something he could have done? Every time he looked at Rhys, fighting for his life, gasping for every painful breath he drew, his highly trained imagination would threaten him with pictures of Rhodry in the hands of the Hawks. Over and over again he banished those thoughts by stamping them with the image of a flaming pentagram until at last his mind was still.

Then, finally, he could think. Although his first impulse was to rush to Cerrmor, not only did he have pressing reasons to stay where he was, but also the journey would simply take too much time. By the time he reached Cerrmor, Jill and Salamander might well be a hundred miles away. Besides, if the enemy had left by water, as certainly seemed the case, they and their victim were doubtless already long gone. It made perfect sense: although they could never get an unconscious man past the harbor guards and customs officers in Cerrmor itself, nothing would be easier than to get him out of the city in a wagon, load him onto a coastal vessel, and take him to some less heavily guarded port, where . . . where what? That 'what' puzzled Nevyn mightily. If the Hawks had simply wanted to torture him to death or even kill him quickly, why hadn't they taken him on the long road down to Cerrmor or even stayed in the Bilge, where torturing a man to death was considered light entertainment and no matter for the gwerbret's men? Why all this business with ships and this slow game of gwyddbwcl that offered them chances to lose at every turn? And above all, who under the god-cursed sky had hired them in the first place?

As baffled as a cornered bear, he shook his head and growled aloud, then resumed his pacing. At least this water journey explained why scrying could find no trace of Rhodry. If they were far enough from land, the dark masters had no need of setting seals over their victim, because not even the greatest master of dweomer can scry over a large body of water, and especially not the ocean. The vast outpourings and upheavals of etheric force disrupt the images, as well as shielding whoever is trying to hide, rather as if someone were trying to use normal sight to peer through thick fog or smoke. As long as the Hawks kept Rhodry some miles out to sea, no dweomer in the world could find him.

"I suppose they're somehow toying with us," he remarked to the fat yellow gnome.

The gnome frowned in thought, then hopped up onto a wooden chest and began to pick its toes.

"We do have one hope," Nevyn went on. "They may be planning on ransoming him or suchlike. If that's true, then they'll keep their foul hands off him, at least until they open the negotiations."

The gnome turned its head, looked at him, and nodded to show it understood. Since this particular little creature had hung around him for many years, it was beginning to develop the rudiments of a mind. All at once it stiffened, then jumped to its feet and pointed at the door. Just as Nevyn turned there was a knock, and a page came in.

"My lady Lovyan wishes to know if you're free, sir. Talidd of Belglaedd has just turned up at our door."

"Then fetch the gwerbret's lady to keep watch on her husband, and I'll go down as soon as she arrives."

Nevyn muttered a few choice curses under his breath, then steeled himself to face the scheming lord.

When he came into the great hall, he saw, much to his relief, that Talidd wasn't the only guest at the table of honor. Lord Sligyn was there, sitting at the tieryn's right hand, swilling ale and glaring at Talidd over the tankard. A stout, red-faced man in his mid-thirties, with a thick pair of blond mustaches, Sligyn rose with a bellow in Nevyn's general direction.

"There you are, herbman! Come and talk some sense into this pigheaded fool of a noble lord."

"I beg your pardon, my lord." Talidd was on his feet in an instant.

"You blasted well should, eh? Spreading all this nonsense about our Rhodry."

Talidd opened his mouth, glanced at Lovyan, and shut it again. Nevyn went cold, wondering if Talidd had somehow discovered the secret of Rhodry's parentage. Dimly he was aware that across the hall, Cullyn had gotten up and taken a few steps their way.

"Will you both please sit down?" Lovyan said, and there was steel in her voice. "What nonsense, Sligyn?"

"That the lad's dead." Sligyn took his place on the bench again. "Don't you try to deny it, either, Talidd. Heard you myself, eh? Nattering away at that tourney Peredyr gave. Pile of . . . uh, nonsense."

Talidd winced and sat down fast, scrupulously avoiding Lovyan's eye.

"Your Grace, forgive me if I distress you. I had a bit much ale that day, and I was only wondering why the king's riders couldn't find the lad if he were still alive."

Sligyn started to blurt out an angry contradiction, but Nevyn laid a heavy hand on his shoulder to make him hold his tongue.

"I take no offense, my lord." Lovyan sounded a bit weary and nothing more. "I've often wondered the same thing myself. Nevyn, do sit down! I can't stand having you all hovering about."

"My apologies, Your Grace." He took a seat next to Sligyn. "As far as anyone can tell, Rhodry's actively hiding from the king's guard. I have no idea why."

An odd look flickered on Talidd's face, a hint of contempt, hastily stifled. Sligyn slammed his tankard down on the table and leaned forward.

"Out with it, man," Sligyn snarled. "I've had enough of your foul sneers and mincing words. Out with it!"

Talidd's face reddened.

"I was merely wondering, Lord Sligyn, just why he doesn't want to be found. He's been a silver dagger for years now, hasn't he? Makes you wonder what he's done."

Slowly and deliberately Sligyn got to his feet.

"Are you insulting my lady's son and her right here to see it?"

"I'm not." Talidd rose to face him. "I'm merely speaking a wondering."

Before Lovyan could intervene Cullyn was there, striding over and stepping between the lords with respectful bobs of bows to both of them.

"My lord Sligyn, my apologies, but if anyone's going to be taking umbrage at insults for my lady's sake, I will. That's my duty as her captain, after all."

Talidd went white and sat down rather fast.

"If Your Grace will forgive me, I fear me I forgot myself. The unsettled state of the rhan is beginning to wear on us all."

"So it is." Lovyan favored him with a small nod. "I promise you that as soon as we receive news of Rhodry, the Council of Electors shall have it, too."

"My humble thanks, Your Grace."

Although Talidd kept his speech pleasant and his visit very brief, Nevyn found himself wondering about the lord. Why was he so sure that Rhodry was dead? Could it be that he'd had something to do with his kidnapping?

"Curse them all!" Salamander said. "May their teeth rot first, then their noses. May their eyes fill with phlegm, and their ears with a ringing. May their breathing slacken, and their hearts tremble within them. May their testicles harden, and their manhood soften."

"And is that what you've been brooding with your breakfast?" Jill said. "I thought a curse was a wrong thing for a dweomerman to work."

"It would be if it had any power behind it. Alas, my curses are but words, idle, empty, and most meaningless, except as a way to relieve my most overwrought and troubled heart." He got up from the table and stalked over to the window. "Curse this fog, too! May it shrivel, may it vanish, may it turn to naught but air!"

Jill looked up from her porridge to see the fog swirling dark outside the window, as if defying Salamander's curse.

"What's so wrong about the fog?" she said.

"None of the coasters will sail in it, and we need a ship."

"We do?"

"We do. While you were sleeping, my turtledove, I was considering wiles and schemes. Your success in the Bilge gave me an idea, or to be precise and thorough, many ideas, of which I have rejected most." He turned, perching on the sill. "Obviously we are meant to chase after this Briddyn. If the Hawks truly wanted to hide from us, we would've discovered naught, no matter how badly you terrified the entire Bilge. Instead they've left clues so plain that even the gwerbret's men could have followed them. So, now, we are left with two choices, to wit, one: Briddyn is a false trail, meant to throw us off the scent; or two: he is the bait to lure us into a trap. Instinct tells me it's the latter."

"Oho! But what if we follow the trail, then avoid the trap?"

"My thoughts exactly. I suspect that they're underestimating us. For all I know, they could well realize that I have dweomer, but I'll wager my last copper that they don't know you do. I'm also sure they don't know how well you can swing that sword."

"Good. It'll gladden my heart to show them."

"No doubt. I . . ." He broke off at a knock at the chamber door. When Jill opened it, she found a sleepy lad of about six.

"My apologies, sir, but there's a man outside, and he says he wants to talk with you, and Da wouldn't let him just come up, so he sent me, and I'm supposed to ask you if he can come up."

"Indeed? What's he like?"

"He's a Bardek man, and he's all covered with scars, and he smells funny."

Smells funny? she thought to herself; what, by the hells? She gave the lad a copper and told him to bring the fellow up. In a few minutes the tavernman from the Red Man arrived at the door. He did indeed smell, but of fear, not of dirt or perfume, the particular reeking sharpness that seeps into a man's sweat when he's terrified. As soon as the door closed behind him, he threw himself at Jill's feet.

"Kill me now! Do not make we wait any more, I beg you. All night I wait, and the waiting drives me mad."

Utterly confused, Jill hooked her thumbs in her sword belt and arranged a cruel smile in an attempt to play for time, but Salamander seemed to understand. He strolled over from the window and stared into the taverner's eyes, while the man gasped for breath out of sheer anxiety.

"I might enjoy killing you," the gerthddyn said in an offhand way. "But perhaps there's no need."

"But I told! I let out Briddyn's name. Never did I realize that you were testing me."

When Salamander chuckled, an unpleasant sort of laugh, Jill suddenly understood: the tavernman thought they were Hawks.

"Naught of the sort," she broke in. "The Brotherhood is just that, a band of brothers. Have you even known brothers who weren't all rivals in their hearts? Have you ever met an elder brother who willingly shared his sweetmeats with a younger? If you did, you knew a rare and holy man in the making."

Color ebbed back into the tavernman's face.

"I see. So you truly do want this Rhodry . . ."

"For reasons of our own, dog!" Salamander kicked him in the stomach hard enough to make him grunt. "But you didn't tell him everything you knew, did you? Tell me now, or I'll ensorcel you and make you jump off a pier and drown yourself."

Wiping his mouth repeatedly on the back of his hand, he nodded his agreement, then swallowed heavily and finally spoke.

"They are taking him to Slaith. I don't know why. But I heard Briddyn mention somewhat about Slaith to his two companions."

Although the name meant nothing to Jill, Salamander grunted in surprised recognition.

"I should have guessed that," he said. "Well and good, dog. Slink back to your kennel. But if you mention us to anyone . . ."

"Never! I swear it on the gods of both our peoples!"

Trembling, sweating in great drops, he scrambled to his feet and shamelessly ran for the door. As Jill shut it after him, she heard him pounding down the corridor.

"Slaith, is it?" Salamander said in a grim voice. "A bad omen, little pigeon, a wretched bad omen indeed."

"Where is it? I've never heard of it."

"I'm not surprised, seeing as few ever have. But I must say, you've certainly put the fear of demonhood into that fellow's craven heart. What am I traveling with, a poisonous snake?"

"Let's hope so. They always say that vipers are immune to venom themselves." She paused, struck by a sudden thought. "But I wonder if that fellow sees Hawks everywhere because he fell foul of them once. Those scars . . ."

"Oh, not that. I forget you don't know much about Bardek. He was no doubt a knife fighter. It's a sport there, you see. You have the knife in one hand, and around the other arm is this padded sleeve you use like a shield. The man who scores the first cut wins. The rich folk there have their favorites, and they shower them with gifts and suchlike. That's doubtless how our friend got the coin for his tavern, but seeing as it's in the Bilge, he must not have been truly successful, or—"

"Oh ye gods, I don't give a pig's fart! Do you have to babble on about everything?"

"Well, actually, I do, because it relieves my feelings and makes me sound like a fool, which is exactly what I want our enemies to think me. Who'll take a fool and a viper seriously?"

"Done, then. You babble, and I'll hiss."

"And it's time I did some babbling down in the harbor. We want to book a passage to Dun Mannanan. It's faster than riding the whole way, and we can buy horses there for the final journey."

"But where are we going?"

"Slaith, of course. Ah, my pretty little turtledove, a most peculiar surprise lies in store for you."

Since sending one lone prisoner on remand to Aberwyn was low in the royal priorities, Perryn rotted in the king's jail for several days, each one more tedious than the last. With nothing to do but sleep and plait bits of straw into little patterns, he was almost glad when Madoc came one morning and announced that he'd be leaving that very afternoon.

"There's a galley going down to Cerrmor with dispatches, and they have room for a horse thief. From there I'm farming you out on a merchant vessel. I wouldn't advise trying to escape. The master of the ship is a formidable man."

"Oh, er, ah, I wouldn't worry about that. I can't swim."

"Good. Now, when you get to Aberwyn, you be honest with my uncle, and he'll see what he can do about saving your neck."

"I suppose I should thank you, but somehow I can't find it in my heart."

Much to his surprise, Madoc laughed at that with genuine good humor, then took his leave.

The trip downriver was fast and smooth, the galley reaching Cerrmor just as Jill and Salamander were leaving it. While they were handing him over to the gwerbret's men, Perryn felt her presence, then lost the track almost immediately. He was hustled up to Gwerbret Ladoic's dun, where he spent a miserable night in a tiny cell turned cold and damp by the thick Cerrmor fog. In the morning, two of the gwerbret's riders came for him, tied his hands behind his back, and marched him lockstep down to the harbor while his every joint ached and complained. Down at the end of a long pier was a big Bardek merchantman, lateen-rigged and riding low in the water. Waiting at the gangplank was one of the biggest men Perryn had ever seen.

Close to seven feet tall, he had enormously muscled arms and shoulders, and his skin was so dark that it seemed pitch-black with bluish highlights. His presence, too, was as formidable as Madoc had called him; in fact, the cold, calm look in his eyes reminded Perryn of the equerry.

"*This* is the royal prisoner?" His voice was so dark and deep that it seemed to rumble across the pier like a rolled barrel.

"He is, Master Elaeno," said one of the guards. "Not much to look at, is he?"

"Well, if Lord Madoc wants to buy a passage to Aberwyn for a stoat, I shan't argue. Let's have him aboard."

Elaeno grabbed Perryn's shirt with one massive hand and lifted him a few feet off the ground.

"You give me any trouble, and I'll have you flogged. Understand?"

Perryn squeaked out an answer that passed for "I do." Elaeno lifted him right up over the side and dumped him onto the deck, then signaled to a pair of sailors as dark and huge as he was.

"Put him down in the hold, but see that he's properly fed and gets clean water on the trip."

Although it was decent of the ship's master to be concerned about feeding his prisoner, it was also a waste of time. As soon as the ship left the harbor and hit the open sea, Perryn's stomach decided to turn itself inside out. As the seasickness washed over him in rhythmic waves, he lay on his straw pallet, moaned, and wished he were dead. Every now and then one of the sailors would come see how he fared, but for the entire thirty-hour journey, the answer was always the same. He would look at them with rheumy eyes and beg them to hang him and have done with it. When the ship finally made port in Aberwyn, they had to carry him off.

Lying on the pier was like reaching paradise. Perryn clung to the rough, dirty wood with both arms and considered kissing it as the nippy sea air cleared his head of the last of the nausea. By the time men came down from the gwerbret's dun with a cart, Perryn felt almost cheerful. Even being shut in another cell couldn't spoil his good humor. The straw may have been dirty, but it covered a floor of real dirt on solid land.

Yet his good mood evaporated when he realized that he was cold and getting colder. The day was gray with high fog, and a brisk wind blew in the barred window. He had no blanket, not even a cloak. Although he huddled into a corner and spread some straw over his legs, he was shivering uncontrollably in a few minutes. By the time he heard someone coming to his door, about half an hour later, he was sneezing as well. The door swung back to reveal an old man, tall, white-haired, and dressed in plain gray brigga and a shirt embroidered with red lions at the yokes. Just as the fellow started to speak, Perryn had a fit of cramps, or so he thought of it. He felt as if a number of invisible cats had leapt upon him and were clawing at him, so deeply and painfully that he yelped and squirmed.

"Stop that!" the old man said. "All of you—stop that right now!"

When Perryn obediently went still, the pains stopped, leaving him to wonder why the old man had addressed him as "all of you."

"My apologies, lad. My name is Nevyn, and I'm Madoc's uncle."

"Are you a sorcerer, too?"

"I am, and you'd best do exactly what I say, or . . . or I'll turn you into a frog! Now come along. I can see by looking at you that you're very ill, and I have the regent's permission to keep you in a chamber under guard rather than out here."

Perryn sneezed, wiped his nose on his sleeve, then got up, brushing away the straw and wondering what it would be like to hop through a marsh all his life. When he happened to catch Nevyn's eye, the old man's glance struck through his very soul, pinning him to some invisible wall while the dweomerman rummaged through his mind at leisure. At last Nevyn released him with a toss of his head.

"You're a puzzle and a half, truly. I can see why Madoc sent you along to me. You're also close to death. Do you realize that?"

"It's just a chill, my lord. I must've gotten it on that beastly ship."

"I don't mean the chill. Well, come along."

As they crossed the ward, Perryn glanced up at the tall broch complex and noticed that the towers seemed to be swaying back and forth. Only then did he realize that he was burning with fever. Nevyn had to help him climb up the staircase to a small chamber in one of the half-brochs. Perryn was shocked at the old man's strength as he hauled him through the door and lifted him bodily onto the narrow bed.

"Get those boots off, lad, while I light a fire."

The effort was so tiring that he barely had the strength to get under the blankets. He was just drifting off to sleep when Elaeno, the shipmaster, came into the room, but tired as he was, no amount of talk could keep him awake.

"He isn't much, is he?" Nevyn said.

"That's what I said when I first saw him." Elaeno shook his head in a mild bafflement. "Of course, being seasick for days never helped a man's good looks."

"He was badly beaten recently, too. You can see the missing tooth and the fresh scars and suchlike. Salamander tells me that our Rhodry caught him on the road."

"I'm surprised he's still alive."

"So am I. Salamander had no idea why Rhodry didn't kill him, and neither do I. Ah well, he *is* alive and our puzzle to untangle as well. Take a look at his aura."

Cocking his head to one side, Elaeno let his eyes go slightly out of focus as he examined the area around the sleeping Perryn.

"That's the strangest thing I've ever seen," the Bardekian said at last. "The color's all wrong, and all the inner Stars are out of balance, too. Do you truly think he's a human being?"

"What? What else would he be?"

"I have no idea. It's just that I've never seen a human with an aura like that in my life, nor an elf or dwarf either."

"Now that's true-spoken, and well worth a little thought. If he's some sort of alien soul trapped in a human body, it would explain a great many things. Unfortunately, we may never find out the truth. He's very ill."

"Do you think you can save him?"

"I don't know. I feel duty-bound to try, in spite of what he did to Jill. He's suffering, after all, and besides, it strikes me that we should find out what we can about this strange being. But ye gods, all I need now is another burden."

"I was thinking about that. We could winter over here if you need my help. I can send messages to my wife on another ship."

Nevyn started to speak, then paused, wondering what was wrong with his voice. All at once he realized that he was very near tears. A startled Elaeno laid a hand on his shoulder.

"I'd appreciate that," Nevyn stammered at last. "Ah ye gods, I'm so tired."

"My lord Madoc, I hardly know what the king thinks anymore," Blaen said. "And I'll admit that it aches my heart. I wonder if I pressed him too hard or suchlike."

"You might have. Our liege is a touchy man, and jealous of his strong will." Madoc hesitated, swirling the mead around in his goblet. "On the other hand, I think Gwerbret Savyl has more to do with our liege's coldness than your lack of tact."

Blaen winced. Although he knew perfectly well that he was no polished courtier, he didn't care to have it pointed out. They were sitting in Madoc's comfortable chambers high up in one of the auxiliary brochs of the palace complex. As well as a pair of cushioned chairs, the usual table, and a large charcoal brazier, glowing at the moment against the night chill, the main room sported a wall shelf with twenty-two books on it. Blaen had counted them in amazement; never in his life had he seen so many volumes together outside of a temple of Wmm.

"Well, that was tactless of me in turn, Your Grace," Madoc said with a self-deprecating smile. "My apologies, but this matter of your cousin is beginning to vex me. He belongs in Aberwyn, but if the king won't recall him . . ." He spread his hands in a gesture of helplessness.

"Just so. I'm afraid to request another audience. If I *have* annoyed our liege, I don't want to make things worse. I must say I appreciate all you've done in my service. You can count on me for aid whenever you need it."

"My thanks, but the dweomer has a great interest of its own in our Rhodry."

"So it would seem." Blaen had a sip of mead, then put the goblet down on the table. When he was at court he preferred to stay sober and on his guard. "I don't suppose I can ask why."

"Certainly. It's no true secret. When Rhodry was a lad Nevyn received an omen about him. Eldidd's Wyrd is Rhodry's Wyrd, or so it ran."

"Oh." Blaen was too staggered to say more. "Oh."

Madoc smiled, then got up to pace restlessly to the window and look out at the night sky, stippled with clouds in the light of a half-moon. At that moment he reminded Blaen strikingly of Nevyn, just in the warrior-straight way he stood and in the look in his eyes, as if he were seeing a much wider view than that from the physical window. The gwerbret wondered all over again if Madoc truly were the old man's blood kin. Although he'd doubted it before, the relationship was beginning to seem plausible.

"So," the equerry said, "I'll see if I can have a word with our liege myself. Never in all the time that I've been here have I asked for a private audience, so perhaps I can get one now. We'll see on the morrow."

When the coaster put into Dun Mannanan, early on a clear day whose crisp wind proclaimed the coming autumn, Jill was profoundly glad to get onto dry land again. In her joy at feeling solid ground under her feet, she barely registered Salamander's stream of chatter as they unpacked their gear and piled it up at the end of the pier. Finally, though, some of his words caught her attention.

". . . can't stay in an inn, it's too dangerous."

"Probably so," Jill said. "I've got a friend here in town, but I don't think he'll put you up."

"What? How ungracious, my turtledove. Why not?"

She leaned close to whisper.

"Because he's a dwarf, and he thinks all elves are thieves."

"And I consider his people to be dullards and sots, and bad cess to him. But you're right enough. We'd best acquire some horses and get on our way."

"We might stop in at Otho's, though." Jill was looking forward to seeing the silversmith again. "He'll be able to tell us the best place to buy stock."

Otho's house was at the edge of town, down by the river. Over the door hung three silver bells that rang in a gentle cascade when Jill pushed it open. They went into the antechamber, a narrow slice of the round house, set off from the rest by a wickerwork partition. In the partition hung a dirty green blanket for want of a proper door.

"Who's there?" Otho called out.

"Jill the silver dagger, and a friend."

Wiping his hands on a rag, the smith pushed aside the blanket and came out. He glared at Salamander in exaggerated suspicion.

"So, young Jill, your taste in men gets worse and worse. You've left one misbegotten elf for another, but this one's a fop to boot!"

Salamander's mouth dropped open, but Jill hurriedly started talking before he could recover from his surprise.

"I haven't left Rhodry at all, Otho! This is his brother, not some lover of mine."

"Humph. Fine family you've married into." He paused, looking the gerthddyn over carefully. "You must be cursed clever with your fingers, lad, to have such fine clothing. I'm not letting you into my workshop, that's for sure."

"Now here! I'm not a thief!"

"Hah! That's all I have to say to that: hah! Now, what do you want with me today, Jill?"

"Just some advice. Is there an honest horse trader in town?"

"Not in town, but there's one about a mile north of here. Bevydd's his name, and he's somewhat of a friend of mine. I've made him many a fancy piece of tack over the years. Tell him I sent you. You take the river road straight out of town to the north, and then turn left at the lane edged with beech trees."

"A mile?" Salamander said with a groan. "Walk a whole mile?"

Otho rolled his eyes up so far it looked like he was going to lose them.

"And doesn't her ladyship have soft feet today? Ye gods, Jill, I'd find some other clan to marry into if I were you."

"They grow on you once you get to know them."

"Like moss, no doubt, or mildew."

"I beg your pardon," Salamander snapped. "I don't have to stand here and be insulted."

"No doubt you could be insulted anywhere you went."

When Salamander opened his mouth for a retort, Jill elbowed him sharply.

"Please forgive him, Otho. I was wondering if you had a map of the Auddglyn I could look at. One that shows what lies to the east."

"Well." He paused to scratch his head with one gnarled finger. "I might have somewhat like that, and for old times' sake I'll go look for it. You keep an eye on this fancy lad out here for me."

Otho pushed his way back through the blanket, and in a moment or two they heard the unmistakable sound of heaps of objects being rummaged through, a rustling, a banging, and the occasional oath.

"May the gods shorten his beard for him!" Salamander hissed. "The gall, calling me a thief."

"Now, now, it's not like it were personal or suchlike."

"Humph! And you've got gall of your own, asking *him* to forgive *me.*"

"Well, I was just trying to smooth things over. Hush—here he comes."

Otho made a triumphant return with a yellowed and cracking scroll in one hand. He took it to the window and unrolled it carefully while Jill and Salamander crowded round for a look. It mostly showed the Auddglyn coast, and Jill got the distinct impression that it had been drawn long before the province was truly settled. To the east beyond Dun Mannanan it showed the island group known as the Pig and Piglets, but the village of Brigvetyn just to the north of them was missing. Even farther on, the eastern side of the parchment was blank, except for a small banner bearing the words "Here there be dragons."

"Dragons?" Jill said. "That must be some scribe's whimsy and naught more."

"Just so," Salamander said. "Deverry dragons all live in the northern mountains."

"What?!"

"Oh, just a jest." Yet he spoke so hurriedly that she knew he was covering something over. "A tale for another time. Now see that little river here, my turtledove? The Tabaver? That estuary is where we're going."

"I never heard that there was any town out there."

"Of course. That's why I said you were in for a surprise."

Salamander was speaking naught but the truth for a change. After they bought new stock, a sturdy gray for Salamander, a battle-steady chestnut for Jill, and a pack mule, they headed east, following the coast road to Cinglyn, about four days' ride away. For this part of the journey, the gravel and packed-earth road was well kept up, and it ran through good farmlands, where the farmers were beginning to harvest the golden summer wheat. Cinglyn itself was on the verge of growing into a small town from a large village; they had no trouble buying provisions there. When it came to knowledge of the road ahead, however, all they got was blank stares or outright mockery.

"There's naught out there," the blacksmith said. "Naught but grass, that is."

"Perhaps so," Salamander said. "But hasn't anyone ever been curious, like? Surely someone's ridden out just for a look."

"Why?" He paused to spit in the dirt. "Naught out there."

For the first couple of days, Jill had to agree with him, and she began to wonder if Salamander were daft. The road dwindled first to a dirt track, then to a deer trail, then petered out entirely some fifteen miles from Cinglyn. Salamander led the way down to the beach itself, and for the rest of the day and on into the next they rode on the hard-packed sand by the water's edge. Wildfolk appeared in swarms and mobbed them, riding on their saddles and horses' rumps, running alongside, swirling thick in the air, rising up from the silver waves that crashed and boomed close at hand. When they made their evening camp, the spirits sat around in orderly rows, as if they were waiting for something. Jill found out what when Salamander obliged them with a song. They listened, fascinated, then vanished the moment he was done.

On the fourth day, though, she was in for a surprise. They left the water's edge and turned inland to find another road. Long disused, it was only a narrow track through the sea meadows of tall grass, but it ran straight and purposefully. Just at noon, they came to an orchard gone wild, where under the tangle of unpruned trees apples lay rotting. Just beyond was a circular grassy mound that looked like the remains of a village wall; inside it Jill could pick out dimpled circles on the earth where houses had once stood. As soon as they came close to the ruins, the Wildfolk vanished.

"What happened to this place?" Jill said. "Do you know?"

"It was burned by pirates."

"Pirates? What would they want with a farming village? I'll wager there wasn't any fabulous plunder here."

"No gold nor jewels, truly, but wealth all the same. Slaves, my innocent turtledove, slaves for the Bardek trade. The raiders would kill all the men as being more trouble than they're worth, and take the women and children over in the carracks. Deverry slaves are rare in the islands, you see, exotic and therefore expensive, like Western Hunters in the Eldidd horse trade. There used to be a lot of small villages out here, scattered up the river into the Auddglyn. All gone now."

"By all the ice in all the hells! Didn't the local gwerbret put a stop to it? Why did it take him so long?"

"The local gwerbret is about a hundred and forty miles away, my sweet. The pirates finally ended it themselves. They'd overhunted the place, and there weren't any villages left that were safe to raid."

"Oh. You'd think that blacksmith in Cinglyn would've know about this."

"Of course he did. He refused to mention it, that's all. That whole town must live in fear that one day the scum will be bold enough to come take them."

The biggest surprise of all lay two more days along. Here the coastal cliffs became lower and lower, finally fading out into a long stretch of dunes, scattered with coarse grass. As they rode east, the grass grew thicker; tiny streams appeared; the ground grew damp, and here and there trees stood beside ponds and rivulets. Quite suddenly they found a road made of logs laid down in the muck. Whenever Jill tried to get some information out of Salamander, he would only grin and tell her to wait. After a couple of hours more, the road brought them to a straggle of fishermen's huts in a sandy cove at one side of a broad, shallow estuary. Drawn up in the harbor were ships, a few tattered fishing boats, and then three sleek carracks and two galleys, all with suspicious-looking accouterments on their prows.

"By the Lord of Hell himself," Jill said. "Those look like corvos and ballistas."

"That's exactly what they are. Remember those pirates I told you about? This is where they winter. They've got a whole town here, they do, just upriver, and farther on farms to feed it. This, my dearest turtledove, is Slaith."

For a few minutes Jill sat on her horse in something like shock and stared at the peaceful harbor. Through the scattered trees along the riverbank she could see other buildings, and far beyond what appeared to be the roofs of a sizable town. Finally she found her voice again.

"Since you know so much about this place, why haven't you told one of the gwerbrets in the Auddglyn about it?"

"I tried. They wouldn't listen. You see, the only way to take Slaith is to have a fleet of warships. None of the gwerbrets out here do."

"They could petition the king."

"Of course—and surrender part of their independence to our liege. No gwerbret in his right mind asks the king for help unless his proverbial back is to the wall. The king's aid brings with it the king's obligations, my little pigeon."

"Are you telling me that the misbegotten gwerbrets are willing to let these swine breed here just so they don't have to ask the king a favor?"

"Just that. Now come along, and leave the talking to me. Saying the wrong thing is a good way to get your throat cut in Slaith."

As they rode down to the harbor, Jill noticed that all along the sand were wooden racks covered with fish drying for the winter. She could also smell a thick reek of rotting fish entrails, heads, and tails, the thinner smell of the fish themselves, and an undertone of swamp stench.

"One forgets about Slaith," Salamander said in a strangled voice. "We should have brought pomanders."

The town proper was about a mile north on the riverbank. The road picked a precarious way through swampland up to an open gate in a palisade of whole logs thickly covered with bitumen to keep the rot away. To Jill that protective covering showed utter arrogance; those walls would burn from a couple of thrown torches if ever the place came to a siege. Although the gate had a pair of iron-bound doors just like a dun, there was no one standing guard at them.

"Getting into Slaith is easy," Salamander said. "Getting out again is another matter altogether."

"And what were you doing here before, anyway?"

"That, my little nightingale, is another tale for another day. My lips for now are sealed."

Inside the walls were about five hundred buildings, set on curving, nicely cobbled streets. Although most of the houses were well made and recently whitewashed, the swamp stench lay thick over everything. Jill supposed that after a while, one got used to it, just as one got used to the stench of the streets in a large city. In the center was a crowded market square that looked just like any market day in the rest of the kingdom, with peddlers and craftsmen displaying their wares in wooden booths, while farmers spread out produce on blankets or displayed rabbits in wicker cages and chickens tied by their feet to long poles. Not so ordinary, however, were the customers, men with the rolling walk of sailors, but all carrying swords, and women whose faces were heavily painted with Bardek cosmetics. As Jill and Salamander led their horses past the market, people looked up, gave them a glance, then carefully looked away again with no sign of curiosity. Apparently no one asked questions in Slaith.

All around the market square were inns and taverns, far more than a town of this size would normally have. They all seemed to be enjoying good custom, too. At one prosperous-looking place there were four horses tied up off to the side in the cobbled yard. With a hiss of breath, Jill grabbed Salamander's arm.

"See that bay gelding? That used to belong to a man we know."

Muttering an oath, Salamander slowed down, but he kept moving, looking at the horse out of the corner of his eyes. The gelding was no longer carrying Rhodry's gear; instead of his obvious warrior's saddle, it had a lightweight saddle that was little more than a pad with stirrups, such as a messenger or pleasure rider would use.

"It has a new owner, sure enough," Salamander said. "Don't stare so, my turtledove. Very rude."

Jill turned away and casually looked over the various inns, but inside she was burning with rage. Everyone on these streets, everyone in this stinking town was her enemy now. She wanted to burn their walls, burn their ships, fall upon them and kill everyone as they ran screaming from the blazing death. Salamander interrupted this pleasant fantasy.

"We're coming to our inn. I'm picking it because it's likely to be empty except for us, but still, watch every word you say."

Down a narrow alley stood a small inn, built along Bardek lines, with peeling shakes on the roof and water stains on the walls. Out in the muddy innyard was a sagging stable, a broken-down wagon, and a pigsty. As they dismounted near the watering trough, a stout man in his fifties or so came out of the main building and looked Salamander over with something like alarm.

"Don't tell me you're back in town, gerthddyn."

"I am, good Dumryc. How could I live without another sight of your handsome face, another view of glorious Slaith, another breath of its rich and wine-sweet air?"

"Still gabble as much as always, don't you? Who's this with you?"

"My bodyguard. Allow me to introduce Gilyn, a true silver dagger, who's killed at least one man for each of his sixteen years."

"Huh. Cursed likely."

Jill drew, swung, and slit his leather apron from collar to paunch with the point of her blade. With a yelp, Dumryc flung himself back and clutched at the flapping halves.

"Next time it's your fat throat," Jill said.

"Well and good, lad. Now put that thing away and come in for a nice, peaceable tankard, like."

Salamander chose them a chamber on the second-floor corner of the inn with windows that overlooked the stable yard in both directions, because it was always a good idea to have a clear view of trouble coming in Slaith. They stowed their gear, locked the door with a stout padlock, then went down to the tavern room. A small boy was stirring an iron kettle of greasy stew at the hearth while Dumryc was chopping turnips with a dagger at the end of a table. Jill and Salamander helped themselves to ale from an open barrel, picked out a fly or two, then sat down nearby.

"And what brings you to Slaith this time?" Dumryc said. "If you don't mind my asking, like."

"I don't, though I'm not yet ready to answer. Gilyn, here, however, is looking for an old friend of his, the sharer of many a campfire and grievous battle. The lad seems to have headed east from Cerrmor, so I thought. Well, mayhap we'll pick up news of him in Slaith, because he's an Eldidd man, as good on a boat as he is with a sword."

"There's always work for a lad like that here."

"Just so. His name's Rhodry of Aberwyn."

"Hum." Dumryc was concentrating on his chopping. "Never heard of him."

"He might not be using that name. He's a good-looking fellow, tall, dark hair, Eldidd eyes, and a silver dagger in his belt."

"Never ran across him." Dumryc grabbed another turnip and chopped it, the dagger moving fast and nervously. "But that doesn't mean anything. He might have found a berth as soon as he got here and shipped out."

"Could be, could be. He's a useful sort of man."

Dumryc smiled tightly at the turnip and said nothing. Salamander gave Jill a smile and raised one eyebrow as if to say that she shouldn't believe a word the innkeep said. He needn't have worried; she didn't need mighty dweomer or suchlike to tell when a man was lying to her face.

After they finished the ale they went out for a stroll around town. The market fair was beginning to break up; the farmers and tradesmen packed what was left of their wares back into wagons while exhausted children whined and fussed, and wives carefully counted over their earnings for the day. A few drunks snored in the strewn straw; dogs nosed about; gaudy whores strolled around, looking over the pirates who were heading for one tavern or another. When Jill and Salamander went to look for it, they found Rhodry's horse gone.

"There's no use in asking around for its new owner," Salamander remarked with a certain gloom. "No one would tell us the truth."

"No doubt. What should we do now? Sit around a tavern and see if we can overhear somewhat of interest?"

"I'm not sure. I—"

"Gerthddyn! Salamander! By the hells, hold and stand!"

A dark-haired man, quite stout, with his long black beard tied up in six neat braids, was hurrying over to them.

"Snilyn, oh, most beauteous of the bilge rats! Still alive, are you?"

"I am, and glad enough to see you, lad. Got some more good tales for us?"

"I do, but this time I brought a bodyguard along."

With a roar of laughter, Snilyn slapped Jill on the back.

"He's a cautious sort, your hire." He grinned, revealing several missing teeth. "But he's right enough, eh? You never know what the lads'll do when they're drunk. Sober, they've got plenty of respect for a man who can tell a good tale, but drunk, well . . ." He shrugged massive shoulders. "Come have a tankard at my expense, Salamander, and your silver dagger, too."

Although they went to Snilyn's favorite tavern, Salamander picked the table, one where he could keep his back to the wall and have a good view of the street out the window. A blowsy blond lass brought tankards of dark ale, then lingered, looking Salamander over wistfully, until Snilyn sent her away with a slap on the behind.

"It's not your tongue she wants to see wag, gerthddyn." The pirate paused to laugh at his own jest. "So, when did you ride in?"

"Just today. We're staying over at Dumryc's inn, because I like an out-of-the-way spot when I'm in Slaith."

"Good idea, truly. What brings you here, if I can ask?"

"Well, now, that's a strange thing. I'd most treasure your advice about somewhat. We're looking for another silver dagger, and when I asked Dumryc about him, he put me off. Let me ask you, and you don't have to answer, but you can tell whether or not I should just forget this lad and never ask again."

"Done."

"His name's Rhodry of Aberwyn."

"Hold your tongue. Don't even ask why."

"Then hold it I will." Salamander gave Jill a warning jab in the ribs. "My thanks."

Salamander began chatting with Snilyn, but Jill sat steaming and silent over her tankard. She wanted to draw, threaten cold steel, and stab and slash the truth out of this scruffy lot. Only the simple fact that she was outnumbered several hundred to one kept her silent. Salamander ordered and paid for another round of ale, took the third that Snilyn pressed upon him, too, gulping it down but staying as sober as only an elf can. He told jest after jest, got Snilyn laughing until the tears came, ordered more ale yet, and soon had an appreciative crowd around him to hear an involved but anatomically impossible story about a blacksmith and a miller's daughter.

"And so his hammer went up and down," Salamander ended up. "And straightened her horseshoe right out."

Howling with laughter, Snilyn slapped Salamander on the back so hard that he nearly knocked the gerthddyn off the bench, then with a muttered apology grabbed Salamander by the shoulders and hauled him back. The gerthddyn threw a companionable arm around him and whispered something in his ear. Although Jill saw Snilyn first flinch, then whisper an answer, she could hear nothing over the noise of pirates yelling for more tales. Salamander let go of Snilyn and obliged with a story even more bawdy than the one before.

It was another hour before Salamander could extricate himself from his admirers, who pressed pieces of ill-gotten silver into his hands as he left. Her hand on her sword hilt, Jill walked a little behind him and kept watch for pickpockets as they headed back to the inn. Once they were off the main street, though, Salamander motioned her up beside him.

"Well, I've got a bit of bad news."

"Indeed? What did you ask Snilyn?"

"Clever Gilyn of the sharp eye." Salamander gave her a grin. "Never underestimate the power of good fellowship, bawdy cheer, and all the rest of it. I also drew upon the power of surprise and let him know that I knew more than he thought I did. The question was, to wit, whether anyone stood to make a profit off our Rhodry, and the answer was, they did, about twenty gold pieces."

"Twenty? That's an enormous lwdd for a silver dagger. They must know he's heir to Aberwyn."

"Lwdd? Ah, you fail to understand. Not a blood price, by beauteous meadowlark, just a price. I see you have led a sheltered and happy life, Gillo, far from the evils and troubles that cruel men visit upon—"

"Cut the horse crap, or I'll slit your throat."

"How indelicate, but very well. Less horse crap; more horse meat. They've taken Rhodry to Bardek to sell him as a slave."

Jill opened her mouth to speak, but no words would come.

"I was afraid of somewhat like this," Salamander went on. "Which is why we're in beauteous Slaith in the first place. Whoever has Rhodry seems to be a most unpleasant sort of person. You saw Snilyn wince at the very thought of him, and I assure you that Snilyn doesn't wince easily. Although he has many a strangely perverted flaw, cowardice is not among them."

"Bardek! Oh, by all the ice in all the hells, how are we going to get there? The last ships across are leaving Cerrmor by now. By the time we get back there—"

"Cruel winter will be whipping the Southern Sea to a frenzy. I know, I know. We need a ship. We can walk, trot, run, and even dance, but we can, alas, do none of these upon the water. It is too far to swim. Therefore, ships are the order of the day. We are in a place with ships all nicely drawn up down at the harbor. What, my little turtledove, does this suggest to you?"

"Now here, these are pirates! If we get out alone on the water with this lot, they could take us and sell us as slaves, too. I can't fight off twenty men all by myself."

"Ah, what becoming modesty! You're right, of course: never trust a pirate. I've impressed said pirates, but that's not enough. When it comes to these lads, only one thing works: terror. Now let's go get somewhat to eat while I think up a plan."

After a meal of griddle cakes with cheese and fried onions, they went back to the center of town. By then the sun was setting, a time when the streets in most towns would be growing quiet and empty, but here there were plenty of people on the prowl, some carrying lanterns or torches and going briskly about their business, others merely standing around on street corners or in alleyways as if waiting for something. A number of people were leading gray donkeys with pack saddles and bridles trimmed with little bells that jingled musically. In the gathering twilight, with a cool sea breeze wiping away most of the stink, Slaith was oddly cheerful, like a town getting ready for a festival, yet all Jill could think of was murder. These innocent-seeming folk had helped ship her Rhodry off to some horrible Wyrd, and all she wanted was to see them dead. Everything became preternaturally bright, sharp: the bells striking like gongs, the torches flaring up like enormous fires, the sweaty faces around her looming and swelling, the ordinary sunset burning like a sea of blood. Abruptly Salamander grabbed her arm, shook it hard, and dragged her into the semi-privacy of a narrow alley.

"What's wrong?" he whispered. "You look like death itself."

"Do I? Ye gods." Jill ran shaking hands down her face and breathed deeply, gulping the cooler air. "I don't know what I did. I . . . I was brooding, like, over things, and all at once the world turned strange, like when I was with Perryn. I must have tapped into the power without knowing it."

Salamander groaned under his breath.

"That's as dangerous as summoning a demon! We can't talk about it here, so try to control yourself."

Jill merely nodded, suddenly very tired. The world around her seemed painted with brighter colors than normal, but otherwise her vision had settled down. They went to a tavern at one corner of the market square, a big place that was one round stone room with an unusually high ceiling. When the serving wench brought them ale, Salamander asked her about the height of the room.

"Oh, the lads just had a bit of a brawl, and they knocked over a lantern into the straw. Whoosh—up everything went, and the floor upstairs along with it."

"Must have been a splendid show," Salamander said. "Excuse me a moment, Gillo. Just have to go out back."

As soon as Salamander was out the back door, the lass sat down next to Jill on the bench. She was a pretty thing, no more than sixteen under the Bardek kohl that rimmed her blue eyes. Her hair was blond, and done up in elaborate curls and set with little shell combs in the Bardek fashion, but she was wearing a pair of ordinary Deverry dresses.

"You must have been ever so lonely on the road with that chattering gerthddyn," she said. "How about a bit of company, Gillo?"

Jill was too stunned to speak. Here was a woman actually taken in by her ruse! Although she was used to fooling men, most women saw through her acting at once. When the lass laid a hand on her thigh, she shrank away.

"Oho, shy, aren't you? His bodyguard, the gerthddyn calls you, but I'll wager it's a bit more than that. Oh well, no offense, mind. There's men like that, and they don't go bothering me, so it's up to their fancy, I always say." She took Jill's tankard and had an absentminded sip. "I always did wonder why the gerthddyn was so coy and shy like with us lasses." She paused for a wicked little smile. "But you so young and all. Don't you think you should try a slice off a different cut of meat, just once, like?"

Too flustered to speak, Jill looked desperately around and saw that they'd gathered an audience, a grinning ring of pirates and wenches. Someone suddenly whispered an alarm: Salamander was stalking in the back door.

"And what's all this?" In a fine show of furious indignation, the gerthddyn shoved his way through the crowd. "You little bitch! Hunting on my preserve, are you?"

Slowly and dramatically, Salamander raised his hand and pointed at the tankard, which the lass was still cradling in her hands. Blue fire shot from his fingers, struck the tankard, and flared, making the ale steam and boil. With a scream, the lass threw the tankard onto the table and leapt up, tangling her dresses in the bench and tripping. The rest of the audience jumped back with oaths and shouts.

"You little slut," Salamander said to Jill. "Bad as a lass, I swear it."

In the crowd a couple of pirates were reaching for swords. Salamander let out a howl of laughter and waved his hand again. Thunder cracked and boomed in the tavern; smoke billowed; blue light shot through the sudden darkness. All the wenches screamed and ran for the door; the men fell back, shouting and cursing. Salamander swirled and tossed a convincing if tiny lightning bolt at the doorway. Screaming hysterically, the wenches ran back into the crowd.

"No one leave," Salamander called out. "You foul-minded fools! You odiferous and fly-swarmed lumps of swine offal! Whom do you think to insult so boldly?"

With a graceful fling of one arm Salamander jumped up onto the table in the midst of a sudden swirl of purple smoke and began to laugh, the deep, musical ripple of delight that only someone with elven blood can summon. Gasping, white-faced, the pirates and wenches clung together in the curve of the wall. The lass who'd started all the trouble crawled away on her hands and knees to join them.

"So." Salamander drawled the word portentously. "Swine! Turds! You thought me a babbling fool, did you? A mere plaything, beneath you in your sordid lusts and bloodshed! Hah! Would a weak man dare walk the evil streets of Slaith?" He paused for a dramatic glare at the crowd. "If I wanted, I could burn this stinking hellhole to the ground, and you bastard-born lice would crisp and fry along with it."

In illustration, he shot a bolt at a barrel of ale, which burst into superficial flames. The wenches screamed again; the men surged forward; but as the fire burned through the wood, the ale rushed out and doused it with the acrid stink of singed hops.

"Does anyone doubt my powers?" Salamander went on.

In unison heads shook a no like grain bowing in the winds. With a cold, cruel smile, Salamander set his hands on his hips.

"Well and good, swine. Return to your paltry amusements, but remember what I am, and treat me with the deference I deserve."

He jumped down from the table and sat down next to Jill. For a long moment the silence hung in the room like the last of the smoke; then slowly, one at a time, the pirates began whispering, turning back to their ale, or, in the case of the weaker souls, slipping out the door. Once the noise returned to a normal level, Salamander put his arm around Jill's shoulders and pulled her close to whisper.

"This should infuse them with a deep if short-lived piety, huh?" He raised his voice again. "Wench! Come take this charred and stinking tankard away and bring me fresh drink!"

Bowing and trembling, the servant lass sidled over and grabbed the still-steaming tankard with a wadded cloth. When she brought back the fresh, she curtsied like a court lady, then shamelessly ran away. Salamander raised the tankard in salute and drank a good bit right off.

"So, my unfaithful Gilyn, you've learned your lesson, have you?"

"I have, at that." Jill had thoughts of strangling him for all the blather. "But I'm not sure which one."

The news spread almost as fast as Salamander's dweomer fire. In little clots, pirates and townsfolk appeared at the door or the windows, stuck their heads in for a look at Salamander, then withdrew them fast and moved on. Finally Snilyn came striding in and shook the gerthddyn's hand with a hearty bellow of laughter. As Salamander had remarked, cowardice was certainly not one of his vices.

"I'm cursing myself for missing the sight," Snilyn said, sitting down unasked. "I would have enjoyed seeing the bastard swine running from you, sorcerer."

"You'll have your chance if anyone gives me any more trouble."

"And a wretched small chance that is, unless, of course, you're staying here long."

"I'm not, truly. In fact, my friend, maybe you can help me. I'm minded to go to Bardek before the winter sets in. Do you know of anyone making one last run that way? I'll pay good coin for our passage."

Snilyn signaled for ale while he considered the question.

"Well, I don't, at that," he said finally. "But you might talk Buthvyn into taking you over. Whether he winters here or in Pastur is all the same to him, and he had a lean summer of it. Depends on how much coin you're willing to spend."

"No doubt an adequate sum. I have a great and burning desire to see Bardek again, the beauteous palms, the shining sands, the rich merchants with their sacks of gold and jewels."

"Must be a tidy profit there, truly, for a man like you. Why, by the Lord of Hell's hairy balls! You could take one of them caravans all on your own!"

"I prefer to charm the gold out of merchants' paws, but you're right enough about the profit. The way I like to live does not come cheap, and this little minx of mine is developing a decided taste for luxury. It's a pity how easily young lads are corrupted."

When Snilyn snorted with laughter, Jill wondered whose throat she wanted to slit more, his or Salamander's.

"But this Buthvyn had best not give us one whit of trouble," the gerthddyn went on. "I can set wood on fire with a flick of a finger, you see. Ships, as you well know, are made of wood."

Snilyn went both silent and decidedly green.

"I see you understand." Salamander smiled gently. "Fear not, I shall make sure that the glorious Buthvyn understands as well. Where can we find this prince of the oceans, this ferocious sea lion?"

"Down at the Green Parrot, but I wouldn't call him all of that, truly."

Buthvyn was one of the tallest men Jill had ever met and also one of the skinniest, his shoulders as narrow as his narrow hips, his long arms like ropes and scarred at that, his face all sharp edges and long, pinched nose. From the eagerness with which he greeted Salamander's proposal, it was clear that he was not a successful pirate. He had a ragged but seaworthy cog, he said, and fifteen lads to sail it, all of whom, or so he swore, were loyal men with closed mouths. Salamander made sure of this loyalty by lighting the wood in the tavern hearth with one flick of his hand. As the flames sprang up and spread on the heavy logs, Buthvyn went pale.

"Straight to Bardek and no shilly-shallying around," the pirate said, swallowing heavily. "As fast and straight as the winds will take us."

"Splendid!" Salamander said. "Can you carry horses, or should I sell our glorious steeds?"

"I would if I was you. Hard trip across for stock, and this isn't no big merchantman. You can get good horses in Bardek, anyway."

"So you can. When do we sail? I detest waiting."

"Tomorrow dawn when the tie goes out. That be fast enough?"

"It is. We shall meet you at the harbor while it's still dark."

When they returned to Dumryc's inn, Jill and Salamander found the tale gone before them. A newly servile Dumryc gave them a candle lantern and bowed repeatedly, like a crow drinking water, as they went upstairs to their chamber. As soon as the door was safely barred, Salamander collapsed onto the mattress and howled with laughter until he choked. Jill hung the lantern on a nail in the wall and glared at him.

"Ah ye gods," Salamander gasped when he could speak again. "That was truly one of the best jests in my life, and I've perpetrated a lot of them, Jill, my turtledove."

"No doubt." Jill put ice in her voice.

"Ah." Salamander sat up, wrapping his long arms around his knees, and let his grin fade away. "I think me you're vexed with this whole ruse, the portentous words, the flaming fires, and so forth, but unless the lads think us as evil as they—and as danger-ous—they won't respect us, no matter how many hints we drop about dark dweomer. I've no desire to be drugged and tossed over-board one fine night when we're out to sea."

"Well, true-spoken, but ye gods, why all the show? Why not just set somewhat on fire and threaten them?"

"Jill." Salamander stared at her with reproachful eyes. "That wouldn't have been any fun."

"They're doing what?" Elaeno was so furious that his thunder of a voice made the wooden shutters rattle at the windows.

"Going to Bardek on a pirate ship." Nevyn still could hardly believe his own words. "That chattering idiot of an elf is taking Jill to Bardek on a pirate ship."

Elaeno opened his mouth and shut it several times.

"Have some mead," Nevyn said. "Normally I don't drink the stuff, but tonight, for some strange reason, I feel the need."

For some nights Blaen had had trouble sleeping. Generally he would dress, then prowl the long mazelike corridors of the king's palace and wonder why he was wasting his time staying in Dun Deverry. Soon he would have to start the long journey back to Cwm Pecl, before the winter snows came to trap him in the king's city far from home. On that particular night, he wandered half-purposely over to Lord Madoc's chambers and found, as he'd somehow been expecting, a crack of light showing under the sor-cerer's door. As he hesitated, wondering whether or not to knock, the door opened to reveal Madoc, wearing a nightshirt over a pair of brigga.

"Ah, there you are, Blaen. I couldn't sleep, either, and the spirits told me you were on your way. Come in for a nightcap."

Although Blaen looked hastily around, he saw no spirits and decided that it was safe enough to go in. Madoc poured them both dark ale sweetened with Bardek cinnamon and cloves.

"Want this heated?"

"Oh, don't trouble yourself. I don't mind it cool."

"Here, then." Madoc handed him a tankard. "Have a chair."

They settled themselves by the brazier, glowing cherry red in the drafty chamber. Blaen took an approving sip of the strong, dark ale.

"I was planning on coming to see you first thing in the morning," Madoc said. "I have some news. The king has finally deigned to tell me that he's sending a herald to Aberwyn tomorrow at dawn."

"By the Lord of Hell himself! Why?"

"No one knows. His liege is apparently vexed with Savyl more than he is with you, and he's saying not a word to anyone about it. All I know is that the herald is carrying some grave and serious proclamation. It could be recalling Rhodry, or it could be summoning the Council of Electors to choose a new heir. By the gods, it could merely be raising taxes, for all that I know."

Blaen groaned under his breath and had a long swallow of ale.

"I've sent word to Nevyn already, of course," Madoc said.

"Splendid. Here, may I put a blunt question? Where is Rhodry? I think me you know."

Madoc considered for a moment, studying Blaen's face as if he were reading a message there.

"I do, at that," he said at last. "Will you swear to me to keep this to yourself?"

"On the honor of my clan."

"Done, then. Rhodry's in Bardek. His enemies took him there and sold him as a slave."

"They what? By every god, I'll have them hanged for this! I'll have them spitted and drawn! The gall! Selling my kin for a blasted slave!"

"Your Grace? May I suggest you sit down?"

Blaen was quite surprised to find himself standing. He took a deep breath and sat down again.

"After all, Your Grace, at least he's alive."

"Just so." Blaen took another deep breath and reminded himself that he couldn't do anything at all in the middle of the night. "I wonder if I can possibly get a ship for Bardek this time of year, one that can carry a good part of my warband."

"You can't, Your Grace, and truly, it would be unwise for you to go after him. I think me you'll be needed more here in the spring, when he returns. Well." Madoc's face turned haunted. "If we can pull him out of this, at any rate."

"I have great faith in the dweomer's power, my lord."

"My thanks. Let us hope it's justified."

By the gentle rocking of the hull, the prisoner knew that they were lying at anchor in one harbor or another. For a while he merely lay on his pallet and looked round the nearly empty hold. When he'd started this voyage, the hold had been full of boxes and bales. How long ago now? Weeks. He wasn't sure how many. When he rose to his knees, the ankle chain clanked and clattered, but it was long enough to let him reach the porthole and pull up the oiled-leather covering. The blinding dazzle of sun on water made his eyes blink and tear, but in a few minutes he could make out a long white beach and a steep cliff face beyond a forest of masts. All the harbors had looked much like this. For all he knew, they'd been shuttling back and forth between a pair of towns. He did know, however, that they were in the Bardekian archipelago. His captors had told him that several times, as if it were important that he knew. He repeated it to himself now, saying it aloud: "I'm in Bardek." It was one of the few things he did know about himself.

He held up his right arm and looked at the pale skin that marked him as a Deverry man. Although he knew where and what Deverry was, he couldn't remember ever having been there personally, but his captors assured him that he'd been born there, in the province off Pyrdon, to be exact. He also remembered both his native tongue and the small amount of Bardekian he'd known before his capture. In fact, one of his few solid memories was of studying that language when he'd been a child. He had a clear image of his tutor, a dark-skinned man with gray hair and a kindly, ready smile, telling him that he needed to study hard because of his position in life. What that position was he didn't remember. Perhaps he'd been the son of a merchant; it was a reasonable supposition. At any rate, although he was far from fluent in Bardekian, that early training was making it possible for him to pick up bits and pieces of the conversations he overheard and to ask simple questions. Sometimes his questions were answered; more often, not.

When he heard noises behind him, the prisoner turned away

and let the porthole cover fall. The man called Gwin was coming down the ladder, and he carried a small cloth sack under one arm.

"Clothes for you." Gwin tossed the sack over. "A tunic, sandals. Bardek clothes. You leave here today. Glad?"

"I don't know. What happens next?"

"You'll be sold."

The prisoner nodded, thinking things over. Since they'd already told him he was a slave, the news was no surprise. He'd even overheard someone saying that he'd fetch a good price, because he was an exotic commodity like a rare breed of dog. While he dressed, Gwin poked among the remaining boxes and bales, but only idly, as if he were making sure he hadn't forgotten anything.

"Gwin? Do you know my name?"

"Yes. Hasn't anyone told you? It's Taliaesyn."

"Thanks. I wondered."

"No doubt." He paused, looking at the prisoner with an odd expression, a certain very thin, very fragile sympathy. "Someone will fetch you soon. Good luck."

"Thank you."

After Gwin left, Taliaesyn sat down on his pallet and wondered why a man like that would wish him good luck, then shrugged the problem away as being as unsolvable as most of the mysteries around him. He said his name over several times in the hopes that it would bring memories with it. Nothing came—nothing at all, not an image, not a sound, not a single word from the life he must have had before that morning, weeks ago, when he'd woken up in the hold of this ship. He could still remember his absolute panic when he'd realized that he knew nothing about himself, nothing about how he'd come to be chained there. For a few minutes he'd felt like a hysterical animal, throwing itself this way and that against the bars of a cage, biting even those who try to soothe it. But the fit had gone quickly, long before his captors had come down to gloat over him. He'd found the knowledge he needed, that morning: memory or not, he was still a man, he had speech, he had thought, and he would fight to keep that sense of selfhood.

Over the weeks that followed, he dredged up a few bits of memory from his past, and he'd woven them into a story that defined what he knew of his self. Now he had a bit more to add.

"I am Taliaesyn of Pyrdon, a merchant's son once, now a slave—but a valuable slave, mind. They tell me I ran up gambling debts here in Bardek. I remember that Deverry law can't save a free man when he's this far from home, so I was arrested and sold to pay the debts. I must be the son of an important merchant; why else would a Deverry man be in Bardek?"

For a moment he considered the question, came up with no answer, and dismissed it. He had three actual memories to fit into the story. The first, of course, was his old tutor in the Bardek tongue, a memory that fit smoothly into the tale. The other two, however, were difficult and troubling. First, there was the beautiful blond lass. Now, although it was logical enough that a merchant's son would have a wife or mistress (because in the memory she was getting into bed with him), why was she taking off men's clothing instead of a dress? The second memory made even less sense. He saw a man's face and shoulders looming in what seemed to be smoke or heavy fog; the man was wearing chain mail and a pot helm, and blood sheeted down his face. With the image came the words: "the first man I ever killed." Merchants' sons, however, didn't kill people—unless perhaps the victim was a bandit?

Taliaesyn smiled in relief. It would make sense if he'd been leading a caravan and that fellow had been a bandit, and as he thought it over, another memory stirred, mules braying in a crisp dawn. Of course. Of course! And if the lass were his wife, traveling with him? Why, it would be hard to ride in long dresses—why not wear men's clothes? He felt a deep satisfaction at knitting the tale together at last.

Yet the satisfaction was only momentary, because he was always aware that his captors might be lying to him. Although their story was reasonable, and in line with the general knowledge he remembered about the world, he could confirm none of it. There was this business of it being so hard to think. At times, he could barely put two words together or remember a thing he'd been told not a minute before; at others, the whole world seemed strange, far away yet brightly colored, and his mind made odd jumps and lapses. As he thought about it, it occurred to him that he often felt that way after being fed. They were probably putting strange drugs in his food. He knew that somewhere in his mind was a reason for thinking that these people were the sort to drug their prisoners, even though he couldn't quite put a mental finger on it. Over the past weeks he'd come to think of knowledge, which he'd always taken for granted before, in terms of a very involved metaphor, that each thing a man knew was like a water lily. Each blossom floated in the sun on top of the pool of his mind, but it was dependent upon its long stalk and roots underneath to connect it to the earth and to all the other lilies. He felt as though someone had swung a scythe through his mind, leaving only a few broken flowers to wither on top of the pond, cut off from any connection or possible meaning. Although the conceit was peculiar, it fit in a satisfying way. Something had sliced through his mind. He was certain of that.

In a few minutes he heard a small commotion on deck, and the ship rocked once as voices called out. Someone's boarding, he thought. It occurred to him that he'd been on ships before, that he knew a certain amount about them, provided they were small ships, like a galley. He remembered, then, being on a war galley, standing near the carved prow and feeling the spray break over him. What was a merchant's son doing on a war galley? He had no chance to examine that disturbing question any further, because someone threw back the hatch at the bow and light spilled into the hold.

The mute climbed down the ladder and made the gurgling sound in his throat that did him for a greeting. A bent and wizened black crab of a man, he'd had his tongue cut out many years before, or so Gwin had said, without adding why. Behind the mute came the man called Briddyn, with his oily hair and even slicker beard, and behind him a tall, dark brown Bardekian whom Taliaesyn had never seen before. Dressed in a fine white linen tunic with one red sleeve, the fellow carried a pair of wooden tablets, smeared with wax, and a bone stylus. As Briddyn gestured at various bales and crates, the other began jotting down figures and symbols on the wax. Customs officer, Taliaesyn thought.

The mute knelt down and unlocked the ankle chain. Taliaesyn's relief at having it gone died abruptly when the old man handed him a collar and pointed at his neck. When Taliaesyn hesitated, Briddyn turned to him.

"Put it on. Right now."

Taliaesyn buckled it round his neck and made no objection when the mute padlocked on the chain. Although he had trouble remembering the details, he knew that Briddyn had caused him pain—intense pain—once before. The not-quite-memory persisted as a gut-wrenching fear whenever Briddyn looked his way with his pale, lashless eyes. The customs officer cleared his throat, then asked a long question, of which Taliaesyn understood nothing.

"Yes." Briddyn handed over a strip of the thin-beaten bark the Bardekians used instead of parchment. "Here."

Nodding, lips pursed, the customs officer read it carefully, glancing Taliaesyn's way every now and then.

"Expensive piece of goods," he remarked.

"Barbarian slaves are rare these days."

It was then that Taliaesyn realized that the officer had been examining his bill of sale. His cheeks burned as the shame overwhelmed him: here he was, a Deverrian and a free man, sold like a horse in a foreign land. Yet already Briddyn and the officer had turned their attention elsewhere. To them he was nothing but a routine transaction, worth neither pity nor mockery. When they were done in the hold, the mute led Taliaesyn up onto the deck after them. While Briddyn and the port officials haggled over duties and taxes, the prisoner got his first good look around him in weeks.

The harbor was a narrow inlet about half a mile wide, cut into tall cliffs of pale pink sandstone. Four long wooden piers jutted out from the shallow beach, where a jumble of shacks and sheds stood among beached fishing boats and palm trees. Up above on the cliff tops were what seemed to be more substantial buildings in the long rectangular Bardekian style.

"A city?" Taliaesyn said.

The mute nodded yes, and a nearby sailor glanced their way.

"Myleton. It's called Myleton."

Taliaesyn repeated the name and added it to his small store of facts. As he remembered, Myleton was on the island, Bardektinna, that had mistakenly given part of its name to the entire archipelago when Deverry men had first sailed its way. Shading his eyes with one hand, he studied what few of the cliff-top buildings he could see. One in particular interested him, an enormous wooden structure at least a hundred feet long and three stories high, its roof curved and swelling like the overturned hull of a ship. Standing next to it was a wooden statue, some forty feet tall, of a man with a bird on his shoulder.

"Temple?" Taliaesyn asked the sailor.

"Yes. Dalae-oh-contaemo. The albatross guide, the wave father."

"Ah. So his temple is in the harbor."

The sailor nodded. With a jerk of the chain, the mute led Taliaesyn away from the fellow as abruptly as if he were dangerous and made him stand near the gangplank. When Taliaesyn happened to glance over the side, he almost cried out. The blue-green water was alive with spirits, faces and hands and manes of hair that formed only to dissolve again, eyes that stared out at him from sun glints, voices that whispered in the foam, long thin fingers that pointed at him, then vanished. Instinctively he knew that he had to keep silent about them. When he glanced furtively around, it was plain that no one else had seen a thing. He felt smug, almost sly; in this, he was superior to his captors, that the Wildfolk knew and recognized him. He only wished that he could remember why. All at once, the deck was full of gnomes, tall blue fellows, brown fat ones, skinny green beings with frog faces and warty fingers, all clustering round in a comforting sort of way. They patted him, smiled at him, then vanished as suddenly as they'd come. He looked up to see Briddyn walking over, studying what seemed to be a bill of lading. Taliaesyn's heart thudded, then settled when it was obvious that Briddyn hadn't seen the Wildfolk —or could he even do so? Taliaesyn thought he might, but he couldn't quite remember why.

"Well, that's all in order," Briddyn said to the mute. "Let's take the slave to the market. No use feeding him any longer."

The mute winked and grinned with a sly glance for the customs officer striding away down the pier. This gesture was the first confirmation Taliaesyn had for his hunch that something was wrong with these merchants. He was sure now that the bill of sale was not quite legal. Although he had the brief thought of calling to the officer, Briddyn was watching him again. The silver lizard clip in his beard winked in the strong sun.

"At times you remind me of a child," Briddyn said in Deverrian. "I can read everything on your face. Do you remember what I did to you when I had you tied to the deck?"

"I don't, truly, not in any detail." Yet the fear made him swallow heavily and force every word through dry lips.

"It's doubtless for the best that you don't, lad. Let me warn you this. You're a legal slave now. Do you understand what that means? If you try to escape, you'll be hunted down, and they'll catch you. No one in this demon-haunted country will life a finger to help a runaway slave. Once they catch you, they'll kill you—but slowly, one small piece at a time. What I did to you was naught compared to the way an archon's men treat rebellious slaves. I heard of one poor wretch that took two months to die. Do you understand?"

"I do."

Briddyn smiled, the lashless eyes blinking once or twice in remembered pleasure. Taliaesyn winced and looked away. The memory was pushing closer and closer to the surface of his mind, a searing pain like fire, and all caused by the pressure of his tormentor's fingers. When he shuddered, Briddyn laughed under his breath, such a self-satisfied sound that Taliaesyn felt his fear break like an old rope. No matter what pain it cost him, he would have to fight back, or he would never be a man again. He looked Briddyn squarely in the face.

"I'll make you a promise. Someday I *will* escape, and when I do, I'll come for you. Remember that: someday I'll kill you for this."

Briddyn laughed again, easily, openly.

"Shall we flog him for that?" he said to the mute, in Bardekian. "No, it would lower his price. Maybe I'll take a minute to show him who's master here, though."

"No." It was Gwin, stepping in between them. "You've done enough to someone who's twice the man you are."

Briddyn went dangerously calm, dangerously still, but Gwin stared him down.

"There's no time, anyway. Take him and sell him, and be done with it."

Muttering under his breath, Briddyn gestured at the mute, who jerked the chain so hard that Taliaesyn nearly stumbled, but under Gwin's watchful eye he never jerked it that way again. As they went down the gangplank and across the beach, all of them stumbling a little in the soft sand, Taliaesyn was trying to remember how he'd earned Gwin's respect, but no memories came. Switchbacking stairs, cut deep into the stone, brought them to the cliff top directly by the temple, but Taliaesyn had no time to inspect it. He got a general impression of a vast arched doorway, carved with rows of human figures and birds, before the mute growled at him and made him hurry on.

The city gates lay directly across a wide road from the temple. As they went in, Taliaesyn's first impression was that they were walking into a forest. Everywhere he looked he saw trees, lining the wide, straight streets and covering them with a shady canopy of interlaced branches, or planted thick around every house and building. Although he recognized a palm tree here and there, most were varieties he'd never seen before: a shrubby kind with tiny red flowers in clumps; a tall, thick-trunked tree with narrow, dust-colored leaves and a spicy scent; yet another with purple flowers as long as a man's finger. Vines twined around the trees and threatened to take over the various wooden and marble statues he saw scattered in the small public squares or at the intersections of streets. Among the greenery stood the rectangular longhouses with their nautical roofs, some guarded by tall statues of the inhabitants' ancestors; others, by pairs of what seemed to be wooden oars, but made large enough for a giant, standing crossed on end.

Sauntering down the streets or crossing from house to house was a constant flow of people, all dressed in tunics and sandals, men and women alike. The men, however, had brightly colored designs painted on one cheek, while the women wore broochlike oddments tucked into their elaborately curled and piled hair. He vaguely remembered that both ornament and paint identified the wearer's "house" or clan.

What surprised Taliaesyn the most, however, were the children, running loose in packs down the streets, playing elaborate games in the public spaces and private gardens alike without anyone saying a cross word to them. They were also mostly naked, boys and girls alike wearing only bright-colored pieces of cloth wrapped around their hips. Watching them made him think that yes, he must be a foreigner here, because back in Deverry children would have been dressed just like their parents and working at their sides in the family craft shop or farm.

As they went along, the houses grew larger and stood farther apart. Some were isolated by high stucco walls, painted with pictures of animals and trees; others, by flowering hedges and vines. All at once they came between two blue walls and out into an open public square, as large as three Deverry tourney grounds. Shallow steps led down to a cobbled plaza, nearly deserted in the shimmering heat. An old man drowsed on a marble bench; three children chased each other around a marble fountain, where dolphins intertwined under splashing water.

"What is this?" Taliaesyn said. "A marketplace?"

"No," Gwin said. "It's the place of assembly, where the citizens come to vote."

"Vote? I don't know this word."

"Vote—choose a leader. On the election day, they put urns around the fountain, one for each candidate. Every free man and woman puts a pebble in the urn that belongs to their choice. The man who gets the most pebbles is archon for three years."

Gwin might have said more, but Briddyn turned and snarled at him to hold his tongue and hurry.

"Over there, little one," Gwin said to Taliaesyn in a soft whisper. "You'll soon be rid of him."

The "there" in question turned out to be a narrow, treeless alley that twisted between back garden walls. As they walked along, the walls grew lower until they disappeared altogether, and the houses, smaller and poorer until they degenerated into a maze of huts and kitchen gardens. Here and there Taliaesyn saw and smelled pigsties, each holding one or two small, gray-haired pigs. Once, as they passed a ramshackle hut, a vastly pregnant woman came out to slop her hogs. When her gaze fell on the prisoner, her face softened with pity for him. Every other person they met simply ignored him, the same way that they ignored the half-starved dogs in the gutters or the gaudy birds in the trees.

Finally the alley gave a last twist and debouched into an open square where weeds pushed aside sparse cobbles and chickens scratched, squawking every now and then at the small children who shared the space with them. On the other side was a high wall, striped in blue and red and obviously part of a compound. In the middle was an iron-bound door. Everything made Taliaesyn uneasy: the thick wall, gaudy but practically a fortification; the stout door, as heavily reinforced as a Deverry dun. Briddyn glanced his way and smiled in a peculiarly unpleasant way, then included Gwin in the gesture.

"Here's where you two say farewell," he said in Deverrian.

He made a fist and pounded on the door, over and over until they heard a voice scream in Bardekian that its owner was on the way. The door opened a crack, then wider, and a slender, dark boy of about fifteen, wearing a pale blue tunic, made a low bow to Briddyn.

"Baruma, master! How can I serve you?"

"Is your father in? I have someone to sell."

"The barbarian? Oh, he'll be very interested."

They followed the lad down a narrow corridor to a long room with a blue-and-white-tiled floor and dark green walls. At one end was a low dais, strewn with many-colored cushions, where a fat man with pale brown skin and black curly hair sat cross-legged before a low table. When they came in, he looked up from what Taliaesyn took to be a game played on a circular board.

"Baruma!" He heaved himself to his feet only to make a deep

bow. "I am honored, honored." Yet, as he went on, speaking too fast for Taliaesyn to understand, he seemed far more frightened than overwhelmed at the honor of entertaining Briddyn.

The two men bargained quickly in shrill voices, waving their hands around, making dramatic grimaces, seeming to threaten each other, but always, Taliaesyn noticed, Briddyn won his points. Finally the slave dealer, whose name turned out to be Brindemo, unceremoniously ordered the prisoner to strip, then ran his hands down Taliaesyn's arms and back, poked his legs like a horse dealer, and even looked into his mouth. By the end of it, Taliaesyn was thinking murder.

"Deverrian, are you?" Brindemo said in a reasonably sound accent. "A dangerous man, then. I speak your ugly tongue. See? One wrong move or word, and I have you whipped."

Then he turned back to Briddyn, who took the bill of sale out of the pouch at his belt and handed it over. Taliaesyn noticed the dealer's eyes narrow suspiciously as he looked at it. When they started speaking again, somewhat slower, Taliaesyn could pick out phrases here and there. It seemed that Briddyn was suggesting that the trader sell him to the copper mines in the high mountains of the southwest or perhaps to the archon's fleet of galleys. His stomach cramped in fear at the thought; he remembered enough to know that slaves sold to those lives died soon—and were glad to. Brindemo gave him one last look, then returned to Briddyn.

"How much opium have you been giving him, honored master?"

"Not much and not for long." He went on to say something incomprehensible that pleased Brindemo, because the fat trader nodded and smiled.

Coins changed hands, then, close to twenty gold pieces as far as Taliaesyn could see. Brindemo took the bill of sale, tucked it into his own pouch, then escorted Briddyn, Gwin, and the mute to the door while his son held Taliaesyn on a short, tight chain. When the trader came back, he considered his new slave for a long, shrewd moment.

"You cannot run away, Taliaesyn of Pyrdon. If you do, the archon's men hunt you down—"

"And kill me. I know that."

With a little nod, Brindemo unlocked the collar and took it off his neck.

"This will chafe and leave ugly sores. We must have you look pretty."

"And will that matter in the mines?"

"Oho! You understand some Bardekian, do you? Better and better. The mines? Hah! Baruma leaves on the morrow. He comes through here, oh, once each year, if that. How will he know where I sell you? The mines pay a price fixed by law. Barbarians are much more expensive than that. You behave, show the good manners, and we sell you to honored home. Sit down. I have an armed man just outside, in earshot, by the way."

"I won't try to escape. I'm too weary, and I don't even know where I am."

Laughing, Brindemo lowered his bulk onto the cushions and motioned for the prisoner to perch on the edge of the dais. He took out the bill of sale and studied it, his lips pursed.

"Your name," he said at last. "Is it truly Taliaesyn?"

"I suppose so."

"What? Surely you know your own name."

"I don't, at that. I don't remember one blasted thing about my life until a few weeks ago."

"What? Were you hit on the head or suchlike?"

"That could be it, couldn't it? A strong blow to the head makes men lose their memories at times. But I don't know. No one told me."

Brindemo tapped a gold-trimmed tooth with one corner of the bill while he looked over his purchase.

"Tell me somewhat. Baruma, did he . . . well, hurt you?"

Taliaesyn winced and looked at the floor.

"I see that he did, then. It will make you easy to manage." Yet there was a thread of pity under the trader's cold words. "I do not like to cross Baruma. Do you blame me?"

"Never."

"But then, I do not like to cross the archon and the holy laws of my city." He studied the bill of sale again. "If I break the law, it is as painful and perhaps even more expensive than crossing Baruma."

"That thing is forged, isn't it?"

"Ah, the opium must be wearing off." He held the bill up to the light coming in the window. "It is very cleverly done, very, very professional, but then, one expects that from Baruma. May he mistake a candlestick for a cushion and sit upon it! Try to remember who you are. I perhaps can help you. You have kin and clan in Deverry?"

"My father was an important merchant there. That much I remember."

"Aha! Doubtless, then, he will buy his son back at an honest price if only he can find him. If. Do your best to remember. I cannot keep you too long—what if Baruma comes back and asks for you?"

Taliaesyn shuddered, but this time, he despised himself for doing so.

"I see you understand." Brindemo gave a shudder of his own. "But I sell you to decent place if all else fails, and then, when the beloved father comes searching, I tell him where. Perhaps he thanks me with hard coin?"

"Of course." Taliaesyn found it surprisingly easy to lie, considering what was at stake. "He's always been generous."

"Good." He reached up and clapped his hands together. "We give you food, a place to sleep."

At the signal a black-skinned man came through a door near the dais. Close to seven feet tall, he was also heavily muscled and wearing a short sword in an ostentatiously jeweled scabbard. Even without the sword Taliaesyn wouldn't have been inclined to argue with someone whose hand was as broad as an ordinary man's head.

"Darupo, bring him something to eat. I'll wager Baruma's been keeping him half starved."

The fellow nodded, gave Taliaesyn a sympathetic glance, then disappeared again. While he was gone, Brindemo returned to his game, moving ivory pegs along tracks in the board in response to throws of dice much like the ones in Deverry. In a few minutes Darupo returned with an earthenware bowl of vegetables in a spicy sauce and a basket of very thin bread, almost like rounds of parchment. He showed Taliaesyn how to tear off strips of bread and use it to scoop up the sloppy mixture in the bowl. For all that the stew was difficult to eat, it was delicious, and Taliaesyn dug in in sincere gratitude. It occurred to him that feeding him well was a sound commercial proposition, because buyers would pay more for a healthy slave than a sick one, but he was too hungry to care about the ethics of the thing. At his dicing, Brindemo sighed suddenly and looked up.

"The omens are wrong no matter what I do." He waved his hands miserably at the board. "I have this dark feeling in my heart, or however you Deverry men say it. I might turn a good profit off you, Taliaesyn of Pyrdon, but I rue the day that the gods brought you to me."

A thin drizzle sheeted across Aberwyn's harbor and turned the cobbles as slick as glass. Wrapped in his splendid scarlet cloak, the royal herald scurried across the gangplank to the pier and made the galley rock behind him. The high prow, a rearing wyvern, seemed to be bowing to the assembled crowd. Down at the land end of the pier, Nevyn started forward to greet him, then hesitated, turning to Cullyn, who was there as head of the honor guard.

"Make sure the marines get something hot to drink as soon as they reach the dun, will you?"

"Gladly. Poor bastards, rowing half the way from Cerrmor in this wet."

Nevyn hurried down to exchange the ritual salutations with the herald, whose self-control was amazing. For all that he was wet, exhausted, and rheumy, his voice boomed out on every syllable, and he bowed with the grace of a dancer.

"I, Orys, come on the king's business. Who is this who receives me?"

Nevyn hesitated briefly, then decided that he didn't truly want to explain the jest in his name at a time like this.

"I am called Galrion, councillor to the regent, her grace, Tieryn Lovyan. The king's justice is ever welcome in Aberwyn."

"My thanks, good councillor. I see horses have been provided." He suddenly smiled, the ritual done with. "Shall we get ourselves out of this wretched rain?"

"By all means, Lord Orys."

In the great hall of the gwerbrets of Aberwyn huge fires roared in both hearths. Standing warrior-straight by the table of honor, Lovyan was waiting for them, with the red, white, and brown plaid of the Clw Coc draped over her chair and the blue, green, and silver plaid of Aberwyn thrown back from her shoulder. When the herald bowed to her, she acknowledged him with a small wave of her hand, but this was no time for a curtsy. She was as much lord here now as ever her son had been.

"Greetings, honored voice of the king. What brings you to me?"

"Grave news, Your Grace." He reached into his shirt and brought out a silver message tube. "I have with me a proclamation of the most serious import."

Except for the crackling of the fires the hall went utterly, breathlessly silent. Since the king had kept the contents of that proclamation a secret from everyone at court, not even Nevyn knew what it contained. He glanced around, noting the men of both warbands sitting stock-still at their tables across the hall; the servants practically frozen in their places; Rhys's wife at the staircase, her face pale; Tevylla and Rhodda, slipping in the back door and hovering there.

"I would be honored, O voice of the king," Lovyan said, her voice firm and steady, "if you would read it out to this assembly."

With a flourish Lord Orys slipped the parchment free of the tube, laid the tube on the table, and unrolled the proclamation with a snap.

"Here be it known, in the province of Eldidd as in every province of our kingdom of Deverry, that I, Lallyn the Second, king by right of blood and right of sword, do, with full compliance of the laws and of the priesthood of Holy Bel, take it as my duty to concern myself with the line of succession of the gwerbrets of Aberwyn, being as the gwerbretrhyn is both a well-loved and an important part of our realms. While Rhys Maelwaedd, Gwerbret Aberwyn, still lives, let no man dare convene the Council of Electors to meddle with the lawful passage of the rhan to his possible heirs."

Nevyn's heart thudded once.

"Furthermore." The herald paused to clear his throat. "Let it be known in Eldidd as in all parts of our beloved kingdom that I, Lallyn the Second, acting under the authority granted to me by Great Bel, king of all the gods, do hereby disavow and overrule utterly in all its particulars the pronouncement of the aforesaid Rhys, Gwerbret Aberwyn, of the ban of clan exile upon his brother, Rhodry Maelwaedd of Dun Gwerbyn."

There was a great deal more, but no one could hear it over the cheering and shouting of the warbands, wave after wave of approval and laughter. When Nevyn looked through the crowd he found Cullyn standing at the rear door with Tevylla. In the uncertain light it was hard to tell, but he thought he saw tears glinting in the captain's eyes. Through all the cheers Lovyan stood perfectly still, her face expressing nothing but a mild relief, a certain pleasure at the thought that justice had finally been done. Nevyn had never admired her more.

Much later, when the herald was taking his well-earned rest in the best guest chamber, Nevyn had a chance to talk with the tieryn alone, in the reception chamber of her suite. There she could allow herself a crow of triumph, and she even jigged a few steps of a country dance upon the Bardek carpet.

"So Blaen won, may the gods bless him! Truly, Nevyn, I didn't know what to expect when Orys unrolled that bit of lamb leather."

"No more did I. So. We have a year and a day to get Rhodry back here to claim his restoration to the clan."

Her triumph disappeared, and she sank into a chair like an old woman.

"Ah, my poor little lad! If only we had you home! Nevyn, by the gods, you're hiding somewhat from me. Where is Rhodry?"

"Your Grace, please, trust me. I don't want to tell you. I beg you: take my word for it that he lives, and let the matter drop there. I promise you that the dweomer will do its best to bring him home for you."

"I don't know if I can accept . . . Well, what is it?"

A frightened page came creeping into the chamber.

"Your Grace? Lady Madronna sent me. His Grace is calling for you."

Hiking up her skirts like a farm lass, Lovyan ran from the chamber, with Nevyn close behind. They came into the sickroom to find Rhys propped up on pillows. His face was a dangerous sort of scarlet, and his breath rattled in his sunken chest. Over everything hung the stink of diseased urine.

"Mother!" He had to gasp out every word. "I heard the servants talking. The misbegotten king's recalled Rhodry, hasn't he? Don't you lie to me!"

"I see no need to lie to you, Your Grace." Lovyan came over to the bedside and held out her hand. He caught it in one of his and clasped it hard, as if he were drawing strength from her touch. "Rhys, please, it's best for Aberwyn. It's best for the Maelwaedd clan."

He made a sound halfway between a snarl and a cough. Deeply troubled, Nevyn hurried over.

"His Grace shouldn't vex himself. He should rest."

"Rest? When the king's made a mockery of me?" His breathing was so shallow that it was hard to hear his words. "Why couldn't he have waited till I died? He could have done that, curse him."

"He couldn't, Your Grace. If you should die without an heir, Aberwyn would be naught but a bone for dogs to fight over."

For a moment that seemed to soothe the gwerbret; then he frowned as if he were thinking something through.

"Where *is* Rhodry?"

"On his way home, Your Grace."

"Ah." He paused a little while, panting, gathering breath, his ribs heaving under the fine wool coverlets. "He's not back yet, is he now? Cursed young cub. He shan't have what's mine, not yet."

"Rhys, please!" Lovyan's voice shook with tears. "Can't you forgive him?"

Rhys turned his head toward her, and the look in his eyes was one of weary contempt, as if he were wondering how she could possibly misunderstand something so obvious. Suddenly he coughed, a choking gurgle, and spasmed, his back arching as he fought for air. Nevyn grabbed him, slid an arm under his shoulders, and supported him until he spat the blood-tinged gobbet of phlegm out. Rhys's eyes sought out Lovyan's face.

"But, Mam," he whispered, "it was mine. Truly it was."

Then he was gone, with one last ripple of spasming, a cough that never quite came. By the door Madronna threw her head back and howled in agony, keened over and over until Lovyan rushed to her and threw her arms around her to let her sob. Although the tieryn's face ran with tears, she was silent. Nevyn closed Rhys's eyes and crossed his arms over his shattered chest.

"May peace be yours in the Otherlands, Your Grace," he whispered, so softly that the women couldn't hear him. "But I have the ghastly feeling that your hatred won't let you rest."

He left the women to their grief and went down to the great hall. At least he could make the formal announcement and spare Lovyan that grim duty. As he was walking up to the honor table he remembered the herald and sent a page to wake him. Although several of the men called out to Nevyn in a friendly way, no one seemed to notice that he was grim, heartsick not so much for Rhys as for what his death meant to Aberwyn. They were all too busy celebrating Rhodry's recall. Once the drowsy herald was present, Nevyn climbed up onto the honor table and yelled for silence. The hall went abruptly quiet, the warbands turning, apprehensive at last, as they waited for him to speak. Nevyn was in no mood for fine words.

"Gwerbret Rhys is dead."

There was a collective suck and gasp of breath.

"Her Grace, Lovyan, Tieryn Dun Gwerbyn, is now regent for her
younger son: Rhodry Maelwaedd, Gwerbret Aberwyn."

The sound was unmistakable, a would-be cheer cut off out of
respect for the dead, laughter that vanished into coughs and mum-
bles, smiles that disappeared into looks of stricken shame. Poor
Rhys, Nevyn thought; I think me I understand you a bit better
now. Yet as he looked over the hall, he wondered with bitterness in
his heart if Rhodry would ever sit in the gwerbretal chair, if his
loyal warbands would ever see again the young lord that they
loved.

Appendix

CHARACTERS AND THEIR INCARNATIONS

Current Incarnation	Ca. 840
Nevyn	Nevyn
Rhodry	Maddyn
Jill	Branoic
Cullyn	Owaen
Blaen	Caradoc
Gwin	Aethan

Aber (Deverrian) A river mouth, an estuary.

Alar (Elvish) A group of elves, who may or may not be blood kin, who choose to travel together for some indefinite period of time.

Alardan (Elv.) The meeting of several alarli, usually the occasion for a drunken party.

Angwidd (Dev.) Unexplored, unknown.

Archon (translation of the Bardekian *atzenarlen)* The elected head of a city-state (Bardekian *at).*

Astral The plane of existence directly "above" or "within" the etheric (q.v.). In other systems of magic, often referred to as the Akashic Record or the Treasure House of Images.

Aura The field of electromagnetic energy that permeates and emanates from every living being.

Aver (Dev.) A river.

Bara (Elv.) An enclitic that indicates that the preceding adjective in an Elvish agglutinated word is the name of the element following the enclitic, as can + bara + melim = Rough River. (rough + name marker + river.)

Bel (Dev.) The chief god of the Deverry pantheon.

Bel (Elv.) An enclitic, similar in function to *bara,* except that it indicates that a preceding verb is the name of the following element in the agglutinated term, as in Darabeldal, Flowing Lake.

Blue Light Another name for the etheric plane (q.v.).

Body of Light An artificial thought-form (q.v.) constructed by a dweomermaster to allow him or her to travel through the inner planes of existence.

Brigga (Dev.) Loose wool trousers worn by men and boys.

Broch (Dev.) A squat tower in which people live. Originally, in the Homeland, these towers had one big fireplace in the center of the ground floor and a number of booths or tiny roomlets up the sides, but by the time of our narrative, this ancient style has given way to regular floors with hearths and chimneys on either side of the structure.

Cadvridoc (Dev.) A war leader. Not a general in the modern sense, the cadvridoc is supposed to take the advice and counsel of the noble-born lords under him, but his is the right of final decision.

Captain (trans. of the Dev. *pendaely*) The second-in-command, after the lord himself, of a noble's warband. An interesting point is that the word *taely* (which is the root or unmutated form of *-daely*) can mean either a warband or a family, depending on context.

Conaber (Elv.) A musical instrument similar to the panpipe but of even more limited range.

Cwm (Dev.) A valley.

Dal (Elv.) A lake.

Dun (Dev.) A fort.

Dweomer (trans. of Dev. *dwunddaevad*) In its strict sense, a system of magic aimed at personal enlightenment through harmony with the natural universe in all its planes and manifestations; in the popular sense, magic, sorcery.

Elcyion Lacar (Dev.) The elves; literally, the "bright spirits," or "Bright Fey."

Ensorcel To produce an effect similar to hypnosis by direct manipulation of a person's aura. (Ordinary hypnosis manipulates the victim's consciousness only and thus is more easily resisted.)

Etheric The plane of existence directly "above" the physical. With its magnetic substance and currents, it holds physical matter in an invisible matrix and is the true source of what we call "life."

Etheric Double The true being of a person, the electromagnetic structure that holds the physical body together and that is the actual seat of consciousness.

Fola (Elv.) An enclitic that shows that the noun preceding it in an agglutinated Elvish word is the name of the element following the enclitic, as in Corafolamelim, Owl River.

Geis A taboo, usually a prohibition against doing something. Breaking geis results in ritual pollution and the disfavor if not active enmity of the gods. In societies that truly believe in geis, a person who breaks it usually dies fairly quickly, either of morbid depression or of some unconsciously self-inflicted "accident," unless he or she makes ritual amends.

Gerthddyn (Dev.) Literally, a "music man," a wandering minstrel and entertainer of much lower status than a true bard.

Great Ones Spirits, once human but now disincarnate, who exist on an unknowably high plane of existence and who have dedicated themselves to the eventual enlightenment of all sentient beings. They are also known to the Buddhists as Boddhisattvas.

Gwerbret (Dev.) The highest rank of nobility below the royal family itself. Gwerbrets (Dev. *gwerbretion)* function as the chief magistrates of their regions, and even kings hesitate to override their decisions because of their many ancient prerogatives.

Hiraedd (Dev.) A peculiarly Celtic form of depression, marked by a deep, tormented longing for some unobtainable thing; also and in particular, homesickness to the third power.

Javelin (trans. of Dev. *picecl)* Since the weapon in question is only about three feet long, another possible translation would be "war dart." The reader should not think of it as a proper spear or as one of those enormous javelins used in the modern Olympic Games.

Lwdd (Dev.) A blood price; differs from wergild in that the amount of lwdd is negotiable in some circumstances, rather than being irrevocably set by law.

Malover (Dev.) A full, formal court of law with both a priest of Bel and either a gwerbret or a tieryn in attendance.

Melim (Elv.) A river.

Mor (Dev.) A sea, ocean.

Pan (Elv.) An enclitic, similar to *fola* (defined earlier), except that it indicates that the preceding noun is plural as well as the name of the following word, as in Corapanmelim, River of the Many Owls. Remember that Elvish always indicates pluralization by adding a semi-independent morpheme and that this semi-independence is reflected in the various syntax-bearing enclitics.

Pecl (Dev.) Far, distant.

Rhan (Dev.) A political unit of land; thus, gwerbretrhyn, tierynrhyn, the area under the control of a given gwerbret or tieryn. The size of the various rhans (Dev. *rhannau)* varies widely, depending on the vagaries of inheritance and the fortunes of war rather than some legal definition.

Scrying The art of seeing distant people and places by magic.

Sigil An abstract magical figure, usually representing either a particular spirit or a particular kind of energy or power. These figures, which look a lot like geometrical scribbles, are derived by various rules from secret magical diagrams.

Spirits Living though incorporeal beings proper to the various nonphysical planes of the universe. Only the elemental spirits, such as the Wildfolk (trans. of Dev. *elcyion goecl*), can manifest directly in the physical plane. All others need some vehicle, such as a gem, incense smoke, or the magnetism given off by freshly cut plants or spilled blood.

Taer (Dev.) Land, country.

Thought Form An image or three-dimensional form that has been fashioned out of either etheric or astral substance, usually by the action of a trained mind. If enough trained minds work together to build the same thought form, it will exist independently for a period of time based on the amount of energy put into it. (Putting energy into such a form is known as *ensouling* the thought form.) Manifestations of gods or saints are usually thought forms picked up by the highly intuitive, such as children, or those with a touch of second sight. It is also possible for a large number of untrained minds to make fuzzy, ill-defined thought forms that can be picked up the same way, such as UFOs and sightings of the Devil.

Tieryn (Dev.) An intermediate rank of the noble-born, below a gwerbret but above an ordinary lord (Dev. *arcloedd.)*

Wyrd (trans. of Dev. *tingedd)* Fate, destiny; the inescapable problems carried over from a sentient being's last incarnation.

Ynis (Dev.) An island.